ALS

The TWO WEEK Roommate

USA TODAY BESTSELLING AUTHOR

ROXIE NOIR

CONTENT NOTE

PLEASE BE aware that this book contains: discussion and mild description of religious trauma, non-detailed descriptions of corporal punishment of a child, discussion of homophobia including a mention of conversion camps, discussion of transphobia, mentions of misgendering and deadnaming, on-page slut shaming, and a non-detailed mention of a parent's death.

THE BELL SIBLINGS

(PLEASE FEEL FREE TO BOOKMARK THIS FOR
LATER REFERENCE.)

Gideon, 32
Matthew, 31
Elliott, 29
Zachary, 28 (twin)
Bethany, 28 (twin)
Hannah, 26
Jacob, 25
Sadie, 24
Ariel, 22
Reid, 20
Drew, 17
Ruth, 15

For everyone who eats the M&Ms in the trail mix first.

ONE

GIDEON

I STAND in the kitchen doorway, fold my arms over my chest, and narrow my eyes. Everything's perfectly in place, just like I left it: the avocado-colored fridge, the beat-up wooden table, the lemon-yellow formica countertop.

No chipmunk in sight.

"I saw you come in here," I tell the kitchen. "You're not staying."

It's so cold I can see my breath, because I didn't have the chance to re-light the wood stove before this squeaky little varmint darted out from behind it, into the kitchen, onto the countertop, and behind the stacks of ungainly, mismatched dishes on open shelving that can't be less than forty years old.

Neither the chipmunk nor the kitchen responds. Why the kitchen? Now I'm going to have to clean every dish in this place, because I have the misfortune of knowing exactly what diseases rodents can carry.

Little bastard.

I put the lantern on the kitchen table, cross my arms, and wait. I scan the open wooden shelves, the stained white stove, the rounded refrigerator that's probably older than me. It sounds like a freight train when it kicks on. Sooner or later that furry fuckface is going to make a move.

I wait for it. I can be patient. I'd say I'm *quite* experienced in being patient for critters.

Said patience is running low when there's a flurry of scrabbling and a glass falls from one of the haphazard shelves. I practically leap across the kitchen, sock feet thumping heavily on a floor that's seen better days, and manage to catch it before the it hits the floor.

I feel victorious for half a second before I realize it's plastic and I could've let it fall.

"Shit," I mutter at the cup in my hand, then scan the counter and shelves again. "Where'd you—"

It's watching me from the very end of a shelf, the patterned paper lining curled up around its feet. Its nose twitches. Its beady little eyes blink, and it's exactly far enough away from me that I have a zero percent chance of catching it.

"You're supposed to be asleep," I tell it. "Chipmunks hibernate. Look it up."

The chipmunk seems uninterested in scholarship, because it doesn't move at all. At least it doesn't seem rabid. Just more social than a chipmunk ought to be, which is its own kind of concerning. Not as concerning as rabies, but I wouldn't call it *good*.

It chatters at me, squeaky and angry. I know when I'm being told off by wildlife. I put my hands up, palms out, like I'm showing the damn thing I'm not armed. As if a chipmunk can tell.

"Okay," I say, the plastic cup still in my hand. If I get this just right, I can trap the sanctimonious dickhead underneath and carry it outside, like I do with spiders that are too big to live indoors. "Just hold still, I'm not gonna—"

It takes a flying leap off the shelf, to the floor, and before I can get more than one step closer it disappears into a hole in the warped baseboards, scrabbling through the walls. I'm still standing there with a plastic cup in my hand. Fuck.

"Don't eat the wiring," I tell the hole. "If you start an electrical fire your furry ass is toast. I'm not saving you."

There's the faint sound of more scratching, and for a moment I stare at the wall, the afternoon light already dimming, like I think it'll come back and say *you're right, I'm being unreasonable, I'll go now.*

It does not.

"Fucker," I tell the hole, and turn back for the wood stove in the opposite corner. I debate plugging the hole with something, because apparently this chipmunk is unaware that it's supposed to be hibernating and would rather run amok in the Forest Service's cabin, but then there's the risk that it'll die inside the walls, and I'd much rather have a living rodent harassing me than a dead one rotting somewhere I can't get to it.

That happened once to some church friends of my parents, and guess who got volunteered to take care of the problem. All I got for my trouble was an overbaked oatmeal raisin cookie and some tossed-off praise about how I was such a helpful young man.

Once the wood stove is going and a few lights are on, everything feels a lot better than it did in the cold darkness. I put my boots in the tray by the stove, hang my coat in front of it, and start downloading my data from my field iPad to the hard drive I brought with me.

Outside, I swear the snow is picking up. Hard to tell at this time of day—it's barely four in the afternoon, but since it's just a few days before Christmas, it feels like nine at night— but I think it's snowing harder than before.

Much harder, actually. When I checked the weather

report yesterday morning it said we were supposed to get flurries late this afternoon. This is not flurries. This is a snowstorm.

This might even be a blizzard. I cross my arms in front of my chest and frown at the window, because fuck *blizzards*. This is southwestern Virginia, and even though we're in the mountains, we're not supposed to get blizzards. It's supposed to snow a little, and then warm up just enough that everything is slush, then maybe we'll get some sleet and freezing rain and when the sun goes down it'll all freeze over and make the roads a slip 'n' slide. Then, three days later, it'll be gone and everyone will pretend they weren't panicking.

But what are you supposed to do in a *blizzard*?

I nearly jump out of my skin when my phone buzzes on the worn wooden table. I swear it sounds like a foghorn.

Reid: It's snowing? A lot????
Reid: What do I do about Victoria and Fluffy???
Reid: Where are your candles and stuff if the power goes out? I feel like the power's gonna go out
Reid: Blankets? Emergency rations? Can Dolly double as a blanket?
Me: R-85 and C-347 are literally wild animals, they'll be fine. They have good shelter.
Reid: They look cold
Me: You're projecting.
Reid: Are you one hundred percent sure I can't snuggle either of them?

I ignore that question. We've been over this, so I tell him that the emergency supplies are in the same place they were the last time the power went out, and he asks where *that* is, and we're still going back and forth when my work phone starts ringing.

Yes, I came to a cabin in the middle of nowhere and had to bring two phones. Satellite technology has made it incredibly difficult to get *one fucking minute* of peace.

"Gideon," Dale says as soon as I answer, no preamble. He sounds a little out of breath. "You're out by Copper Hollow, right?"

"I'm not far," I tell him.

"You come across that girl?"

I'm staring out the window, snow swirling as the blue-tinted darkness falls. Dread settles over me like a blanket.

"What girl?" I ask.

"The girl chained to a tree."

I'm already by the stove, stepping into my still-wet boots, because—

"There's a girl *chained* to a *tree*? What the fuck?"

"You didn't come across her?"

"*No*," I say, and my voice echoes off the wood-paneled interior of the Forest Service cabin that, up until now, felt pretty cozy. "Why the fuck is there a girl chained to a tree?"

"I think she's protesting that new mine on Swayback Mountain. People are real mad about it but it's right outside of the National Forest so there's not—"

"She's an adult?"

"Yeah?"

I take a deep breath and close my eyes for a minute, because when Dale said *girl* I was picturing a nine-year-old in a bad situation, not a grown woman who did this to herself. She's probably not doing great right now, but still. At least she's not a kid.

"I haven't seen a *woman* chained to a tree, no," I tell him, a little calmer as I grab my coat with one hand. "If I'd seen a woman chained to a tree in this weather, she wouldn't be chained to a tree anymore."

"Shit," he mutters, and then I can hear him talking to someone in the background, snatches of conversation coming through. I put the satellite phone—which is just a regular smartphone connected to a small satellite receiver, I remember when a satellite phone required its own backpack—on speaker and lace my boots up. At least my socks are dry.

"Yeah, her friend hasn't heard from her," Dale says, and I can tell he's trying to sound calm but he... doesn't. "Everyone down here who's any sort of emergency personnel is busy pulling people out of ditches or worse, do you think you could—"

"I'll go find her," I say, pulling the double knot on my right boot tight. "Send me the coordinates."

Three minutes later I've got GPS coordinates as well as semi-detailed directions from Dale, if you count *the creek where we had to take down the beaver dam in '83 and I thought one of those things was going to gnaw my leg clean off* as directions, and I'm heating up the Forest Service's truck while folding the map to precisely the right spot. Already, it's half-dark, the snow is swirling hypnotically in the headlights, and all the roads up here are barely dirt tracks anyway. They're hard enough to find in full daylight when it's not snowing.

For the record, I don't want to be doing this. I was all set to heat up some dinner, maybe make some tea, wash every dish that the chipmunk touched, and then settle in with a book and go to bed by nine. That's the whole point of volunteering for grouse observation duty for two weeks during Christmas: peace. Quiet. Solitude. As much as I don't want that chipmunk living in the walls of the cabin, it didn't ask me any pointed questions about whether I'm ever going to get married or come back to church. The chipmunk won't passive-aggressively ask me how everyone in my household is doing and then deadname my brother Reid.

The road to High Meadow Mine is about three miles as the crow flies and about forty harrowing, white-knuckled minutes in the truck. There's one point where I'm absolutely positive I'm about to fall ass over teakettle down an embankment, but somehow at the last second I remain on solid ground. Thank fuck for four-wheel drive, I guess.

The sky's a deep purple when I finally make the last turn from a dirt road to a gravel road—yes, there's a difference, there's a *major* difference—and see about ten signs that read "NO TRESPASSING, PRIVATE PROPERTY, BEAU-MONT MINERALS LAND, STAY OUT." They glow as I drive past them, practically holding my breath and leaning forward over the steering wheel like a ninety-year-old with glaucoma. A little further and there are the hulking yellow machines, oddly pretty when they're doused in snow like this, lined up along the side of the road.

I can't say I disagree with this woman for not wanting Beaumont Minerals to mine here. Even though it's about half a mile outside the national forest, it's still pristine and pretty, practically untouched. I just wish she hadn't chained herself to a tree with a snowstorm coming, which might be the stupidest thing I've ever heard in my life.

The gravel road ends abruptly: a few orange-and-white sawhorses across the road, and that's it. Just trees. I stop the truck and look around, because it sure seems like no one's here. If someone were, they'd have stood and waved or gotten my attention somehow, right?

Unless they were dead. Or incapacitated.

"Fuck," I whisper to myself, pull my hat down, and get out of the truck but leave the lights on. The wind in the trees is the only sound for miles, even my footsteps dampened by the snow. If there were someone else here, they'd be making noise, but there's nothing as I take a step past the barricade, almost into the trees.

God, this isn't the wrong entrance, is it? I thought there was only the one, and I'm at the coordinates Dale gave me but I know technology is fallible sometimes. Everyone's heard stories about a hiker in need of rescue whose GPS showed them on a ridge but they were actually ten feet to the right and fifty below in a ravine, waiting for help that wasn't coming because—

There's a soft rustle and I nearly jump out of my skin.

"Hello?" I shout, which I should have done several minutes ago, probably. It doesn't always occur to me to talk.

"Uh, hi?" says a woman's voice.

I turn so fast I nearly lose my footing and walk toward the voice, my shadow cutting dark, diffuse shapes across the trees when I walk in front of the headlights.

"I'm from the Forest Service," I say, shielding my eyes against the falling snow as I scan the trees for her, still walking. "There's a blizzard out here—" no shit, Gideon, "—and I need to get you to safety."

The rustling gets more spirited, but she doesn't answer. Finally, I see something bright blue between two trees, out on the fading edge of the headlights, and I step into the shadows.

A pod person straight out of a science fiction double feature stares back.

There's a second where I honest-to-God believe it's some sort of cryptid—this is deep woods, there are tales, this is how half of them begin—but then my eyes adjust and I realize it's a woman in a sleeping bag, standing against a tree, a chain around her middle.

Then my eyes adjust *more*, and I look at her face, which is the only part of her I can see, and I blink some snow out of my eyes, and I look *again,* and—

"Andi?"

The sleeping-bag-pod-person pauses for a moment, squirms a little, clears her throat, and says, "Gideon?"

TWO

ANDI

THE MOMENT I hear Gideon's voice, I start hoping it's not him. It's pretty easy to mistake a voice, right? Especially if you've seen someone once in the past twenty years, and the two of you exchanged a maximum of fifty words?

But it is. The man standing in front of me is definitely Gideon Bell, someone I would recognize across a crowded bar after three beers, or two cars over and one behind at a stoplight, or in the dark during a snowstorm wearing a large winter coat zipped up to his chin and a knit hat. He stares at me like I'm some sort of backwoods monster who's about to pounce on him and eat his eyeballs if he doesn't eliminate me first. For a moment, I think he might try, and that makes me panic, so I do the same thing I always do when confronted with an awkward situation like this.

"Hey!" I say, giving him my sunniest and most disarming smile. "Fancy seeing you here."

I didn't think it was possible for him to stare harder, but he does.

"Andi," he says again.

"Hi."

"Why the *fuck* are you chained to a tree in the middle of a snowstorm?"

"It's a long story," I say, as breezily as I can manage while fully inside a sleeping bag, chained to a tree, in a snowstorm. "How have you been? I ran into your sister Hannah the other day and she said you have a new nephew? Congrats!"

Gideon stares, his frown deepening, and I get a little more nervous. I'm now sweating inside my sleeping bag, which is a very not-ideal situation because the moment the adrenaline of this encounter fades away, it'll make me colder and I really don't need to be colder right now.

For the record, I'm ninety-five percent sure Gideon is going to rescue me, not head back to his nice warm truck so he can pretend this never happened. There's being a self-righteous dick, which he was, and then there's leaving a helpless damsel to the elements, which I'm pretty sure he won't.

He shakes his head like he's clearing it, then steps toward me and to the side, eyes on the chain that's keeping me bound to the tree.

"Where's the key?" he asks when he finds the lock. I shiver a little with relief.

"In my pack," I say, nodding toward it, leaning against the tree on my other side. He walks around me silently, twigs and snow crunching under his heavy boots. "It's in the front pocket—no, there's a smaller one, it's kind of hidden. Yeah, there, and then there's a couple little pouches inside and it's in one of them."

I think. Gideon digs around in it for a bit, readjusting himself and the pack so he's in the light from his truck, taking off a glove to root around even better.

"It's kind of small," I offer, as if he's never seen the key to a regular-size padlock before. "And if you need, I think there's a

17

flashlight in the other front pocket, which actually might also be where the key—"

Gideon stands and starts walking back to the truck.

"HEY!" I shout, full-blown panicking. I duck my head into the sleeping bag and sort of crouch down so I can get one arm out of the hole where my face was, because the key is in there *somewhere*. I used it earlier today. "I swear it's in there, I'm sorry it's kind of buried, just don't—"

"I'm getting bolt cutters," he hollers back, and then mutters something else I don't quite hear.

I pause in rifling through my pack one-handed, contorted so I'm peeking through the face-hole with my arm also extended through the face-hole, which is cinched pretty tightly to keep the snow out. Technically, it's also stuck that way right now, which is something I'll have to admit to Gideon soon.

"Oh," I shout, voice muffled by the sleeping bag.

By the time Gideon gets back I still haven't found the key, but I've managed to get myself upright again and muster all the dignity I can manage in this situation. It's not much. He cuts the chain off me without ceremony, nods once, then grabs my pack and swings it onto his back.

Then he stops and gives me another *look*, probably because I'm still in this sleeping bag and at this point, it's getting suspicious.

"Truck's about fifty feet away," he says. "You okay out of the sleeping bag for that long?"

"Well," I say. There's no way to break this news that makes me look good or even okay. "I'm stuck."

He stares again, face totally blank, though I'm starting to think that this particular blank face is an *are you kidding me right now* blank face, not a truly neutral expression.

"In the sleeping bag," he says, not quite phrasing it as a question.

"The cord that cinches the face part closed got stuck in the zipper," I explain. "And I was working on untangling it when you got here, but I hadn't quite gotten it out yet."

He steps closer to me and slings my pack to the ground in one easy movement.

"Can I?" he asks, pointing at the cord-and-zipper tangle right next to my face. I nod. He pulls a small flashlight from his pocket and steps even closer, looks at me, and nods before taking the zipper in one gloved hand. "You might want to close your eyes, this one's bright," he says.

I do. Even through my eyelids the light's very bright. Even through the sleeping bag Gideon is very close, so close I can hear his soft breathing and his quiet little thinking sounds as he tugs at the zipper, at the cord, like he's trying to see every angle of the mess I've made. I'm sure I'm imagining that I can feel his warmth.

"Andi," he finally says, low and quiet. "The hell did you do?"

I open my eyes and it's bright, but not blinding. He's got one glove off and is experimentally pulling at various loops of the tangled cord. None of them are budging.

"I was getting close," I lie. "If you kinda pull that big loop there—" I point, "I think that's the key to getting it unstuck."

My hand is shoved through the hole next to my face, and our fingers brush. Gideon frowns harder, and without saying anything, wraps his whole hand around my finger.

"Uh," I say, and he takes it off only to grab my whole palm, his hand warm and rough and somehow disapproving.

"Shit, you're freezing," he mutters, mostly to himself. He takes his other glove off and shoves them both under his arm along with the flashlight, sandwiching my hand between his. "New plan. Truck first."

I look past him to the Forest Service truck, headlights blazing through the trees so bright I can't see past it. I'm starting to understand how people think they've been abducted by aliens, because this is probably how it starts.

"Okay," I say. "If you don't mind grabbing my backpack I think I can hop—"

"I'm carrying you."

"No," I say, and he raises his eyebrows a tiny fraction of an inch and doesn't move otherwise. I sigh. "Do I get *any* dignity?"

"Hopping is dignified?"

It's a good point, unfortunately. I close my eyes and take another deep breath.

"I accept my fate," I tell him, and he nods once.

"Good," Gideon says. He lets my hand go, shoves his gloves and flashlight into a coat pocket, and then there's a shoulder in my stomach and an undignified squeaky grunt escapes me as I'm lifted in the least sexy configuration of *face down, ass up.*

"Try not to move too much," he says, and grabs the handle of my backpack as well.

"Kay," I manage. I maintain the position in dignified silence as he crosses the fifty feet to the truck, opens the door, and flops me into the passenger seat, where I do my best to wriggle upright, though the nylon sleeping bag is very slippery and that becomes its own challenge.

Without speaking, he hops up next to me and leans over, one hand planted on the seat next to my thigh, his torso practically draped over my legs.

"Hi," I say at the sudden contact.

"I'll get the heat going," he explains, and ah, yes, there's the jangle of keys as the engine turns over. "Forgot the bolt cutters, be right back."

The passenger door shuts and I'm alone in the truck, in a sleeping bag, with the engine and the heat going as Gideon disappears into the dark, and I do my best not to think about— well, anything. I try not to think about how cold I am. I try not to think about what a good opening for a horror movie this would be. I try not to think about the fact that my rescuer is *Gideon Bell*, twenty years older than my memories of a barefoot kid on sunny summer days. I try not to think about the fact that I knew it was him, fifty feet away, in the dark, in a snowstorm.

Instead, I focus my energy on wriggling around until my arm is poking out of the face-hole so I can turn the dome light on and get back to work on the knot from hell.

I make zero progress before the back door opens and Gideon tosses my backpack in, then climbs into the driver's seat and looks over at me.

"I think I've almost got it," I tell him, inaccurately.

"Looks the same."

"Positivity is important," I say, wondering if I should use my teeth. "Haven't you read *The Secret*?"

Gideon snorts, which is probably the response that question deserves, but he leans in again and then his face is inches from mine. I can feel the cold air leaking off him and then the first blush of warmth: pink nose and pink cheeks and pink lips, moss-green eyes, long, pretty eyelashes. A short dark beard and dark hair that's just long enough to start curling at the ends, slashes for eyebrows. I wonder if they still express every thought that crosses his mind, or if he's learned to control them. I'm still trapped in a sleeping bag and probably suffering from hypothermia and it's *obviously* all my imagination, but still. *Still*.

"Hold on," he says after a long moment, then grabs both sides of the zipper and tugs in opposite directions. Nothing happens.

"I did try that," I say.

"I think it's fucked."

"Is that the technical term?"

"Technical enough," he says, leaning back so he can reach into a pocket. "C'mere."

I flinch back when he opens a knife and reaches for me.

"It's for the cord, not you," he says, disbelievingly.

"It's a surprise knife!"

Gideon closes his eyes for a moment as if gathering patience, and I subtly shift back to where I was as best I can. It's hard, because I've started shaking, suddenly colder than I was when I was outside.

"Andi," Gideon says. "I need to use a knife to cut the cord on your sleeping bag so you can maneuver out of it and buckle yourself safely into this truck before we attempt a journey through a snowstorm, which is only getting worse the longer we sit here and fuck around."

There's a blunt edge to the way he says it, matter-of-fact and clipped like he's reading out safety instructions to a group of tourists. To strangers.

"Sorry. Do it," I say, and I'm trying not to shiver but I can't help it and the more I try to control it, the worse it gets.

Gideon's eyes flick to mine. He pauses. His grip on the knife shifts, a tiny movement I wouldn't notice if we weren't this close.

"I'll be careful," he promises, deep and soft and gentle, cutting through the white noise of the truck engine and the heat on full blast, and... it works. Despite everything, I'm soothed.

"I know," I say, and he is. At least with me. He cuts the

drawstring and I emerge halfway from the sleeping bag like it's been eating me alive, sweaty and freezing and still shaking even though I've got a coat on. Without a word, Gideon turns all the heat vents to point at me, then grabs a camp blanket from the jump seat behind us and hands it to me, my legs still in the sleeping bag.

"Put this on once you've warmed up a little," he says. "You're shaking."

"Thanks," I say. "I—yeah. I didn't know I was this cold."

Gideon looks me over for a long moment, half-turned in the driver's seat, the dim overhead light casting him in odd shadows. He looks like he wants to say something, but all I can do is stare and try not to shake too badly.

"You've got," he finally says, and gestures at his hair.

I pat my head with one hand. All I find is hair. I think my hat's somewhere in the sleeping bag, along with a glove.

"No," he says. "It's—close? The other way."

"I'll get it later," I say, giving up, but Gideon reaches over with one warm hand, fingers whispering into my hair, and gently tugs something free, then holds it out to me: a twig with a prickly leaf on it. Holly, maybe.

"Thanks," I say, and when I take it, I have a sudden flash of memory.

We were ten. It was summer, midday, hot as anything, and we'd trekked through the woods behind our houses to Threebridge Creek. It was further than we were supposed to go since the land belonged to someone else, but there was no fence and therefore no good reason to stay out.

We took off our shoes to splash through the water, and five minutes later I stepped on a piece of glass. It was deep and hurt like hell and bled like crazy, and we were in the middle of the woods where we weren't supposed to be.

I panicked. It felt like I'd sliced my foot in half. Everything was slippery with the gushing blood, and I was pretty sure that I was going to die or at least get in really bad trouble.

But Gideon was there. Gideon, at all of ten years old, stayed calm and had a bandana in his pocket. He sat me down and rinsed away the blood and told me I wasn't going to die, wrapped it tightly and reminded me I'd be fine and then helped me hobble back to my house, where Rick took one look at it and drove me straight to the emergency room.

That was Gideon, back then: gentle, soothing, and honest when something was going to hurt.

"All right," he finally says, and turns his attention to the windshield, releasing the parking brake with a *thunk*. "Hang on. This isn't gonna be pretty."

$$\cdots \cdots \star \bigstar \star \cdots \cdots$$

IT ISN'T. Well, it is, in an aesthetic *the snowy forest is beautiful and serene* kind of way, but the ride itself is pretty gnarly, over a road that can't be more than a disused track when there's not a blizzard going on. With this much snow we can't even see the ruts and rocks, so Gideon has to guess or go on memory, and that's not a great system.

Within five minutes I've given up on acting cool and am actively hanging onto the Jesus handle with my right hand and the side of the seat with my left, both feet braced in the wheel well. I might crack a molar. Uselessly, I remember the "fun" fact that drunk people tend to survive car accidents more than sober people do because the alcohol relaxes them, and I guess being relaxed helps in crashes or something.

I will die for sure if we crash, is what I'm saying.

Meanwhile, Gideon is frowning at the snowflakes through the windshield as though each one has personally insulted him. Which, I don't know his relationship with snow. Maybe they have. Maybe he insulted them first. I wouldn't put it past him. It takes all my self control not to ask that, because right now is very clearly not the time to distract him.

And now, a brief sampling of other things I don't say:

"I'm really glad you're probably not an axe murderer."

"Is this a stick shift?"

"Do you still think I'm going to hell?"

"Does this have four-wheel drive?"

"Which is worse, snow or sleet?"

"What have you been up to for the past twenty years? I haven't asked anyone about you because I'm afraid I won't like the answer."

"Did you make your hat? It looks handmade."

"I knit a scarf once. It wasn't as nice as your hat."

"Driving through snow always makes me think of trying to watch Skinemax late at night after my parents went to bed and it was staticky, but I could *almost* see naked people. Sorry. You probably didn't do that."

"When *was* the first time you saw another person naked in a sexual context? Just curious."

"Do you know where we're going?"

"Where *are* we going?"

"Are you sure this is a road?"

"Are we lost? And is it my fault?"

"Wow, this is a pretty steep downhill!"

"Wow, we're going pretty fast!"

"Tree! Fuck. TREE!"

Except I say that last one out loud, because: TREE. We slide to an abrupt halt about half an inch in front of a huge oak tree, all the stuff in the back of the truck sliding and slamming around with some ugly metal-on-metal screeches.

Then there's a long moment of complete, utter silence, the only movement the snow falling outside and a tree-shaped air freshener swinging from the rear-view mirror. I reach out and stop it.

"Sorry," Gideon says after a long, tense silence. We're so close to the tree that only the sides are lit by the headlights, the center of the tree darker, then nothing else but the glow of the snow beyond. "You okay?"

"Yep," I tell him. My voice is about an octave too high, and I'm probably going to have a seatbelt bruise tomorrow, but I'll live. At least I've stopped shaking with cold, thanks to the heat and the sleeping bag and my several layers. "I'm buckled in. You okay?"

"Fine," he says, and lets out a long, shaky breath. His face doesn't change as he shifts into reverse, drapes his hand over the back of my seat, looks through the rear window, and revs the engine.

We don't move.

Actually, that's not accurate. The truck rocks back and forth a little, like it's trying very hard. Gideon frowns. The engine gets louder. Nothing happens, but I'm sure it'll just take another second, any second now the tires will find some traction and we'll start moving and get around this tree and then we'll be on our way.

Nope.

Gideon is perfectly silent, face blank, as he checks the gearshift, putting the truck into neutral and then back into reverse, then looks at his feet on the pedals as though they might somehow be the problem.

He tries it again. It doesn't work again, and now I'm starting to full-blown panic, sweating a little, my hands in fists in my lap because we're stuck in a vehicle in a blizzard and this is very much all my fault for *chaining myself to a tree.* Who even does that? What is this, 1972? I couldn't make a viral video or something?

"Here, I can get out," I offer, hand on my seatbelt. "And."

And *what*? Push? Gideon just grunts, easing off the gas, letting the truck rock back, and then hitting it pretty hard.

"Maybe it'll be easier if the truck's lighter," I say, and Gideon says nothing, fully focused on reversing this truck. The next time it rocks forward, it bumps into the tree and we both jump a little.

"Fuck," he mutters, then heaves a deep breath and jerks the gearshift into park so hard I think I hear something crunch. "Stay there," he says, and gets out of the truck.

THREE

GIDEON

"I CAN'T BELIEVE you don't have snow chains," Andi says, and I swear all the hairs on the back of my neck rise at the sentence. "You have bolt cutters but no snow chains?"

She doesn't even say it like it's an accusation, just a conversation. As though we are having a regular conversation here, in the dark, in the middle of a snowstorm, next to a truck that shows no sign of moving any time soon.

"There are supposed to be snow chains," I explain, crouching down again. Of course, Andi didn't stay in the truck like I told her to. Of course, she's been flitting around, hiking boots crunching the snow, for the last forty-five minutes. She has, at last count, offered twenty-two suggestions and offered her help no fewer than thirty-one times, and I swear all I want in the world is sixty seconds of silence to think and also contemplate the many mistakes that led me to this point.

I get about three seconds. I use it to be glad she's got appropriate cold-weather gear on, at least, and that she's stomping around and keeping her body temperature up.

"You should have an inventory checklist," Andi says, on her tiptoes, peering over the side of the truck as though maybe snow chains have magically appeared in the back. Her strawberry blonde hair is in a braid that slithers over one shoulder. For half a second I think of how it felt on my fingertips, back in the truck. "So that when you—"

"*Andi,*" I snap, and it comes out more forcefully than I mean for it to. She stops mid-sentence, and then we stare at each other for a moment, her blue eyes wide in her round face, cheeks mottled pink from the cold. Fuck.

"Right, you probably thought of that already," she says without a hiccup in her cheerfulness.

I clear my throat into the deep silence of snowfall in a winter forest. "Yes," I say.

She's silent for another moment before turning back to the truck like nothing happened, and now I'm annoyed *and* guilty.

"You've got some tie-down straps in here," she says, telling me something else I already know. "Maybe we could wrap one around that tree back there and somehow use it to help pull the truck out?"

I don't answer right away. Instead, I take a few moments to shove at the branches we've wedged beneath the tire—which are not doing shit for traction—and keep my mouth shut so I don't say something I don't mean. Even though it's her fault that I'm here, in a blizzard, fruitlessly trying to get my truck moving again. Even though she's the one who *chained herself to a tree* without checking the weather. Even though a little bit of simple forethought or common sense would have prevented all this and I could be comfortable in the cabin right now, reading *The Murderbot Diaries* and drinking chamomile in front of the fire, which is what I fucking deserve.

It's been an hour and a half at most, and we're somehow back into our childhood patterns: Andi sets out on an adventure, and I follow her. As a kid, I must have followed Andi through half the forested land in Burnley County just because she said it would be fun. She was almost always right. I can't think about this now.

"That won't work," I finally tell her without looking up.

I doubt anything short of an act of God will work; I went into a skid that got worse when I hit the brakes to avoid the tree, and now the truck is facing slightly downhill, its front bumper gently resting against a huge oak tree. Turns out all-wheel drive doesn't mean shit when you're on a barely-maintained fire road in the middle of a blizzard and you hit a patch of iced-over mud.

"They've got those ratchets with the teeth that catch when you pull them the right way," she says, as if this is something new and exciting and not a fact I've known for almost my entire life. "So, if you can get the truck to move a *little* maybe we could get the straps to tighten and—"

"It's not going to work," I say, standing.

"It might."

"No," I tell her, very calmly brushing snow from my gloves. "It won't."

She exhales hard, breath fogging in the cone of light her headlamp casts. "It's worth a try," she says. "Do you have a better idea? Otherwise, we're just—*stuck*."

Truth is, I want to try. I know it won't work but it turns out old habits die harder than I expected and she's here, now, suggesting something, and despite all evidence to the contrary I can't help but think: *could be fun.*

Which is stupid of me.

"No, it's not *worth a try*," I tell her, folding my arms over my chest. "These straps can't hold a *five-ton truck* and in the course of trying to get it to work, one of us will probably injure ourselves attempting the impossible and *then* we'll be well and truly fucked because it'll also be darker, colder, and the snow will be deeper. Any other genius ideas while you're at it?"

I'm not shouting but I say the last sentence way, way louder than was necessary and Andi's eyes go wide, her face pale in the bright light and oddly angled shadows of her head-lamp. How dare she? How *dare* she get us into this stupid, dangerous situation and then have the nerve to look like a cornered animal when I tell her that?

I'm tempted to say all that out loud. It would probably feel pretty good right now. I don't, because I'm an adult and this is already strained enough.

"No," she says at last, voice steady, chin up. I take another deep breath in a seemingly endless succession of deep breaths and look around, the beam from my headlamp sweeping over snow and trees and... that's pretty much it. I turned the truck's headlights off—if the battery ran out we'd be even more fucked than we already are—and the paleness of tree trunks against the blackness beyond makes the forest feel shallow, like it's all set dressing with no depth. I breathe again and manage to engage the part of my brain that wants to do some-thing besides shout.

"In the past year I've had to rescue three cars from a ditch," I tell her, now at a normal volume. Andi stares right back at me without moving.

"You drove into three ditches?"

"No," I huff, my breath catching the light for half a second. "Three of my idiot siblings drove into ditches. I pulled three of my idiot siblings *out* of three ditches. I've never driven into one ditch, let alone three."

"Oh," she says, and she sounds way too skeptical. "Right."

"I got this truck all the way to you and almost all the way back," I point out. "That was a fucking miracle. No. Not a miracle. That was a feat of skill."

"I wasn't saying—" My face must do something, because she holds both her gloved hands up and takes a small step back. "Sorry. Your driving is perfect."

"Point being, I understand the forces involved in moving a stuck vehicle and a tie-down strap or even ten tie-down straps aren't gonna do it right now," I say, adjusting my hat a little because it's making my forehead itch. "And some Chuckle-fuck McFucknuts didn't put the snow chains back in last winter, so this isn't going anywhere."

Andi takes a shaky breath and glances sideways at the truck. "Shit," she breathes. "So, we're stuck here."

"Can you hike?"

"What?"

"Can. You—"

"We can't leave the truck."

"I doubt anyone's gonna steal it," I say, opening the driver's side door. The dome light comes on, and I blink hard. "And if they do, they've earned it."

"No, that's like—the first thing you learn from every single outdoors guide, website, and ranger talk," Andi says, her voice pitching a little higher. "If you get lost, you stay with your vehicle and don't wander off into the woods at night in the middle of a blizzard!"

"We're not lost," I tell her, leaning over the driver's seat.

"We're way deep in the woods at *night* in the *snow* in the middle of nowhere and that's how people die of exposure!"

I do not point out where I found her earlier.

"It's a mile," I call back. "Maybe a mile and a half. One hour, tops, even in the snow."

"To the road? No, it's not."

"To the cabin."

"What cabin?"

I pull my GPS unit and my backup GPS unit from where

they were plugged into the center console, then dig through the glovebox for the paper map.

"The cabin where we're staying in," I tell her, snapping the glovebox shut.

When I turn around, her face is very pale, her eyes are very wide, and she's standing very still.

"Oh," she says. She's watching me like she needs to be ready for me to do something, then speaks with a forced calm. "I see. I had thought we were going to the Parkway."

"That's the opposite direction," I say, baffled. "We've been heading away from the Parkway for miles."

"I didn't realize."

"How did you not—" I stop myself. I know the answer, which is that most people don't know which direction is which when they're in the middle of the woods. They don't even know it in their own neighborhoods. "Here's the plan: we hike the mile back to the cabin, which has shelter, heat, and food. Tomorrow or the day after, once the roads are clear, I take you down the mountain and into town. There's no way the Parkway's been cleared, and there's no way we'd make it the twenty miles into town."

Andi chews on her lip for a few moments, glancing away, breath fogging in front of her.

"Okay," she says. "I still think we should stay with the truck. Every survival guide is very clear—"

"What do they say about chaining yourself to a tree in the winter?" I snap. I'm louder than I should be, again. "Is *that* more advisable than hiking to safety or is it—"

"That was also stupid and I was also scared!" she shouts.

Everything goes silent, her words swallowed by the snow. Now her face is blotchy and red, even in the weird light from her headlamp, her jaw clenching, and—

Fuck.

I'm being an asshole.

I've got good cause for being an asshole, but suddenly I'm paying attention to Andi instead of looping the thought *this is her fault how do I get us out of this* over and over again and Jesus, fuck, she's not just scared, she's scared of *me*. Andi's never been *scared* of me before.

Fucking... shitfuck. I feel like dirt scraped off the bottom of a shoe. I feel like the ground should be swallowing me whole.

"Andi," I say, and I try to sound as warm and fuzzy as I can, which isn't very warm and fuzzy at all but at least I'm trying. "First, we're not lost. Here."

I turn on the GPS, wait for it to boot, and show her the screen. She glances at it, then glances up at the sky, as if that'll help orient her. I swallow and try to channel every bit of help-ing-a-wounded-animal-calm I can get a hold of.

"Okay," I say, and pull a glove off with my teeth so I can mess with the screen. "This dot is us, right now, and this little cabin-shaped symbol is the cabin."

Andi looks at it for a moment, biting her lips together, then glances north. Then she glances northeast, toward the cabin.

"Those survival guides are aimed at amateurs," I point out, very patiently. She takes the GPS unit from my hand, removes her own glove, and keeps poking at it. "Not wilderness professionals with two GPS units, a map, and a lot of familiarity with this exact location."

She shifts her weight, and the snow squeaks beneath her feet.

"This says it's about zero-point-nine miles to the cabin," I go on. "Where there's heat, water, hot food, and real beds. There's a little bit of tricky uphill, but nothing too bad."

I lean over and zoom in a little on the spot where a few squiggly lines are running close together on the map.

"This right here is—"

"I can read a topo map," she says tightly. I pull my hand back and grind my teeth together while it gets darker and colder and we stand around like two jackasses instead of getting a move on toward safety.

She's like a... wounded hawk right now, or something, lashing out because she's scared and cornered, and in this metaphor I'm trying to extend the raw meat strip of peace.

"Sorry," she says, after a moment. "Yes. Thank you. It's a steep uphill."

She hands the GPS back to me and takes a deep breath and rubs her eyes and generally looks miserable, though that could be the terrible lighting. To my discredit, it makes me feel better that she's having a hard time right now, because at least she's taking it seriously.

"Okay, let's do it," Andi finally says. "If it all goes horribly wrong I've got a tent and a really nice sleeping bag with a broken zipper, so I'll probably make it through the night."

"Thanks for your concern," I tell her, sliding the GPS into my pocket. She makes a face.

"Sorry," she says again. "Look, I know this is my fault. I just don't want to make everything worse. Not that I'm sure how it could be worse. This seems pretty bad and like it's everything I've been trying to avoid every time I go hiking."

I lean back into the cab of the truck, grab her sleeping bag, and start stuffing it into her frame pack.

"Could always be worse," I call back over my shoulder. "Neither of us has any broken bones or concussions right now, there are no mountain lions I know of in the area, all the bears should be napping."

"That you know of," she repeats. "*Should* be napping."

"Nature is unpredictable," I say, turning my back to the driver's seat and squatting so I can get the frame pack on. I swear I have to adjust every single strap on the thing. Andi watches me, her arms still crossed over her chest, her face tight. She's got both gloves back on, the snow flashing through the beam of her headlamp.

"Are you gonna carry that no matter what I say?" she asks.

"Yes."

"Can I at least carry something so I don't feel like you're doing all the work?" she asks, so I hand her a small backpack from the truck's cab. It has two water bottles and some emergency granola bars in it.

"Thanks," she says, deadpan with that line of panic still running underneath. I stand, adjust the pack a little more, pull the straps tight. It's too short for me, but it'll be fine for a mile.

"We'll be fine," I tell her, swinging the door shut. Everything goes darker without the dome light on, dim as it was. Now I can't see anything that's not in my headlamp's beam, and I don't like it, but the alternative is worse.

"Yeah," she says, and she nods, but she doesn't look convinced. "Let's go."

FOUR

ANDI

IF I DIE on this hike, at least the headline will say *Area Woman Dies While Semi-Competently Hiking to Safety*, not *Area Woman Dies While Chained to Tree; Motivations Remain Unknown*. I don't particularly think I'm going to die—Gideon seems pretty competent and, again, I do have a tent and sleeping bag with me—but I didn't think it was going to snow, either.

I very much did not think I'd get rescued by Gideon Bell, but I guess the cosmos or whatever has a sense of humor. Or maybe a sense of drama? A sense of irony? I'm too tired to know what it is, but it's something.

Whatever it is, I sure never thought I'd be here again, tromping through the woods with Gideon, wondering how much trouble we're going to be in. It's so familiar that I keep thinking *I hope Dad doesn't ground me this time* before remembering that I'm an adult and that can't happen. Even though the trouble we could get into now is *die of exposure* or *get eaten by a mountain lion*, at least Dad won't use his Disappointed Voice on me.

Well. He might, assuming I survive this and can contact him later.

Gideon's father didn't have a Disappointed Voice. He never got grounded when we got home too late. He never told me about his punishments, but somehow, I still knew that they were worse than mine in a vague, kid intuition sort of way. I never put together what that meant until I was in college and hadn't seen him for half a decade, though, once I started processing everything that happened. When we were five, or eight, or ten, it didn't seem weird that he had to call his parents *Sir* and *Ma'am* or that saying *I'll do that in a second* was considered backtalk or that he'd get in trouble if one of his siblings didn't do their chores. That's just what the rules were at Gideon's house.

It wasn't until college, when I was old enough and removed enough that the story became an event in my life instead of the single point everything else twisted around, that I realized it was probably why he was over at my house so much. I didn't think about it at all when I was a kid, because that was the natural order of things: Gideon came over, ate something, and then we'd roam through the woods until one of us had to go home. He was quiet, even as a kid, usually happy to play along with whatever Unicorn Pegasus Princess or Dinosaur Stomp Destruction game I came up with. We were adventurers. We were pirates. We were settlers on the Oregon Trail, orphaned children living off the land, or magical people who could turn into birds, and those were our weekends and summers for years.

Gideon was clever, resourceful, and handy. He always had a pocketknife on him—even when we were in kindergarten, something else I had to process later—and sometimes we'd pull down tree branches and make shelters for ourselves, small, shady places to hide away from the world. He was a genius at damming creeks, climbing trees, and dressing minor wounds. He knew what all the birds were called and any time we saw a snake, he'd get so excited he couldn't contain himself.

We were best friends, I think; at the very least I didn't have a better friend. He was in a different category than my friends from school or dance class or girl scouts because he was constant, a baseline, a foundational bedrock. He was the only friend I had who'd known my mom. We told each other secrets, the kind that kids have: he told me about how he'd stolen his younger brother's Hot Wheels because he was jealous, that he didn't want his mom to have any more babies, that he'd eaten the last cookie and let his sister take the fall for it.

I told him about how I'd once tripped a girl on purpose during recess and how bad I felt, about the time I stole a purple marker from the school, that sometimes I hated not having a mom. The only secret I never told him about was Rick and my dad, but I guess he figured that out anyway.

We were best friends until suddenly, we weren't.

· · · · · ★ ★ ★ ★ · · · · ·

WHEN IT FEELS like it's been long enough, I pull out the GPS Gideon gave me, just to check. I feel a little lost in time and space and seeing that our dot is closer to the cabin dot and further from the truck dot helps me feel... less lost in time and space.

Gideon glances back over his shoulder without stopping.

"We going the right way?" he asks, like he doesn't know, which he'd better be lying about.

"As long as this is right," I say.

He bounces on a step, adjusting my pack a little. I bite

back an offer to take it from him, because I know he'll refuse and maybe get annoyed about it.

"It's satellite-linked," he says. "Weather doesn't matter. It's right."

I slide it back into my pocket and focus on walking: the snow crunching below my feet, the creaks and groans of the snow-laden forest around us, the sweat trickling down the back of my neck. I'm in decent hiking shape, but cross-country through the snow is something else.

"Gideon," I finally say, when my lungs are starting to hurt. He glances over his shoulder. "Can we take a break?"

He stops without answering, the beam of his headlamp traveling over the landscape in front of us. It's mostly trees and snow except for one rock, which he points to.

"There?" he asks, and I nod.

Ice-cold granite on my butt has never felt so good. We both guzzle some water. I'm overheated, so I take off my hat and gloves for about thirty seconds before I realize that now I'm freezing, so I put them back on. We both stare, silently, into the darkness of the woods. After a moment I turn off my headlamp. Gideon looks over at me, then does the same.

"Don't want to waste the battery," I say.

"Dark is good," he answers, and then we're quiet again. Shapes form out of shadow, all shades of the same gray-blue: the lightness of snow and the darkness of the trees; the glow of the moon behind clouds and the inky black of the branches against it. It's spooky. It's beautiful.

"I'm sorry," I finally say.

"I needed a break too," Gideon says, drinking again from a water bottle.

"No, for needing rescue," I say, because *obviously*.

He doesn't answer or look over at me, breath fogging the air, visible when it rises.

"I know this is bad and it's my fault," I tell the trees in front of me, not looking at Gideon. "I should have thought ahead, or planned better, or taken a GPS or a satellite phone or something instead of just assuming everything would be fine and there was nothing to worry about."

There's a long pause, because Gideon's quietness hasn't changed.

"Why *did* you chain yourself to a tree on Christmas Eve?" he finally asks.

"Technically, I chained myself to a tree on December twenty-third."

He looks over at me, unimpressed.

"Because Chloe asked if I would do it with her," I say, which is not a great explanation. I rub my face with my gloved hands. "I said yes because I don't have a lot of friends here yet and I like her, and because Lucia and Frank are on a Mexico cruise and Dad and Rick couldn't make it down and I didn't go up, so it's not like I had anything better to do."

I blow out a breath, watching it steam in the dull moonlight.

"Also, I like the environment and fracking is bad for it," I say, as an afterthought.

Gideon is frowning at a tree, which I get the feeling he does a lot. "Chloe Barnes?" he asks. "Friends of the Chillacouth, Chloe Barnes?"

"Yeah, she founded it, or something," I say. "She organizes a lot of these headline-grabbing environment things."

"Was she *here*?" he asks, swinging his head around to look at me, and I realize he's alarmed.

"Yeah, but she had to go back into town because she forgot she also volunteered to help with the canned goods drive at the Hootenanny," I say. "She was gonna come back, but then it snowed. Shit. I hope she's okay."

Gideon hasn't moved a muscle.

"She left you here," he goes on, voice oddly flat. "Chained to tree."

"I have the key," I point out, because I do. Somewhere. "And I told her she could, it's not like she just disappeared on me."

"Chloe Barnes," he says, slowly, "Talked you into *chaining yourself to a tree* for a good cause, and then she *left* you for *the Hootenanny*?"

Okay, fine, it does sound bad when you put it that way, but I don't want to throw Chloe under the bus right now. She's passionate about causes and a little impulsive, but she's not evil.

"We should keep walking," I tell Gideon, and we get back to it without saying anything else.

· · · ★ ★ ★ ★ · · · ·

"WHAT KIND OF FOOD?" I ask Gideon's back, once he seems like he's calmed down about Chloe.

He grunts, but it's a grunt with a question mark.

"At the cabin," I go on, breath frosting in the air, my voice nearly swallowed in the quiet, snowy night. "You said there was food."

"Canned chicken noodle soup," he says, over his shoulder.

"Which kind?"

He walks for a few more steps, like he's focusing.

"Campbell's, I think," he says. "The regular one. Not some healthy bullshit."

"Fuck, that sounds *amazing*," I grumble, because it does. "How much further is it?"

I pull out the GPS I'm holding so I can answer my own question.

42

"We're close," he says, still trudging.

I stop in my tracks, frowning down at the screen.

"We're *there*," I say, because our dot is smack in the middle of the little cabin symbol.

However, I am not smack in the middle of a cabin, so something's gone wrong. At night in the woods in deep snow, probably with a pack of wolves lurking just out of sight beyond those trees. I don't think there are wolves in Virginia, but I'm willing to bet some materialized just for this occasion.

I'm sure it's fine.

"Not quite," he says.

"This says we—" the GPS's screen adjusts a little, and our dot is now *past* the cabin. "Passed it?"

"We didn't pass it," he mutters, pulling the second GPS out of his pocket. "Did you see a cabin?"

"I can't see more than twenty feet in any direction," I point out.

"These aren't accurate down to the foot," he says. "They're useful as a directional guide, but sometimes they—"

"Forty minutes ago, they were God's *extremely* accurate gift to lost hikers!"

Gideon ignores me and keeps frowning at his GPS. Then he frowns at the trees. It's not making me feel any better.

"We're at least close, right?" I say. I'm not about to panic so much as I'm about to sit down in the deepest snowbank I can find and cry, because I'm hungry and exhausted and I fucked everything up. "Maybe if we walk in a spiral pattern or something?"

"Hard to do with this many trees," he says, still not really paying attention. "I think the clouds messed with the signal a little."

"I thought the weather didn't affect these because they're satellite."

"Well," Gideon says, and does not elaborate. He seems tense, looking at the GPS and then up at the sky, around at the forest, peering back at the trail of our footsteps. I have no idea if we're on a road, or a trail, or if we just picked a direction and walked. Gideon was all, *trust me I'm a professional*, so I did, and now I'm ready to sob into some snow like a hapless maiden in a Scandinavian fairy tale.

I don't. I remain upright and merely think about how nice snow sobbing might feel right now.

"Turn off your headlamp, I can't see," Gideon says, a few seconds later, which makes no sense but I don't argue. Once our eyes adjust he circles around a little bit, looks at the paper map, and then shoves it back into his pocket.

"Sorry about that," he says, and starts walking in another direction. "We overshot a little."

I follow him because what the hell else am I going to do?

· · · ★ ★ ★ ★ ★ · · ·

"AH," he says, five minutes later, and comes to a complete stop so sudden I almost plow into his back.

"We're there?" I ask, praying that this particular Gideon Noise means *here is the promised shelter*, not *look at that interesting lizard.* Are lizards even out in the winter? Probably not. I duck my head around him and see nothing in the beam of the headlamp.

"This is the bear tree," he says, pointing at a tree trunk that looks... oily, and like it's seen better days. "Almost there."

I simply accept this without question, but Gideon is right this time: thirty seconds later we come into a clearing with a building in the center.

More specifically, a murder cabin.

It's small, dark, and quiet, and has a forbidding front

porch and a forbidding front door and, somehow, forbidding curtains hanging in every forbidding window. It's a full-on murder-ass murder cabin, and I've never been happier to see a building in my entire life.

"Thank *fuck*," is all I manage to say. Gideon makes a noise between a mutter and a grumble.

Inside, the cabin is... let's go with *cozy*. It's got a covered wooden porch across the front, two curtained windows looking out onto it, and boards underfoot that bounce more than I'm strictly comfortable with. The door isn't locked. Inside is dark but warmer than outside, a faint orange light coming from a closed wood stove in one corner. The room is split into flickering darkness and deep black shadow.

None of that makes it feel like anything but a murder-ass murder cabin, but right now I'd face down any number of Satanic cultists in need of a human sacrifice if it means I can sit and eat some soup.

"See," Gideon says, slinging my pack off his back. "Told you."

FIVE

GIDEON

BY THE TIME we get into the cabin, Andi is exhausted, cold, nervous, hungry, grumpy, and not particularly cooperative. Luckily for her, I've got eleven younger siblings, so I'm an expert in getting tired, hungry, grumpy people to eat dinner and go to bed. I put more wood into the stove. I order her to sit right next to it, remove her shoes and outer layers, and stay there while she warms up. She doesn't seem thrilled at taking orders, but she also seems happy to be sitting somewhere warm, so she does it.

While I heat up soup, I call dispatch again and tell them I found the girl and she's fine. I don't mention the truck, because there's nothing anyone can do about it tonight, no point in worrying anyone, and I can take care of it. I *do* mention Chloe Fucking Barnes, and tell Dale that the next time I see her anywhere near a tree I swear to God I'm issuing every citation I can think of, inventing a few more, and possibly calling in the FBI to investigate an attempted murder for leaving Andi like she did. I can't stop thinking about how hard she was shaking.

When I finish that, all Dale says is, "And you're all right?"

I frown at the soup heating on the stove.

"Fine," I say, because I'm obviously calling him and having a normal conversation, how else would I be?

"Good to hear, Gideon," he says, and I think he's laughing at me. "Take care of yourself. Merry Christmas."

"Right," I say, which is impolite, so I fix it with, "Thanks. Merry Christmas to you too," and hang up.

While I wait for the soup to finish heating, I text Reid that I'm still fine.

Reid: Dolly misses you

Reid: Also I might have given her slightly more treats than you said were technically allowed

Reid: She keeps glaring at me

Me: She's a cat. That's her job.

Reid: Think of it as bribing her not to eat me in my sleep

Me: If she wakes you up at 3am demanding crunchies, you did this to yourself.

Me: DO NOT give her 3am crunchies, then it will never end.

Reid: What if she gives me her murder glare, though

I leave my brother to his longstanding feud with my cat and let my friends' group text know that I made it back in one piece with a bonus houseguest. The responses are mostly emojis, followed by some earnest *glad you made it back safe* sentiments.

"Andi!" I shout, grabbing two mismatched bowls from a cupboard. "Soup!"

"That smells *incredible*," she says of reheated canned soup as she enters the kitchen.

"Eat, then call…" I start, and *fuck*. I nearly said *your dad*,

47

as if that's something I can just say to her, and I can't because this is so nice, right now: Andi being friendly and pleasant and glad to be alive. There's no way she's forgotten what I did but at least right now, we're not talking about it.

"...anyone you need to call," I finally settle on, pretending that I was so absorbed in the process of pouring soup that I couldn't talk and concentrate at the same time. "I just told dispatch that I've got you, so they're probably contacting people now."

We wolf the soup down in silence, sitting on opposite sides of the scarred wooden table. At the end Andi lifts the bowl and drinks the last few mouthfuls of broth, and that's another flash of memory: her doing that with cereal milk and her dad laughing about the milk mustache she'd get. After a moment, I drink the rest of my soup, too.

"Thanks," she says, the fingers of one hand lightly drumming the table, her braid over one shoulder. She must have redone it because it's smooth now, not the staticky, wild halo it was earlier. Her cheeks are still pink, though, twin blotches of color that go nearly to her jaw and make her pale blue eyes look even bluer. The color's coming back into her lips and there's a tiny, red scratch on her chin I hadn't noticed before. It makes me feel oddly unsettled.

"You can borrow my phone," I tell her when I realize I'm staring. I grab both bowls and jerk to my feet, the chair scraping over old hardwood. "I'll get it."

"Do you want to call your parents first?" she asks. Her voice is light, but I can hear the tension in it, see it in the ramrod-straightness of her spine. "I mean, it's your phone, I've got other stuff I need to do. There's no rush."

I nearly ask her why I'd call my parents, because the thought hadn't occurred to me.

"They're probably worried," Andi says when I'm silent

48

too long, everything about her carefully neutral, hands folded on the table in front of her. "Also, it's Christmas Eve, so..." she trails off, but there are years of weight in that ellipsis. I shake my head.

"Phone's all yours," I say, deposit the dishes in the sink, and grab the phone from where it's been charging from a solar battery. "Here. Sometimes the satellite connection cuts out but it's usually pretty good. You can use it like a regular phone, just—yeah. Have fun."

I turn away before I can say more stupid things or continue the discussion about why I'm here on Christmas Eve and not at my parents' house watching nieces and nephews run around, hopped up on sugar, while my sister Beth tries to corral them into making a nice picture or singing Christmas carols and my brothers Zach and Matt stand off to one side, letting the women do the parenting, while they subtly compare their children's accomplishments.

But that's not what Andi remembers, because she moved away before any of that. If she remembers anything it's popcorn strings and sugar cookies and cozy pajamas, songs sung next to the Christmas tree, everyone listening as my father read the nativity story. I wonder how often she thinks of it. If she thinks of it. I wouldn't.

I'd say it was nicer back then, but time casts a long shadow backward, and the truth is that we didn't know any better. We were all still kids who more or less fell in line.

These days there's only so much I can take of them pretending my brother Elliott doesn't exist and so many times I can ask them not to deadname Reid, so I usually pick one winter holiday to spend with them. This year it was Thanksgiving.

She's gone into the other room of the tiny cabin, and I can hear the creak of the floorboards under her feet. I put the bowls and the pot into the sink full of freezing cold soapy water and tell myself that I'm not listening to see who she calls.

But I hear, "Hey Rick, it's me," anyway, and it hits me right in the chest. That tender spot between the lungs, and it's so unexpected that breathing feels funny for a second, like all my bodily processes forgot what they were doing for a moment and now I'm breathing with my heart and pumping blood with my lungs.

What the *fuck* is wrong with me that hearing her say *Hey, Rick,* has me holding onto the edge of the sink and staring into the dishwater like it's got some answers?

"Wait, Rick, can you—" Andi says, and pauses. There's laughter in her voice. I grip the sink a little tighter. "Is Dad there? Can you put him on so I can just talk to both of you at once?"

It's not—it's—I don't know. It's the funny ache of releasing a grip you've held for too long, a relief and a new pain, all at once. It's the answer to a question I hadn't let myself ask for twenty years: no, I didn't rip them apart, because Andi is on the phone with her dad and her stepdad, and they're in the same house, and she's telling them over and over that she's fine, she's safe, she's *fine,* she's sorry.

When I was a kid, I was always told to give it to God. *It* was whatever bad thing I'd done or whatever bad way I felt; as if I was supposed to simply hand *it* over and be free. I tried. I always tried, and it never really worked; I could hand things over again and again, but they always seemed to come back and stick like burrs in my conscience. It was because I wasn't doing it right, wasn't trusting God enough, didn't have the right kind of faith.

After Andi left—after her family got chased away and it was my fault—I didn't try any more. For the first few years I was still too self-righteous to think I'd done anything wrong, and after that I didn't think I deserved to be rid of it. Even after I grew up, after a stint in the Army and a college degree, after therapy and a steady job and my own house, I never let go. I never told anyone who didn't know already. I never gave up the guilt, but I did push it down.

But Andi still says *Rick* the same way she says *Dad*, and I'm so grateful for this small mercy that it hurts.

Christ, I'm a mess. I'm tired and haven't eaten enough or drunk enough water. It's been a long, stressful day and it's still not over because the truck is still a mile away and I don't know when we're getting out of here. It's exhaustion and stress and being blindsided by twenty-year-old sins in the middle of it all, and after some sleep and some breakfast I'll feel normal again.

I reach my hands back into the freezing dishwater and get back to work, only to hear Andi laugh.

"Because I'm tired after my near-death experience and dramatic rescue, and only want to tell you about it—no, I wasn't really near death. Yes, I promise."

I wash the dishes as quietly as I can and try not to listen. I even start humming Christmas carols to myself, despite firmly not being a Christmas Carol Person, so I can't hear her talk to her parents. Every so often, though, she'll laugh or exclaim something and then I can't help but start listening again to the bright, happy cadence of her voice in the next room.

Strange, how she sounds exactly the same, like sunny summer days, like goading me into going past the property markers and deeper into the woods, like walking across a fallen tree over the creek, ten feet in the air, and knowing I'd follow her. She was always right. I always did, even if I paid for it later.

"Yes, a cabin," she's saying, in the tone of voice that

suggests it's not the first time she's said it. "A ranger came and got me and drove me back here. The Parkway's closed, anyway, and it's too far to drive in the snow."

She says all this like she's the authority on the matter, like she knew this all herself and wasn't stuck in a sleeping bag, cold and freaked out when I found her earlier. Her bravado could be annoying, but instead it's kind of charming.

"I don't know, Dad, it's a cabin," she says. I need something to do besides eavesdrop, so I start wiping down the counters and then the table again. "It's kind of cute and old-timey. There's a wood stove, there's a kitchen, all the lamps are oil lamps. The fridge is avocado green, you'd hate it."

I wipe down the ugly fridge, too.

"The ranger?" she asks, and for all that I'm determined not to listen in there's a note of alarm in her voice. I realize she was pacing back and forth because the soft creaking of the wooden floor stops. Suddenly, it's very quiet. "Why?"

There's a long silence. I don't breathe and don't make noise, then think that I *should* be making noise, so I pace over to the sink and toss the dishcloth in, rearrange some of the dishes in the drying rack.

In the other room, Andi clears her throat and drops her voice, so I have to strain to hear it when she says, "Uh, it's Steve."

Pause.

"Wheeler?" Pause. "No, I didn't get his badge number. Do rangers even have that? He might not be a ranger, he said he was up here to... study something. About birds and global warming?"

I think, inanely, that I never told her why I was here but that it's a good guess; for a moment, I wonder how on earth she got my name wrong.

It takes me a minute to realize that she doesn't want them to know who she's with. Of course. I probably wouldn't either.

· · · · ★ ★ ★ ★ · · · ·

"THIS IS FINE," Andi's saying, sitting on the edge of a twin bed and digging through her pack. It seems to have no organizational plan whatsoever. "Why wouldn't it be fine?"

"I like the couch," I claim.

"I don't bite."

"I know."

"I'm not—" she starts, waving her hand in the air like I'm supposed to derive meaning from it. "Look, I don't think you're gonna *do* anything. It's just beds. It's just sleeping, whether you're five feet away on that bed or ten feet away on the couch."

I shift uncomfortably in the doorway, because, logically, I know. It's not logic that's the problem. The problem is the stifling feeling that sleeping in the same room as Andi is one more thing I'm doing to her, and I've done enough for a lifetime.

"I think it's better if I sleep on the couch. That's all," I say, but Andi pauses to stare at me.

"What is it you think I'm gonna do?" she asks.

"Nothing," I say.

"I can keep my cooties to myself."

"*Cooties?*"

"I promise not to tell anyone that I tainted your honor by sleeping in the same room as you, even," she says, and there are circles under her eyes and an edge to her voice and it's been such a long day. "Just sleep in the fucking bed. It's not even the same bed."

Part of me wants to, because that would be the normal

thing to do. It's what anyone would do, but I'm not anyone. I'm the guy who came out here to be alone for two weeks and who doesn't want to be with his family on Christmas; who's never slept with anyone literally or metaphorically.

I'm the guy who's thirty-two and still a virgin, technically, which I feel like she'll somehow *know* if I sleep in the same room as her.

"I'm not worried about you *tainting my honor*," I tell her, and turn away. "I'll be on the couch. Sleep well."

"I'll sleep on the couch," she calls after me.

"No."

"I'm shorter," she argues, rising. "I come way closer to fitting on it than you do."

"You spent last night chained to a tree."

"So obviously, I can sleep anywhere."

She looks pissed, tired and bedraggled, her strawberry-blonde hair still in a braid, flyaways escaping. There are circles under her eyes and she looks strange and angular and pale in the shadows from the oil lamp on her bedside table, but I can't stop looking. I can't stop feeling like some part of me has gotten detached and knotted up in the past couple hours and I haven't a clue how to fix it.

When we were kids, I followed her anywhere. Being with Andi felt like chasing a sunbeam: she was always *going*, always laughing, always full of ideas for adventure, so bright I could never look away. She never wanted me to take care of her, and I always loved her for it. Even now, literally rescuing her from a snowstorm, it somehow doesn't feel like *taking care*.

She was the best part of my childhood, and I was the worst part of hers. Maybe the couch is penance.

"Do you need more pillows?" I ask, because I think there's one more in the chest, but it's just as sad and flat as the one already on her twin bed. "I figured you'd sleep in your sleeping bag, it'll be warmer than the blankets they've got here."

She gives me a long, serious look. I swear the shadows under her eyes deepen. *Steve Wheeler*, I think, and swallow hard because I wonder if she's thinking the same thing.

"No thanks," she finally says. "If you get too uncomfortable in the middle of the night, feel free to—"

"I'll be fine," I tell her, and turn away to brush my teeth and leave her in peace.

SIX

ANDI

IF I DIDN'T KNOW BETTER, I'd think I was having this argument with a Yeti.

"Of course I'm coming with you," I tell the creature who just walked into the cabin, either Gideon or the Abominable Snowman. "You can't just go off alone into the woods like that, it's dangerous. What if you get hurt?"

Gideon/Abominable crouches to unlace his boots. There's a long, annoyed silence until he steps out of them, leaving them in the tray by the door.

"I won't get hurt," he says, unzipping his jacket and hanging it on a hook.

"I'm so glad you've got magical future-sight powers," I say, which is a stupid comeback, but I've been awake for all of five minutes after sleeping for thirteen hours, so I'm not at my wittiest. "I'm still coming with you."

"I'm fine on my own," he says, crossing the room in sock feet, sturdy-looking pants, and what looks to be multiple layers of flannel. "You should stay here and rest, you just spent two nights chained to a tree."

"I'm rested," I tell him as he walks past me, bringing the

cold air with him. I shiver and cross my arms over my chest, because I'm wearing long johns and nothing else and I don't need my nipples to help me win this argument. Not that I think they would, since Gideon seems singularly uncharmed by me.

"No," he says again, this time from the kitchen. "Do you like bacon?"

"Everyone likes bacon, and yes, I'm coming," I say, following him as far as the doorway, arms still crossed. "What kind of question is that?"

"Vegetarians don't," he points out, opening the avocado-colored fridge and peering in.

"They like it, they just don't eat it," I say, and finally realize something. "Is there electricity up here?"

"No. How do you like your eggs?"

"How does that fridge work?"

He glances over at it from where he's standing at the counter, like he's unsure which fridge I'm referring to.

"Propane," he says. "It's connected to a tank outside."

"So, there's electricity."

"There's a fridge and a stove," he says. "Scrambled, over-easy, or what?"

I decide to question the mysteries of the cabin at another time, and rub my hands over my face, trying to wake up a little more. Weirdly, sleeping for thirteen hours will really take it out of you.

"Over-easy," I say. "Thanks. I'm gonna go get ready to hike to the truck with you."

"No, you're not," he calls out as I head back into the tiny bedroom, but I can tell he doesn't mean it.

· · · · · ★ ★ ★ · · · · ·

IT'S CLOUDY BUT BRIGHT, all the available light reflecting from the snow on the ground, and I wish I'd brought my sunglasses. At least I remembered sunscreen, a lesson I learned the hard way after my one and only skiing experience left me with the weirdest sunburn I've ever had.

Did you know that the underside of your nose can sunburn so badly it blisters? Did you know that *really* fucking hurts?

We walk in silence for a while, Gideon first, along the still-visible footsteps in the snow from last night. It stopped snowing at some point while I was asleep, but there's enough wind to puff the snow off the ground and from where it's piled on the tree branches. It's very pretty. It's very, very quiet.

In the quiet, I start thinking. Mostly about how dumb it was to chain myself to a tree because I wanted to be friends with someone. A little about how lucky it was that Gideon came to my rescue, because though I do have a sleeping bag and a tent and enough water and calories to stay alive for a few days, I'd be miserable at best.

And I think about how it was *Gideon* of all people who rescued me, and how maybe we're over what happened, now, twenty years later, though neither of us have said anything, and maybe the past is in the past and doesn't matter anymore. We're all present in the present moment and whatnot and no one is dwelling on things that happened a long time ago and that we can't change.

But also, I told my parents that I was with someone named Steve Wheeler—a person who doesn't exist, as far as I know—and Gideon definitely overheard me because the cabin is very small, and now I have to live with yet another awkward, unspoken thing between us.

"What's a bear tree?" I ask, because he mentioned it last night and I might lose my mind in the quiet.

Gideon clears his throat and takes his time to answer.

"It's a tree that bears like to rub themselves on," he finally says, talking over his shoulder to me. "They do it partly to mark their territory, and partly just because they're itchy. I think the one near the cabin has particularly satisfying bark, and it's in the middle of the range of several females."

I take a moment to extrapolate some of that information.

"So that tree is part back-scratcher and part Tinder for bears," I say. "How come humans don't have something like that? It's a great idea."

He glances at me again, and the path has leveled out a little, so we're both stomping through a foot of snow more or less side-by-side. I wonder if we should have snowshoes or something. Tennis rackets, maybe? I'm not sure I've ever actually seen a snowshoe in real life, given that I grew up half in Virginia and half in New Jersey and have never once been a trapper living alone in a rugged wilderness.

Until today, at least, though I'm still not a trapper. Not that I'm above it at the moment. I'll eat a squirrel if I need to.

"Have you tried gluing a back scratcher to your phone?" he asks, and it's hard to tell through the beard and with the hat and the coat zipped all the way up, but there's a movement at the corner of Gideon's mouth that *almost* looks like a smile.

"I didn't realize it was an option until today," I tell him. "So, the cabin is a hundred feet from a black bear pickup spot. Can they open doors?"

"They're not around right now," he says, which I notice doesn't answer the question. "They mostly hibernate in the winter."

"Mostly."

Gideon exhales, his breath puffing out and disappearing upward until it's indistinguishable from the steel-gray of the clouds above, flat and monochrome.

"This far south, black bears don't hibernate as strictly as they do further north, since our winters aren't generally as harsh," he says. "The cubs stay in the den, but adult bears often come out between long naps and do some foraging during the winter months."

"And here I thought that having a foot of snow on the ground at least meant a bear-free vacation."

"They're just black bears," he says. "As long as you don't go near the cubs, they're—"

"I know, I know, it was a joke," I say, because I also partly grew up in the Blue Ridge and am well-versed in our ursine friends. "Are there any *actually* dangerous animals out here?"

"A few," he says, grabs onto a tree trunk, and leans past it. "Hold on."

I realize he's leaning out over a steep hillside, and that it's the same one we climbed up last night. It looks much scarier from this direction, and also completely different. I'd never have recognized it. Truthfully, the landscape in the snow looks so strange and flat that I didn't even realize I was about to fall right down it.

"Oh," I say, helpfully.

"This is why I wanted to come alone," he says, but it's more matter-of-fact than annoyed.

"So no one would know if you fell and broke a leg?"

"So I wouldn't have to worry about *you* falling and breaking a leg," he says, putting down the pack that he's carrying and opening it. "I'm fine."

It's at least the third time I've heard some variation on that from him in less than twenty-four hours, and it's starting to sound like a mantra. I wonder if Gideon ever worries about himself. How often he considers that *he* might be in danger. Whether he takes himself into account at all, or whether anyone else ever does. Whether anyone else ever really has.

"It's a tie-down strap!" I say as he pulls a long, red strap with metal buckles from the pack.

"Yes."

"I *told* you."

Gideon gives me a long-suffering look and wraps the strap around the base of a tree, securing it with the ratchet. He's knotted it every eighteen inches or so, and he tests it by leaning his weight away and pulling as hard as he can.

It makes his pants—which are thick and very practical and not sexy pants, like, at all—go tight around his thighs, which... I notice.

"Okay," he says, swinging his pack back onto his back and buckling it across his chest. "I'm going first. When you come down, hang onto the strap. I think you'll be fine anyway, but it never hurts to take an extra precaution."

"Did you only bring it because I came along?" I ask, and Gideon just gives me a look and starts down the slope without answering.

We both get to the bottom without incident, though there is one part where I slip and slide several feet, banging one knee in the process. When I get to the bottom Gideon frowns at me—what a surprise—and watches disapprovingly while I brush myself off.

"Want me to take a look?" he offers.

"At what?"

Another disbelieving look, which Gideon seems to hand out like candy on Halloween.

"The knee you just smashed into a granite outcropping," he says.

"I didn't smash it and it was a rock, not an outcropping," I say. "I'm fine." It hurts, and it'll definitely bruise, but I've survived bruises before and I'll survive them again. Gideon sighs and starts walking.

The ground here is a little trickier, a slope that's rockier and has more fallen branches than before, so we go silent for a while. Gideon won't quit glancing over at me like I'm going to collapse at any moment, and I wish he'd quit it.

"You didn't answer me," I finally say after *are you going to survive this short walk in the woods* look number two hundred and thirty-eight. "About what dangerous animals are out here."

"In theory or in practice?"

I don't know what that means. "Both?"

"In theory, mountain lions," he says, stepping over a large rock. Something crunches underfoot. "If you come up against a hundred and fifty pounds of big, angry cat, you don't stand much of a chance. But they hardly ever go after humans."

"Oh," I say, and look around at the snowy forest. I don't see any mountain lions, but I'm not sure that counts for a lot. Cats are notoriously sneaky. "Hardly ever."

"Practically speaking, hogs," he says.

Crunch. Crunch. Crunch.

"Sorry, did you say hogs?" I finally ask when it becomes clear he's not going to explain himself.

"Feral hogs."

"You're saying *hogs*," I press on, because I'm not one hundred percent sure I'm hearing him correctly. "Hogs like pigs?"

"Yep. But feral," he says, and pulls out the GPS to glance at it. "Big, mean, hungry, and not much fear of humans."

"Mountain lions, bears, and wild murder pigs," I say. "Oh my."

"Feral."

I roll my eyes while he's looking away.

"*Feral* murder pigs," I say. "Sorry, I was focused on the *murder pig* part."

"Generally speaking, wild animals will stay away from humans," he says, and points up ahead. "There's the hollow where the truck is, up ahead. Formerly captive animals who've been released and reverted to nature don't have that same fear. Which is why you're much more likely to see a feral hog than a mountain lion."

"Exactly how likely is *much more likely*?" I ask, because I'm starting to regret this line of questioning. I'll be out of here tomorrow for sure and *maybe* this afternoon if I'm lucky, how much do I really need to know about wild murder pigs? I'm more likely to accidentally strangle myself on a tie-down strap.

"Well, you're extremely unlikely to see a mountain lion," he says. "I've only seen one once, with binoculars. Here, be careful."

We're on the slope leading down to where the truck is stuck, and it's not nearly as steep as the other one, but he braces himself and holds out a gloved hand. I take it, even though I don't really need to, and as we descend Gideon holds my hand a little tighter than necessary. At the bottom he lets go without looking at me.

"All right," he says, surveying the truck. "Can you drive a stick?"

SEVEN

GIDEON

"MORE GAS!" I call, the truck lurching in the snow. "You gotta ease off the clutch a little and then really stomp on—"

The truck shudders as the engine cuts out, jolting as Andi slams on the brake. I can hear her swearing through the open driver's side window, so I walk over.

"It needs a little more gas when you let off the clutch," I say, motioning with my hands to demonstrate how one drives a stick shift vehicle. "What's happening is—"

"I know how to drive a stick shift," she says, her jaw tight.

"You said you'd forgotten."

"I *said* it had been a few years and I might be out of practice," she says, giving me a sharp look. "And I also said I've never driven a truck this size, in the snow, when the wheels keep slipping and you won't quit standing behind the damn thing and I'm afraid I'm going to hit you."

"I'm beside it."

"It's *very* slippery, and if I run you over, we're probably fucked."

I rub my face with my bare hands, my gloves in the pockets of my coat, currently hanging over a tree branch because I'm sweating like a feral hog trying to get this truck out of here.

"If you run me over, you've got the satellite phone and both the GPS units, so you can radio for help and get to safety," I say. "Dale will talk you through it, he's very professional."

Andi blinks at me, her pale blue eyes a contrast to the bright pink hat she's wearing. Her nose and cheeks are red and she's got strands of hair sticking out below her hat, and in the bright snowy daylight she has the lightest freckles, and she frowns at me and—shit, I'm staring, *again*, and that tangled, detached feeling is back.

"If I run you over, I'm probably going to freak out too much to think clearly," she says. "Given that you would be— you know. Pretty bad off."

"You're not going to hit me," I say, very calmly, even though I'm not even sure why we're discussing this. "And if you do, and I'm incapacitated, then you should use the satellite phone to call dispatch, and they'll tell you what to do and send help. You'd be fine."

The look she gives me is indecipherable.

"What about when they bring me in for murder?" she asks, taking a hard left straight into Irrational Land.

"If you ran me over by accident?"

"Come on. There's one other human in a fifty-mile radius—"

"Ten-mile, *maybe*."

"—and I manage to hit him with the only vehicle available? No witnesses? No good reason for me to be out here? That's suspicious as fuck."

I have no idea why we're talking about this, but I lean against the truck window anyway.

"Andi," I say. "*Are* you here to murder me and make it

look like a freak accident?"

"No," she says. "I'm just saying that's the conclusion people might come to if I run you over by accident because you won't take two more steps back."

"I'm starting to consider throwing myself under the wheels and framing you if we don't get back to it soon," I tell her.

"How would you *frame* me?"

I grab a shovel and break apart some snow behind a tire. I don't really need to, but standing still when there's work to be done makes me restless.

"You just told me how everyone would suspect you," I point out. "You've got means, motive, opportunity—"

"Motive?" she says, and I freeze, because that was a fucked-up thing to say and I obviously shouldn't have. I don't mean that I actually think Andi's going to do it. I mean that, if I were a detective looking into reasons she might kill me, people have gotten murdered for less.

I look up, still crouched on the ground and she's still staring at me from the truck window, and the worst part is she doesn't even look mad. She looks *concerned*, and alarmed, and on her pretty face the expression is almost tender—

"Gideon," Andi says, and I stand up.

"Right," I say. "Start her up and try it again, and this time you've really gotta let off the clutch slow and step on the gas."

Andi mutters something about this being the first time in ten years she's driven a stick so she's doing great, actually, as I grab the firewood we brought with us from the cabin, each log conveniently wedge-shaped.

· · · ★ ★ ★ ★ ★ · · ·

IT'S SLOW-GOING, dirty, and an unpleasant combination of cold and sweaty. It's in the upper twenties, which is below freezing but not cold enough for the snow to have much traction, so the ground is turning into mud slush, my least favorite surface. Every time Andi gets the truck a few more inches back it's my job to shove a wedge in front of the wheels so it doesn't roll back, and half an hour in, at least she stops gasping in alarm every time I do it. There are rocks and branches and stumps underneath the snow that I can't see, and despite my heavy boots I've stubbed every toe six times, I think.

"Almost there," I tell her, and stand back. "One more good shove and we're on flat ground again." Thank *fuck*. The road —well, "road"— through here is flat and easy enough to navigate, but the spot where I slid off and gently bumped a tree has a distinct downward slope.

Andi just nods, checks that the truck is in gear—something she's done every single time even though, to my knowledge, she's never taken it out of gear—and hits it. Both the rear wheels find purchase on the flat part of the road, the truck steadily if slowly moving backward. For a moment I let myself feel relieved that we managed to get this out without making it worse, getting frostbite, or having to tell the Forest Service what happened, and—

The wheels must hit an ice patch or something because suddenly it's sliding right toward me and Andi is shouting, the front bumper gleaming with light reflected off the snow.

"Brakes!" I shout, getting the fuck out of the way, only my foot snags on something and next thing I know I'm spitting out snow, swearing, and trying to shove myself back to standing so I don't get run over.

The moment I try to move my left ankle, pain shoots through it all the way to my knee.

I gasp, eyes shut, freezing hands clenched in the dirty snow. Shit. *Shit.* In the periphery, a truck door slams.

"Gideon!" Andi shouts, and she sounds terrified again, the second time in two days I've freaked her out like this. "Shit, are you okay?"

"Fine," I tell her, both hands still in the snow, my left leg at an angle I can only describe as *incorrect.* When I finally manage to look down at my foot, the toe of my boot is still under the root I tripped over. Great.

And now Andi's here, her knees hitting the snow, her hands up and floating six inches from my right side, like I'm a dangerous but fluffy animal she wants to touch and can't.

"What happened?" she asks, breathless.

"I tripped," I say. I still haven't moved, pain still spiking up my leg. There was a definite *snap* when I went down, but I'm ninety percent sure it was a twig, not bone. "You're supposed to steer into a skid."

"Shut up," she says, and now she does put her hands on me, one on my shoulder and one in the middle of my back. They're warm even through my coat, somehow, and I close my eyes for a moment because despite everything, this feels good. "Is it your leg? Can you stand?"

"In a minute," I tell her, and she sighs like she's annoyed, but she doesn't say anything or move her hands. In a few deep breaths, I manage to flip myself over so at least I'm not on my hands and knees anymore, legs straight out in front of me. That hurts too, but wiggling my toes isn't too bad.

"That looked awful," she says. "Are your hands okay?"

"I'm fine."

"Can you move your toes?"

"Andi, I'm—"

"If you say *fine* again, I swear to God I'll run you over for

68

real this time," she says lightly, and then smiles at me. It's a strangely sweet smile for the death threat she just issued and the combination makes a fuse blow in some deeply buried, unimportant part of my brain, but I'm in no state to think about it right now. "Murder charges be damned."

"I just turned it," I say, which I'm pretty sure is a lie. "I'll be fine to drive in a minute. Don't worry, we're not sleeping in the truck."

She's quiet long enough that I look over at her. Andi's closer than I realized, one knee in the snow and one against her chest, half her strawberry-blond hair tied behind her head and the other half escaping from below her technicolor beanie, waving around her face in the breeze, and she's got that *look* again, the one I'm not sure I like.

"That's not what I'm worried about," she says, and she sounds a little strange again, like she's explaining something important to an alligator that might attack at any moment. "I can also drive, obviously, if your ankle is broken or something—"

"It's not broken," I say, mostly sure I'm right. I've broken bones, and they usually hurt worse than this, the pain already fading a little as long as I don't move it. "It's my left ankle. I can drive."

"It's a stick," she says.

"Oh, is it?" I snap, and she presses her lips together like she's stopping herself from saying something. I clear my throat. "Sorry."

"It's fine."

The silence that settles over us is familiar: it's awkward, and we're not talking about it. After a while I shift, getting my right leg under myself, and Andi stands and offers me her hand.

I must look at it a little too long, because after a beat she says, "Gideon, for *fuck's* sake," so I take it, and after a moment of standing, manage to hobble to the truck without too much swearing.

EIGHT

ANDI

BY THE TIME we get back to the cabin, Gideon's jaw is clenched so hard I'm afraid he'll crack a molar. When we got into the truck he managed to convince me that he wasn't that hurt and also that he knew the road and how to drive on it in these conditions, and I figured that hitting—or *gently bumping*, Gideon's words—another tree would be worse than letting him operate the clutch, so I gave in.

"Let's get you inside," I say, but he closes his eyes and tilts his head back against the seat. His jaw flexes. His throat works as he swallows, and his coat is open enough that I can see the tendons moving under the beard stubble, his skin winter-pale all the way down to the hollow of his throat. It looks warm and soft, and for a moment I'm stuck there, watching the subtle, delicate flex of his neck as he breathes.

"In a minute," he finally says. He doesn't open his eyes, though his hand on the gearshift moves. He's not wearing gloves. I'm starting to think he doesn't like them, and *now* I'm looking at his hand: short nails with mud underneath them and thick, calloused fingers, a single freckle on the thumb he's got hooked over the top of the shifter knob. There's something

I like about it, but that's a weird thing to think about anyone and definitely a weird thing to think about Gideon, so I shove it out of my brain, open the door, and walk around the truck to the driver's side.

"I don't need help," he says when I open the door.

"Great," I say. "Hold onto my shoulder and hop down onto your right leg anyway."

There's some grumbling and hissing as he turns in his seat, and it's not like this late model Forest Service truck is particularly high off the ground—we're not talking hydraulics here—but it's still a truck, and he hesitates long enough for me to get annoyed.

"Gideon," I say, and grab his hand, planting it on my right shoulder. "For *fuck's* sake."

He grumbles and lands on his right foot, only wobbling a little, and lets my shoulder go immediately because God forbid I provide Gideon with any help, apparently. He walks to the cabin under his own power, obviously favoring the bad ankle and just as obviously trying to hide it.

Inside, he gets his coat and hat off, glances down at his feet, and hobbles over to the couch, boots still on, left leg straight out in front of him, heel resting on the floor as he leans an elbow on the arm of the couch and runs his hand through his sweaty hair.

To my credit, I don't immediately ask if he's okay. He might stab me with a fire poker if I do, so I settle for taking off my own outer layers, shoving my hair into a tangled bun that I'm going to regret later, and sitting on the wood floor in front of him.

Gideon stares at me like I'm a pet who's about to talk, or grant him wishes, or something.

"*What*," he finally says. Good *lord*.

"How bad is it?" I ask, nodding at his left leg.

"It's fi—"

"*Gideon.*"

We glare at each other for a moment. Glaring isn't exactly my specialty, but he's being enough of an exasperating dick that I've got no problem right now.

After a moment, he huffs out a short sigh.

"It's not that bad," he says. "I just need a minute."

I, a human being with eyes *and* a brain, don't believe him, so I reach out, grab the cuff of his pants, and start rolling it up. His leg jerks and he hisses again, but he doesn't manage to move it much, and I wrap my hand around his ankle, right above his boot.

"Does that hurt?" I ask, glancing up at him.

"Not really."

"Does it really not hurt, or are you still lying about it because you think—"

"You barely touching my ankle actually doesn't hurt, believe it or not," he snaps, one elbow still leaning on the arm of the couch, his hand in his dark wild hair, and it would be a relaxed pose if every muscle in his body weren't so tense right now.

"How about this?" I ask, pressing just above his ankle bone with my thumb. His leg twitches again and he inhales sharply, so there's my answer.

Gideon meets my eyes when I look up, his face resigned and wary, his eyes steady on mine. The cabin has plenty of windows, and even though it's a cloudy day the blanket of snow outside diffuses the light and even inside it's bright as anything, the perfect all-around glow of Christmas morning or a magazine shoot.

Seated at his feet, a hand around his ankle, gazing at each other, I feel like a Renaissance painting. Some sort of supplicant, except we're both tired and muddy and bitching at each other on a couch that's probably older than either of us.

"I'm taking your shoe off," I tell him, and he grunts in response. When I look up, he's rubbing his hands over his face, finally relaxed back against the couch. It takes most of my self-control not to roll my eyes and sarcastically tell him that *he's welcome*, so I settle for just rolling my eyes where he can't see.

"My feet are gross," he says once I get the knot in his laces undone and start unwinding them.

"You're gross."

"Your face is gross," he mutters, like we're eleven again, and I snort.

He's right, though. His feet are kind of gross, once I get both boots and socks off, but worse things have happened to me. Including a couple of times that I bled all over Gideon, so this is fair.

"It's swollen," I say, comparing it to his other ankle. His feet are several shades paler than his legs, even in December, the dark hairs on them surprisingly soft. I wonder if his beard is also soft, which isn't a particularly useful thought.

"Yep," he offers, still draped over the couch.

"Can you move it?"

"I'd prefer not to."

I prod a little more, gently, and he grunts a few times but doesn't kick me in the face or anything.

"It's not broken," he says, after a bit, his big toe twitching. "It'd hurt worse if it were broken."

"Where's the First Aid stuff?" I ask, standing, and Gideon points at the tiny coat closet. He lets me wrap his ankle in an Ace bandage and fasten several ice packs from the freezer around it as well as around his knee, which he begrudgingly admits he wrenched a little when he fell.

Finally, I sit back to admire my handiwork, such as it is. Most of my expertise in this sort of thing is limited to drunk friends who did something dumb, and it's been several years since an incident of that sort, so I'm out of practice and also boring now.

"Thanks," he says, when I scoot backward across the floor and settle against the armchair, because I don't feel like going through the effort of getting all the way in. He leans his head over the back of the couch, the tendons in his neck obscured by the bright light, though his Adams' apple moves when he speaks again. "I might not be able to drive you into town tomorrow. If the Parkway's even cleared. We're not very good at snow around here."

To my credit, I don't say *no shit, Gideon.*

"Well, it's Christmas," I point out, a fact I'd kind of forgotten until right now.

"Right," he says. "That."

He doesn't move from where he's flopped: one pant leg rolled halfway up his calf, ice packs wrapped around his knee and two on his ankle, leaned against the back of the couch, head tilted back over the cushion. The sleeves of his plaid flannel shirt are pushed up and he's got something black and long-sleeved on underneath it, his hat on the couch next to him, melted snow soaking into the blue fabric.

I must be exhausted from the last couple days, because I suddenly find it appealing in a way I don't find Gideon appealing. There's something insouciant in the way he's draped on the couch, like a mountain lion relaxing at the top of the food chain. Gideon's not particularly tall—five ten, maybe five eleven?—but looking at him now, I realize he's *solid*, wide-shouldered and powerful in a way that feels impolite to think about.

So, I don't.

"Why are you here on Christmas?" I ask, suddenly loud in the quiet cabin, trading one awkward thought for another.

"Ruffed grouse census," he tells the ceiling, then swallows. "You?"

"I told you, Chloe Barnes needed company," I say.

Gideon lifts his head just enough to give me a look, and I shrug, like his answer was any better of an explanation.

"Lucia and Frank went on a cruise to Mexico because, and I quote, *fuck this performative capitalist nightmare, see you in January*," I say. "And my dad just started a new job and doesn't have much time off, so we figured it made more sense for me to visit in the spring, when I wouldn't be battling holiday traffic."

"Ah," Gideon says, and goes quiet again.

I stretch my legs out, cross my ankles and arms, and frown at him, not that he sees it because he's either asleep or staring at the ceiling. On Christmas. In an off-grid cabin that can't be more than five hundred square feet, in the middle of nowhere, with a busted ankle.

I don't really mind missing Christmas. To be honest, it's kind of nice to skip Christmas once in a while—I don't have to think about presents, or a tree, or decorating, or hosting people, or cleaning up afterward, or whether I'm making the season magical enough or whatever. It can really be a whole *thing*.

But Gideon's family was always a big Christmas family, at least when I still lived here. The whole month of December was usually Christmas Month: kids making and putting up decorations, Gideon having to go to one church social event after another, repairing whichever precious old ornament had broken this year. A flurry of costumes for the nativity play his church did every year, mending white robes and gluing together tattered, ancient angel wings. I never did find out which part he played.

I wonder if that still happens. Gideon's youngest siblings are probably in their late teens by now, so I doubt they're the baby Jesus, but he's got tons of nieces and nephews. I wonder if he still glues together angel wings and ceramic mangers.

I wonder if they still get a wild Christmas tree.

Of everything Gideon's family did for the holidays, that's what I remember the best because it was what I liked the most: the weekend after Thanksgiving, Gideon, Matthew, and their dad would go into the woods and cut down a Christmas tree, and sometimes I got to come, too, as did his other siblings when they were old enough: Elliott the last few years I lived here, Zach the final time.

I have no idea why they let me come. None of Gideon's sisters ever did, though maybe that's because they were too young; of the twelve kids, the eldest four were all boys. But I loved tromping through the woods with axes and handsaws, debating the merits of every fir tree we saw and finding the worthiest. The trees we got were never as pretty as the ones you could buy at Kroger or the Christmas tree lot down Old Lawyers Road—a little gangly and a little patchy and never quite right—but I always liked them better anyway.

Getting the tree always felt like an old pagan ritual, wild and out of place among the strictures and scriptures of Gideon's house. Even after they tamed the tree with lights and popcorn garlands and thrice-repaired ornaments, it still felt wild. Like an old god in their midst, bestowing the ancient blessings, a little dangerous and a little out of control. His parents would've hated that I thought that.

"Is it my fault you're here and not chopping down a Christmas tree?" I ask after a long silence.

"No," he says.

"So, it was your plan to be in an off-grid cabin counting grice or whatever during the biggest holiday of the year?" I prod.

"Grouse, and yes," he says.

I let it be silent for a minute, just in case he'd like to add something.

"Are you being serious right now?" I ask when it becomes apparent he wouldn't.

"*Yes*," he says, a little more forcefully than I think is warranted.

"Your family's not doing anything?" I say, casually prodding. It gets a big sigh from Gideon, who doesn't move his head but does scrub his hands over his face.

"They're doing the usual and I elected not to attend this year," he says. "Reid was very excited to host his first Friendsmas at our place, so I decided to get out of there so they could have the place to themselves, and also so no one would show up and guilt trip me or give me big sad eyes about coming to Christmas."

"Oh," I say, absorbing the layers of information. Reid must be the younger brother who lives with him who Lucia has mentioned once or twice; I don't think he was born yet when we moved away.

"But that got canceled for obvious reasons and he spent Christmas under five blankets, watching Muppet Christmas Carol on his laptop and probably eating chips and marshmallows for Christmas dinner," he goes on, sounding mildly annoyed. "Hopefully he didn't give Dolly any marshmallows."

"Dolly's an animal?" I hazard.

Gideon moves for the first time in several minutes, sitting up to pull his phone from his pocket and leaning forward to show me his lock screen. There's a faint smile on his face and some sort of creature on his phone.

"My cat," he says of the animal who is stretched out on a comforter next to a paperback of *Crazy Rich Asians* and positively dwarfing it.

"That's not a cat, that's a five-year-old in a Muppet costume," I say, and Gideon frowns.

"Rude," he mutters, settling back again. "We think they're part Maine Coon."

"They? You have more?" I ask. "Do you have an army of giant cats who do your bidding?"

"Have you ever met a cat who'll do anyone's bidding?" he asks, shifting against the couch.

"My roommate had one who would sit and shake," I say, which is true-ish. "Well, it was more of a high five."

Gideon doesn't look impressed.

"Dolly's mom showed up at a friend's place and had kittens," he says, after a beat. "He adopted the mom, I took Dolly, and some other friends took her siblings."

"That's the cutest thing I've ever heard," I tell Gideon, and he rolls his eyes and puts his phone away but I'm pretty sure he also blushes.

NINE

ANDI

TO PUT IT LIGHTLY, Gideon is not a good patient.

To put it honestly, he's a grumpy nightmare who seems bound and determined to fuck up his ankle as much as possible and who thinks that I, an adult woman in her thirties, can't make a simple dinner of spaghetti, sauce from a jar, and frozen peas. He limps around while claiming he just wants to feel useful as he narrates the extensive contents of the pantry to me, and I finally yell that I spent ten years living in Brooklyn with three roommates and a grocery budget of about fifty bucks a month, I'm *very good* at weird "whatever's in the fridge" dinners, and he needs to go sit on the couch and put his foot up before I hit him with a wooden spoon.

I don't hit him with the spoon, but it's a near thing. I also choose to ignore the scratching sound that seems to be coming from the wall near the doorway because I don't want to deal with Gideon coming in here and harumphing about whatever it is. Probably a squirrel on the porch or something.

He wins our standoff about who's sleeping where that night, mostly because he's already on the couch and no matter how annoyed I am about it, there's no way I'm going to be able to carry him to a bed, so I leave it. He's in a bad mood, and no matter how hard I try, that puts *me* in a bad mood that I can't help, which leaves everyone irritated and no one happy and both of us still stuck in a tiny cabin with no chance of getting out in the next few days, at least.

That night, it takes me forever to fall asleep, lying on a lumpy twin mattress under my sleeping bag with a zipper that I finally had to dismantle to get apart. My brain feels like an asteroid belt or something: giant, worrying chunks flying every which way and sometimes crashing into each other, knocking loose smaller chunks that are still plenty big enough to cause concern.

I moved back to Sprucevale a couple of months ago, and in that time, I've seen William Bell, Gideon's father, once. My aunt Lucia is friends with the editor of Sprucevale's tiny newspaper, so when the reporter who usually covers the school board meetings called in sick, she asked if I'd be willing to attend and write it up since at the very least, I can string a sentence together.

I wasn't expecting what I got, which was William Bell and two of Gideon's brothers—Matt and Elliott, I think, but it's been so long—in all their button-down, pleated-slacks glory enumerating a long list of books that they wanted the school library to ban. A couple people spoke against them, and they lost the vote, thank God, but it rattled me all the same. It was proof that Gideon's father hadn't changed in twenty years, and that at least two of his sons had grown into his likeness.

At least Gideon wasn't there, I remember thinking. *At least I don't have proof that Gideon grew into this, too.*

What I want right now, and what I don't have, is proof of the opposite. That Gideon is just being an asshole right now because his ankle hurts and he's stuck here with a surprise guest, not because he dislikes everything about me and still thinks I deserve to go to Hell.

Here's what I want to believe: that the reason Gideon won't share this bedroom and won't mention my queer parents is because he's an awkward, quiet guy, not because of sin or whatever. I want to believe that he skipped Christmas with his parents because he sees them for what they are. I want to believe that his little brother lives with him because Gideon is kind and open-hearted and offered his home when the kid needed somewhere to go, but I don't know anything about the story. Maybe Gideon's house is just closer to his job.

I just need to keep my head down and my mouth shut for a few more days until I can get out of here, and then I never have to worry about any of this again.

· · · ★ ★ ★ ★ ★ · · · ·

"IT'S NOT AN OUTHOUSE, it's a composting toilet," I'm telling Rick as I stand in the kitchen, watching twilight fall through the window. "It's in the regular bathroom and everything, I guess we have to... empty it... every so often? Hopefully, I'll be out of here before it's my turn."

"Wow, fancy," Rick says. "It's a wonder you want to go home at all."

"The sink and tub have drains?" my dad asks, on their house's other extension. "Where do the drains go?"

I glance down at the sink, like the drain in it will have that information written on it.

"The... ground?" I guess.

"I'm sure there's a septic tank," Rick informs my dad.

"Could just drain into the creek," my dad says.

"They'd never plumb a residence that way."

"It's not a residence, it's an emergency shelter," my dad

says. "Do you remember that place you and I went to the Poconos for—"

"First of all, that was your sister's nephew's hunting buddy's off-grid hideout that I'm a hundred percent certain he had as some sort of doomsday prepper backup plan," Rick says. "He didn't exactly build it to code. The Forest Service has *standards*."

"I don't think it drains into the creek," I offer, even though I'm not sure. Seems like it wouldn't.

"Then who's up there servicing the septic tank every fifteen years?" my dad asks.

"I imagine they hire someone," I say, and my dad grumbles a little.

The two of them are still worried about me, and being the people they are, they express that worry via increasingly detailed questions about the infrastructure and logistics of where I'm staying. After I moved into my first Brooklyn apartment at twenty-three, Rick spent a whole weekend cleaning the traps under every sink and installing carbon monoxide detectors in every room. I can always tell how anxious my dad is feeling when he visits me based on how many toolboxes he brings along, just in case I need something.

Knowing all of this doesn't make their questions about the plumbing here any less frustrating. I don't know how it works, I just know that it does, as far as I can tell.

"Is it still snowing?" Rick asks, clearly changing the subject.

"A little, not much," I tell him. "I think we're in the clear for a couple—"

I break off when I hear the couch in the next room creak and my irritation spikes through the roof.

"Hold on," I tell my parents, then cover the phone's microphone. "I CAN *HEAR* YOU STANDING!" I shout, because

Gideon is supposed to be sitting on the couch, reading his book, with his busted foot propped on a chair and wrapped in ice packs because I would like to leave this cabin someday soon, which means I need his ankle to operate a clutch.

He, however, seems absolutely fucking determined to put as much strain on it as he can. Earlier today I had to stand in the doorway and refuse to move so he wouldn't go outside and clear the snow off the porch steps, which is the dumbest thing I can imagine doing with a sprained ankle.

Two seconds later Gideon appears in the doorway, jaw set, and gestures sarcastically at the bathroom.

I clear my throat and feel like an asshole.

"Sorry," I say.

He limps across the corner of the kitchen and closes the door behind himself, and I go back to the phone.

"Sorry," I say again.

"Was that Steve Wheeler?" my dad asks instantly. "How's that going? Everything okay?"

"Totally fine," I semi-lie.

When I get off the phone five minutes later, Gideon's back in the other room, sitting on the couch next to the wood stove with his foot propped up, when I go to give Gideon his phone back. Mine's not hooked up to the satellite doohickey, since in order to do that, I need to download something and in order to do *that*, I need to be hooked up to the satellite doohickey.

"Thanks," I tell him. "Also, you've got a billion notifications, you should probably answer people."

He glances down, frowns, and scrolls.

"How are your... parents?" he asks without looking up. It's the first time he's acknowledged that there's two of them.

"They're good."

"Glad to hear it," he says, then gestures at his foot, which is elevated and wrapped in ice packs, as per my protocol. "See?"

In a moment of saintly forbearance, I don't point out that healing his ankle is also beneficial for him and that I'm hardly being an asshole by wanting him to be healthy. Gideon looks down at his phone, the screen off, like he's thinking.

"They worried?" he asks, maybe the first time all day he's initiated conversation.

"Yeah. You know," I say. "Parents."

Then he looks up at me, still fidgeting with the phone in his hand, and his expression is familiar and unreadable and god, this is all so weird and awkward, what am I even *doing*. Jesus.

"You heard the Steve Wheeler thing," I admit. It's not a question; the cabin is maybe five hundred square feet. He can hear everything.

"It's fine," he says.

"I didn't want them to worry more, is all," I explain. "They're already kind of freaking out, and..."

"They'd worry more about me than a stranger they've never met?"

I don't answer, just look away for a moment.

"Right," Gideon says, and scrubs his hands over his face, muffling his voice. "Yeah. I get it. Parkway should be clear in a day or two and then you can leave."

"Thanks," I say, and walk back into the kitchen.

I stand there for about thirty seconds, feeling like shit, then walk back into the other room.

"I'm sorry you heard that," I say, which is true. "I didn't mean for you to."

"Want me to pretend I didn't?"

"Can you?"

"Sure," he says, and leans forward to start messing with the ice packs around his ankle. "Of course. Done."

I last about ten seconds.

"I didn't say that because I think you'll do anything, it was because they're already worried that I'm out in the wilderness in a snowstorm and I didn't see any reason to make it worse—"

"I said it was fine. We can stop talking about it."

I feel like I might explode, or at least shout *stop saying fine it's not fine this is all very weird if you say you're fine one more time I swear I'll scream*, but instead I say, "Sure," and head back into the kitchen so I can pace around a little more, feeling frustrated and pent up and a little crazed. It doesn't work.

"I'm going for a walk," I announce, heading back into the main room.

"Now?"

"No, tomorrow, I just thought I'd let you know," I tell him, pulling a sweater over my head. "Yes, *now*."

"You can't leave," he says, and there's a note of panic in his voice. "It's freezing, it's past sundown, it's hard enough to find your way—"

"I'm not *leaving*, I'm stepping outside for a minute because this cabin is about five hundred square feet and I need some space," I tell him with all the calm I can muster.

"Do you know how hard it is to find someone in the woods when there *hasn't* just been a blizzard?"

"I have a general idea, yes," I snap, because my patience is gone. "Maybe that's the point."

Gideon looks horrified. Maybe I'm imagining it, but I think his eyes go wide and his face goes pale. "Andi," he starts. "It's surprisingly easy to die of exposure even in conditions—"

"I'm not going for a hike," I say, practically growling it through clenched teeth. "I'm going to go out there—" I point

86

for some reason, as if there's a direction that isn't *outside*, "—and I'm going to stand there in the snow and enjoy not being in the same space as you for a while. Maybe if I decide to get really crazy, I'll stomp around the cabin a little. I'm not going anywhere besides *not here*."

He looks so relieved that it's like I didn't just explicitly tell him that I want to be where he's not. Maybe he's used to that sort of thing.

"Take a flashlight," he says, and somehow, instead of biting his head off and saying *of course I'm going to take a flashlight, obviously I'm going to take a flashlight, I'm not a five year old* I just nod.

"I'll be back," I promise, very calmly.

"Don't leave visual range of the cabin," he says.

"Do you want me to wear a beacon?" I ask, sarcastically.

"Do you have one?"

I don't answer and settle for zipping up my coat instead, then pull on my scarf, hat, and boots.

"Try to wait at least thirty minutes before you send a search party," I tell him, and then leave before he can say anything else.

TEN

GIDEON

A SLAMMING door sounds like a cataclysm when it's this quiet. I swear it shakes the whole cabin. Rattles the windows. There's a moment where I feel like the whole place ought to simply fall in and bury me, but it doesn't; instead, her footsteps cross the porch and scuff on the path beyond and then I can't hear her any more.

I stand and limp to the window at the front of the cabin, where I shove back the ugly floral curtain and watch her stomp away from the cabin, through the snow, and then stand there, her hands in her pockets. After a moment I decide to trust her and let the curtain go.

I spend the next ten minutes limping back and forth the length of the entire cabin because Andi isn't here to tell me to sit down. I silently curse Andi and Andi's stubbornness and Andi's stupid magical thinking and Andi's willingness to lie to her parents. I curse her for acting like she does and for being the way she is and for the tangled-up way I feel around her and for crashing back into my life like this when I wasn't prepared. I stop short of cursing her for all the years she was gone, because I can't curse her for that.

By the time I'm finished cursing, I've calmed down a little.

Once I'm done stomping I stand in front of the wood stove, soaking up the warmth and staring at the fire through the window. There's something imprinted on the iron top of the stove, and the light in here right now is too low to see what it is, but I've never looked at it before. Probably flowers or wheat or a horse or something else pleasantly domestic and reminiscent of some past era, just like everything else in this cabin.

Including me, probably. Maybe that's why I like it here so much. I never grew out of the pseudo-olden-times of my upbringing, the one my younger siblings don't remember, the childhood where I got eggs from the hens every morning before I started school, where half the time the washing machine was broken so we took turns washing things in the tub, where everything was mended within an inch of its life and it had to be nearly freezing before we were allowed to turn on any heat except the fireplace and regardless of all that, my parents kept having kids. God would provide, they always said, and then when friends brought over firewood or neighbors gave us hand-me-downs or relatives fed us, my parents would give the thanks to God.

It was a long time before I realized my family wasn't normal. It was a long time before I realized that almost no one else my age had to go pick a switch when they were about to be punished. It was a long time before I realized that no one else was responsible for waking up in the night with a toddler sibling when they were only six themselves, that no one else with a little brother or sister was in charge of changing them and their sheets if they had an accident at night. Turns out most first-graders don't really know how to change a diaper or clean a scraped knee or calm down a hysterical two-year-old.

It's here, with the oil lamps and the wood stove and the

fading wallpaper, that I feel more like I'm in the right place than anywhere else. It's old, and it's a little hard and a little odd, but there's no one to worry about but myself and I can handle all that.

Usually there's no one to worry about but myself. I swallow hard, still staring into the fire, because I know what I'm about to go do, and I don't want to. Every instinct I've got is telling me that I need to leave it alone, that she'll come back and we'll be at our weird detente again, where she pretends she's not still angry with me and I pretend I don't know that anything ever happened, but I don't think I can. I feel like my skin might split open if I stay quiet much longer, and it's probably better to face her wrath for the next few days than keep all this bottled.

I stare at the top of the wood stove a little longer. I think the picture stamped into the metal is a basket of flowers, after all. The faint promise of springtime in the dead of winter.

I sigh and start the ugly process of getting my boots on, because I know what I have to do.

· · · · ★ ★ ★ ★ ★ · · · ·

SHE'S fifty feet from the front door of the cabin, off to one side, sitting on a fallen tree. I know she hears me coming because it's dead quiet out here and walking through the snow is loud, but she doesn't turn around. She doesn't even look over when I sit next to her.

"I had enough sense not to wander into the woods like a lost child in a fairy tale," she says, eyes ahead.

"I know," I say. The tree is maybe eighteen inches off the ground, pretty low, and I prop my feet in front of myself and put my hands in my coat pockets. There's a lighter in one and a rock in the other, and I rub my thumbs over both. "I didn't think you would."

"Yes, you did."

Okay, she's right. When she said *I'm going out* I jumped to the worst-case scenario and assumed that she was going to do something drastic, like try to get back to the Parkway alone, at night, in the snow, and I panicked.

"I wasn't thinking clearly," I tell her.

"Other people have sense," she says to the trees in front of her. She hasn't glanced over this whole time. "Other people know what's good for them. Even if you don't."

"This counts as icing it," I tell her, moving my foot slightly so my ankle throbs less at least for a few seconds. She glances down at my foot, then up at me. I can't see her freckles in the faint moonlight, diffused through the clouds, but I can see her eyes and her mouth and I know the look on her face.

It's been twenty years, and I still know the look on her face.

"I owe you an apology," I say, more bravely than I feel.

"It's fine," she says, voice flat and tired. "We're both stressed and keyed up because of this whole mess."

"Not about that," I say, which isn't quite right. "Well, for that. But also—"

Her gaze feels like a floodlight. I fight the urge to shade my eyes from her, hide while I say what needs to be said.

"For outing your dad and Rick," I finish, and brace myself.

The woods go very, very quiet. It feels like the trees hold their breath and the breeze stops blowing. Andi's gone perfectly still, eyes on me, colorlessly pale in the night. I can feel my heartbeat in my busted ankle and it's six, eight, ten before she moves, looking forward, staring into the trees.

"You don't owe me anything," she finally says.

"Owed or not, I'm sorry," I say. "I should have kept my mouth shut."

I've thought a thousand times about how this conversation would go, and now's the part I have to brace myself for: her righteous fury for fucking up her life. For tearing her family apart and turning a town against her. For making her move hundreds of miles away from the only place she'd ever lived and making her start over while she was in middle school, the worst time to start over.

I wait for it, and it doesn't come. Andi doesn't speak or move for so long that I start to wonder if I didn't actually say anything, just thought about it. When she does, she stands from the log, walks to a pine tree, yanks a small branch off, then comes back and sits again. The air's sharp with the scent of it and gets sharper as she pulls the needles off, one by one, dropping short dark lines into the snow.

There are a thousand more things I want to say—*I didn't mean to wreck your life, I thought I was helping, I was so scared for the three of you*—but it's not my turn right now.

"You were a kid," she finally says. "It shouldn't have been your secret to keep."

"But it was," I say. "I did for years."

Her gloved hands stop moving, the pine branch going still again.

"Years?" Andi asks, her voice strange. Suddenly I'm electric with nerves, a twisting, tugging sensation like someone's dragging a string though my veins and I pull my feet in, ankle protesting, and lean my elbows on my knees.

"Three, maybe four," I say. I've got a lighter in one hand that I don't remember taking out of my pocket, but it feels good to flip it between my fingers.

When I look over at Andi she's staring at me, unblinking, pupils blown, eyes like twin lunar eclipses.

"You knew for *years*?" she asks, voice hushed.

"I came over once without calling first," I say, the words spilling out of me. I've never told her this, never told *anyone* because when it happened I was horrified, and afterward I felt guilty for keeping the secret for so long, and then later, when I was grown, I felt guilty about how horrified I'd been. "It must have been morning. Rick was making coffee in the kitchen wearing pajamas, and your dad came in and gave him a kiss. I was eight, maybe nine. Old enough to know what it meant."

I'd tried other solutions, of course: maybe they were brothers, or cousins, or... Andi's dad was secretly a space alien with different customs or a prince from a far-off land, like Canada, where it was normal for rumpled-looking adult men to sleep at a good friend's house and use the kitchen like it was their own and kiss each other on the mouth.

Back then, I believed in demons. I knew the devil walked among us. Looked like us. Acted like us. The devil was charming, charismatic and even kind, sometimes, but still the devil. The vigilant could recognize him anyway. The Godly would be brave enough to cast him out.

I thought it was a test. I thought it was a chance to prove that I was Godly enough.

"You knew for *years*," Andi says, and she's got a look on her face like she's scratching out page after page in a notebook in her head, tearing them out, throwing them into the trash. Frantically rewriting. "You knew for that long and didn't tell anyone? And then—"

She stops, mid-sentence, like her words have run dry and there's a moment where I'm angry with her for blaming me, I'm angry with her dad and Rick for being so careless, I'm angry with everyone for making any of this matter at all.

"I put it out of mind for a while," I say, which is more or less true. "I thought a lot less about kissing when I was nine than when I was twelve, but in that year before I finally told I felt like it was all I heard about. Who I could look at, who I could think about, what I wasn't allowed to look at or think about. Keeping the secret felt worse every year."

"And that reminded you," she says. "Gideon, I didn't—you never said anything."

"I know," I say. "I beat myself up for that all the time. There you were, sinning away, and I could've saved you but couldn't work up the courage to tell you the good news about Jesus Christ even once."

Andi snorts, and I finally look over at her: twirling the bare twig between her fingers.

"That would've gone over like a lead balloon," she says.

"I didn't usually think about Jesus much when I was with you," I admit. "I thought way more about catching frogs and finding lost Confederate gold."

"You ever find that?" she asks, and there's laughter in her voice. I want to swim in it.

"Sure. Tons of it," I deadpan. "Can't you tell?"

"Is *that* how you're funding this glamorous lifestyle?"

"I stopped looking after you left," I say, flicking the lighter again. "Might still be out there somewhere."

"You never know," she says.

"I think my parents thought I might be gay because I was a weird kid who loved Dolly Parton, so they talked a lot about how evil it was so I... would change my mind, I guess?"

"Exactly how that works," Andi says.

"Joke's on them, they picked the wrong kid," I say. "They ended up sending Elliott to a conversion camp when he was fifteen."

Andi gasps, loud in the quiet, dark night, turns her floodlight gaze back on me. "Oh *fuck*," she says. "Is he—okay, now?"

"Well, they could only afford the day camp where the abuse was emotional and psychological instead of physical," I tell her, and I sound sarcastic and brittle, even to myself. "Apparently, the beatings are more expensive. And God knows our house didn't have the space for a prayer closet, so, lucky him."

She's staring at me, the leafless twig still between her fingers, and I have to look away. Thinking about what I did and didn't do as a teenager can feel like strangulation, long, shadowy fingers of my old self wrapping around my neck. Turns out no matter what, we can never leave ourselves behind.

"I," I start, and I don't want to tell her this. She knows everything I did to her and her parents back then and she can still smile when she looks at me, sometimes; why confess more? "At first, I was glad," I say. "I wanted him to stop being gay so he wouldn't have to go to hell. But he didn't get changed, he only got hurt. Obviously. And I didn't know what to do, so I joined the Army and left the minute I could. He lives in Boston now and doesn't talk to our parents. I don't blame him."

"I wouldn't either."

We sit in silence for a while, and for the first time all day, it's comfortable, like the quiet is a blanket we're both wrapped under, minds whirring.

"I thought if I told my parents about your dad and Rick, they'd help them... not like men," I admit. "I thought, I don't know, that your dad would start dating a woman instead and he and Rick would be regular friends, and you could have a normal family and none of you would go to hell anymore."

I exhale hard enough that the flame on the lighter goes out.

"God, that sounds so stupid," I mutter.

"You were a kid."

"I was twelve. It's not that young."

"You were pretty sheltered," she says, and now she's watching me flick the lighter on and off, too. "It's a miracle they let you hang out with me."

"They thought your dad was a sweet, Godly widower who was doing his best to raise a daughter alone and that I could be a strong moral influence in your life," I tell her.

Andi bursts out laughing and it's so, so loud in the snow-soaked night that something startles in a nearby tree, but it's good, like a burst of music. I can't help but smile at her.

"Wow, they got that wrong," she says.

"I was a great influence."

"You taught me how to climb barbed-wire fences and carve sticks into spears with a pocketknife."

"You could've learned that anywhere."

"But I didn't. I learned from you."

I put the lighter back in my pocket because my hand is freezing, and I stretch my legs out again. My ankle protests, and I force myself not to make a face.

"I thought you'd be angry," I tell her.

Andi blows out a breath, the twig in her hand bobbing up and down.

"I used to be," she says. "I was for years."

I wait, silent. Something I'm good at, for once.

"I couldn't stay angry," she says. "You were kind of a dick about it, don't get me wrong—"

I snort, closing my eyes. She's right.

"—But it's hard to be a grownup and stay mad at a kid for making exactly the judgement call he was raised to make," Andi says. "Dad and Rick put me in a lot of therapy. I'm still angry with your parents, and with my dead grandmother, and

I'm *pissed* at the Burnley County school board, but not with you. Not anymore."

I have no idea what to say to that, so I say, "Thank you."

"Unless you still think I'm going to hell," she amends.

"I'm not sure I think there's a hell." I'm not sure about much, these days.

She turns her head again, elbows resting on her knees, braid dangling over her shoulder, and looks at me.

And for the first time since I found her chained to a tree, I let myself really remember how we were before: two kids exploring way deeper into the forest than they should have, crawling across logs and splashing through creeks and climbing trees. Andi taught me to be curious. To be brave. To believe in unicorns and buried treasure. The memories are gold-tinted, always the perfect summer afternoon, and the sudden yearning hits me like a rubber band snapping against my skin.

"I missed you," I say, and everything I've told her tonight is true, but this is the truest of all.

"I missed you too," she says, and smiles, and the warmth of it flickers through my bones.

ELEVEN

ANDI

"THIS IS STUPID," Gideon grumbles, sorting through fifty-dollar bills. "They're national parks, the whole *point* is that you can't own them and rent them out to people."

"What do you think campgrounds are?" I ask, still holding my hand out.

"That money goes to the upkeep and maintenance of the campground itself," he says, frowning some more and reaching for the twenties. "National parks don't turn a profit off of those. The popular ones are more expensive because more people means more personnel and more maintenance. No one is enriching themselves off of national park campgrounds."

"Sounds like you should write a strongly worded letter to whoever made this game," I say, and wiggle my fingers because he's sure taking his time over there. "Pay up."

Gideon looks at the money in his hand, looks at the money left on his side of the board, and looks at me, eyes narrowed.

"You can't argue your way out of this," I tell him. "You landed on the Grand Canyon, I saw it, you saw it, everyone here can count to seven perfectly well—"

"I'm not trying to find a loophole in the rules, that's *your* thing," he says, all grumpy and offended. "When you're not stealing from the bank."

"We agreed on house rules!" I say. My hand is still out and still bereft of the Monopoly money I'm owed. "Not my fault if you don't remember your own rules."

"We never had that rule," he says. "You made it up for this game and now you're trying to trick me into thinking we had it all along."

"Gideon," I say, patiently. "Would I do that?"

"Absolutely."

For a minute, I consider telling him he's right. He's not, of course—*you can steal from the bank as long as no one catches you* is a time-honored Monopoly house rule, one we played with almost from the first time we played Monopoly together.

But saying *don't you remember* feels delicate and tentative, like crossing a canyon on a bridge made of toothpicks. Just because we finally talked last night doesn't mean he wants to be reminded. It's one thing to apologize in the cold, silent dark of night and another to run wildly down memory lane.

I've always had a bad habit of running without looking, though.

"We always played with the heist rule," I remind Gideon. "You don't remember the time you got two hotels on Boardwalk and you thought you were about to win for once, but then it turned out that Zach had stolen like five grand because no one was watching him, since we thought he couldn't be that sneaky?"

Gideon blinks at me for a moment, and I'm not at all sure this bridge is holding. I hold my breath.

"Shit," he finally grumbles. "Yeah. Was that the time Matt kicked all the pieces off the board?"

I exhale and can't help but grin.

"That might have been when he was having a really bad game and finally got a bunch of buildings built, and then next turn you rolled a double six, declared a monster attack, and knocked them all over."

"That's right," Gideon says, looking far away for a moment. "God, he was pissed. I don't think we ever found the top hat."

"Anyway, the heist rule is legit, and you still owe me money," I say. "C'mon."

Gideon considers me and my outstretched hand for a moment, then taps the bundle of bills against his opposite palm, leaning back against the sofa. We're playing on the floor of the main room, mostly because this is where the wood stove is, and he's got his bad leg stretched out to one side, the ankle still a little swollen but thick with ace bandages beneath a wool sock. Between that and the sweater he's wearing, Gideon looks cozy as fuck in a very *woodsman who can keep you warm* kinda way, which feels impolite to think.

"Or," he says, slowly. "I have a proposition."

Heroically, I don't make a joke about strip Monopoly. He'd get all blushy and embarrassed, and then I'd feel bad, and we're having such a nice time.

"Go ahead," I say, finally retracting my hand and sitting up, cross-legged.

"I'll give you four hundred, and the next time you land on one of the green properties, I'll give you half off," he says.

I lean over the National Parks Monopoly board and pretend to consider this. On one hand, it's not a bad deal; on the other, there's no guarantee that I'll land on one of those any time soon, and what if he's craftily making this deal so he can somehow win in the next turn and I'll never collect on my end of the bargain.

On a third hand, I've seen someone win Monopoly exactly twice in my life.

"Half off the rent on a green property, *and* you do the dishes after dinner tonight."

Gideon snorts at my very fair idea.

"If I'm doing all the dishes, I want free rent," he says, pointing at the shoe token currently on the Grand Canyon.

"Absolutely not," I say. "How about you give me five hundred and loan me a sweater."

"Are you cold?" he asks, frowning. "Fuck's sake, Andi, just say something, I can put more wood in—"

"They look cozy," I say, which is... the truth, I think. I said that without thinking about it too much, and now I realize what an odd bargain it was, and I should probably backpedal and take the deal, but also?

Now I really want to borrow a sweater.

"I'll give it back when I get out of here tomorrow," I say, since the reports from dispatch are that the Parkway is basically clear and should be totally safe in another day.

"Four hundred and a sweater, returnable upon your departure," he says.

"Four-fifty."

Gideon flips through the wad of brightly-colored money in his hand for a moment, like he's thinking, and then nods.

"Deal," he says, and we shake hands.

"Pleasure doing business," I tell him, taking the money. "I like the blue one."

"You want the sweater *now*?"

I finish tucking several twenties under my side of the board and glance up at him.

"I don't want you backing out," I say.

"I wouldn't back out," he says, awkwardly getting to his knees, then getting his good foot under him.

"Just tell me where it is," I say, because I forgot that getting off the floor with his ankle was a whole process. "I can go—"

"I'm not letting you rifle through my things," he says, already walking into the bedroom, muttering something about the organization of my frame pack, which is fine, thanks very much.

I steal two hundred dollars from the bank while he's gone.

"This one?" he asks, coming back and holding up a deep blue cable-knit sweater that's chunky and lovely and looks very warm.

"Yes!" I make grabby hands at him, and he makes a whole thing of sighing and rolling his eyes as he walks over to me. I settle it on my lap, take off the fleece I was wearing, and pull it over my head.

And—oh, it smells nice. Sharp and woodsy with a hint of smoke, or leather, or tobacco, or something. One of those scents that they put in fancy candles that sounds gross and then smells good.

"Are you huffing my sweater?" he asks, lowering himself to the floor again.

"No," I say, inhaling with the neck of his sweater pressed to my nose. "It smells like expensive candles and fancy play-grounds after it rains."

Gideon stares at me for a moment.

"What," he says.

"Expensive candles," I repeat. "And the *nice* playgrounds in the swanky "

"It's wool. I keep it in a cedar chest so the moths won't eat it," he says, still staring.

"Oh," I say. "It smells like cedar chest, then," I finish, and he's still giving me this look like he's regretting every moment of this borrow-a-sweater deal, and also like I'm suddenly speaking in a foreign language, and *also* like I'm a small child who needs to be dealt with delicately lest I have a sudden meltdown.

It smells like him, I guess, but it also doesn't. I can't quite say what Gideon smells like in my memories of him, but his cedar-chest-and-nice-candles sweater isn't unlocking anything in my brain the way scents sometimes can. It's brand new, and the wool is already warm from my body heat, and the shoulders are too wide and the sleeves are too long, and it smells *new* and really, really good, and I'm having a confusing time.

Gideon watching me like I'm television isn't helping.

"It's my turn, right?" I finally ask, and he nods.

· · · · ★ ★ **★** ★ ★ · · · ·

BECAUSE GIDEON IS, at heart, a gentleman, he lets me take my sponge bath and brush my teeth first that night. The sponge bath is actually a pretty decent way to get clean—it's soap and water, after all—but my hair is currently hopeless. My plan is to keep it in a braid until I can finally take a glorious, glorious shower when I get home tomorrow.

Because I'm a stubborn asshole, I take up residence on the couch while he's taking his own sponge bath and brushing his teeth. He's consistently refused to either a) just sleep in the other twin bed in the bedroom, or b) let me sleep on the couch, so I have no choice but to take matters into my own hands.

I'm snuggled deep in my sleeping bag, almost comfortable, and reading *Tender is the Storm* when Gideon walks through the door, stops, and frowns.

"Your face is gonna get stuck that way," I tell him without looking up.

"Why are you on the couch?"

"Because I'm going to sleep here," I say, turning the page. I didn't finish reading it and I'm gonna have to go back, but I like the dramatic effect. "Your sleeping bag is in the bedroom, on an actual bed."

"Andi," he says with exaggerated patience, a mood I recognize from watching him deal with small children for many years.

"Gideon," I say, finally looking at him over the top of my book.

He crosses his arms over his chest and tries to look... stern, or intimidating, or grouchy, or something, I guess. I grin and wave.

"This isn't over," he grumbles, then walks into the bedroom. There's some rustling, and I go back to my book, unconcerned.

There's a small, reasonable part of me that knows I shouldn't be pushing it like this. Gideon and I used to know each other; we don't, anymore. Our truce—our friendship?— feels fragile and sticky as spiderwebs, and I should be gently building trust and establishing rapport or whatever people do in these situations.

But there's this face Gideon makes when he pretends to be annoyed with me but isn't, or at least when he's not as annoyed as he's pretending to be, and that face delights me like little else.

Some of it is pure, giddy relief. Some is cabin fever and boredom. Some is pure, simple enjoyment at getting a reaction out of him, and I've chosen not to examine that last thing too closely. He was the closest thing I had to a sibling when I was a kid, so *noticing* how he looks in sweaters and well-fitting hiking pants feels a little odd and uncomfortable, like I'm some Jezebellian pervert and he's still the church-going innocent he once was.

Though I'm pretty sure he doesn't go to church anymore,

and I can only assume that in the last twenty years he's gotten up to some perversion of his own. Which is another very impolite thought, Jesus, I'm done with that now.

Also, he won't even sleep in the same room as me, which suggests that he probably feels the same way as far as appropriate thoughts are concerned.

"Off," he says, walking back into the main room, carrying his own sleeping bag and pillow. He stops by the side of the couch, looming over me, and in the low light of the wood stove, two oil lamps, and the headlamp I'm using to read, it's actually a little intimidating.

"No," I say anyway.

"Andi," he says. "We've already established a precedent here. I sleep on the couch, you sleep on a bed."

"Here's the thing, though," I say, and finally quit pretending to read. "I'm on the couch already, so you may as well go sleep in a bed, particularly because your ankle is still healing and I need you to drive me into town tomorrow."

"I can't let you sleep on the couch."

"I bet you can."

Gideon gives a resigned sigh, then turns and drops his sleeping bag and pillow on the floor behind himself. Then he pulls his sweater over his head—I'm still wearing the blue one I borrowed—and unbuttons and pulls off the flannel shirt he's got on underneath.

All he's got on now is a dark gray long-sleeved thermal shirt—the kind with the waffle weave— that he's wearing a base layer, and the thing about base layers is that they're close-fitting. That's, like, the point of base layers. They're tight so you can put more clothes over them.

Which is to say: now I'm staring at Gideon's back in this tight shirt as he rubs his hands over his face, which makes all the muscles in his back and shoulders bunch and flex in the dramatic, flickering lights.

I stare. My brain momentarily clears into light static and a distinct feeling of dismay at my reaction. It's not—I shouldn't. I really shouldn't.

"Andi," he groans, all low and rough, into his hands, and I can feel my eyes go wide. What the *fuck*. "C'mon."

I almost say *yes*, but come to my senses.

"I live on this couch now," I announce, burrowing as far as I can into the cushions.

"Don't make me do this."

"Go sleep in a bed like a regular person," I tell him, the sleeping bag all the way up to my chin. "Isn't the whole point of this that you can't sleep in the same room as me anyway? Shoo."

He heaves another deep sigh, and it moves his shoulders and back a little, and it's alarmingly appealing, is what it is.

"Don't *shoo* me," he mutters, and turns, and shirt is actually quite tight and he's so pretty and stern and he *pushes the sleeves up to his elbows*, and who the fuck gave him permission? Wasn't me.

"If you don't want me to *shoo* you, then—HEY WHAT THE FUCK?!"

Gideon crouches, shoves his hands under me, and lifts me off the couch like I'm a pile of laundry in need of folding, and it's unfair and undignified and also very hot and that's a hell of a combination.

"Warned you," he says, turning for the bedroom.

"Okay, *no*," I say, squirming against him. I succeed in knocking my sleeping bag off, but not much else. "You can't just—"

"Try not to struggle too much, I don't want to hurt my ankle again," he says calmly.

"Then put me *down*."

"I will."

"Now, asshole."

"The less you struggle, the sooner I'll put you down," he says, turning sideways to go through the bedroom doorway, his arms tightening around me, and he's very solid and very warm and wow, his face is close right now. And he's touching my butt, technically, and his fingers are splayed along my ribcage in a spot that's kinda grazing my underboob, and I'm glad for the low light because I'm ten thousand shades of red right now.

"Why won't you let me help you?" I shout, and grab the door frame. Gideon grimaces, hissing through his teeth, and I let go instantly. "Sorry," I gasp. "Are you—"

The fucker just gives me a smug smile, walks two more steps, and dumps me onto a twin bed so hard the frame creaks.

"*Ow*," I say, and instantly, he looks worried.

"Sorry, are you—"

I grab his wrist and pull. Gideon stumbles toward the bed and catches himself with his other hand so he's leaning over me, and before I can think about it I knock that arm from under him and shove.

Gideon is heavy. He's also full of complaints, but he's off-balance for a few seconds so I take advantage of it and push him as hard as I can to the other side of the narrow, tiny bed, wriggling out from underneath him so I can get back to the couch.

I've almost made it—just one foot stuck under his thighs—when he lurches forward, hooks and arm around my waist, and slams me back onto the bed.

"Ow!" I yelp, mostly for effect.

"Sorry," he says, but doesn't seem particularly sorry

because he's still got a forearm braced across my ribcage, and he uses it as leverage to push himself to sitting.

"I can't breathe," I say, and now he's flipped himself over, still holding me down, and we're face to face and it's very close to dark, and I'm having nothing but bad ideas.

"You can breathe enough to complain," he points out, which is rude, even if it's true. "You gonna stay down this time, or—"

I wriggle enough to free one leg, hook it around his hips, and shove with my entire body so hard that he rolls and hits the wall, which makes it shake, which makes both of us freeze for a second, like we're waiting for the whole cabin to fall down around us.

Thankfully, it doesn't.

"Be *careful*," I say, pushing myself up so I can use my weight to grab his shoulder and pin him, sort of.

"That was your fault," he says, seamlessly grabbing my wrist and rotating it so it's behind my back, which pushes me wildly off-balance enough that I very nearly face-plant into his chest. I'm breathing hard, and a lot of my body is touching a lot of Gideon's body, and he's definitely winning this dumb wrestling match, and oh my god what was I *thinking*. Gideon's the oldest of twelve. He can probably wrestle a smaller person into gentle, unharmed submission in his sleep.

"No, it was yours, because you're being unreasonable," I tell his pecs, warmth rolling off them in waves. He's breathing a little fast, too. "Ow," I add as an afterthought, even though it doesn't hurt.

Gideon snorts and pushes me onto my side, and suddenly we're face-to-face in this twin bed, one arm pinned behind my back. Our knees are touching, and if I struggle at all, the rest of us will be touching, too. Out of self-preservation, I quit struggling.

"Andi," he says, and he sounds a little out of breath, a little gravelly, a little annoyed.

I wait for him to go on, but he doesn't. We just... lie there, in the almost-dark, inches away from each other. My heart is thudding away, and I'm trying not to pant into his face, and I'm trying not to move at all because we're so close that any movement at all will lead to *touching* and I really, really want to touch him. I want it way more than I should, to touch Gideon who doesn't even want to sleep in the same room, and whose hair is falling across his face and who has the loveliest eyes and eyelashes, and who's looking at me right now like—

My brain shuts off, overridden by a wave of terror and elation. I don't move. I barely breathe, because if I breathe too much we might touch even more. His fingers around my wrist shift, his thumb stroking across the heel of my hand, still holding it behind my back.

"Gideon," I whisper. My voice isn't working. He swallows and it's so quiet that I can hear it perfectly, see the hollow of his throat move in the dark. Oh, god, I'm such an asshole.

"You can't win this," he finally says, and lets my wrist go, the spell broken. "I'm sleeping on the couch."

He gives me one final *look* and then throws a leg over me and shoves himself off the twin bed. I lie there, still breathing hard, blinking at the ceiling, feeling ten kinds of confused and twenty kinds of flustered.

Thank God I'm leaving tomorrow.

TWELVE

GIDEON

I SIGH at the bacon in the cast iron skillet as my phone buzzes *yet again* on the countertop. I'm grateful for satellite technology in general—it's why I managed to rescue Andi, after all, and that turned out to be good—but it also means that everyone in my life knows they can get a hold of me even now, and I hate that.

I also regret telling people that I'd be briefly coming into town today, because Reid wants me to stop by the house and check up on the rehab critters, and Silas is trying to cajole me into staying overnight so the four of us can have our gift exchange, and now Javi is swearing in the group chat because his presents for us aren't finished yet, whatever they are. With Javi it'll either be a poorly glued together popsicle stick coaster or a perfect, detailed carving of my cat Dolly that he spent months perfecting. He's not big on middle ground.

"Okay, I'm packed," Andi says, walking through the kitchen and into the bathroom. "Oooh, bacon?"

"Yup."

"Thanks," she says, and emerges from the bathroom holding her toothbrush and toothpaste, because she's a liar who *wasn't* packed yet. "Holy shit, is that blueberry pancakes?"

"Go finish packing," I say as she comes up beside me, at least a foot away, craning her neck and getting nosy about breakfast, and it doesn't matter that we're nowhere near touching because goosebumps race up my right side anyway. I swear I can still feel her hand on my wrist, stronger than I was expecting, pulling me on top of her.

It kept me up half the night. It's exactly why I didn't want to room with her, because if she'd been a couple feet way, it would've been the whole night. Even if she's not mad at me any more, it doesn't mean she wants me thinking *thoughts* about her all night from four feet away. The least I can do as penance is go into the next room to stare wide-eyed at the ceiling while thinking about how she was stronger and more ruthless than I expected.

I know how she meant it: the same way as she meant the Monopoly game, as friends who grew up together. We used to invent rules to make board games more fun and we used to roughhouse every so often, back when we were kids. I was eight and didn't really understand that attraction existed, much less feel it about Andi. Even when I was twelve and she moved away, attraction was kind of abstract, the understanding that I liked looking at women in movies and on posters.

But last night, for a few seconds, she was warm and breathing hard enough to push her ribcage into my arm and it was nothing like looking at a woman on a poster.

"I'm finished," she says. "Where'd you get blueberries?"

"The blueberry store, and you're not finished packing, your toothbrush is in your hand *right now*."

Andi catches my eye and then rolls hers dramatically.

"Why do I ask you anything?" she says, but there's that

undercurrent of laughter in her voice that I've realized is usually there, and I don't have a good response for her, so I don't respond at all.

"Looks good," she says, and before she leaves, she swipes her finger through the remaining pancake batter and sticks it in her mouth.

"Hey!" I shout, but she's already gone, so I frown at the bowl instead.

Thank fuck she's leaving today.

· · · · · ★ ★ ★ · · · · ·

"GIDEON," Andi says, her mouth full. "These are amazing. I need the recipe."

"They're all right," I say, and focus on putting a piece of bacon onto a bite of pancake, because I can feel myself blushing, which is ridiculous. It's just a pancake. Andi said almost the exact same thing about the chicken soup I reheated for her the first night. She probably likes everything. I shouldn't be this pleased that she likes my pancakes.

"If these are all right, I shudder to think what good pancakes taste like," she says between bites. "Is it an out of body experience? Do you take a bite and instantly co—uh."

And now we're both bright red. Great.

"It's a mix, I just added frozen blueberries," I say, not making eye contact. I don't think I can. "And couple other tweaks."

"It's especially good with the bacon," she says, and we both fall silent for another moment. "The food up here is better than I'd have thought. Pancakes, bacon. That omelet yesterday was better than I can manage on, like, a regular stove."

"I make do," I shrug, and take another bite of pancake.

"I figured we'd be eating cereal and canned milk or something," she goes on. "Granola bars and freeze-dried eggs, that kind of thing."

"It's a cabin, not prehistoric times," I point out.

"Did they have a lot of granola bars in prehistory?"

I sigh again and don't look at her, because I know she's still doing that thing where she laughs at me with that look on her face that crinkles her eyes and that smile that means she's expecting me to join in, and I can't quite deal with it right now.

The thing is, she's right. The two mornings before I rescued her from the tree, I had granola bars and instant oatmeal for breakfast, and I ate them standing over the kitchen counter and looking out the window. No real point in cooking when it's just me, but her being here gives me an excuse to whip something up. Besides, the last time we took the truck out we ended up hiking a mile back to the cabin, and I'm not expecting that to happen again, obviously, but Andi may as well eat a real breakfast just in case.

We finish up in silence, but it's a pleasant, friendly silence, so I like it. I grab her plate and take it to the sink when my phone buzzes on the table, then buzzes about six times in a row.

"That better be important," I say, submerging the plates in the sink.

"It's from... uh, 'wizard emoji, ninja emoji, Wildwood Society BFFs, crystal ball emoji, candle emoji, toilet paper emoji?'"

"Mother*fucker*," I mutter, wiping my hands on a towel and crossing the kitchen to grab my phone, because I'd forgotten that Wyatt got ahold of it last week. "Those assholes."

"Are you a freemason?" she asks, chin on one hand. "I

have so many questions, like what's the deal with the eye in the pyramid on money?"

"I'm not a freemason," I tell her. "It's just—it's a joke."

"That's what you'd say if you were a freemason," she points out.

"No, it's not," I say, swiping my notifications open, because no one can leave me alone. "Being a freemason isn't a secret. My great-uncle was a freemason. He was always complaining about the meetings."

"Can he explain the weird stuff on money?"

"He's dead," I say as my phone buzzes again.

"Because he spilled the secrets?"

"Because he was ninety-three," I say.

Silas: We can use my place. Levi's mom gave me leftover pie.

Silas: And I have way too much hot sauce from my dad.

Javier: So, you're suggesting hot sauce on pie?

Silas: No

Wyatt: I'd try it

Javier: Weirder things have been good.

Wyatt: Pepper jelly is a thing, sweet and hot totally go together

Silas: If you come over you can't talk about sweet and hot

Wyatt: You know you're my favorite sweet and hot thing, don't be jealous

Javier: Excuse me

Silas: ANYWAY

Silas: Maybe around four, depending on Gideon?

"Everything okay?" Andi asks, her chin still in her hand, looking worried. I shake my head.

"Fine," I tell her, and stick my phone into my pocket. "You ready to head out?"

"Yep!" she says, stands, and heads into the other room.

I inhale for what feels like the first time all morning. I know I should give my friends an answer—and I should go hang out with them—but deep down, I don't want to spend the night at home. I want to drop Andi off and come straight back here, because if I go home Reid will have a thousand questions about me rescuing Andi from a tree, and if I see my friends *they'll* have questions about the same thing, and then they'll all want to know who Andi is and why I've never mentioned a childhood best friend if we were that close, and I'm not ready for all that. Reid knows the general sketch of what happened, but he was a baby when it all went down, and I think Silas and Wyatt might remember the kerfuffle, but I'm not sure they know it was my fault.

And—last night. I need to be alone with it for a little while, at least until I feel better about it. I'd wonder what I was thinking, but I wasn't. I shouldn't have picked her up off the couch, first of all, and I shouldn't have put her on a bed and I shouldn't have *let her pull me onto the bed* and I absolutely shouldn't have pinned her arm behind her back like that, and I need a couple of days to work through everything I did wrong.

Gideon, she whispers, and my rational mind still isn't fully back online.

· · · · · ★ ★ ★ · · · · ·

"YOU COULD GET your ankle checked out while you're in town to drop me off," Andi says, glancing down at my feet as the truck jolts over the uneven dirt road back to civilization. There's still snow all over the ground, but this road is much more serviceable than the barely-there dirt track I had to take to rescue her. I think the Forest Service comes and puts more gravel on it at least twice a decade, so it's basically luxury travel.

"I'm fine," I tell her. "Barely hurts at all any more."

"You could even stay down for a few days instead of going back to a cabin in the middle of the woods where no one will hear you scream if you hurt it again," she goes on, ignoring me.

"I'm *fine*," I remind her. "I'll be careful."

"You were being careful when you sprained it the first time," she says, which I don't have a good response for.

"I've got the satellite phone," I say. "You want me to check in with you every few hours?"

I'm being sarcastic, but as soon as I say it aloud, it's... appealing. I wouldn't mind if Andi texted me sometimes while I'm up here. Just to check in.

"Would you?" she asks, eyebrows raised. "Have you answered your friends yet or did you just frown at your phone and assume that would be enough of an answer?"

I sigh, carefully navigating around a dip in the snow-covered road the size of a large pig, and don't respond because she's technically correct and I'm not going to dignify her technical-correctness with an answer.

"Is that no?" she finally asks, staring straight ahead. "To me texting you?"

"What? No," I say quickly, glancing over as much as I dare. "I mean, yes. Text me, it's fine."

"Well, as long as it's fine," she says.

"I'd like it," I say, and from the corner of my eye I can see the skeptical look she shoots me. "Really. I would."

"When are you coming back?" she asks. "Maybe we could—"

She cuts off mid-sentence because I brake hard, both of us

leaning into our seatbelts, the pine tree air freshener swinging wildly from the rearview mirror. The truck slips a little, but this road isn't nearly as bad as the one to the mining site, so disaster doesn't strike this time.

Well. Not that kind of disaster, at least, but the road in front of us is... no longer a road.

"Uh," Andi says. "Shit."

THIRTEEN

ANDI

"WELL," Gideon says, and lets the word hang in cold, snowy silence for a while.

"Is this an avalanche?" I ask, after a bit, because I'm honestly not sure. I thought avalanches happened in, like, the Sierra Nevada or the Himalayas or something. The Blue Ridge mountains just don't seem dire enough to have them.

"Yup," he says. "Don't go any closer, I don't know if—"

"Gideon," I say with exaggerated patience.

"I just don't want you getting hurt," he grumbles, after a minute, and of course I feel like an asshole.

The road's gone, for a good fifty feet where it snakes through a hollow in the mountains, then picks up again on the other side. Where there should be road there's a flat slope of snow, downed trees, rocks, and dirt, a big blank space on the side of the mountain, suddenly open to the sky. It's short enough that I could easily walk over it, except walking on a recent avalanche is a terrible idea.

There's no way the truck's getting over it, and we're still a bunch of miles from the Parkway.

"Any chance there's another route?" I ask, though I'm pretty sure I know the answer.

"None I'm willing to take," Gideon says. He takes his knit hat off, runs his hand through his hair, then puts it back. "If you want to hike out, there's a couple trails we could take, then call for a ride once we're at the bottom," he says. "It's a good ways, though. And we'd need an earlier start so we couldn't start until tomorrow."

I don't miss the fact that he says *we*, but I also don't bring it up. Of course, Gideon assumes that he'd be escorting me to safety on a bad ankle and then *hiking alone back to the cabin on that same bad ankle*, and I'm not even going to acknowledge that.

"It'll probably melt in a few days," I say, because this is my first winter back in Virginia in a very long time, but isn't that how it works here? It snows, and instead of dealing with it everyone just waits seventy-two hours for the snow to melt?

"I'm willing to bet the road's out," he says, still looking out at the mass of snow and debris, arms crossed. "Even once the snow melts, it's gonna be..."

"Once the snow melts, we can go the back way," I say, which elicits no reaction from Gideon. "The way you got to the mine site where you found me?"

"You mean the way where we already ran off the road once?"

"It was dark and actively blizzarding," I point out.

"And in a few days it'll be muddy and slippery or muddy and frozen over," he says. "I wouldn't go that route unless I really had to. Pretty dangerous for vehicles."

Now he tells me, and there's twist of guilt somewhere behind my ribcage.

"Oh," I say. "Sorry."

"You don't have to apologize more."

"Did I apologize at all?"

"Only about twenty times that night," he says. "And a couple times since then."

I blow out a foggy breath toward the trees still over us and the sky above them. The avalanche tore a window through them, so even though we're still standing in forest, it's lighter than it would otherwise.

"Then I un-apologize and I'm not sorry for making you drive that road and get your truck stuck," I say, because Gideon is being difficult and I can *also* be difficult, dammit. "I'm proud of my actions and I'd do it again."

That, at least, gets a snort and the tiniest smile out of him.

"At least don't do it on my watch," he says. "I can only lose so many years of my life to the stress."

"Noted," I tell him.

* * * * * ★ ★ ★ * * * * *

AFTER A HAIR-RAISING twenty-point turn in the snow on the side of a mountain that involves a lot of shouting and more than a little bickering, we head back to the cabin, because what are our other options? Gideon claims it's got enough supplies to last out the winter, and while I'm not sure I completely believe him, even I can tell the pantry has enough cans for a pretty long time.

"Home sweet home," I declare when we step through the front door. "Cabin, I missed you."

"Keep moving, you're in the way," Gideon grumbles. He's holding the frame pack he wouldn't let me carry and trying not to look amused.

"Do you want me to track snow into the house or do you want me to move?" I ask, untying my laces. "It's up to you."

"How much longer do I have to put up with this?"

"I think you mean to say *how much longer do I get to luxu-riate in the pleasure of your company*," I correct, standing up again in my sock feet. "Go ahead."

Gideon's faintly pink, probably from the excitement of the drive and the sudden warmth of the cabin. "I'm not saying that," he tells me, shifting the frame pack as he toes off his own boots.

"C'mon," I say, blocking the path to the rest of the cabin. "*How much longer will I have the pleasure—*"

"Is that tent still in here?" he asks. "Can I go live in that?"

"I can't believe you'd rather move out than admit my company is kind of okay."

He's pinker now, and trying not to smile.

"Fine," he says. "Your company is kind of okay. Can I come past the doorway now, please?"

· · · · · ★ ★ ★ ★ · · · · ·

GIDEON IS on the phone for a million years, so I take his sweater again and try not to start worrying. All the same, I have visions of the snow piling up over the door frame, the two of us completely stuck in the cabin for god knows how long. At worst we'll hike out in a few more days, once Gideon's ankle is healed enough, and someone will come collect the truck at a later date.

Meanwhile, I've got nothing to do—like, truly *nothing*, which feels bizarre—so I grab *Tender is the Storm* again. I didn't get very far last night, but there's a naked man on the cover, which seems promising.

I'm on page six when Gideon marches into the room and holds his phone out at me.

"For you," he says, which turns out to mean a phone call from a number that looks vaguely familiar.

"Andi!" my aunt Lucia says as soon as I answer. "Good, you don't sound like you're freezing to death."

"You talked to Rick and Dad?" I say as Gideon nods once, then retreats to the kitchen.

"I just got done answering twenty questions about what kind of insulation I thought a remote Forest Service cabin might have," she says. "I told them I had to go before they could start asking how well I thought the floors might be sealed."

I look down at the floor. It's a hardwood floor that's seen better days.

"Fine, I think," I tell Lucia, who laughs.

"More interestingly, I got to answer a lot of questions about Steve Wheeler," she goes on.

There's a brief silence. I make a face into it.

"Yeah?" I say, determined not to give anything away.

"Oh, they want to know everything," Lucia goes on cheerfully. "Whether he's from here. Where he went to high school. Whether he went to college. Who his people are, because Blake and Rick couldn't place a Wheeler clan, but they *did* move away ages ago, so their memories might be at fault with that one."

"I... can ask?" I say, even though it's pointless, because Lucia clearly knows I'm lying.

"Is there a particular reason you didn't tell them you're up there with Gideon Bell, or is it the same reason you haven't wanted anything to do with him the last couple months?" she goes on, sounding determinedly casual. I can practically see her leaning over a houseplant and subjecting the poor thing to her scrutiny while she skewers me via satellite phone.

I let my head drop back against the arm of the couch, bodice ripper falling to the floor.

"Fuck," I say.

"Sweetheart, it's literally front-page news," she goes on. "Below the fold, but still. 'Forest Service Employee Enacts Daring Rescue.'"

"I didn't want them to worry," I tell the ceiling. "More, at least."

Lucia sighs dramatically, the way only a southern sixty-something woman who has Seen Some Shit can sigh.

"Look, I didn't think it through," I go on.

"You don't say."

"How was I supposed to know it was going to be *in the newspaper*?" I ask, because honestly. "Isn't there anything else going on in Sprucevale right now?"

"Course there is," she says. "They held a vote to name the snowplow, and *Snow Money, Snow Problems* won, but the old farts in charge don't want to use that so now they're fighting. That's above the fold."

"My daring rescue lost to a snowplow?"

"The debate's very heated," she says. "And Andrea, if you didn't want them worrying, that ship has sailed and is halfway to Australia by now. Do you know how many voicemails I had when I got back? Twenty-three, and I'm shocked it wasn't more."

I cringe at *Andrea*, because while Lucia never wanted kids of her own, she can sure say a full name like it's a guilty verdict.

"Don't tell them, I'll do it," I say.

"I don't get involved in your business," she says, inaccurately. "But make no mistake: it *is* business. And I'm more worried about why you lied about who you're with."

"Because of," I start, acutely aware of Gideon's footsteps in the next room and the thinness of the interior walls. "...what happened."

Lucia's quiet a moment.

"Ah," she finally says. "Is that also the reason you never want to talk about him?"

Guess I wasn't subtle about changing the subject whenever he came up, then.

"You noticed?"

"Andrea."

"I figured there was a good chance he'd turned out like the rest of his family and I didn't want to know if he did," I say, as quietly as I can.

"And?"

"He didn't."

"Well, I'm glad you're not up there with a shit-for-brains bigot who can't think past the end of his own dick," she says. "I'm not on speaker, am I?"

"What if I said yes?"

"I reckon it would be time to start apologizing," she says serenely. "Though I meant every word I said."

Lucia does *not* get along with Gideon's father, William Bell.

"Gideon's fine and it was dumb to lie," I tell her, because I need to get off this topic, like, ten minutes ago. "How was the cruise?"

· · · · ★ ★ ★ ★ ★ · · · ·

GIDEON WANDERS BACK into the room as I'm saying goodbye to Lucia, his tablet and a book under one arm. He's got a green sweater on today, just as cozy and warm-looking as the other two, and I nearly tell him that it really brings out his eyes but don't.

"Reid's the brother who lives with you?" I ask instead, looking down at the screen of his phone.

"Yeah."

"He sent you a picture of a plate of raw meat," I say, handing the phone over. "I don't know if that's urgent or something."

Gideon takes the phone, looks at the poorly lit picture of red meat strips arranged neatly on a white plate, and mutters something to himself while he texts back.

"He's not training Dolly to enjoy the taste of flesh, is he?" I ask, stretching my legs out on the couch and wiggling my toes in my socks.

"Cats are carnivores," Gideon says, still half-distracted by what I hope isn't Reid's dinner. "She already enjoys the taste of flesh."

"Remind me never to burgle your house."

"You needed reminding?" he says, and puts his phone in his pocket, then crosses his arms and looks at me, half-sprawled on the couch.

"Can't hurt," I say as he walks over and waves one arm at me in a *make space* gesture. It's odd how used to him I already am, but it's also nice. Funny what patterns you remember about a person.

"It's for R-185," he says, sitting on the other end of the sofa. I'm still half-reclining, my head on the armrest, legs haphazardly crossed in the middle of the couch.

"Of course," I say, because what the fuck is that? A terminator?

"Who, if you'll *let me finish*, is a bald eagle who broke her humerus when she got tangled in a fence two months ago, and the raptor sanctuary didn't have space, so I'm letting her rehabilitate in my back yard."

"There's a bald eagle in your back yard?"

"In a cage," he says quickly. "A big one. Big enough for her to walk and heal up until the wildlife center has space for her.

Anyway, Reid had to thaw some more of her food and wanted to make sure he did it right."

"You have a pet bald eagle and didn't tell me until right now," I say. "What's her name?"

"R-185."

"That's a designation," I say, being very patient with Gideon.

"She's a wild animal."

"She's eating steak in your back yard," I say, and on a whim, put my feet in his lap. His thighs are warm beneath my Achilles tendons, and also... solid. Quite solid.

Gideon looks at my feet for a long moment. It's long enough that I'm about to move them because that was kind of a weird thing to do in the first place, like, are we that kind of friends? But then he settles his right hand on my left ankle, his fingers wrapping all the way to my Achilles, his thumb on the bony knob.

I don't move.

"Uh," Gideon says, like he's lost his train of thought. "Well, she has to eat something. Raptors are obligate carnivores and she's in no shape to hunt. So."

"Still sounds like a pet," I say.

Gideon sighs and tilts his head back against the cushions, holding onto my ankle while he lets himself slouch, like he's making sure I'm not going anywhere. After a moment, I realize his thumb's tracing a circle around the knob of my ankle and he gives me an exasperated look. Maybe I'm imagining it, but I think there's a hint of a smile somewhere in there and it gives my heart a weird stutter.

It's the most relaxed I've seen him this whole time and if I didn't know better, I'd think maybe he was *happy*. I try not to overthink it.

"Reid calls her Victoria," he admits. "Because he's a big

softie and I'm worried that when we have to give her to the wildlife center, he's gonna be upset."

There's moment of quiet where I try to imagine getting emotionally attached to a bald eagle. I'm sure people have done it, but all I can imagine is majestic-yet-beady eyes looking at me and thinking about murder.

"I'm more worried about C-347, though," Gideon goes on, his thumb still moving, his hand warm through my wool sock. There's a sliver of his pinkie that's cool against the skin of my leg, and it's taking up more of my attention than it should.

"Is that one a crustacean?"

Gideon shoots me another weird look, which is probably fair, so I put on my best *innocently curious* face. "C is for *canid*," he says. "It's a fox who was shot in the hind leg and had to have it amputated."

A tripod fox. Oh my *god*.

"Reid calls him Fluffy," Gideon admits, and I think he's trying to sound annoyed but his voice has gone all soft and warm, talking about his little brother and the wounded animals he takes care of, thoughtlessly holding onto my ankle in this sure, calm way, like I need to be settled and he's the one to do it.

"Are there pictures?" I ask, and Gideon rolls his eyes.

"Andi," he says, all patient and offended-sounding as he pulls his phone out with his other hand. "Of *course* there are pictures."

FOURTEEN

GIDEON

FOR SOME REASON, I let Andi win the argument the next day over whether I can go *do my job* or not. I'm up here during the winter for the sole purpose of conducting a survey on the nesting habits of the ruffed grouse, and so far I've surveyed precisely *one* of several probable nesting areas.

I tell her that, obviously, and point out that my ankle feels *much* better and it's wrapped up properly and also I'll be very careful, but she just folds her arms and blocks my way to the front door, as if I could not a) use the back door in the kitchen, or b) simply lift her up and move her, something I've already proven I can do.

In any case, I'm attempting to compile data on a tablet—a pain in the ass, but the laptop takes way too much power to bother bringing to the cabin—when she bursts through the kitchen door, a tiny flurry of snow swirling through at her feet.

"Did you know there's a sled?" she asks, all breathless, still in the doorway, holding up a plastic sled just over the threshold so it's technically outside.

"Close the door, you're letting snow in," I tell her.

"It looks pretty nice, actually," she goes on, turning back to the sled she's still holding up, her braid sliding across her back, her cheeks and nose faintly pink from the cold, her fuchsia hat dotted with melting snow.

"It's a Wal-Mart plastic sled."

"Yeah, but it's the *expensive* Wal-Mart plastic sled," she says, enthusiasm undampened. "You know, they always have the super-cheap ones out front in the bin for ten bucks, and those are the ones that crack if you look at them funny, but if you go to the winter outdoors section in the back you can get a nicer one for thirty dollars? This is a *thirty-dollar* Wal-Mart sled."

"What are you, a cat? Come in or go—"

"Yeah, yeah," she says, lowering the sled to the porch and *finally* stepping inside so she can close the door. "We're not paying to heat the outdoors, stop letting the outside in, what was I, raised in a barn?"

"I didn't say any of those things."

"You didn't have to," she says, bending to take her boots off, but she's smiling at me like it's a joke and I'm in on it, so—I guess it is. "There's some wild stuff in that shed."

"Why were you in the shed?" I ask. "You should be careful, there are probably black widows—"

"It's December, they're all dead," she points out, taking off her hat and coat and draping them over a kitchen chair, which isn't where they go. Underneath she's got my blue sweater on, and she pushes the too-long sleeves up her arms like it's already a habit.

It's a couple sizes too big for her, chunky and formless, but it looks good anyway. She's all flushed and cozy and warm, and wearing my sweater like it belongs to her, and I'm somewhat alarmed to discover I don't hate it. The opposite, actually, which is even *more* alarming.

"Could be snakes," I say, instead of all that.

"They don't hibernate?"

"They'd stop hibernating right quick if you dropped a shovel on one."

"I can outrun a frozen snake," she says, opening the fridge, as if that's even the issue here. "I'm gonna make tomato soup and grilled cheese for lunch, you in?"

"I can make it," I say without thinking.

"*You* can sit your ass down at that table and wait to be served," she says, pulling the ingredients out. "Keep playing *Stardew Valley*."

"I'm not playing *Stardew Valley*," I say. "I'm compiling the GPS data from—what?"

She's grinning this reckless grin at me, braid over one shoulder as she rifles through a drawer for the can opener.

"I'm just teasing," she says. "You don't have to look so mad."

"I don't look mad," I grumble, shutting the tablet and pushing it to one side because I'm clearly not going to get anything done. "It's in the drawer next to the sink."

"Ah," she says, pulls it out, and shuts the drawer with her hip. It's not the sort of thing I should notice, but at this point I've got a whole goddamn list of things I shouldn't notice about Andi but do anyway.

Like: the slight gap between her front teeth when she smiles at me, smaller than the gap she had as a kid but still there, like she had braces but they didn't fix everything.

Like: the way she wears leggings that dig into her waist a little, and thinking about that soft, fleshy bump is why I burned dinner last night.

Like: how she was stronger than I expected when she wrestled me on that bed and how I liked that more than I should have.

"You sure I can't help?" I ask, because the alternative is to sit here and watch her, and that feels dicey at best.

"If you really want to do something, stick your foot on a chair," she says without looking up from the soup she's pouring into a pot. "Rest that ankle because after lunch, we're going sledding."

"I've got work to finish," I say, glancing at the iPad even though I also put my foot on a chair. "I'm already a couple of days behind on tagging, and if I want these data sets to mean anything in the spring, I can't afford to lose more time. I can't just go sledding in the middle of the day."

She glances over her shoulder as she puts a slice of cheese into her mouth and smiles around it.

"Suit yourself," she says, and goes back to making lunch.

· · · · ★ ★ ★ ★ · · · ·

"ALMOST THERE," I say an hour later. I've got the sled under one arm and Andi crunching through the snow in front of me, and I don't want to talk about how this happened.

"There's still a lot of trees," Andi is saying, hands in her coat pockets, breath fogging out in front of her, cheeks and nose and lips all pink again.

"It's a forest."

"You said there was a good spot!"

I sigh because I'm a sucker with no spine and even less ability to say *no* in the face of the way Andi looks when she thinks she's got a good idea. She had the sled at first, but it's kind of big and it was awkward for her, so after the fifth time she knocked it into a tree and dropped it I picked it up.

"Here," I tell her. "Just after that rock."

"How far from the cabin are we?" she asks, plunging ahead.

"Maybe three-quarters of a mile," I say, watching her braid swing across her back. "If you check the GPS I handed you before we left, it'll tell you exactly—"

She stops and her face lights up. Coincidentally, I forget what I was saying.

"This is perfect," she says, and turns to me, she's smiling with her eyes crinkled, the kind that threatens to turn into a laugh at any second, and it feels so good I have to look away.

"Should be okay," I tell her, coming up alongside with the sled. "I've never actually been sledding up here, but I know a couple other rangers have. Nice slope, no debris."

The spot's open to the sky, maybe twenty feet wide and two hundred long. In the summer it's a pleasant little meadow with a steep slope, but in the winter it's a decent place to sled if you don't want to run into a tree. Or so I've heard.

"You should go first," she's saying, pushing her hat down a little further onto her head, the ties on either side swaying in the breeze.

"So I can find out if there's stumps under the snow?"

"Because you carried the sled and found the spot," she says. "You should have first crack at it."

"It was your idea."

"That I badgered you into carrying out."

She's right, but that doesn't mean I'm giving in.

"Andi," I say, folding my arms and dredging up all the hard-won dealing-with-toddlers patience I've acquired in my life, "stop arguing and sled down that hill while there's still light to do it by."

"It's two in the afternoon," she says, but she takes the sled from me and plops it into the snow, aims for the hill, and begins the process of lowering herself as the sled slides around, as sleds are wont to do. "I haven't been sledding since

I was a kid," she admits, laughing, breath puffing toward the sky. "How do you—"

"Here," I say, and crouch to hold it still. When she gets in it puts her face six inches from mine, and it's not as close as that night in the dark, but it feels warm despite the cold. "You want a push?" I ask when she's in, nylon rope gripped in both hands.

"You were joking about the stumps, right?"

"I don't think there's any," I tell her, down on one knee, my hand on the back of the sled behind her. Without meaning to I slide my gloved thumb along the fabric of her coat, the whisper of it so loud in the snowy quiet. "Ready?"

"Bombs away," she says, and I push her over.

Andi shouts all the way down, a high-pitched *wooooo!* that breaks through the stillness like someone opening a heavy curtain and letting the light in. When she finally comes to a stop at the bottom she's doubled over in the sled, her forehead on her knees, and I'm about to shout down when the sound of her laughter trickles up to me.

I'm smiling. I can't help it.

"That was great!" she shouts, standing. "See?"

"See what?"

"Sledding was a good idea!" she shouts, starting back up the hill, sled dragging behind her.

"I never said it wasn't," I call down, and she somehow rolls her eyes with her whole body, still tromping back up.

"Yes," she says, when she gets to the top. "You did." She's out of breath, eyes bright, skin flushed as she holds out the sled rope.

"Doesn't sound like me," I say, and take it.

"What?" she says, swallowing like she's trying to control her breathing. "You said it was *ridiculous*."

"I wasn't wrong."

"You're *smiling*," she says, like I could be doing anything else when she's this close and this happy.

"I'm allowed to smile."

"Here," she says, and points at the flattened snow from her sled run. "Sit. It's your turn."

FIFTEEN

ANDI

AT THE BOTTOM of the sled hill, Gideon comes to a stop, then carefully leans out of the sled and plants a stick next to the nose of the sled, adding to several other stick-markers in the snow, a good twenty feet short of where the trees start again.

Then he turns back to look at me, half-rolling out of the sled, and when he's on his knees he raises both arms into the air.

"I got it!" he shouts up at me.

"That's not further than my last one!" I shout back.

"It's at least two more inches," he says, pointing at some sticks in the snow.

"I don't believe you!"

"Come down here and check!" he says, getting to his feet and brushing the snow from his pants. I hope his ankle is okay, but he hasn't said anything and it's not like I can do much about it out here.

"Come up here and bring me the sled!" I shout back, and he starts trudging up the hill. We've managed to make an okay path up one side of the slope, and after at least an hour of sledding we've both taken off our outer layers, which are currently on one of the granite boulders near the top of the slope.

"You can check all you want," Gideon says when he gets to the top, half out of breath. "I beat your record, fair and square."

"It's not fair, you're heavier," I point out. "You've got more... momentum."

It's momentum, right? High school physics was a long time ago, and I'm vaguely recalling some experiment where we proved that a ping-pong ball and a bowling ball fell at the same speed. Velocity. Whatever. It may or may not apply to this situation.

"Life's not fair," he intones, and he sounds serious but there's a hitch at one corner of his mouth, his pretty green eyes barely crinkling. I haven't seen Gideon smile this much at a stretch since we've been together up here, and it makes me feel like the first time you plug in the Christmas lights. It feels like having him back.

"Thanks," I deadpan. "Any other enlightening words of wisdom about sledding?"

"*You* were complaining about fairness."

"I wasn't complaining," I say, and now I'm grinning at him because this is winding him up, I know it, and it's kind of fun. I like getting under Gideon's skin more than I should, and I feel bad about it, but he doesn't seem to mind that much and I kind of can't help it. "Just making an observation."

That gets a flat, unimpressed look, but I'm close enough to see the way his lips just barely move as he tries not to smile. They're pink with cold but they look warm, and I think about that for a moment longer than I should.

"We should go soon," he says, rubbing a hand through his hair and looking at the wide blue sky. "I'd like to be back well before sundown."

"We have time for one more?"

"Sure," he says, and gives me a *your turn* gesture toward the sled.

"Both of us," I say on a whim.

"We won't both *fit*."

"Sure we will," I say, though I'm actually not confident, either.

"It'll break."

"If it hasn't broken yet, I don't think it will," I say, again with more confidence than I technically feel. "C'mon. We'll beat our distance record. Get in."

Gideon makes a big show of sighing and shaking his head and acting like he's giving in to me as a big favor, but I'm onto him. He likes fun as much as the next person and just thinks he shouldn't for some reason that I'm not going to examine right now.

"Scoot back," I tell him, and he does, upright in the sled with his knees wide, both feet planted in the snow outside it.

I guess I sit between his legs, and I can feel my face flush a little more because I hadn't thought that far ahead, but I'm suddenly nervous about it and even more nervous that I'm subconsciously giving into my newly discovered Gideon-is-attractive thoughts. Which seems rude to Gideon, who's clearly humoring me until I leave.

"Are you getting in?" he asks, and yes, I am, sitting up ramrod-straight between his legs, trying to touch him as little as possible in this sled that is very much not designed for two adults.

Then Gideon ruins it by wrapping an arm around my waist and pulling our bodies together from hip to shoulder, and even through the layers he's so warm and solid that I shiver. His arm tightens when I do, so when he says "Ready?"

in my ear, voice like rough-hewn wood, all I manage is a wide-eyed, breathy, "Yeah."

He pushes us off and then we're hurtling down the hill, and I was right about momentum or whatever because we're going way faster this time, the ground zooming by. I shout, just for the hell of it, and I could be crazy but I think I can feel Gideon laugh silently behind me, his arm solid around my waist.

Seconds later we're at the bottom of the hill, flying past all the sticks we stuck in the snow, definitely beating the last record Gideon set—by a lot, actually—and oh, *shit*, we're going way too fast and the trees are coming up and—

"Oh *shit!*" I yelp at the same time as Gideon says "Fucking—" and then we both fling ourselves to one side, landing in the snow in a tangle of limbs and profanity. A moment later, there's the plasticky *clunk* of the sled hitting a tree and bouncing off harmlessly. I'm half on Gideon, his arm and one leg under me, and I roll off with all the grace I can muster.

"Sorry," I gasp. "Are yo—"

"Did you—"

We stop and look at each other, both breathless and snow-covered. It's stuck in his beard and his hat and his gloves as he rolls onto his back and I push myself onto my knees.

"You okay?" he asks.

"Fine," I say. "How's your—"

I cut off because Gideon's *grinning* as he sits up, brushing the snow off, and it's infectious. I can't help grinning back, and I can't help wanting to take this moment and bottle it so I can bring it out whenever I want. Gideon does a lot of things, but he doesn't really *grin*.

"That was fun for you?" I tease. "Leaping from a moving vehicle?"

"That's what you think just happened?"

"It sounds better than *I talked Gideon into something reckless.*"

"It's not reckless, it's just sledding," he says, and reaches toward me. "You've got—"

He doesn't finish the sentence, just runs a gloved hand along the inside of my collar of the fleece I had on under my coat, knocking the snow out. The fabric of his gloves brushes the back of my neck, and it's not skin on skin, but I get goose-bumps anyway.

"Thanks," I say, but his hand lingers there when I look up and suddenly realize how close we are, my knee brushing his thigh, his face inches from mine. He's stopped grinning but those telltale crinkles are there around his muddy green eyes, the soft indents that are on their way to becoming laugh lines someday, and there's a thought. Gideon, with laugh lines.

Gideon's hand is gentle but firm around my wrist in the dark. The bloom of heat in every point of contact: my knee against his thigh, his elbow over my waist.

I feel like a deer in the headlights, like something huge and maybe catastrophic is barreling toward me, but all I can think about is how beautiful the light is. Gideon's still looking at me, his pretty eyes still smiling. The crash is inevitable.

"There's," I say, and raise one hand to the snow melting in his beard, but my glove's covered in snow and I only get more on him, and I'm distracted by his mouth, his gloved hand still on the back of my neck, the memory of his arm around my waist and his hand on my wrist and his thumb tracing around my ankle. I shouldn't, but his eyes flick to my mouth.

I shouldn't, but I lean in and kiss him before I can think any more.

His mouth is just as soft and warm as it looks. The snow

in his beard and the tip of his nose are cold against my cheeks, and it's sweet and gentle and I can't believe I'm doing this—

Gideon's not kissing me back. He's gone still as a statue, frozen in place. I jolt back like I've been scalded.

"Fuck," I babble, my heart hammering so hard I can feel it in my throat, my face cold and then hot. "I'm sorry. I'm so sorry, I don't know what—"

I'm mid-apology when his lips hit mine again and the words *a mistake* disappear into the warmth of his mouth, sweet and tentative and needy, all at once. He kisses me and pauses, lips a millimeter away like he's thinking, and I close the distance. It's back and forth like that, each press deeper and warmer and giddier. I can't believe I'm doing this. I can't believe I'm getting away with it.

I can't believe it feels so *good*, sitting in the snow, both of us a little off-balance as we work out the angles where our mouths fit together best. I scrape his lip with my teeth and mumble an apology. In response, he puts a gloved hand on the side of my neck and I gasp, a rush of cold air against my warm, wet lips.

Gideon grunts, pulls away, and before I can wonder what's going on he grabs a finger of his glove with his teeth and yanks it off. Then his hand is on me again, cold fingers sliding into my messy hair and his warm palm against my neck.

I make a noise I'm not sure I've ever made before. There's a drop of melted snow from his glove on his lower lip, and when I get close enough I lick it off and then his tongue is sliding against mine, hot and slow, like we can memorize this. I don't make another noise, but I want to. I do pull a glove off and work my fingers into his unruly dark hair, knocking his hat off as he pulls me closer, mouth never leaving mine.

It's better than it's got any right to be, both of us sitting in the snow in the middle of the woods. Gideon kisses me unhurriedly, lazily, like there's nothing else he'd rather do. He pulls his other glove off and tugs me forward by the waist until I'm half in his lap, tangled on the snowy ground, and it's dizzyingly warm everywhere we're touching and cold everywhere else.

Finally, I can't ignore how numb my butt is, and I pull back, swallowing as if I can mask the way I'm panting for breath.

"I, uh," I start, and instead of pulling back his mouth traces a line along my jaw, beard tickling my neck as he brushes a kiss against the spot below my ear and I forget what I was going to say. God.

"What," he murmurs, and I swallow.

"I can't feel my butt," I say, and he stops, the tip of his nose cool against my ear. I shiver, my fingers wrapped around the back of his neck. I can feel him breathing.

His lips are still brushing my skin when he says, voice low and scratchy, "We should get back."

"For sure," I agree, doing my best to sound normal and failing. "It's... late?"

For a moment he barely moves, one hand in my hair as he kisses my neck again, mouth hot as a brand even as I shiver. He stays there, lips barely brushing me, as he moves his other hand from my waist down, over my hip, settling atop one thigh and holding on.

He's not squeezing. He's not *gripping* me, just holding on in that patient-but-firm way he seems to do everything, hand spanning the muscle, the heat soaking through the pants and leggings I'm wearing and sinking into my skin.

"Okay," he says into my neck, and now he *does* squeeze my thigh, a bolt of warmth and something else scaling my spine. "Up."

He untangles himself. I'm suddenly cold everywhere he was touching me, and he's all business, brushing his hair back, adjusting his fleece, finding his gloves. I point to his hat, still behind him where I pushed it off, and he hands me mine.

In a minute we're both standing, re-arranged like nothing happened, except my skin still tingles where his lips were and he's flushed across his cheekbones, his mouth deep pink, his hair even more riotous that usual where it's sticking out from under his hat.

I should say something. I should acknowledge what just happened, that it happened. Gideon looks a little nervous and a little lost and I should tell him that I liked it. That I meant it. That I'd happily do it again and more when my butt's less cold; that I've been thinking about kissing him kind of a lot but didn't really mean to actually do it.

My heart feels like it's thumping sideways, like it's somehow gotten stuck the wrong way around it's Gideon, I just kissed *Gideon* and I liked it and despite everything, I wasn't prepared for this. Someone should say something. *I* should say something—

"If the tortillas are still good, we can make burritos tonight," I blurt out as Gideon wraps the sled rope around his hand. "Do you like burritos? I think they're super."

Gideon clears his throat and looks up at the top of the slope, then glances over at me. His face is perfectly neutral, so I give him a cheerful smile because that's what my face does on autopilot, sometimes.

"Yeah," he finally says. "Burritos sound good."

SIXTEEN

GIDEON

THERE ARE TORTILLAS. There are refried beans. There is cheese.

We make burritos. We don't talk about what just happened.

"Have you ever put grouse in these?" Andi asks, standing in front of the stove, poking at beans with a spatula. Her hair is in a fresh braid, over one shoulder, and she's down to leggings and thick socks and my blue sweater that she stole.

I'm on the brink of losing my mind about it and she's acting like nothing's happened. Maybe nothing did. Maybe when people don't get told practically from birth that thinking sinful thoughts will send you to Hell, they kiss people in the snow and it's not a big deal.

Maybe this is only a big deal to me. The thought makes my chest twist unpleasantly, so I shove it aside.

"Grouse?" I echo.

"Sure. You said they were game birds," she says, shrugging as she stirs, balancing on one foot and tapping the toes on her other foot on the floor behind her. Fuck. What was I doing?

"That doesn't mean I cook and eat them myself," I say,

grabbing a cast iron pan from the cabinet. I'm supposed to be making dinner, not wondering whether her skin's also a little pink under the sweater.

"Might be good. And if you're catching them anyway..." she trails off, shrugging.

"Have you ever actually been hunting?" I ask, walking up to where she's blocking practically the whole stove, leaning and tapping, sweater sleeves rolled up around her wrists.

I take another step forward and tap her on the hip to get her to move over, and she gives me a smile like sunlight. *Fuck.*

"Nah, never appealed," she says as I put the pan on the other burner and turn it on. "Rick used to go when I was younger, and I think a bunch of his family do it, but I never went. Lucia has friends who give her venison in exchange for tomato plants, though."

"Well, processing birds is an enormous pain in the ass without the right equipment, and the equipment's not worth it unless you do a whole lot of it," I say, watching the pan and not Andi. "But if you'd like to catch one, get the feathers off, and butcher it for grouse tacos, be my guest."

I stare at the pan, willing it to heat faster. Andi's quiet right next to me, so close that every time she moves scratchy wisps of wool rub against my bare forearm, and it's making my entire arm tingle.

This has never happened to me before.

Not the physical parts. I have, in fact, kissed women. I've been naked in sexual situations that resulted in orgasm. Not often, but enough. That said, my relationship history is... by-the-book.

Meet a woman, somehow. Ask the woman out. Go on dates. Kiss. Maybe more, all on a timeline that feels pre-determined, like I'm checking boxes. Inevitably call it off before it gets serious and wonder, for the millionth time, whether it's something wrong with me. It's been different, once or twice, felt less like checking boxes and more like anticipation, but those never lasted, either.

I'm *supposed* to be dating. Hell, I'm *supposed* to be married with a couple of kids by now, like my siblings Matt or Zach or Beth, and there's been no small measure of concern over the fact that I'm not. At a certain age, I've come to understand, you're supposed to simply pick someone and start reproducing, and neither part of that equation has ever appealed to me.

I'd rather be alone than settle, and I had a vasectomy when I was twenty nine. My family doesn't believe me about the first and doesn't know about the second. Except for Reid, who drove me and then spent a weekend making fun of me while I complained about my balls.

The last time I kissed a woman without a date first was in college, where I did some alcohol-fueled fumbling that I never felt great about the next morning. Even those were few and far-between. I started college when I was twenty-four and had already enlisted, gotten out, and worked the kind of job that made me decide to use the money from the GI bill, so I was older than most of the kids there. The only urge I ever got about drunk eighteen-year-olds was to make sure they got home safe.

Truth is, the alcohol was good at shutting up the tiny voice that's always whispered *this is wrong* about every physical encounter I ever had.

"Do your parents still have chickens?" Andi asks, and I realize I've been staring a hole in a frying pan.

"No," I say, plopping a tortilla onto it. "Someone left the door to the coop open when I was sixteen or so and a fox got in there."

Andi gasps, appropriately.

"Wasn't pretty," I agree. "I didn't think I'd get the smell out of my nose for a week. Gave Sadie nightmares. She'd named all the hens."

I don't bring up that my brother Elliott and I were the ones who wound up cleaning the blood and feathers or that when Sadie had a nightmare, it was me she'd come looking for. Andi throws me a glance like she knows anyway.

"I saw her," Andi says. "Lucia's friends with the managing editor at the Sentinel-Star, and they needed someone to cover a school board meeting, so I did it."

"I didn't know you were a reporter."

Andi laughs, glancing over at me like we're sharing a joke. I wonder what would happen if I just kissed her right now, whether the moment has passed, whether she's decided it was a bad idea or what. I don't know what the rules are here, and I'm adrift.

"Oh, I'm not," she says. "I'm a grant writer, but that means I can string sentences together decently and they were desperate, so I went." Andi pauses, clearing her throat, not looking at me. "Your dad and brother were there. Actually, I thought it was Elliott, but I guess not if he lives in Boston."

"Matt, probably," I say, and carefully place a tortilla on the hot cast iron pan. "He and my father still... agree on a lot of things."

"Ah."

"This was the meeting where they wanted to ban books?" I ask. The tortilla is puffing up in a few spots, so I grab it with my fingers and quickly flip it.

"There are tongs," Andi says, frowning at me. "Don't—"

"Quit fussing, I'm fine," I tell her.

"I'm not fussing."

"That was textbook fussing," I say, and I can see her roll her eyes on the edge of my vision.

"Was *not*," she says. "Anyway, yeah, they were trying to get a bunch of books taken out of the school library for immorality. And it's not like Sprucevale Public Schools are a bastion of progressive thought, it was like, the book about the penguin chick with two dads."

"Sadie say anything?" I ask, taking the hot tortilla out and plopping it onto a plate, then handing it over to Andi.

"No, she was just there. I saw her talking to Matt later and it looked... tense. I didn't say hi, I didn't think she'd remember me and wasn't in the mood to talk to Matt just then."

"Understandable," I mutter. I'm also not often in the mood to talk to Matt, who's only a year younger than me but seems to have had a completely different childhood.

"They didn't get the books taken out, but it was close," Andi says, loading beans and cheese onto the tortilla as I heat another one and pointedly don't watch her try to roll the one she just overfilled. "Shit, I'm terrible at this."

"I'm sure they'll try again. My father doesn't enjoy being told *no*," I say, and lean toward her. A few stray hairs stick in my beard, and the spot where I kissed her neck in the snow earlier is right *there*, so close, and I have no idea what the fuck I was doing in the first place.

"Yes, I fucked up the burrito," she says. Right. "Take some of the filling so I can—thanks."

"My father is," I start, rolling my own much neater burrito, but I'm not quite sure where to go from there. "I don't agree with him on most things."

Andi finally finishes wrangling her mess into a burrito, then licks refried beans off her thumb. It shouldn't be as enticing as it is.

"Me either," she says, and we head to the kitchen table.

· · · · ★ ★ ★ · · · ·

THAT NIGHT, she doesn't even try to convince me to sleep in the bedroom with her. She says goodnight after she brushes her teeth, and then there's a long moment where we look at each other—her in the threshold to the bedroom, me on the couch reading a book—and then she smiles like a flash of sunlight, says goodnight, and turns away.

I feel a little like I'm being asked to make small talk in a language I don't speak, and instead of saying *yes, isn't this lovely weather* I'm telling her that some animals eat their young when they feel threatened because their instinctual calculation is *if someone's gonna get the energy from consuming these, it may as well be me.*

When I was eighteen, I started feeling bad for what I'd done to Andi and her parents. I know it's too old. I know I should have felt bad right away, but it took joining the Army and getting sent halfway around the world for me to finally understand just *how* wrong I'd been and how small a world my parents had made for us.

All kinds of people join the military, is the thing, and it turns out most people aren't evil. People are mostly people. They do some good shit and some fucked up shit, and people who thought the same way as my parents sure didn't have a monopoly on doing good shit. Once I realized that, everything else started to crumble.

I should have reached out to her. I found her Facebook profile and her LinkedIn; I could have contacted her, but I didn't think I'd ever see her again, so why dredge up the past? I imagined her furious at me, and I imagined her sobbing, or screaming, or being frostily polite if we had to interact, but I never imagined her kissing me in the snow until my brain felt fuzzy.

I'm not expecting to fall asleep easily, but I do, and sleep like the dead.

· · · · ★ ★ ★ ★ · · · ·

"SO, IT'S LIKE GRICE VOLLEYBALL," she says, looking up at the net, breath puffing in front of her. There's so much wrong with that sentence I barely know where to start.

"Grouse," is the first thing I say.

"Sure. Grice," Andi says, grinning at me.

"The plural of *grouse* is also *grouse*," I say, even though I know she knows this and furthermore, I know she's only saying *grice* because she thinks it's funny, or something, and correcting her is completely useless.

"So, it's volleyball with grouses," she says, and I close my eyes and sigh, and she laughs. To be honest, I'm mostly closing my eyes because I know if I look at the way she sparkles when she teases me or the way she turns a little pink when she laughs, I'll also start smiling and I can't have that. Not when she's out here incorrectly pluralizing birds.

"It's nothing like volleyball," I say, another thing that I know she knows. "They fly into the net, drop into the pocket, and we get them out and tag them. No one is spiking a bird over the net."

"Maybe *you're* not," she says, and I ignore that because I have no constructive response, just grab the pack I brought and hoist it onto my back.

"Now's the boring part," I say. "We sit a hundred feet away and check back every ten minutes to see what we get. You brought a book, right?"

"Two," she says, and follows me as I trudge uphill toward a cluster of boulders that should be far enough away not to scare the wildlife.

The net—which does look a little like a volleyball net, fine —is stretched between two trees maybe ten feet apart, basically invisible in the forest. We're about a mile and a half from the cabin, relatively near a spring and also a stand of fir trees that the grouse seem to particularly enjoy.

Five minutes later, we're sitting on an old quilt we brought from the cabin and leaning against a gray granite boulder. I didn't tell Andi, but in addition to all the net setup, lunch, and a thermos of coffee, I stuffed an extra blanket into the bottom of this pack in case she gets cold. It's mid-twenties today, so not terrible, and we're both dressed warmly, but it's not like we're getting our body temperatures up by hiking.

The first hour goes by uneventfully. For a long time nothing gets caught in the trap, and I start to wonder if there's something wrong with it, but then we catch a blue jay, and soon after that, a very indignant titmouse.

"You should put birdseed out to lure them," Andi says, the fifth or sixth time we're hiking back up to our hideout.

"It's not good form to feed wild animals," I say. "Dangerous to make them dependent on humans for their food, particularly out here where they're unlikely to encounter more of it any time soon."

"One snack does not a dependency make," she says. "Think how much faster this would go with a lure."

"You brought the GPS, right?" I ask. "You can go back to the cabin, don't feel like you have to stay."

"Why? This is fun," she says, and we've both got our hands in our pockets, but she nudges me with her elbow, glancing over, flushed and conspiratorial like there's a secret only the two of us know, and for a moment every single thought leaves my brain. "I've never played a net sport with greese before."

"It's not—" I start, and she's laughing again, but this time she wins and I smile.

SEVENTEEN

ANDI

I HOLD my hand out to Gideon, both of us sitting on the quilt that's keeping the ground from freezing our butts *all* the way off. I'm glad he talked me into dressing as warmly as possible—which included his sweater that I'm borrowing, something Gideon is demonstratively grumpy about but seems to actually kind of like, which I simply cannot think about right now—because sitting around in the freezing cold is, in fact, a very chilly pastime.

"You take the almonds, I'll take the dried cranberries," I'm saying.

"What are the white things?"

"Coconut, I think."

Predictably, Gideon frowns a little at that, even as he selects several almonds from the palm of my hand. "What kind of bougie trail mix has coconut?" he asks, popping them into his mouth.

"Sorry, should it have only had acorns, wild blueberries, and whatever suspicious mushrooms you can forage for your-self in the dead of winter?" I ask, tossing the rest of my handful into my mouth. Dried coconut and cranberries are perfectly good in trail mix, thank you very much.

"First—"

"Here we go," I tease, and Gideon's lips twitch like he's trying not to smile, a facial expression I've become an expert on.

"—foraging mushrooms is a very bad idea unless you're an expert mycologist, which I'm not," he says. "Most poisonous plants here aren't deadly, but the fungi will fuck you up. Secondly—"

"If you ever start a metal band, that should be its name. *Fungi Will Fuck You Up.*"

"There's not much danger of that happening," he says, trying not to smile *again*, and God, the way my stomach twists when he does that. "*Secondly*, it's not the dead of winter. We're barely a week in."

I sigh and tilt my head back against the boulder, resting my forearms on my knees, my ratty braid over one shoulder. Half my hair is sticking out of it, but there's no point in fixing it right now.

"No one is forcing you to eat my trail mix," I point out, even as he tilts the bag into his hand, frowning at what's probably the incorrect ratio of ingredients. I can't tell whether his fervor for getting exactly the right bits out are because his opinions are that strong, or because he wants to avoid eye contact while we're sitting this close.

Which—is fine. Honestly. I get it. I enjoyed whatever happened yesterday, but I also know that it was probably because of the adrenaline from sledding, and the fact that we've both been cooped up for a while, not to mention we were probably a little dehydrated. These things happen! Not a big deal.

Also, okay, suddenly being back with Gideon like this,

more physically proximate than even those summers when we were together all day every day, is a mind-fuck of the highest order. He's a total stranger and I somehow know everything about him. I've spent twenty years moving on from our friendship and here he is, again, familiar and alien all at once. Sometimes it feels like no time has passed and sometimes it feels like it was forty years, sixty, that we didn't know each other. I don't know what to do and I don't *not* know what to do, but it seems like kissing him was probably incorrect.

Even if I really, really liked it, and I'd swear on a stack of bibles that he did too.

"I'm glad you came," he says suddenly, when he's finished eating his handful of Approved Trail Mix Ingredients, leaning his head against the boulder behind us.

For a moment, I'm surprised into silence.

"Yeah, well," I say, eloquently. "I mean."

"It can get a little boring out here," he admits. "As much as I like not having to deal with people…"

I copy his pose and raise both eyebrows. Now we're both leaning against the boulder, the sun weak through the clouds, the branches reaching toward the sky half skeletal and half bushy evergreens, like the forest could never make up its mind.

Gideon's looking at me very seriously, that insouciant swagger somehow back in the line of his body against the rock, the splay of his legs on the ground. The moment stretches, ready to snap and for half a second I wonder if I'll ever get to kiss him indoors, in fewer layers.

His phone alarm goes off. We both sit up straighter then stare as he pulls it from his pocket and turns it off.

"Well," he says, rising to his feet. He's got his binoculars out, gazing over the boulder at the net trap, and it's not like I have a thing for birdwatchers, exactly, but I might have a thing for the calm, confident way Gideon approaches tasks. "I think we've got one," he tells me. "You coming?"

· · · · ★ ★ **★** ★ ★ · · · ·

IT'S A GROUSE, and it is *pissed*.

Gideon goes to his knees in front of the net, stretched between two trees. He puts his gloves in his pockets, takes careful stock of the situation, and then sighs.

"You really got yourself worked up, huh?" He says it in this low, soothing rumble that goes up my spine. "All right. I'm gonna get you out of this, try not to get your—oh, you're spittin' mad, aren't you. Can't say I blame you."

I stand a few feet back and watch, because the few other birds we've caught today were a pretty straightforward affair: Gideon pulled at the right few spots in the net, and they flew away. But the grouse is considerably bigger—the size of a small, skinny chicken—and it is absolutely not interested in being comforted by Gideon.

"Course the first one we got had to be a firecracker," he says. "Usually, they give up after a few minutes, but she's real spirited."

"You need help?" I take a cautious step closer, since I don't want to piss the bird off more, and see that Gideon's got one big hand around her shoulders, mostly immobilizing her neck and wings, while with the other he untangles the net from around her feet.

"I can get it, but if you don't mind," he says. "She's not making this easy."

I kneel in the snow beside Gideon and take my own gloves off. He's still talking to this bird in this low, soothing voice that makes my skin pinprick as he works both hands around her body, keeping her wings in.

"Okay," I say, and the grouse fixes me with an angry, beady stare, as if to say I *fucking dare you.*

"I've got her, take as long as you need," Gideon says, so I get to work.

She's got the black cords of the net wrapped at least twice around each foot in knotwork that it's pretty hard to make sense of, given that every few seconds she scrabbles at me with her talons. They're not deadly claws or anything, but she does get me once and I yelp, snatching my hand back.

"You okay?" Gideon asks, frowning, as the grouse squawks.

"Fine, just surprised," I say, and shoot her a glare. "Hold *still*, it'll be easier for everyone."

She doesn't, but we get her untangled anyway with a fair amount of swearing on my part and lots of low, soothing murmurs on Gideon's. I'm not saying I want to be a grouse, but if he talked to me like that, I think I'd do anything he said.

"There we go," he says, and holds her up in front of himself, looking her over. "That wasn't so bad."

The bird and I both make a noise.

"Female, about a year and a half," he says. "This will probably be her second clutch of eggs this spring, which is good. More chicks survive with experienced hens. Looks to be in good health, average size, no molting."

The bird struggles again, and a few small feathers drift to the ground. Gideon's hands around her don't budge, firm and gentle and soothing.

"All right," Gideon says, and I have no idea whether he's talking to me or the grouse. "Now comes the fun part."

He shifts his grip like he's gonna take one hand off, but the moment he does, the grouse kicks up a fuss so hard she nearly gets away and Gideon's hands clamp back down.

"Shit," he says, and glances over at me. "She's really got it in for me."

"You trapped her in a net and subjected her to indignities," I point out as he gets his hands back around her, all stern and frowny.

"No more of that," he says, low, authoritative, and gentle. Not that I notice. "You ever put a radio tag on a bird before?" he asks me in his regular voice.

"Sure. All the time," I say. "What else am I supposed to do on a Friday night?"

Gideon shoots me a look that's not at all soothing.

"Pliers are in my outside coat pocket, and the tags are in the breast zipper pocket," he says. "I'll talk you through it."

He does, though he's considerably less soothing and patient with me than he is with the bird, and I try not to take offense. A few minutes later she's successfully got a thin metal radio tag band around a leg, and no one has been irreparably scarred.

"Is that it?" I ask, sliding the pliers into my own coat pocket. Gideon clears his throat and there's a pause so slight, I almost don't notice it.

"Could you take a picture?" he asks. "My phone is, ah, in my pocket. Of my pants."

"Which one?" I ask.

"Right. If you don't mind. Please."

Gideon is blushing furiously and making eye contact with the bird as if his life depends on not looking at me. Not that I can talk, because I'm also blushing, maybe because he's blushing. We're all having a very blushy time right now, except this grouse, who looks as though she's somehow exacting revenge.

"Sure," I say, and delve into his pocket before I think about it any more.

It's just a phone, just in a pocket, and it's absolutely no big deal except it's all the way down at the bottom of the pocket and Gideon's thigh is very warm and very hard and very *there*, and I've been doing my best not to notice anything about his thighs for several days now. It hasn't been working. This isn't helping.

Fuck, I'd like to touch more of his thighs.

"Okay, here," I say, pulling the warm phone out. "Just— uh, like this?"

"Get the tag and her distinguishing features," he says, as if I know what distinguishing features look like on a grouse. It's not like she's got a mermaid tattoo on one forearm, but Gideon directs me and thirty seconds later, I'm done.

"You might want to step back," he says, rocking to his feet. "Sometimes there's a real flutter when I let them go."

I've never seen a bird look so angry on takeoff before, but there's a first time for everything.

"So that's it," I say, still watching the sky where she took off.

"For now," Gideon says, brushing his hands off on his pants. "Once I get her data into the system, we'll track her movement patterns and come spring, her nesting behaviors, but that's all for right now. Let me see your hand."

"What?" I ask, mind still half on the bird, but Gideon takes my hand and frowns at the parallel scratches running across the back. I'd already forgotten that they were there, three puffy pink lines. One has a few small drops of blood beaded in it. That talon must have been the longest.

"Fucking birds," Gideon mutters, sliding the pad of his thumb close to the scratches, rough on my skin.

"We *did* trap her in a volleyball net."

"It's not—" Gideon looks at up at me and huffs. "It's for her own good."

"Is it? It seemed like it was for you to do science."

He's still holding my hand in his, the warmth slowly leaching out into the cold air, his thumb still rubbing thoughtlessly over my skin, a frown still creasing his forehead. I want the laugh lines back. I almost reach out and touch him, and it's thrilling, destabilizing, because I *could*, and I've got no idea what would happen next. Maybe he'd kiss me back. Maybe he'd shove me away. Maybe he'd panic and somehow teleport to the nearest ranger station. It's been twenty years, I don't know what Gideon's capable of.

"It was for her own good in the greater scheme of things," he says, and the forehead lines disappear and the crinkles in the corners of his eyes deepen, and there it is. "Keep an eye on this. You're probably fine but birds can carry diseases. You know."

I want to point out that I've gotten worse injuries brushing my teeth—embarrassing, but true—but instead I promise to keep him updated on all minor scratch developments, so finally he relents and we retreat to the boulder and wait for more birds.

EIGHTEEN

GIDEON

"WELL, it's a sign of how far society has fallen, because we're denying our heritage," I tell Andi. "Obviously."

"Because it's trees instead of mining equipment?" she asks, incredulous.

"The trees are catering to the wealthy elite hippie environmentalists," I explain as I follow her up the back steps and onto the cabin's back porch. It's smaller than the front porch, but covered, and just big enough for a small table. I put the net, ropes, and stakes on it, all neatly rolled into a package.

"And the old shovel and pickaxe are as blue collar as a country song," Andi finishes for me, and I snort. "The fight was seriously that bad?"

She kicks one boot against the doorframe, knocking snow off, and I make a face at her for doing it *right* by the back door where it'll be the first thing one of us steps in if we come back out. Andi rolls her eyes at me and switches to kicking a post on the other side of the porch, but she's smiling about it.

"*Thank* you," I say pointedly, because we're trying to be civilized, here. "And yes. Blood in the streets. Brother fighting brother. Houses torn asunder. Susan Curtis is no longer welcome at either Hank's Pub or the Brick Wall Tavern, and I've heard if you say her name around Bobby Calhoun, you'd best settle in because he'll talk your ear right off."

"Because they finally got a new *Welcome to Sprucevale* sign and put trees on it."

"You say that like those stakes aren't life or death."

Andi makes a face as she steps out of her boots and onto the doormat. I open the screen door and hold it for her as she picks her boots up and carries them in, placing them into the boot tray. I refrain from pointing out that in exchange for two seconds of discomfort she doesn't have to clean muddy slush off the floor.

It's warmer in here, though not by too much.

"I guess," she says, unwinding her scarf. "Lucia was also telling me about the battle over naming the snowplow. Apparently that one made the front page of the Sprucevale Sentinel-Star over my daring and dramatic rescue."

Andi slides me a look I can't quite parse because she's still got her hat on, and because she's flushed and pink from the sudden warmth, and because it's mostly teasing but there's something else in it, too. Maybe there's a flicker of heat. Maybe I'm imagining it because I want there to be.

"Good thing or I'd have heard about it even more," I say, also dropping my boots into the boot tray, the two of us huddled into a small space by the back door between the counter and the pantry. "As it is I've got Matt and Zach asking me pointed questions, Hannah and Sadie excited that the cool girl is back in town, and Reid wondering why his older siblings are being so weird right now."

Andi laughs, plunking her hat on the top of a coat hook and rubbing her hand over her hair, which is both plastered against her head and sticking up in every direction.

"What did you tell them?" she asks, unzipping her coat.

I'm right behind her and she turns her head slightly so I can hear, her braid threatening to slide over her shoulder. I reach out and nudge it so it does, and then on impulse I trace one lock of hair as it weaves through the two others, holding my breath. Andi doesn't step away. I breathe again.

"That reception's pretty bad out here," I say, and drop my hand. Andi goes to shrug out of her coat, but one shoulder catches on something. She makes an annoyed noise and before I can think, I reach out and fix it, then pull the coat off her arms, the backs of my fingers tickled by the wool of my sweater she's still wearing.

"Thanks," she says, voice hushed and a little breathless, maybe, or maybe I'm imagining things, but I hang her coat with one hand and run the other back up her arm, to her shoulder, to the back of her neck. My fingers are still cold but her body warmth is bleeding through the heavy fabric, unfurling into me.

"Sure," I say, the best I can do right now. Her shoulders relax as I trace over one, her head tilting back a little. I can't see her face but I know her eyes are closed and her lips are parted a little, and imagining it makes me feel like I can't quite breathe right. Her hair's half out of the braid, escaping in every direction, sticking to the back of her neck, so I drag one finger along the warm skin there, sticky with heat, pulling her hair from where it had migrated under the neck of her sweater. My sweater.

I've got calls to make. I should put more wood in the stove, heat this place up, figure out what we're going to eat for dinner, but Andi's skin feels like an electric current under my fingertip and she tilts her head as I trace it across her neck. There are short, dark curls at the edge of her hairline and the tendons are standing out like an invitation.

It is. Isn't it? I've never had a thought in my life, never had anything in my head except the urge to put my mouth on Andi's neck and see what it feels like.

I take the invitation. Andi makes a soft noise when I do but it's loud in this room, in this snow-covered cabin, in the middle of this forest. She's warm, her skin damp from the sudden flush of heat, and smells like sunscreen and snow. Her shoulders shift as she breathes and I hook a finger under the neck of my sweater that she's got on, gently pull it down, following my finger with my lips. The sweater's too big on her and the neck pulls past the hollow above her collarbone, to where it meets the point of her shoulder. I stop when I hit a bra strap, my face buried in the crook of her neck.

There's a voice in the back of my head. It's always there, always evaluating my actions and usually deciding I've come up short. Sometimes it shouts and sometimes it murmurs, and right now it's not so much a voice as a tug in the space behind my rib cage, a slow swirl of heavy guilt, the sense that if I want this so much, it must be wrong.

I push it down and run my teeth over the tendon in her neck, softly. Andi's breath catches and her head falls back against my shoulder as she relaxes into me. I slide my other hand down her side, hesitate a moment, then push it into the warmth between her body and my sweater and settle it on her hip.

The guilt tugging at me burrows in as I spread my fingers and sink them into her until I can feel the point of her hip bone, shifting as I suck at her skin, gently, then flick my tongue over the spot. The guilt lessens when she puts her hand over mine, thick wool between us, holding it there, so I gather my courage.

"You look good like this," I say, my lips by her ear. My voice comes out half an octave lower and twice as rough as I meant it to, like it's scraping its way out of a coal mine.

Andi swallows. Her hips shift again. "With hair I haven't washed for a week?" she asks, and I can hear her smile.

I nip at her ear without thinking, soft and gentle but with teeth all the same. I've never heard a noise like the one she makes.

"In my sweater," I say.

"You like it?"

"Obviously. Is that why you took it?"

"No, but that's why I'm going to keep wearing it."

A noise comes out of me as I put my mouth on her neck again, with teeth and tongue this time, and Andi laughs, all breathless and fluttery.

"*What*," I say, letting my voice buzz against her skin.

"Did you just growl at me?"

Probably. "Of course not," I say. "I don't growl. I'm not an animal."

Then her fingers are in my hair, sliding against my scalp, sending little bursts of pleasure down my spine.

"That's too bad," Andi says, and pulls my mouth to hers.

It's a bad angle and she's pulling my hair and my neck isn't really supposed to bend like this, but I want to drown in it anyway. All day I've been carefully not thinking about this, forcing myself to contemplate birds and rocks and snow and sticks and Jesus Christ, *anything* but the heat of Andi's mouth against mine, but now I can have it.

She slithers against me, mouth barely leaving mine, and then she's facing me and the angle is right and our mouths slot together. It's slow, torturous, like I'm bursting at the seams, the slide of her tongue against mine a promise and a reward all at once.

Somehow, she's against the wood-paneled wall. Somehow, my hand slid up her torso and it's on her side, ribcage rising and falling beneath my palm. There's a thin layer of fabric between us, drenched in warmth, and I twist it in my fingers while I kiss her again. Her hands are in my hair, around the back of my neck, grabbing at my shoulders, her back against the wall. There's a tug at my chest and I break the kiss, look down to realize she's unzipping the fleece I've still got on.

"Is this," she says, lips dark pink and cheeks light pink, strawberry blond sweat curls against her neck. There's a red spot on her neck that looks like it might bruise, barely, and my train of thought crashes into it.

She stops unzipping.

"Yes," I say, in a voice I barely recognize, and then I'm pulling it off and dropping it behind myself as Andi runs her hands down my arms, still covered by the thin blue base layer I wore today. Her blush deepens and her lips are parted and I'll never wear anything else if this is how she's going to look at me.

I get my mouth back on hers and my hands under the sweater, higher, dragging the thin fabric below with me. Our bodies are pressed together and there's flashes of cold skin against my belly where she's toying with the hem of my shirt, and my brain feels like it's losing signal and becoming static.

In my pocket, my phone starts vibrating. I ignore it in favor of running one thumb along an elastic line on Andi's ribcage—bra? she's got a lot of layers on, I've lost track—and Andi makes a noise and tilts her hips and grabs my wrist and pushes my hand higher.

It's—fabric, mostly, stretched tight against the swell underneath it, but the layer under my hand slides against the layer below and Andi gasps into my mouth so I do it again. My phone's still buzzing. It can buzz for all fucking eternity if it wants, because this time I go slow enough to feel the slight peak of one nipple under the heavy fabric, so I scrape a thumbnail across it. The noise Andi makes is perfect.

My phone stops vibrating. Ten seconds later, it starts again.

"Someone's calling you," Andi says into my mouth. I make a noise in response and do nothing about my phone. After a bit, it stops ringing.

It starts again.

"Answer it," Andi says, breathless.

"I'm busy," I say, and mouth at her neck again, running my tongue over the red spot I left earlier.

"What if it's important?" she asks. I lick the spot again.

"It's not," I tell her, and she sighs.

"For fuck's—" she starts, and then she's squirming her hand into my pocket, but before I can contemplate *that*, she's pulled my phone out and is frowning at it.

"Forest Service Dispatch," she says, holding it up. "Do they usually call you just to chat?"

I grunt, take the phone, and I'm still pressing her against the wall when I answer simply because I don't want to stop.

"Bell," I answer, my forehead against the wall over Andi's shoulder. I've still got my hand splayed over her ribcage, rising and falling beneath my palm, and I move it until the bump of her nipple is under my fingertips. I can't move away. I can't stop touching her, because if I stop this might end and we might start talking about burritos again, and I can't risk it.

"There you are. I was starting to worry," Dale says, friendly and folksy as ever, voice crackling down the line. Through the air. Whatever. "Listen, I wanted to update you on the situation."

It takes me several seconds to process that, because Andi's hand just sneaked under my shirt, cool fingers on skin, and her nipple hardened under my fingers. Fuck. What?

"What situation?" I ask.

"Well, it's not looking like anyone's going to be fixing the road up to y'all in the next couple days," Dale says. "Truth be told I'm not sure I can put a timeline on that fix at all."

I draw a circle around Andi's nipple with one fingertip and wait for Dale's words to filter through.

"Okay," I finally manage.

"You've got food, water, firewood?"

Andi makes a small noise in her throat, head tilted back against the wall, eyes closed. I pull the phone away from my mouth and turn to face her, lips almost against her ear.

"Shh," I whisper, and she swallows without opening her eyes. God, did she like that? "Plenty of everything," I tell Dale.

"All right, then, you've got some options," he goes on. "You folks know about the weather we've got coming?"

"What weather's that?"

"The cold snap," Dale says, as if he's surprised I don't know. Which is fair. I *should* know. "Supposed to get down into the single-digits tonight and then dump another six inches of snow starting late tomorrow."

"*More* snow?" I ask, because that actually got my attention.

Dale sighs on the other end.

"Meaning," he says, resigned, "that your best bet for hiking back to civilization before the weekend is to start early tomorrow. I can send someone to pick you up at Hogswallow Picnic Area by the trailhead, the Parkway's clear enough for that."

I pull back enough to make eye contact with Andi, and I don't move my hand, but I still it. We're both breathing a little harder than we should be, her lips deep pink and her cheeks flushed, eyes watching my face.

"Give me a sec to talk to—Andrea," I tell Dale, stumbling over her full name because I don't know if *Andi* is too familiar and I'd be giving something away; I don't know what exactly I'd be giving away or whether she'd mind and it seems best to leave that all be for right now.

"You heard?" I ask her, muting the phone.

"Yeah," she says.

There's a small, short silence that feels like a slingshot being pulled back.

"Is your ankle—"

"It would be dangerous—"

We both stop again, our faces still a few inches apart, Dale waiting patiently on the other end. I nod at Andi.

"Your ankle might be not be up to it yet," she says, voice low and quiet. "It's a lot of tricky downhill, right?"

"Yeah," I agree, my heart beating so hard I can feel it in my neck, in my fingertips where they're gripping the phone a little too hard. "We'd have to make really good time or risk getting caught in the snow."

"And it'll be in the single digits, he said," Andi goes on. "There's a risk of. Uh. Frostbite, probably."

"And the weather could do anything."

"It could."

"Probably best to stay here a little longer," Andi says, tipping her head back against the wall, looking at me through her eyelashes. "For safety."

"Safest thing to do," I agree, thinking about the way her throat flexes when she breathes. I bring the phone back up to my ear.

"I think we'll wait it out here," I say. No response. I sigh, unmute the phone, and repeat myself.

"Sounds like it's for the best," Dale agrees. "And anything could happen. You know what they say about the weather here."

I slide my hand up again, still underneath Andi's shirt,

and she makes another tiny noise when I scrape a thumbnail over her nipple, even through the thick fabric. I have no idea what anyone has ever said about the weather.

"If you don't like it, just wait ten minutes," Dale goes on, thankfully oblivious.

"Right," I agree.

"Stay warm," he says. "I'll keep you updated on the avalanche situation, but I've got a feeling y'all are gonna be hiking out and coming back for the truck at a later date."

Dale goes on a little about the logistics of clearing a road, and I half-listen at best because Andi is heavy-lidded and flushed, watching me through her eyelashes, running one thumb through the trail of hair below my bellybutton. Every part of this makes that guilty feeling tug harder at me, that sickly sense of *you shouldn't be doing this*, but it's outweighed by the warmth of Andi's leg, slotted against mine.

"Thanks for calling," I say when I think Dale's done talking, though it's hard to be sure when you're not really paying attention. "We'll keep you updated on our status."

"Be safe," he says, and the line goes blank. I toss my phone toward the couch and have my mouth back on Andi's before it lands. We kiss hot and slow for a few more minutes, and I don't want to stop, but the world starts to crowd in.

Not to mention the formless, baseless sense that I shouldn't be doing this. There's no reason why not, just the feeling that I like it, so it's bad and I should stop.

After a while more Andi puts a hand on my face and I pull back, touching our foreheads together. Her back's still against this wall and I'm practically folded around her, like she's a gravity well I'm crumpling into.

"It'll be dark soon," she says. It's not late but she's right; sundown comes early this time of year, especially in this weather. "Do we need to do anything?"

I take a deep breath and will myself to remember anything that needs to be done besides *kiss Andi again*. "We should get more water and firewood, at least. If it gets cold enough the creek might freeze and we won't want to go out to get firewood."

She's quiet for a moment. I can feel her forehead scrunch under mine, and then she says, "I've been drinking creek water?"

"Filtered."

"I've been drinking *filtered* creek water?"

"It's good for you."

"Fish pee in that," she points out, and I draw back a little more, enough to straighten her shirt and my sweater that she's wearing. "And animals drink it, and stuff *dies* in there, and..."

Or all the things that have happened in the past week, this is somehow the one that's scandalizing Andi the most. I'm trying not to smile about it.

"The tadpoles and fish pee get filtered out," I tell her. "Not that you need to worry about tadpoles this time of year."

"I don't think I was meant for roughing it," she says, but she's half smiling again, hooking a finger around my belt loop in a way that feels so natural I almost don't notice. "When we get back, I'm taking the longest shower and turning the heat up until the house is *tropical*."

"You're doing great," I reassure her. She makes a face, but it's cute.

NINETEEN

GIDEON

THE WIND STARTS a few hours after sunset and the snow comes with it. There's a "birds of Virginia" thermometer on the back porch, facing the kitchen window, and we can practically watch the red needle fall fifteen degrees. It says it's seven out when I finally stop watching.

The beginning of a storm always makes me unsettled and anxious, like somewhere there's a door I forgot to close or tools I forgot to put away. It's probably left over from the bad storms growing up, when thunder would shake the house and someone would need to go close the shed doors or make sure all the chickens were in the hen house. I still hate the beginning of *The Wizard of Oz*. Watching Dorothy try to open the storm cellar after she's been locked out makes me nauseous with panic.

I wipe down the counters. Re-wipe them. Glare at the hole in the corner where the chipmunk disappeared last week. I haven't seen it again. I wonder if it's okay, then remember that it's a nuisance, then hope it hasn't frozen to death. I pace back and forth a little, and finally, I give up.

"I'm gonna go check the outside," I tell Andi, pulling on my coat. She's in the bedroom, pulling things out of her frame pack and tossing them onto one of the beds. There's no organizational system I can discern.

"What's outside?" she calls back.

"Just making sure everything's tied down."

"Don't be gone long, I dunno if I can drag you back in if something happens."

"I'll be—"

"*Fine*, yeah, I know," she says. "Ten minutes."

"Done," I tell her, and step out.

It's fucking *cold*, the wind sinking through my layers like I'm not wearing anything, so I jam my hands into my pockets and swear under my breath and head for the truck.

There's nothing in particular I'm looking for, nothing I think I've left out or open, so I give it a once-over: windows closed, parking brake on, toolbox in the back closed and locked. Same for the shed and the firewood lean-to against the side of it. None of the trees look likely to fall onto the cabin, though that's always hard to tell. I trek over to the creek again even though I was there to fill our five-gallon containers earlier, but there's nothing besides the sound of water over rocks. When I shine the flashlight onto it, the ice crystals forming against the banks glitter back at me.

I head back around the other side of the cabin because I like to make a complete circumnavigation of a place. The bedroom windows are still dimly lit, partly white from the electric lantern and partly yellow from the oil lamps. Using both is a slight waste of resources, but we've got enough lamp oil and spare batteries that I won't give Andi grief about it.

I'm trudging past the windows, maybe ten or fifteen feet away, when movement catches my eye and I glance over. I'm exactly in time to see Andi pull a long-sleeved shirt over her head and toss it onto the bed, nothing on underneath besides an electric blue sports bra.

I stop. I inhale sharply enough that the cold air hurts my lungs, then force myself not to cough and don't think about why. There's an alarm going off somewhere in the back of my brain because I'm looking at a woman in an undergarment and that's bad, it's always bad, so much skin and not enough fabric in the way.

The alarm's old and worn down and muted, but it's there all right and I think it'll be there forever, screaming at me while Andi scratches one shoulder with her opposite hand, her braid trailing messily down her back. She's winter-pale and wearing leggings that come above her belly button; when she leans over the bed her braid falls forward and the waist-band of her leggings cuts into her soft skin. I want my mouth there. I'm dizzy with lust.

I'm perfectly still, just beyond the dim pool of light spilling from the window. I'm watching her from the dark while she rifles through her clothes and doesn't know I'm here. I shouldn't have stopped. I shouldn't be watching. I shouldn't be *lusting*. Andi holds up an item of clothing, sniffs it, drops it to the bed, and then hooks her fingers under the band of the sports bra and tugs.

A gentleman—a good person—would avert his eyes. I watch, lips parted in the darkness, trying to memorize the way she looks as she wiggles, hopping a little, and then her breasts bounce free. They're full and round and pale, the lower curve kissing her ribcage, her pink nipples puckered in the cold. There's a red line around her torso where the elastic was digging into her skin, and even from here I can tell it's got stri-ations in it, tiny ridges and valleys in her flesh.

I wonder what they'd feel like under my fingertips, my tongue, and ball my hand into a fist. I haven't blinked. I've been holding my breath for fear that she could hear me if I breathe, though now she's trying to pull the bra over her head, both arms in the air and her face covered, her braid tangled somewhere in the electric blue and she's twisting and turning and *jiggling*—

She's stuck, and I'm transfixed. I'm getting hard. I keep watching as she takes a deep breath and wriggles a little more and then finally pulls the bra off, shaking her head and making a face as she throws it onto the bed and then grabs something else.

Finally, I break away. Before I mount the steps to the porch I sit down on them for a moment, take off my gloves and hat, and let the cold bite into my skin. It doesn't feel *good* but it does feel right, like maybe it can freeze that out of my brain. I stood there. I *watched*, and that old voice says *it's wrong to want* and a newer, correct one says *it's wrong to watch without permission*.

I consider throwing myself into the creek. Instead, I stand and open the door to the cabin.

I've barely got my coat and boots off when the bedroom door opens and Andi's standing there in thermal underwear, the shirt rainbow-striped and the bottom avocado-patterned. I have no idea where she gets these things, because the stores I frequent sell long johns in three colors: white, gray, and black.

"Oh good," she says, and she's smiling, and her braid is over one shoulder, her feet bare and her top just tight enough with nothing underneath that I can see her nipples pointing at me. I want to lift her top and lick the marks her bra left behind. "You made it."

"That wasn't in question," I say, running a hand through

my hair and making eye contact. I can feel my face going red, and I hope it looks like I'm flushed from the cold.

"Your brother Reid called," she says, nodding toward the kitchen, where my phone's charging from a battery. "I almost answered, but then I figured..."

She leaves *I'm not sure how he feels about me* unsaid, which is fair.

"Thanks," I say, and head into the kitchen because no one can leave me alone.

· · · ★ ★ ★ · · ·

"THEY'RE NOT REALLY A MIGRATORY SPECIES," I tell Reid for what has to be the thirtieth time. "And especially not the ones here. She's *fine*."

He makes his grumpy-slash-concerned face at me, the picture jerky because he insists that I videochat from the middle of nowhere via a satellite connection.

"She looks cold," he insists. "Here. See?"

"I don't—" I say, but he's already taking his phone to the back door, holding it up to the window, and flicking on the floodlights overlooking my back yard. In the very back of the cage on the left—sized more like a large dog run than a cage—is a lump inside a wooden crate, turned on its side and perched high up on a pole. I'm pretty sure the lump is glaring.

"She looks fine," I tell Reid. "Eagles overwinter in New England and Minnesota, where it regularly gets much colder than this."

"In the wild, they huddle together to share body heat," he says, with the confidence of someone who's read a Wikipedia page. He flips the camera around so he can glare at me again. "Vicky's alone out there."

God, it's *Vicky* now.

"She's sheltered."

"You've got a whole collection of heating pads and hot water bottles," he says, walking through the house. "Tell me which ones are for animals and which ones are for when you go camping with your buddies and move rocks or whatever for two days straight and then spend a day lying on the couch complaining about your back when you get home."

"I don't do that."

Reid snorts. "Sure."

Behind me, I hear the bedroom door open, followed by padded footsteps. When I turn, Andi's standing in the doorway to the kitchen, wearing my sweater again, eyebrows raised. I carefully don't think about jiggling or how I've seen her bare nipples without her permission, because if I did, I might spiral.

"It's Reid," I tell her, and then tell Reid, "This is Andi," and yes, introductions are extra-awkward on a video chat with a dicey connection.

"Hi," she says, and comes over to sit next to me. "You named the animals?"

"They needed names," he says, a little defensive.

"Oh, I'm on your side," she says, and I think it gets a small smile out of Reid.

"They are *wildlife*," I mutter, not that anyone's listening.

"It's for show. I heard him call them Victoria and Fluffy just yesterday," Andi says, and I frown at her. "I think he doesn't want to get attached."

"That's not it," I protest. "It can be dangerous to start anthropomorphizing wild animals, because you're less likely to treat something named *Fluffy* as a threat even though he's got just as many teeth as C-347."

They both look at me for a long moment.

"Are you the cool girl Sadie and Ariel keep talking about?"

Reid asks, ignoring my good point to change the subject. Andi laughs.

"Dunno. I hope so," she says. "I used to live next to you guys when we were kids, but I think we moved away before you were born. Ariel and Sadie were really little. I'm surprised they remember me."

"Mostly Sadie," Reid says. "But Ariel believes everything she says."

"I do remember them ganging up on Jacob," Andi says. Jacob's about two years older than Sadie, and they've never gotten along very well. "Your mom had a baby, like, two months before we moved, but I think that was—"

"That was Reid," I interrupt, and fuck, I should have mentioned this to Andi before so it wouldn't put Reid on the spot like this. "He transitioned a couple years ago."

"Oh! Neat," she says. I think a pixelated Reid blinks.

"Thanks?" he says.

"But yeah, you obviously don't remember me," Andi goes on. "You were tiny when we left. Are you the youngest? You're not the youngest."

"No, there's two more," Reid says, and doesn't look thrilled about it.

"Drew and Ruth still live with our parents," I add.

"You know how there are songs to help people remember all the presidents? Or the capitol of every state?" Andi asks, leaning back in her chair. "You guys need that for your siblings."

Reid snorts, but he sort of smiles, too.

"There's only twelve," he says. "You can't remember twelve names?"

Reid hassles Andi for another minute, until she's laughing, and I put up with it for a few minutes while I watch the battery on the iPad dwindle.

"Okay, okay," I say, attempting to regain control. "Wrap it up. What do you need?"

"Critter heaters," Reid reminds me, and I roll my eyes.

But Reid is bound and determined to show two wild animals all the comforts of home, so after a few minutes I give up and instruct him on microwaving a few heating pads and bringing them along with some blankets into the animals' cages without anyone ripping his hand off. Andi wanders off, probably because this is boring.

Luckily, Victoria and Fluffy—R-85 and C-347—are used to him and uninterested in making a fuss.

He's still got me on video chat when he goes back into the house, and as soon as the door slams, there's a demanding meow.

"Yes, your majesty," Reid deadpans. "I think she smells blood," he says to me, since he just got finished bribing the outdoor critters.

"How's she doing?" I ask, though Reid's already flipping the camera around to show a giant off-white cat sitting neatly by a food bowl, looking imperious. "Is Reid treating you right?" I ask her.

Behind me, there's a gasp.

"Is that Dolly?" Andi asks, coming back to sit next to me. "Hello. Goodness, you're regal."

"Don't inflate her ego," Reid mutters.

"You bossing Reid around?" I ask Dolly, who blinks.

"Yes," he says, and Dolly yawns. There's a toothsome display. "She wants to know when you're coming back so she can bite *you* at five thirty in the morning."

"Dolly, you wouldn't," Andi says. She's leaning on the table, her chin in one hand, gazing at my enormous cat. I think she's about two seconds from reaching out and petting the screen.

"She would and does," Reid mutters. "It's like living with a panther or something. You're gonna come home and she'll be feasting on my body that she's dragged to the top of a bookcase."

"*That* fluffster?" Andi says. "She would never."

Reid and I snort in unison, and Andi cracks up.

"Even Gideon knows his princess cupcake would eat a person if her dinner was a few hours late," Reid says, flipping the camera back around so we can see him.

"Princess cupcake?" I ask, incredulous.

"You think I don't hear the things you call her?"

"I've never in my life called Dolly a—"

"Oh, my *god*, it was a metaphor or something," Reid says, rolling his eyes so hard I'm afraid they might get stuck that way. I take a deep breath and remind myself that human brains don't finish maturing until a person's mid-twenties and that at twenty, Reid is basically still a teenager.

"That's not what a metaphor is," Andi points out.

"Both of you."

"We're running the battery on the iPad down," I announce, because I'm suddenly unsure that I'd like Andi and Reid getting along too well just yet. Seems like a situation where I could be easily outnumbered. "We'll talk in the morning if you need to."

"I'll keep you updated on Vicky and Fluffy," he says, and now he's making his *trying to look serious and failing* face. "Stay warm up there. Share body heat if you need to."

My face instantly goes hot.

"Okay. Thanks," I mutter, reaching for the *end call* button.

"Make safe choices!" Reid shouts, just as it disconnects. I sigh, face still burning, even though I can *feel* Andi laughing silently next to me.

"He's got your number, huh?" she asks, still laughing.

"I have no idea what you're talking about," I grumble, and she heads into the bathroom to brush her teeth while I stay at the table, staring at the blank screen of the iPad and try to pick apart guilt and shame and desire and embarrassment, but I only succeed in knotting it all together.

TWENTY

ANDI

"DO you turn into snakes at night?" I ask, arms folded, standing in the doorway to the bedroom. "Is that the problem?"

He pauses where he's rearranging the wood in the wood stove, then turns to stare at me.

"What?" he finally asks.

"Or some kind of hideous monster?" I go on. "Like that Greek myth where the woman married a god but wasn't allowed to look at him at night."

We stare at each other, and with each passing millisecond I'm less certain I know what I'm talking about.

"You mean Cupid and Psyche?" he finally says, because of course Gideon knows this.

"Sure."

"She wasn't allowed to look at him because he was *too* pretty."

"Is that—"

"*No.*"

There's a note in his voice that makes me stop what I was about to say and go silent instead. Gideon's been a little extra gruff and a little extra awkward—above his usual baseline of gruff and awkward—since he got off the phone with Reid, and damned if I know why. I just know that usually when I badger him about sleeping in a separate bed in the same room, like a reasonable adult, he blushes and almost smiles and rolls his eyes and then packs me off to bed by myself.

But now he's shoving wood around again and I'm standing in this doorway, wearing avocado-patterned pants and his sweater, wondering what happened and how I'm supposed to fix it. Is it because we kissed? Is it because I said it was *neat* that Reid transitioned, like the world's biggest dork? Was I insufficiently obsequious to his cat? Are we both just cold and tired?

"We don't even have heating pads here," I finally say, and to my relief it comes out light and teasing.

Gideon sighs. "*Now* what point are you trying to make?"

"That the couch is probably bad for your back," I say, mentally thanking Reid for that bit of ammunition.

"It's fine," Gideon says, and swings the glass door to the wood stove shut. "And do you really think that mattress is so much better?"

Well, having slept on one, no.

"I want the record to show that I tried to offer you comfort, like, thirty times," I tell him, and finally, that gets a faint smile as he brushes his hands together, turning toward me. The relief I feel is ridiculous. Maybe he's not mad at me; maybe he doesn't regret everything we did. I could ask but it's easier to accept his smile and push past it.

The light in here is low: two oil lamps mounted on the stone fireplace itself, the electric lantern casting a white angle on the far wall, where our coats are hanging, and the dancing orange light from the wood stove. Gideon's lovely in it, all his hard lines softer, his hair gently curling around his ears. I swear his eyelashes look a mile long right now.

"Thank you," he says, and it's a little stiff, a little formal. "Do you need more blankets?"

"I think I'm okay."

"Night, Andi."

"Night, Gideon," I say, then go into the bedroom and get under approximately seventeen blankets.

· · · ★ ★ ★ ★ ★ · · ·

SEVENTEEN BLANKETS ISN'T ENOUGH.

I would never survive in the wild.

· · · ★ ★ ★ ★ ★ · · ·

OF COURSE, all we've got at this cabin is instant coffee. I probably shouldn't complain that I got rescued from a blizzard and all I get to drink is instant, but I slept like shit last night and complain I shall.

"Ugh," I say quietly, to myself, and stir in another spoonful. It's already kind of gross, so why not make it espresso-strength? At least it'll do something then.

"Can you be ready in ten minutes?" Gideon calls from the other room, where he's doing something or other that sounds like it involves a lot of stomping around.

I'm not sure I can be a functional person in that much time, but I'm annoyed with Gideon because he's annoyed with me for unclear reasons and being tired isn't helping anything, so I shout back, "Sure!" and then take a giant gulp of mediocre coffee.

"Good!" he shouts back.

"*Good,*" I mutter to myself, very quietly, in a terrible

impression of Gideon because it makes me feel slightly better. "*Andi, get dressed faster. Andi, stop being so—*"

I turn away from the counter, make an undignified noise, and drop my coffee mug on the floor because there's an animal watching me from the kitchen table.

"You okay?" Gideon calls, and I can *hear* his concerned frown. It's guilt-inducing.

"Fine!" I shout back, still staring at the animal, still very tired and now with bonus coffee all over my lower legs. "There's, um, a marsupial in the kitchen?"

There's a brief silence.

"Or is that possums?"

I'm, like, ninety-five percent sure it's not supposed to be here but Gideon's got an eagle and a fox in his backyard, so who the fuck knows. There's a rush of footsteps, and then the critter leaps off the table.

I squeak again, still very dignified, and it escapes into a hole in the baseboards just as Gideon appears in the doorway.

Helpfully, I point.

"Was it the chipmunk?"

"I think so?" I say, because it's too early and I'm too tired to be identifying critters properly. "*The* chipmunk?"

He walks over to the hole and frowns at it, like that'll help.

"It's supposed to be hibernating but it's living in the walls," he says, arms crossed, sighing.

"Oh. Well, that's fine," I say, and start picking up the broken mug.

"Doesn't New York City famously have rats?" he grumbles, still glaring at the hole. "One chipmunk isn't that bad."

"The rats aren't in the walls of *my apartment*." That's not exactly true—there was *one* incident, years ago, that I'd rather not recall—but it's close enough.

"It won't hurt you. I just haven't chased it out yet," he says, and runs a hand through his hair. "And yes, opossums are the only marsupial native to North America."

I dump the broken mug in the trash, wipe up the rest of the coffee, and set about making more.

· · · · · ★ ★ ★ ★ · · · · ·

"JUST USE BIRDSEED!" I say, and it's loud enough to startle a nearby bird into taking off. Gideon's tromping up a slight incline toward me, coming back from yet another empty net check.

He simply sighs in response, because this is not the first or even the fifth time we've had this conversation.

"They're not going to become birdseed addicts," I say, my hands jammed in my pockets and entire head scrunched as low into my scarf as I can get it. "It's *one* time, it's a super simple lure, they get a snack today and then they come back tomorrow and there's no snack and they fly somewhere else."

He scrubs one gloved hand over his face and adjusts his hat over his forehead. Gideon's got shadows under his eyes and an oddly short temper today, an extra edge to his usual gruffness. I'm not sure what to do with it, but I slept like shit last night because I was too cold to sleep well but also refused to disturb Gideon's precious Andi-free slumber by asking if I could sleep in the living room, so I'm not sure I care about his bad mood.

We also haven't kissed again, nor have we even *almost* kissed again, and I get that this is a pretty strange situation, but come on. Give a girl a horny look sometimes.

"Setting aside that we don't even *have* birdseed—"

I crouch, grab a bag of trail mix off the ground, and hold it out. Gideon eyes it.

"Absolutely none of that is in their natural diet."

"Then maybe it's time they learned to party."

"You're welcome to wait back at the cabin, you know," he says, and that edge to his voice is a little sharper and it sounds like *I don't want you here*.

"And do *what*," I say, and I sound like a bratty teen and don't care. "I already read everything I'm interested in and you'll get annoyed if I try to stream anything on the iPad over the satellite."

"Aren't there puzzles?"

"*Ugh*."

Gideon waits.

"I don't like puzzles," I say. "Why would you print a whole picture and then cut it up into tiny, weird pieces and mix them up only to put it back together? Nothing happens when you finish, you're just back where you started only you've got about ten fewer hours of life left."

"If you stay, you can't keep talking about birdseed."

"Do you want me to go back so you can be alone?" I ask, and it comes out have annoyed and half pathetic, and neither of those are my good half.

Gideon huffs, breath puffing into the air, and he walks closer to me and sits on the ground, leaning back against a rock.

"Not really," he says, looking up at me, and it feels better than it should. I sit with a sigh, my shoulder brushing his, my head back against the big rock behind us.

"Sorry," I say, and he nods, then pats my knee. *Pats* my *knee*.

"It's okay," Gideon says, but we don't talk much for the rest of the day, either.

TWENTY-ONE

ANDI

BEFORE WE GO to sleep that night—Gideon in the living room, on the couch that's too short for him, and me in the bedroom—I ransack the place for more blankets, not that I think they'll do much besides crush me under their weight.

It's been a weird, awkward day that turns into a weird, awkward evening, and I try to tell myself that we're both tired and exhausted and un-showered and trapped in a tiny cabin that doesn't have electricity, and that's all obviously true, but that doesn't keep me from feeling like there's something else. Like I came on too strong, maybe, or I'm a bad kisser, or talking to his brother reminded him that he's not supposed to be kissing girls unchaperoned or something. Instead of asking I decide to go to bed and possibly deal with it in the morning.

Besides my sleeping bag, I've got a fleece blanket, a comforter circa 1965, a quilt that's seen better days, a quilt that had seen better days twenty years ago, and a wool blanket that I'm pretty sure was meant for horses but that I'm not complaining about. It takes me forever to warm them all up barely enough to drift off, but eventually, I do.

I wake up shivering. It's dark as the grave, something my

grandmother used to say, back when we still saw each other. The wind is blowing something fierce, some part of the cabin whistling in it. After a few moments I realize the curtains are open and there's just enough dim moonlight to see the outline of things. I curl up into myself, double-check that all my blankets and limbs are still there, but it doesn't help. There's a loud *pop* from the living room as the wood stove burns lower, and I exhale, chewing my lip.

A gust of wind rattles the window, and I decide: fuck it, and fuck Gideon and his puritanical ideas about rooms.

Outside the blankets is, obviously, even worse. In about thirty seconds I swear my hands are shaking and my teeth are chattering as I rummage through my frame pack as quietly as I can, trying to yank out my sleeping pad without waking Gideon.

I've barely dropped the pad and all my blankets on the floor in the living room—where it's at least forty degrees warmer, thanks to the wood stove—when he stirs on the couch, then pops up suddenly on one elbow.

"Andi?" he says, voice scratchy.

"I'm Bigfoot. Go back to sleep," I whisper, like it matters.

In the orange glow of the wood stove I can see him run a hand through his dark hair, as if it'll get his brain online.

"You're cold."

"It's, like, negative thirty in there," I explain, and he sighs.

"It's not negative thirty," he says, rubbing both hands over his face. "I doubt it's even below zero."

Gideon gives me a long, indecipherable look, and I can't tell if he's thinking or just half-asleep. I glare back, bracing myself to argue about where we're sleeping.

Then he gets up and walks into the bedroom, which, fine, he can sleep the Antarctic ice cave if he'd rather be in there than *share a room*—

There's an ominous creak, followed by a bang and Gideon muttering *ow, fuck.*

"What are you—oh," I say, still on the floor next to my camping pad, surrounded by my pile of blankets, as he side-steps through the door with a twin mattress in his arms.

Oh.

It's unwieldy, being a mattress, and he keeps swearing every time it hits something, so I get up and help him. I get a muttered *thanks* before we plop it on the floor, and then we're standing on opposite sides of this twin mattress, looking at each other. I've got on several layers of sleep gear, and all Gideon's got on is that same thin, tight base layer and a pair of thermal pants that don't leave a lot to the imagination, even in this low light. *Thighs.* God.

He runs a hand through his hair again, highlighted in the orange glow.

"Floor's not very warm," he offers. "If you're cold, you need more insulation."

"You're not cold?" I ask, and he just shrugs thick shoulders, folding his arms over his chest. The light catches on every single muscle in them, outlining his body in dramatic shadows.

"I run hot when I sleep."

I swallow and maintain eye contact, but I can't think of anything worth saying. It's some ungodly, timeless hour of the morning. It's black beyond the windows. My brain is half-awake at best, thoughts swirling lazily past like snowflakes, melting when I try to grab them. I feel unmoored, unanchored, like this cabin might be a child's diorama and at any moment the roof will come off and faces will appear.

"Thanks," I finally say. "For the mattress."

"You okay?"

I shove the heels of my hands against my eyes, trying to

trick my brain into waking up because I know I'm not dreaming, but this doesn't feel *real*.

"Are *you* okay?" I finally ask, copying his stance: feet wide, arms folded. "Or are you going to go sleep in the freezing room so we don't have to breathe the same air tonight?"

He glances at the door to the bedroom like he's considering it.

"No," he finally says. "Do you need help with the blankets?"

God forbid I get any kind of real answer from him.

"I'm fine," I tell him, and he nods, then heads back to the couch. I rearrange my sleeping bag and all seventeen thousand blankets, and I'm not quiet about it.

I need sleep, is all; I'll wake up tomorrow and all this *weirdness* will be sorted. I tell myself that as I blink up at the ceiling.

Sometime between five and five hundred minutes later, Gideon clears his throat softly, and I roll over to look at him. He's lying on his back, staring up at the ceiling, legs slightly akimbo because the couch is a couple inches too short.

"I saw you naked," he says, his voice flat and controlled, like he's confessing sins.

"I haven't *been* naked," I say, after a moment. It's too cold to be naked. Any required clothing removal I've been doing piecemeal, top and bottom separately, staying as dressed as possible.

"Topless, then," he goes on. He's still not looking at me. "I was outside, and you were in the bedroom, with the lights on, and the curtains were open."

"When?"

"Yesterday."

I start laughing. I don't know what else to do. I stop when he gives me a look so horrified and betrayed that I feel bad.

189

"Is that why you went outside?" I tease, but it's the wrong thing to say because even in the firelight, he turns beet red.

"Of course not," he says. "It was an accident, at first, and I should have turned back."

"But you didn't," I supply.

"No."

"Did you watch me get stuck in a sports bra? Without my knowledge?"

Gideon puts his hands over his face and takes a deep breath, his sleeping bag heaving over his chest.

"Yes," he admits.

I push myself up on one elbow and watch him for a moment. It's a fairly low couch, so he's only a few inches further off the ground than me, and he's shadowed and disheveled and tortured-looking, and I think: someone's really done a number on Gideon.

For the record, it doesn't bother me that I forgot to close the curtains and Gideon got a peep show that was maybe twenty seconds longer than it could have been. I lived in Brooklyn for ten years and I've *never* been great at closing curtains; presumably worse people than Gideon have gotten an eyeful. If the reverse had happened, I probably would've watched too.

I think of earlier, trying to wriggle out of my stupid sports bra, Gideon watching from outside the window. I think of what I'd do if it happened again and I knew it, and my pulse picks up, my stomach suddenly fluttering.

"Did you like it?" I ask, my voice soft because I don't dare to be louder.

Gideon freezes, then rolls to match my position, up on one elbow, facing me.

"What?" he asks, and I swallow.

"Did you like it?" I ask again.

190

There's a hitch in his breathing: quiet, subtle, unmistakable.

"I did," he finally says, and I sit up on the mattress, pushing the blanket pile off myself. Gideon's watching me, his green eyes nearly black in the dark, his lips parted.

"For the record, you could've just asked," I say, and tug on one sleeve.

It's not particularly easy to take off a sweater in a sexy way, and it's not any easier to remove two sweaters, a long-sleeve t-shirt, and a tank top. I get the three top layers off at the same time, the only sound in the room the snap of static and Gideon's soft breathing. The tank top is thin and tight and the way Gideon's staring at me makes me bold enough to take it off in one final flourish.

Once I toss it away, I realize I'm topless and a little cold and on a twin mattress on the floor in a cabin in the middle of nowhere, and I have no idea what to do with my hands. I settle for leaning back on them while I watch Gideon look at me, unmoving.

I'm not sure how much longer I can be this brave when he finally shoves off his own blankets, falls to his knees from the couch, and crawls the three feet over to me. He crawls until he's straddling my legs, knees on the floor and pressed against the side of the mattress, then leans in and kisses me.

When he wants to be, Gideon is so soft. There's nothing hesitant in the way he kisses me, but it's sweet and gentle and firm, all at once. I think of the birds he took out of the net, how he held them without hurting them or letting them hurt themselves, and flick my tongue against his lips.

The kiss deepens by shades, a bit at a time. He's not pinning me down but I'm pinned nonetheless, unable to move my arms or the force of him will topple me backwards. He shifts and puts a hand on my back, rough and calloused, with that same firm tenderness that makes me gasp quietly and squirm, pressing myself into him. He's got that thermal shirt on again, and it feels so good against my nipples that a noise escapes my throat.

Gideon makes an answering noise, plants a hand on the mattress, runs his fingertips along my spine. They're improbably warm—*I run hot*, he said—and they send trickles of heat down my backbone. He pulls his mouth away from mine and pauses, millimeters of space between us, before closing his teeth around my bottom lip and biting just hard enough that I feel it.

Then it's gone, and his hand is sliding over my ribcage and I gasp in a deep breath, and the movement rubs my nipples against his shirt and I shudder, fingers going tight on the mattress. Gideon puts one hand against my sternum and presses me back.

I go. He does it the same way he's done everything in the last five minutes: gentle and sure and sweet and unyielding. I drop to my elbows, looking up at him, his hand hot as an iron on my chest as he looks me over, his pupils blown in the dark. There's a lock of hair that's come down to curl over his forehead, and between that and the look on his face he's the portrait of desire as I let my elbows go from under me.

My head goes back further than I'm expecting, and I remember it's a twin bed. There's a blanket here to shield my head from the floor but I'm tipped slightly backward, looking at the corner where the wall meets the ceiling, and I'm about to shove myself up again to reposition but Gideon's mouth is on my neck. It's soft and hot and his beard scratches and tickles and there are teeth, sometimes. I hear myself make a noise and he does it more, scraping them over my collarbone as he shuffles one knee onto the mattress, the weight of it next to my left hip.

He takes the other hip in a hand, firm and gentle and certain, like I'm a bird he won't hurt but won't let fly away. I have my hands, finally, and I sink my fingers into his hair. I can't see him because my head is tipped back, but I can feel him pause, the sudden coolness where his mouth was a moment ago.

Then there's a quick, sweet press of lips against the inside of my wrist, and a second later, a flash of heat flicks over my nipple. I'm expecting it but I still gasp and arch into the solid heat of his hand still pressing against my sternum, telling me to keep still.

I try, but I can't. My breathing is ragged and I'm squirming, back arching, as Gideon explores my nipple with his mouth, using his lips and tongue and *teeth* with a focused intensity that makes me feel like he's taking notes.

Under him, I'm melting, turning from a person into a liquid. There are noises coming out of my mouth I've never heard before and all I can do is pretend I'm not making them, because Gideon is kissing a trail of fire across my chest and does the same to my other nipple, only this time he moves the hand on my sternum just enough to casually slide his thumb over my other nipple.

I make a noise like a squirrel stuck in the mud, a sort of gasping whimper because my head's still back at a weird angle, but I wriggle one leg free and wrap it around Gideon's hips. He doesn't pause what he's doing but he does stroke my thigh from hip to knee, hitching it a little higher as he does, the heat of his hand sinking through two pairs of pants.

Soon, I get my other leg free and around him, but he doesn't let me take his weight. I can tell he's hard and it would be a relief if he'd start rutting against me, but he doesn't. Not even when he trails kisses to the hollow of my throat, up my neck, and under my chin. I swallow against his lips and he licks me, then gets an arm under my back, and tugs me onto the mattress, spinning me so my head is on the pillow.

We stare at each other. My brain is so blank I don't think I could come up with words if I had to, and Gideon looks at me like I'm an animal he's trying to classify. He runs one thumb over my lips, leans in, kisses me again. We kiss like that until we're on our sides with no space between us, huddled on this twin mattress. He hasn't removed his shirt and I haven't put one on, but I like it. It makes me feel delicate, adored, like I'm being carefully displayed.

Gideon pulls the sleeping bag and blankets over us. He rests one hand on the naked skin of my waist as we kiss again, but doesn't move it further.

I don't know when we stop kissing and fall asleep, but we do.

· · · · ★ ★ ★ ★ · · · ·

I WAKE UP ALONE, still topless, and under a mountain of blankets, the bright white light of snow-covered winter filtering through the curtains that look onto the front porch. Gideon's sleeping bag is still crumpled at one end of the couch, and I blink at it a couple of times, trying to process several thoughts at once but instead they all get snarled into a big lump in my brain.

I settle for staring at the ceiling for a few minutes. It's wood paneling, or maybe just wood, like everything else in this decidedly 1970s-feeling cabin. I wonder how old the cabin is, whether it was built then or if that was the last time someone redecorated. Was it always owned by the Forest Service? Did it originally belong to someone trying to make a living up here? Or maybe some grumpy loner who decided to be done with people and come live on a mountain?

There's a faint *clank* as Gideon sets something on the stove, and I reflect for a minute on that *grumpy loner* thing. I guess I ruined his solitude, but based on the events of yesterday, I'm going to take a wild guess that he doesn't mind too much.

I lay there for a few more minutes until I smell coffee, which I consider my cue to get up and look for my shirt. That's too far for me to reach while still under the blankets, but Gideon's sweater is pretty close, so I grab that just as Gideon walks into the room.

He stops when he sees I'm awake. I've got the blankets up over my chest, but my shoulders are out, arms already through his sweater sleeves.

"Oh," he says, his voice quiet in the still morning. "You're awake."

"What time is it?" I ask, as if it matters, but I need to say something.

"Almost eight," he says. "I figured we'd have some breakfast and then head back out for more grouse."

I pull his sweater over my head, which might flash some boob. I don't know. I'm pretty sure it doesn't matter at this point.

"Do I smell coffee?" I ask, pulling my braid out of his sweater, then pulling it down around me as I shove the rest of the blankets off. I've still got two pairs of pants on—leggings and sweats—and between the woodstove and the blankets and the sweater, I'm a million degrees.

"I made some," he says. "Figured I'd fry up the last of the bacon before it goes bad."

"Bacon takes forever to go bad."

"Then I'll fry it up for no reason."

"*Because you want some* is reason enough, you know," I tell him, kicking blankets away and standing. Gideon just shrugs and almost smiles, all gruff and adorable and I remember the way he kissed the inside of my wrist last night, in the near-dark.

"Am I correct in assuming you'd also like some?" he asks.

I reach my arms overhead, stretch, and yawn. It makes a noise like a chupacabra crossed with a demon bat, probably, and Gideon goes faintly pink across his cheekbones, hands stuffed into his pockets.

"Yes, of course," I say, and hook my thumbs in the waist-band of my top layer of pants. "You know my position on—"

I pull the sweatpants down. Gideon turns away and walks into the doorframe.

"Ow, *fuck*," he mutters, and before I can ask if he's okay, he's back in the kitchen and I've got sweatpants around my ankles, staring after him. For half a second, I consider being offended, but that seems dumb, so I settle on being... charmed, I think.

"I'm wearing leggings," I say as I walk into the kitchen a minute later, the smell of bacon already wafting through the cabin.

He glances at me, then back at the stove.

"I know," he says, cheeks and ears still pink, and you know what? Fuck it. Fuck letting him be uncertain and awkward about whatever *this* is, this thing where we make out and then act like we didn't and then get half-naked and act like we didn't. Time to do what I want and deal with the conse-quences.

I walk over and wrap my arms around his waist from behind, hooking my chin over his shoulder. Gideon freezes. I almost apologize and pull away because clearly this isn't it, clearly he hates this, but then he relaxes into me.

Tentatively, so tentatively I'm not sure it's happening at first, he puts one hand over mine. My heart *flutters*. I press my luck and give him a quick kiss behind his ear, and Gideon squirms.

"Smells good," I say.

"It's *bacon*," he says, and I roll my eyes even though he can't see me.

"Yes, we established that," I say. "It's bacon, which everyone likes and which smells good. I was making *conversation*, so now you're supposed to—"

I don't get to dictate his half of it, because he's put down the spatula, takes my face in his hand, and turns to kiss me on the lips. It's a quick kiss at the wrong angle, but my stomach feels like an entire flock of grouse takes off inside it.

"I know how to converse," he says, head still turned, his face an inch from mine.

"Do you?"

"Go get ready for hiking," he says, all low and fake-gruff, like he's not secretly the sweetest person I've ever met. "We're leaving right after breakfast."

I kiss him on the cheek before heading into the bathroom.

TWENTY-TWO

GIDEON

BEFORE WE CAN ACTUALLY LEAVE, my phone rings, and because I'm cursed to be reachable at all times, I answer. It's Reid, and apparently, I've missed a lot in the past day.

"*Why* is the women's bible study group refusing to meet at mom and dad's house, again?" I ask, twenty minutes later. I think I'm being very patient, but Reid huffs. He does not, technically, roll his eyes, but it's close.

"Because, according to Sadie, Mom made Beth miss choir practice to replant her rosebushes," Reid explains very slowly, as if explaining this to a small child.

"It's *winter*."

"They're in a greenhouse or something, I don't know."

"Okay. Boycotting for missed choir practice. Got it."

I don't, but that's probably fine. I still don't know why he's telling me all this third-hand gossip.

"And Beth had to re-plant the rose bushes because Sadie told Mom who really ran them over eight years ago," he continues. Even though I was in my mid-twenties and not living at home, I remember the incident well, mostly because my parents wanted me to get to the bottom of it. That didn't go well, either.

"And Sadie was getting back at Beth because Beth found condoms, et cetera, in her bedroom and went off about it," I finish, because *that* part of the story I managed to understand the first time. I do not elaborate on the *et cetera* because I'm still on my first cup of coffee and also, thinking about what else my little sister has in her bedside table may, in fact, cause me to die. "And she was snooping because…"

"She's a self-righteous nosy twat who thinks it's her job to police the rest of us?"

I take another sip of coffee because as much as I try—unsuccessfully—not to get involved in my siblings' disputes, I don't exactly disagree with Reid's assessment.

"And now Sadie's upset," I finish, still in the just-trying-to-get-the-facts portion of my morning. Andi is still getting dressed, and given the discussion I'm having with Reid, I'm hoping she takes a while longer. She doesn't need to know how fucked up this situation is or just how deeply I'm still enmeshed in my family's bullshit.

"Yes," Reid says, giving me a *look* through FaceTime. "She says Mom gave her a lecture about sex before marriage, Matt's wife took her aside for a little *girls-only* chat that I'm pretty sure involved the phrase *get the milk for free*, Zach won't look at her, and Beth is furious that her sweet, obedient little protege is actually no such thing."

For the record, Sadie is twenty-five, teaches middle school math, and doesn't live at home. I imagine that in regular families, Beth would have quietly closed the drawer and never mentioned it.

Actually, in most families, I doubt Beth would have opened someone else's bedside drawer in the first place. Lucky us.

"Oh, and Jacob called her a Jezebel, so she punched him," Reid finishes. "In the arm. Pretty hard, though."

Reid, who adores and would do anything for his older sister, is grinning about it.

"Great," I mutter. "He needed more to bitch about. How's Sadie... holding up?"

"She's pretty upset," Reid says. "Her and her boyfriend who she's apparently fucking were over here until pretty late last night. He's nice. Seemed supportive, if out of his depth."

"What, he didn't follow the politics of planting rosebushes and choir practice?"

"God help him, he tried," Reid says. "And Sadie is, like, *into* this dude, so I think she's also mad that Beth basically tainted his reputation with the rest of our family before he even met them."

"We're talking about taints already?"

Andi pads through the doorway in thick socks, leggings, and my sweater, her fingertips barely sticking out of the sleeves. I wonder if she's got anything on under the sweater or if it's nothing but her soft, warm skin. I wonder if I left beard burn last night.

I know, without looking, that I'm stoplight-red.

"It's nearly nine," Reid says from the iPad. "If not now, when?"

"Fair," Andi says, and bends over to look at the iPad, bringing her cheek close to mine. "Hey, guys."

"Morning," I murmur, trying valiantly, desperately to stop thinking.

"Good *morning*," Reid says, and when I finally glance back at the screen, he's wearing a delighted, half-grinning, half-eyebrows-raised expression that makes me instantly wary. I can't get any redder, but I *can* feel more embarrassed, it turns out. "I was just telling Gideon the latest developments in our family soap opera."

"Don't worry about it," I tell her, something tightening in my chest. "It's nothing, it's stupid, it's boring—"

"I'll get more coffee," Andi says, and her hand drifts across the back of my neck as she walks away. This makes twice now, this morning, that she's just *touched* me out of nowhere. Maybe if it happens a third time it won't send my whole brain offline.

"Gideon?" Reid is asking, still grinning like a shithead. I clear my throat and frown, because that's what I do, right?

"I should go, actually," I tell Reid, and it's got nothing to do with getting off the phone before Andi comes back. "Unless you have questions about any of the animals—"

As if summoned, there's a *mrrrrrr* sound and Dolly's enormous head appears in front of the camera. Imperiously, she scans the room, then appears to zero in on Reid, who looks wary and takes another sip of coffee.

"She wants you to pet her," I say.

"I think it's a trap."

"She's a cat."

"She's a cat who's tempting me into petting her so she can tear my hand off and... sacrifice it to the old gods, or something."

"Your hand would be a terrible sacrifice."

"My hand would be a *great* sacrifice."

"MRRAAAAAAAH," says Dolly, and Reid makes another face.

Slowly, he reaches out a hand and rubs it gently across the top of her head. I can hear her purr even through the spotty connection. Andi comes back with her own chipped mug, drags over a chair, and sits with one foot tucked under the other, her knee touching my thigh. When I can think again, I slowly put my hand on it, and she gives me a small, secret smile.

"So, what's the soap opera?" she asks Reid, who's currently frowning and scratching Dolly under her chin. One of them is having a very good time right now.

"It's complicated and really not interesting," I say. "Just drama."

"My sisters Sadie and Beth are fighting because Sadie's getting laid," Reid says. Andi glances at me with one eyebrow raised. Does my face get hotter? Maybe.

"And Beth's not?"

"Beth's got three kids," I tell Andi.

"That doesn't mean she's *getting* laid, it means she's *been* laid a minimum of three times," Reid points out as Dolly leans into him.

"But it's a problem that Sadie's getting laid," Andi says, glancing over at me again. "Isn't she..."

"Twenty-five? Yes," I say, and push my fingers through my hair, mortified that *this* is why my whole family is fighting right now, because what kind of people care if an adult woman has sex? "But our parents thought she was still... devout," I say.

"Sadie swore up and down that she was waiting for marriage, even though she wasn't," says Reid. "And for some reason, they believed her, and meanwhile Beth really *did* keep it under wraps until the wedding night, and thought that at least one of her sisters would turn out okay, so she feels betrayed. And probably mad that Sadie's having a way more fun life than she is."

"I see," Andi says, and I don't really think she does—this is the kind of shit that goes down deep and back years—but I appreciate the effort."Meanwhile, Ariel is on the warpath on Sadie's behalf, Zach, Matt, and Jacob are half shocked and half getting blamed that they didn't, I don't know, guard their sister's honor, and Hannah is trying to smooth everything over because she's the middle child," Reid says.

"Most of you are middle children," Andi points out. "*You're* a middle child."

"She's the middlest," Reid says, as Dolly flops over in his lap. His hand pauses a minute, then very cautiously continues petting. "She's so middle our parents don't even know she has a girlfriend."

Andi makes a neutral noise and drinks more coffee.

"Which you can't tell them," Reid blurts out, suddenly looking a little panicked that he might have told the wrong semi-secret to the wrong person; most of my siblings have *something* they're hiding from each other and/or my parents, and in a family of fourteen remembering who's allowed to know what can get tricky.

"I definitely won't," Andi says. "I promise." She doesn't have to say *if I ever talk to them again it'll be too soon.*

"I can draw you a family tree later," I offer, just to change the subject a little.

"And of course, everyone wants Gideon on their side because he's the Sweden of the family," Reid finishes, and Andi looks at me in slight confusion.

"Switzerland," I say to Reid. "Sweden's the one with fjords, Switzerland is the neutral one with banking."

"I always fuck that up," he mutters.

"And I'm on Sadie's side, obviously," I reassure them both. "Though I wish she hadn't faked it quite so hard."

"Really? *You* wish she'd been more honest?" Reid says, bitterness leaking through into his voice.

"There's lying and then there's *lying*," I say. "She's the one who kept the purity ring on and went to church with them."

Reid looks down and pets Dolly without responding.

"I haven't been to church in years. I'm not faking anything," I tell him, ignoring the same tug of guilt I feel every time we talk about this.

He's quiet for a long moment, concentrating very hard on giving Dolly ear scratches.

"Right. Sorry. Never mind," he finally says without looking up, and I bite back the next ten things I want to say.

"How are the outdoor animals?" I ask instead. He gives me a look.

"Fine," he says. "Appreciative of heating pads."

I sigh and accept this.

· · · · ★ ★ ★ · · · ·

"HEY," Andi shouts, hours later, her voice half-swallowed by the snow and the trees and the sky. "What do feral hog tracks look like?"

"Same as regular hog tracks," I call back, giving a knot one last tug.

"You can't possibly think that was a helpful response."

I walk over to where she's squatting, boots crunching through the snow. It's in the forties today, at least ten degrees above freezing, so the snow is crunchy and sticky, the whole forest dripping.

"Like an oval with a sharp notch in the front," I say as I crouch next to her and look down at the snow. "Yup. That's a big 'un."

"How big?"

I shrug. "Real big?"

"Why do you sound so southern all of a sudden?"

"I've got news for you," I tell her, and she laughs, even as she's glancing around the forest. "You'd hear it if it were nearby," I reassure her.

Andi doesn't look reassured.

"How big is *real big*?"

I shrug and hold my hand about three feet off the ground.

"I'm not a hog sleuth," I point out. "I can't tell you that it's got a chipped tooth and had berries for breakfast by looking at its tracks."

"What use are you?" she teases.

"I can tag the hell out of a grouse."

We stand, brushing snow off ourselves. It falls to the ground in clumps.

"How dangerous *are* they?" she asks. "You did say they were the worst thing out here."

"No, I said the worst thing was a mountain lion, followed by a momma bear," I correct. "I just said you're *more likely* to come across—"

She flicks some snow off her sleeve right into my cheek, and my sentence gets all tangled up.

"It's fine," I finish. "They probably won't attack unless provoked."

"Probably," she says, looking back at the tracks. "Great."

TWENTY-THREE

GIDEON

IT'S evening when Andi walks into the kitchen with an armful of clothing and looks over my shoulder at the iPad, where I'm backing up bird data.

"Nosy," I say, and she makes an indignant noise.

"You're using it right out in the open where anyone can see it," she says.

"Doesn't mean you have to look at my private computer activities," I say. I'm trying to tease her but I think it comes out a little too serious, and next thing I know, Andi's bright red and not quite meeting my eyes. I don't know what to think about any of it.

"Just for that, I'm not offering to toss your laundry in with mine," she says.

"You're doing laundry again?"

"I'm out of," she says, and then stands a tiny bit taller. "Unmentionables."

We look at each other for a long moment, and I've seen her half-naked and had my mouth on her bare skin, and I've got no clue what to say.

"I think you just mentioned them," is what I go with, and

glance at the pile in her hands. Sure enough, there are under-pants and sports bras in every color of the rainbow and several whimsical patterns. I look at them for a moment too long, then realize I'm looking at her dirty laundry and look *anywhere* else.

Andi just sighs and sort of laughs. "I'm trying to be a lady, okay?" she says.

"How's that going?"

Andi scrunches her face. "I'm about to wash and hang *unmentionables* in the bathroom I currently share with a gentleman, I've been taking baths with a washcloth and a sink for the past ten days, and my hair has so much grease in it I could fry a small turkey," she says as she walks into the bath-room. "I've felt more ladylike, I'll tell you that."

"There's a bathtub," I point out, still talking to her through the doorway.

Andi tosses her laundry in the sink, looks at the bathtub, and then looks at me.

"You could take a bath," I go on, pointing out the obvious.

She grabs the hand-cranked laundry machine from under the sink and starts filling the tank from the water filter, then gives me the world's most skeptical look.

"The water's freezing and in short supply," she says. "I'm fine, I promise. Or do you need me to scrub harder during my sink baths?"

"We've got a stove and a creek," I say. "No reason the water can't be hot and plentiful."

Andi pauses, then turns the water off. She's quiet for a long moment.

"That's a huge pain in the ass," she finally says in a tone of voice that I'm pretty sure means *I've never wanted anything more.*

I walk to the bathroom door and lean against the frame,

glancing past her at the tub. It's pretty small—maybe two and a half feet by four feet, basically a wooden basin with a drain in the bottom—but that makes it easier to fill.

"I'll make you a deal," I say. "Let me toss a few things in with your laundry and I'll get you some hot water."

"That's not a fair trade."

"Sure it is, if I don't have to look at your greasy hair any more," I tease, and Andi huffs and rolls her eyes.

"Your hair is *also* gross," she mutters. "*You're* gross. Go get me whatever it is you want me to wash."

A few minutes later, there's a giant stockpot full of water heating up over two burners on the stove and the sloshing sounds of the hand-cranked laundry machine coming in from the bathroom. I'll need to refill the water tank in the kitchen, but that's a problem for daylight, not right now. While it finishes heating, I lean against the kitchen counter and pretend I'm not watching Andi as she pulls her *unmentionables* from the washer and hangs them on the lines strung over the bathtub, their presence already oddly familiar since she only brought enough for a few days.

Everything about Andi is like that: startlingly new and oddly familiar at the same time, like an old melody with new words. Like I know it, deep down, even if I don't know exactly how to sing along yet. Andi's just like I remember down to the millimeter, down to the hitch in her laugh, the freckles in her eyes.

When I woke up this morning, I was a million degrees and half-off a twin mattress, one arm under Andi's head, her back to me. I came awake in stages, like you do: heat, light, the hardness of the floor under my left leg, Andi's bare skin in front of me, rising and falling as she slept. I don't know how long I watched her for, cataloguing the night before, making sure I slotted the memories away properly—*did you like it?* Jesus—warmth and the thump of her heart under my palm, every noise I could draw out of her. I thought about it until she stirred, not quite awake yet, and I could pull my arm from under her, drop a kiss on her bare shoulder, and get up.

Then I locked myself in the bathroom and got myself off, hard, fast and quiet, biting my lip against the desperate noises I wanted to make. It didn't take long. I was barely done before the guilt set in—not deep, but always present—and I made bacon as penance.

When the water's ready, Andi clears out so I can lug it into the bathroom and pour it into the tub without splashing too much anywhere, then top it off with the water in the bathroom tank. When I'm done it's hot enough to turn my hand red, but that won't last long.

I grab the pot and look around. No Andi.

"Bath's ready," I call, then hear something fall in the pantry.

"There's bath stuff in here," she says when I poke my head in. She's on her tiptoes, a flashlight in one hand, the other elbow-deep into a shelf above her head.

My first instinct is to tell her to watch for snakes. I remind myself we're indoors.

"It's getting cold," I tell her.

"Hold on," she says, lurching upward on her tiptoes, the sweater she's wearing sliding down her neck and exposing a patch of collarbone. It's my sweater, of course, because that's practically the only thing she's worn for days now, as if she's committed to making me lose my mind.

The leggings she's wearing aren't helping, nor is the way her stance highlights every tensed muscle in her legs. Nor are the effortful grunts she's making as she reaches for whatever it is she's—

"Aha!" Andi says, finally coming back to earth, holding something up and grinning. "I knew it!"

I squint into the darkness of the pantry, because her flashlight is unhelpfully pointed at the ceiling.

"Bubble bath!" she says, and her smile's a confection, even in the odd light. "I think, at least. The label's kinda worn off."

She hands it to me and comes out of the pantry. The label is so old it's just white. This bubble bath might remember the Reagan administration.

"There's no way this still bubbles," I tell her, but Andi just shrugs, still grinning.

"Only one way to find out," she says, and before I know it, she's leaning in to kiss me on the cheek, lighting my entire face on fire. "Thanks."

Then she's gone, the bathroom door closing behind her, and I'm out here not thinking about her being naked and slick and warm in the—fuck.

· · · · ★ ★ ★ · · · ·

I'M PACING. It's stupid, but I'm pacing, because Andi's currently taking a bath—she is *taking* a *bath* for fuck's sake—and I've been wondering all day how to make last night happen again, but I feel like I'm trying to negotiate in a language I barely speak.

I have, technically, done this before. I've been naked with women and brought them to orgasm, thanks, and I've enjoyed myself, but I've never before spent a full five minutes staring at a rock and thinking about the exact texture of someone's nipple against my lips. I didn't even realize it was an option.

What if I just—knocked. To see if she needs anything. I go before I can think better of it.

For a moment I pause at the bathroom door, my forehead

against the wood, because—I don't know. I don't know where I am and I don't know where I'm going and this is familiar, too, finding myself somewhere new and unknown, side-by-side with Andi. Up until now I've understood relationships as a progression, as *this* and then *that*, neat steps toward a logical endpoint. This feels like diving off a cliff.

"Come in," she calls when I knock, and I stick my head in.

Andi's somehow gotten the bubbles piled high, over the rim of the tub in places, head poking out of one end, the pale knobs of her knees barely visible underneath suds. The room's warm and humid and smells of something fruity and floral that I can't place.

"Hey," I say, and clear my throat. Then I clear it again. "You need anything?"

Andi looks around the bathroom for a long moment, eyes darting, like she's trying to find something and can't.

"Yes!" she finally says, and points so hard with one arm that water splashes out of the tub. "That washcloth over there. Please?"

I close the door and grab the washcloth, and when I turn back to her she's got her arms folded on the edge of the tub and suds piled on one shoulder and she's pink from the heat of the water. All my thoughts pop like a soap bubble. From somewhere, I dredge the last of my bravery.

"Want me to get your back?" I finally ask.

"Would you?"

"Why do you think I offered?" I mutter, but it's on autopilot because yes, I would, of *course* I would, so I fold the bathmat in half, pull my sweater off, and kneel next to the tub so we're face-to-face.

"Hi," Andi says, and her hair's wet and secured on top of her head in some kind of bun and she's naked under the water, her skin shining and slick, faint freckles on her cheeks and along the tops of her shoulders and she's smiling at me like we've got a secret. I'm certain my heart's never beat this hard before.

"Hi," I echo, the only word that comes to mind.

There's a few moments of perfect, quiet stillness before I put one finger under her chin and kiss her. She's warm and pliable and up close she smells even more like a soap store in a mall, but in a good way.

"Turn around," I say, when we break the kiss and she does, the water sloshing around in the tiny tub. When her back's to me there are freckles on the back of her neck, darker than the ones on her shoulders, a few small moles dotting the expanse of skin. I push up my sleeves and run a thumb over one, soft and slightly raised.

"You should get these checked out. Just in case," I say, and then her head dips and her shoulders shake and I sigh. "Shut up," I mutter, but I'm smiling.

"No," Andi says, and I run the washcloth across her back.

Her skin turns even pinker everywhere I rub her in slow, careful circles: around her shoulder blades, over her shoulders, down her spine and under the bubbles. The back of her neck. I go over every inch of her skin twice, and when I don't have that excuse any more, I abandon the washcloth to the tub and slide my bare hand over her skin. She's hot and wet and there's no room left in my brain for anything but this, at least not until she leans back, settling against the side of the tub.

The knob of her neck is right there, freckled and bright pink, and I press my lips against it. It's impossibly warm and wet and slippery and Andi says *oh* softly, but it's loud in the quiet bathroom. She tilts her head back over the edge of the tub against my shoulder and looks at me, face pink and lips parted and eyes half question mark, half invitation.

"Thank you," she says, my heart beating so hard I fear for my ribcage.

"Of course," I say, and flatten my palms against her shoulders, the tips of my fingers just below her collarbone, warm and slippery and pink with heat. My brain's half the feeling of slick, soft skin below my fingers and half a cloud of roiling anxiety telling me I don't know what I'm doing and also that I like it, so I shouldn't.

"Anything else?" I ask, and Jesus, that sounds like I'm ringing her up at a gas station mini-mart. "I mean, do you need more help... bathing?"

"Are you offering?" she asks, and turns her head, nosing along my neck.

I think of at least five variations on *you're a dirty girl* and they're all awful. Christ, how do people do this?

"My sleeves are already rolled up," is the thing that comes out of my mouth, and Andi starts laughing, the sound bouncing around the tiny bathroom, the buzz of it under my fingertips. I bite back a smile and draw a circle on her skin with one fingertip. "I'm just saying, I'm prepared and willing to get elbow-deep." I clear my throat. "In the water."

"As long as it doesn't inconvenience you," she teases, sliding a warm, wet hand around the back of my neck. "While you're here, may as well help me finish bathing. It's only practical."

"Otherwise, I rolled my sleeves up for nothing," I agree.

"Can't have that," she says, and settles herself against the side of the tub with a wriggle I'm going to think about forever. "Wash me off, Gideon, I'm such a dirty girl. Wow, that sounded different in my head."

I can't help but snort, my face against her wet hair, and Andi sighs but she leans against my shoulder again, head back. It wipes my brain clean, water and skin and heat and the floral, fruity scent that will probably give me a Pavlovian erection for the rest of my life, and—the anxiety cloud is gone. Not gone. Smaller. In a corner.

It stays smaller, quieter, as I splay one hand across her chest, my thumb in the divot of her throat, and slide the other under the water. It's warm and so is she, and she's slippery with the bubble bath, and the noise she makes when I move my palm over her nipple buries itself in my hindbrain so I can think about it forever. It's flat with the warmth, but I stroke my thumb over it slowly, circling, and it stiffens until I can pinch it between two fingers, gently at first, then harder until she squirms.

"Too much?" I murmur. Andi swallows, her eyes closed.

"Almost," she says, and I let off a little. "But not quite. You could do it again."

I do. I touch her almost everywhere I can reach and catalog the results, sorting them into categories so I can come back to them again and again. Andi gasps and moans quietly and bites her lip sometimes, tells me *harder* and *softer* and *more*. Her hand digs into the back of my neck and a rivulet of water makes its way down my spine, inch by inch.

Andi inhales sharply when I reach the inside of one thigh, her legs already spread underneath the water. Her skin's soft and the way she yields when I squeeze makes me a little dizzy along with the way she moves, hips rolling. I think she braces her foot against the other side of the tub and leans even further into me, one pink nipple peeking above the water. I'm so hard it hurts, and the slight friction where I'm pressed against the outside of the tub isn't doing shit.

"Can I," I start, and swallow hard. "Get you off?" I finish, stroking the spot where her thigh meets her hip. I can't see anything under the water so I'm doing it all by feel, my arms in the tub up to my biceps, my shirt soaking wet, water dripping onto the floor.

"Yes, please," she says, the politeness of the words destroyed by the way she sounds, all ragged and breathy. For me. Because of what I'm doing with her, here, in this tub, and the thought makes me lightheaded.

"Show me what you like," I tell her before I can ruin this by thinking. "And show me how you like it."

"Fuck," she whispers without opening her eyes, then grabs my hand, her fingers on top of mine. It's a little clumsy but then I'm stroking her lips, sinking between them for a moment, sliding upward until her whole body gives a tiny, involuntary jolt that makes my mouth go dry.

"There?" I ask, lips against her ear, and stroke her clit again, this time with two fingers. Andi just turns her head and nods into my neck, her hips pushing up and into my hand as I move in slow, lazy strokes.

Andi makes beautiful, perfect noises against my neck. Every couple of strokes she jolts again, her hips bucking, her hand digging into me. Her breathing picks up, faster and harsher, and she *whimpers*, I swear to God she whimpers and there's real chance that I'm going to—

"Can I—?" she says, her hand back on mine, though she doesn't wait for an answer, just positions my fingers at a slightly different angle, changing the pressure.

"Like that?" I murmur, trying to obey her with every cell in my body.

Andi just huffs and I can feel her bite her lip, positioning me again. I've never paid more minute attention to something in my life, but she makes a frustrated noise and wriggles, her hand around my wrist, pushing my hand into her like she needs more.

"Sorry," she whispers, after a moment, voice edged with desperation. "Sorry, fuck, I'm so close, it's just—"

Her hand slides under mine, our fingers fitting together as she rubs herself in small, tight, fast circles and moans into my neck. I pull my head back so I can see her, my hand never leaving hers.

"This is how I make you come?" I ask, her eyes heavy-lidded and her lips parted. "Just like this?"

"Yeah," she whispers, her eyes fluttering shut.

"Fuck, Andi," I whisper, my brain a perfect blank but my mouth working anyway. My fingers tighten microscopically on hers and an urgent, desperate noise comes out of her mouth. "You look—this is so fucking hot, Andi, I want to—"

She cuts me off with another noise and turns her head to one side, mouth open and back arched and our fingers not stopping for a second. It's unmistakable and glorious and *loud* and hands-down the hottest thing I've ever seen. I watch her jolt through the aftershocks, biting her lip like it'll muffle the sounds she's making, settle a hand on her inner thigh when she moves hers away, and then her other hand is tangling in my hair, hard enough that it nearly hurts, and she's pulling my mouth to hers in a hot, wet, open-mouthed kiss.

Holy shit. Holy *shit*.

"Jesus Christ," I say, against her mouth. My hand is on her soft, plush inner thigh, and I squeeze. Andi makes a tiny noise, then huffs out a laugh.

"That was," I start, but then we're kissing again, both of us half-twisted over the wooden lip of the tub, messy and wild. "Can you do that again?"

"Do what?" she asks, her face bright red. She's still breathing fast. "Come?"

"Yes," I say, and my mouth is back on hers, my hand stroking her inner thigh.

"Probably not right now unless you, uh, have a vibrator with you?"

"Fuck," I grumble, and determine to start carrying a vibrator with me at all times. "You sure?"

"Rolling up your sleeves didn't work," she says, tugging lightly on one. I look down. It's still above my elbow, and Andi is still naked and wet and warm, so I have no idea what she's talking about. "You got wet anyway."

She is correct. "Oh," I say eloquently, and rub my other hand down the front of my shirt. It's also wet, but I'm having a hard time attaching that fact to any particular meaning right now.

Andi turns around in the tub, legs bumping the sides and water sloshing, until she's facing me with her forearms resting on the wooden edge of the tub.

"You could take it off," she suggests.

TWENTY-FOUR

ANDI

GIDEON STARES AT ME. His lips are deep pink and slightly parted, red across his cheekbones, his dark hair curling at the ends. He's still got one hand on his chest where there's a deep, dark V of water on his tight gray shirt. He's on his knees on the bathroom floor, and in the silence sudden trepidation slices through me.

Shit, is this too much? Am I going too fast? I'm telling him to take his clothes off and get into a bathtub with me, while he's probably got plenty of baggage around sex because how could he *not* with the way he was raised?

"Or, if you—"

I stop because Gideon abruptly sits back on his heels and pulls his shirt off, and there's nothing quite like watching a hot man take his shirt off because you asked him to. Told him. Whatever. It shows off all his arm muscles, his wide shoulders rippling as he yanks it over his head then gives his hair a little shake. The hair on his chest is a shade darker than the hair on his head, all of it slicked down over a broad torso that's just as heavily muscled as the rest of him, thick in a way that suggests a lot of lifting rocks and chopping wood or whatever. The slick, dark hair narrows over his stomach, a dark line past his belly button and under the button of his jeans.

When I finally look at his face again, which takes me a minute, he's watching me. His expression is intense, all curiosity and caution and desire, but he's got his knees spread a little past shoulder width and his hands relaxed on his thighs, and there's really no mistaking the bulge under his zipper.

I wish I had a photographic memory so I could have this snapshot forever. Gideon, on his knees, wet and hard and half-naked, casual as anything and maybe the hottest thing I've ever seen. I wonder if he has any clue how hot he is. I'm pretty sure he doesn't.

"Thank you," I say, which I immediately recognize as terrible dirty talk but Gideon snorts softly and blushes and glances away, like I'm being ridiculous and not sincerely grateful that I get to see him in this state.

"You're welcome," he mutters after a moment, and I like it so much I lean up over the edge of the tub and kiss him with one hand around the back of his neck. Water sloshes gently over the side of the wooden tub when I do. It probably gets Gideon's knees wet. My upper half is out of the water now and in the freezing air, puckering my nipples and covering me with goosebumps, but Gideon strokes his warm hands over my shoulders and down my back, making me sigh into his mouth.

I explore him with my hands, and he lets me: he's warm and damp everywhere, muscled but soft. He makes a gratifying little noise when I follow the trail of hair to the button on his pants and then stop, fingers pressed against the skin there, pausing, savoring the moment and making sure he doesn't tell me to stop.

He doesn't. He pushes his fingers into my wet hair and kisses me harder and with his other hand, he takes my wrist and guides my hand to his dick, then groans into my mouth as I slide my palm down his shaft. He's hard as iron and pushes his hips into my hand, still holding onto my wrist.

"Come in," I say. "Water's great."

He nods, I think, then pulls back. Gideon's eyes are on my face as he pops the button and pulls down the zipper. He palms himself, once, over black underwear, then blushes like he didn't mean to do it. I swallow down the words *do that again* but bookmark the thought for later use: what would Gideon look like, on his knees, getting himself off while I watched?

I shift until my back is against the other side of the tub, watching as he stands and steps out of his pants. When he hooks his thumbs under the elastic of his boxer-briefs and tugs, his cock springs out, thick and swollen and leaking a little. Jesus Christ. His blush goes all the way to his chest, and he runs a hand through his hair when he's fully naked.

"It's still hot," he says when he steps into the tub, like he's surprised. It's really, really not big enough for two adults, so our knees bump together and he's got one arm slung along the side, his arm muscles shiny with water.

"Does that mean you don't need warming up?" I ask, and since we're fit together in here like human Tetris blocks, I reach down and put my hand on the inside of his knee. He inhales softly but sharply and his eyelids flicker.

"I could be warmer," he says, voice low and velvety and I wonder for the hundredth time if he has any clue that he's sexy as fuck.

Gideon gives me a skeptical look as I maneuver until I'm straddling his lap, the water sloshing, the bubbles mostly disintegrated by now. He guides me with hands on my hips, then slides them up my sides once I'm settled.

"Like this?" I ask, and wrap a hand around his cock. Gideon inhales hard and his eyelids go to half-mast, his hands tightening on me. His hips buck just hard enough to ripple the water in the tub, and I take it as an invitation to stroke him from root to tip.

"Yeah," he grits out, voice a harsh whisper. "Like that."

Gideon doesn't make a lot of noise as I get him off in hard, slow strokes. Sometimes he groans quietly, his breathing irregular. Sometimes he makes these choked-off noises like he's trying not to moan as he grabs my hips and fucks up into my hand, the movement small and controlled, like he wants to help himself and can't.

One time he says *God, fuck, Andi* and the only thing I can think of to say is *yeah?*

I could fuck him right now. I sure think about it, how it would be the easiest thing in the world: to rise up a little more on my knees and sink down onto him. I think about how he'd probably moan out loud then, how maybe he'd grab my hips and hold me down on him, how good it would probably feel.

I don't, for a million reasons, but I want to.

Gideon arches his head back when he's close, his face going mottled pink. When he looks at me again his pupils are wide and his hands are gripping my thighs so hard I might have bruises tomorrow. I stroke him faster, harder, until he wraps one hand around mine, setting the rhythm and bucking his hips, and comes with a long, low groan, head tilted back.

It's impossibly hot. All I can do is stare down at him, head back and eyes closed, replaying that sound on a loop in my head, the way his whole body tightened and bucked between my thighs. After a moment I lean in and put my lips right on the pulse point of his neck, skin water-cooled, and I can feel how hard his heart is beating right now.

Gideon jerks a little when I take my hand off his dick, but then he's lifting his head again, all flushed and hazy, his hand tangling in the back of my hair as he brings our mouths together.

After a few minutes, I pull back. He's watching me, less hazy now, something uncertain in his face. I almost ask, but instead I say, "I gotta move, my knees are killing me."

"Shit," he rumbles, voice like a coal mine. He clears his throat and sits up a little straighter. "Here, is that—this tub wasn't made for two people," he finishes.

"I don't think it was made for one person," I say, settling against the opposite wall of the bathtub. Gideon settles one arm around my knee, his hand coming to rest on my thigh, his other arm stretched along the side.

"It's an old cabin. People used to be smaller, you know," he says, voice still low and lazy and relaxed, eyes heavy-lidded.

"I don't think the average adult was ever four feet tall."

Gideon just grunts, his thumb stroking slowly over my leg, and I never really want to move again. Sure, the tub is really uncomfortable, the water is closer to *lukewarm* than *hot*, and yes, there's semen floating around in it now, but I like this sweet, safe, secret moment.

· · · · · ★ ★ ★ · · · · ·

THAT NIGHT when I finish brushing my teeth, I notice there's a piece of bread and a little bit of cheese by the hole in the baseboards in the kitchen. I'm tempted to tease Gideon about it when I head into the main room, but he's dropping a pillow and sleeping bag onto the second twin mattress that's now next to mine. When he finds me looking at him, he just shrugs and runs a hand through his hair, not quite meeting my eyes. No reason to mention the chipmunk.

"Couch isn't very comfortable," he grumbles.

There are a hundred things I could say to tease him, starting with *so all I had to do to get you to sleep in the same room as me was jerk you off in a bathtub?* But I don't say any of them. I'm glad he's here—intentionally this time, with forethought and everything—and I don't want him to regret it.

"Neither are these, honestly," I say, skirting both beds and sitting on mine to pull my socks off, because sleeping with socks is weird no matter how cold it is. "Putting them right on the floor helps, though."

He nods, absentmindedly. Runs a hand through his hair again and then leaves it on top of his head like he's thinking, lit by the golden orange of the fire in the wood stove and the piercing brightness of an electric lantern we've got on the mantle. He's solid, wearing tight base layers again, his muscles highlighted in the strange light, and he's lovely with those pretty eyes and the graceful lines of his body; he's standing there like he's cautious, uncertain, but earlier today I watched him calmly wrestle a young male deer free of the grouse net with barely a flicker of alarm.

"Is that enough wood or should I put more in?" he asks, nodding at the wood stove.

"I don't think you *can* fit more."

"Sure, I could."

"It's fine," I say. I'm sitting on my mattress and wrap my sleeping bag around my shoulders. "Come to bed."

The tiny smile that ghosts across his face at that might be the sweetest thing I've seen all day. "We should get more wood tomorrow," he says as he kneels at the edge of the mattress and arranges his own sleeping bag. I do the same and also get my pile of blankets in order, because some of us are going to need seventeen layers to get through the night.

"Do we have to chop it?"

"What? No. There's a huge pile out there," Gideon says. "It's right by the shed, you didn't see it when you were digging out the sled?"

I probably did. Mostly, I was hoping I'd get to watch Gideon chop wood.

"Oh, right," I say. "I guess it'll last a while."

"We just need a few more days," he says, on his back, staring at the ceiling. "They're still working on clearing the Parkway, but a road crew should be able to come up and deal with us before long. And if not, the hike out isn't too bad and once the Parkway is good to go, someone can meet us at the Hogswallow trailhead and get us back into town. I can come back later for the truck if I need to."

I know I need to go down the mountain and back to every day life, for a shower if nothing else. I'm also excited for light switches, the internet, and using a microwave again. I can't take infinite time off from my job, even though I'm lucky and the university I'm a grant writer for is on winter break anyway.

But *out there* is also a mess. I still have to go contend with the fact that I impulsively chained myself to a tree so I could make friends with someone who didn't even stick around. When I go back, I'm going back to my aunt Lucia's spare bedroom, which is also currently my home office. After I came down to help her out when she broke her knee six months ago, I didn't mean to not leave, I just... didn't leave. I thought I'd have a plan by now, but I don't.

Not to mention that plenty of people will have plenty of questions about what's going on with me and Gideon and whether it's a good idea.

But that's all *out there* and right now I'm *in here*, and *in here* has the dreamy quality of a snow globe or a town on a Christmas-themed model train set. It feels charmed and untouched and uncomplicated, and there's an appeal to trading one kind of ease for another.

"I know your parents are worried," Gideon says, finally turning his head to look over at me. "I could hear Rick asking how old you think the subflooring in here is when you talked last night."

"He's positive it's completely rotted and I'm one heavy step away from falling into an old mine shaft or something. I don't know why he thinks this cabin is built on top of an old mine," I add, because Gideon's frowning and I don't really want to get into my stepdad's neuroses right now.

"It's not," he says, sounding a little defensive.

"Hopefully," I say, and he snorts, and then before I can stop myself, I ask: "Have you talked to yours?"

"Only the once," he says, so he must be talking about four or five days ago when I overheard a conversation that couldn't have been longer than three minutes, tops. I'd be worried about him, but he seems to be in constant contact with everyone in Sprucevale that's not his parents: his brother Reid, at least two of his sisters, a group chat that blows up his phone at least once a day until he turns it off, and Forest Service dispatch. Gideon's been doing a *lot* of grumbling about how the solar-powered batteries he's been using aren't meant for this kind of heavy use.

"It's improper," he says, after a bit. He rolls onto his side and looks at me, one arm under his pillow, all warm and rumpled in the firelight.

"What is?" I ask. At this point, there's a list.

"Sleeping in the same room as a woman I'm not married

to," he says. His voice is a soft, deep rumble. "I might be tempted. People might talk."

"I don't think avoiding the bedroom worked to avoid temptation," I point out, and I can see Gideon's blush even in the low light. He doesn't break eye contact, though.

"No," he says, simply. "Sometimes," he starts, then stops. Thinks. "Things can get so ingrained in you as *wrong* that after a while, you forget to think about why it's wrong and it just *is*."

Something pops in the wood stove. I think a log falls. Gideon adjusts his head on the pillow, his eyes never leaving mine. I don't move and barely breathe for fear he'll stop talking if I do.

"And even after you know better, even after you've learned, that *wrong* feeling isn't gone. It fades, but it's always this—this dread in the back of your mind, and it'll disappear when you shine a light on it, but the second you look away, it's back."

I watch him for a long moment. Gideon's quiet and lovely in the firelight, and I don't want to think beyond that. It's easier, right now, to pretend that there's nothing complicated about him or about this; that this morning's family drama is entirely separate from him, gloriously naked and coming in the bathtub with my name on his lips.

It's dreamlike here, unreal, weightless. It feels like these moments couldn't possibly have consequences.

"Does this feel wrong?" I ask, voice low, even though I'm not sure I want to know.

Gideon sucks in a long breath.

"Yes," he says. "No. Not for good reasons." He pauses. "Feels right, too."

I don't know what else to say, on the floor of a cabin, cold outside and warm in here, in these moments that feel like a dream. Everything I think of sounds like an empty platitude, like I'm telling Gideon something he already knows, and it's not like *knowing* is the problem.

In the end, I don't say anything, but I reach out and push his dark hair behind one ear. He catches my wrist and presses a kiss to my palm, and I'd be lying if I said it didn't break my heart a little.

TWENTY-FIVE

GIDEON

"SO ANYWAY," Andi says, shaking the bag of trail mix like she's looking for something specific. I don't point out that this behavior is against the rules of trail mix. "That's why it's the Sunday crossword's fault that Lucia broke her knee."

I hold out my hand for some non-specific trail mix, as God intended, and consider this for a moment.

"Sounds like it was the fault of whoever left the hose out the night before for her to trip over," I say.

"Yeah, but that's a boring story and you know Lucia," she says, and I don't, at least not very well, but I like her based on how fond Andi is. "Why tell a story where you forgot to put something away when it could be about heroically knowing the name of the lead actress in *Zorba the Greek*?"

"Pretty heroic," I agree. "I wouldn't get it if you gave me a hundred guesses."

"Irene Papas."

"Nope." I toss more trail mix into my mouth, discover it's all raisins, and look down at what's still in my hand. "You have to give me at least *one* M&M per handful," I tell Andi. "That's the rule."

"Trail mix doesn't have rules," she says, but she looks guilty. "Trail mix is anarchy."

Silently, I hold my hand out to her. After a moment, she makes a face, shakes the bag again, and pokes through it. Eventually, I get *one* yellow M&M.

"I think that's the last one," she says. "Don't eat it all in one place."

"Andi," I say, as seriously as I can. "Did you eat all the M&Ms out of the trail mix?"

"Obviously not, since you're about to eat one," she says.

"Did you eat all the *other* M&Ms?"

"I don't think that's relevant," she says, and settles her back firmly against the boulder we're leaning against. "Anyway, Lucia's doing very well now, thanks for asking."

I toss the raisins and one M&Ms into my mouth, chew, and swallow before I get brave enough to ask the next thing. It's not a good combination, for the record.

"But you stayed?" I ask, and I hope I'm right, I hope she doesn't say *actually I'm going back to New York* next week. For all the time we've spent together the past two weeks, we somehow haven't talked much about our lives back in the world.

Andi sighs and tilts her head back. My stomach clenches.

"Yeah," she finally says. "I guess? I don't really have a plan, and I broke my lease anyway because—"

She cuts off suddenly, goes still and quiet. I wait. I'm good at that.

"It was kind of impulsive," she says, after a beat. "My roommate and I weren't getting along, and then Lucia broke her knee and coming down here to help out seemed like a good way to get out of there, so... here I am."

"Ah," I say, because something needs to be said. I remind

myself to breathe through the buzzing of relief in my chest, the wild thumping of my heart.

"New York is hard unless you're rich," Andi goes on, still not looking over at me. She sounds defensive, like she thinks I'm judging her. "A lot of my friends moved away to have kids and stuff, and the ones who are still there are really *driven*, you know, one's a human rights lawyer, and one works for the Met, and one is probably going to be running Simon and Schuster in ten years, and I'm... chaining myself to trees in blizzards."

"Some people might say that's *very* driven," I point out, and Andi snorts.

"It really wasn't," she says. "It sounded kind of fun and I'd never done it before, so I said yes. The way I do everything."

I watch her for a moment, the profile that's become desperately familiar over the past week. It's warm enough today—in the low 40s—that she's got her scarf and her hat off, stray hairs drifting around her face. *It sounded fun and I'd never done it before*, she said, and the thought makes me feel weightless.

"Was it?" I ask, and she turns to look at me, sky-blue eyes reflecting the gray sky. Shit. "Fun," I finish.

"The first night was kind of exciting, while Chloe was there and we were chained to a tree," she says. "But then she left and it started snowing and some asshole picked me up and then made me hike for *miles* through the snow to a tiny cabin with no electricity."

"You're *welcome*," I say, and I can't keep the smile out of my voice, and it's okay because Andi laughs.

"It's been an adventure, that's for sure," she says, and I don't say *it always was, with you*. "But I'm also pretty excited for a shower tomorrow night."

"Just a shower?"

"That's after I flip every light switch in Lucia's house. And turn the heat up to eighty. Ugh, and check my text mess—"

She's interrupted by a loud, screaming grunt that echoes through the woods and makes Andi freeze, her eyes wide.

"The *fuck*—"

"Hog," I say, already getting to my feet, brushing my hands on my pants as I look around for it.

"Is it possessed?" Andi asks, also getting up.

"Maybe," I say, and then: "Fuck."

It's about a hundred feet away, tangled in the grouse net and churning up mud with its hooves, and grunt-squealing to raise the dead.

It's also, very possibly, the biggest fucking hog I've ever seen.

"Oh," Andi says, staring. "Fuck."

And after a few more moments: "You know, I thought it would have tusks."

"That's boars."

"Do we have those too?"

"Not this far north," I say, distracted, standing behind this boulder and watching this pig scream in the mud and fight the net. "They're native to Europe and Asia. They were intro-duced to North America as big game animals so people could hunt them and now they're invasive."

"Oh."

The net's made to trap birds that top out at around twelve pounds, not a thrashing hog that probably weighs more than I do, so I was hoping it would snap the thing and leave but I'm not that lucky. It's only succeeded in tangling itself up even more, the net still attached to trees on both sides, and now this is my job.

"Fuck," I mutter again, and Andi looks over at me, both

eyebrows raised. I sigh. "Stay here," I tell her. "Can you get on top of this boulder?"

Andi nods.

"If it starts coming over here, do that," I say. "It'll probably run away once I cut it free, but just in case."

"Can I help?"

"Yeah, by staying out of the way."

She makes a scrunched, slightly grumpy face at me, but doesn't argue.

The hog's got its front two feet tangled in the net, and the closer I get to it, the louder it squeals. With two days above freezing, all the snow is half-melted, sticking around in dirty scraps and muddy puddles, and the hog's managed to churn up a good one.

"Okay, okay, Jesus Christ," I tell it as I pull out my knife and flip it open. "Simmer down, the knife isn't for you. Why does everyone think the knife is for them?"

In response, I get the world's most unpleasant noise. I sigh and step toward it, studying the net to see if I can free it without getting much closer. Feral hogs haven't outright *killed* very many people, but they've maimed and bitten plenty.

I get to work, sawing through the points of tension in the net in the hopes that it'll loosen its hooves. At first the thing just thrashes harder, furious and probably terrified, and then seems to calm down a little.

All at once, it gets loose. One second it's pulling at the net, snapping it back and forth; the next net is destroyed and sagging between two trees and the hog is getting its feet under it, slipping in the mud.

The second it's up, it heads for me. It's not charging—more of a trot, really—but two hundred pounds of pissed-off pig is never good.

"Hey," I say, backing away, the knife still in one hand.

"Shoo." It doesn't. "Go on, get."

It stops short, its front legs planted wide in the snow, and snorts. The hog is a mottled brown and covered in bristly fur; it looks like a pig that lives in the forest, and that's exactly what it is.

Pigs will, incidentally, devour an animal so completely there's nothing left. There's a reason murderers feed bodies to hogs sometimes, a fact I can't help but remember while this thing stares me down.

"Get outta here," I tell it, waving my non-knife hand, and it's a mistake.

Because it *charges*.

"Fuck!" I shout, turn, and sprint for the nearest tree. There's a second where I slip in the half-frozen snow-mud and I swear I can feel its breath on my ankle, but then I'm upright and scrambling, the knife dropped in the process. The lowest branch of the tree is higher than I'd like but adrenaline's on my side, and when I grab onto it the rough bark scratches the shit out of my hands.

I hang on anyway, the stupid fucking hog a few feet behind me, and half-pull, half-kick myself up until I can get a foot over the branch and wrestle myself on top of it. Below me the hog is snuffling at the knife on the ground, making a noise like pissed-off, rusted-out brakes.

"GIDEON!" Andi shouts, her voice shot through with panic and half-swallowed by the snow, and I jerk my head up to find her fifty feet away and crouching on top of the boulder, thank fuck, four feet off the ground and firmly out of hog range.

"I'm fine!" I shout back. My heart is slamming against my ribcage and I have to close my eyes for a second and breathe, then swallow, then breathe again before I open my eyes to see that Andi's still okay.

"WHAT THE FUCK?" she shouts, and all I can do is shake my head, because I don't know what the fuck either, but I sure don't like it. The hog is still below me, and as I watch it finishes nosing at my pocketknife and raises its head, like it's scenting the wind or something. It gives a small, interested grunt.

And trots directly for Andi's boulder.

"ANDI!" I shout, alarm pouring through my veins.

"I know!"

"Don't move!"

"I KNOW!"

My knuckles are white around the branch and there's sweat pouring down my back, half adrenaline and half exertion. Andi stands slowly from her crouch, eyes on the hog as it hustles over, hands up and out like she's placating it or something. My heart's in my throat, and no matter how much I tell myself that she's fine, hogs can't climb for shit, she's *fine*, my heart stays there as the hog trots around the boulder and disappears.

Andi turns to watch it, her back to me, and I feel like I've been dipped in ice water. I start trying to remember all the diseases hogs can carry. I start thinking about how I'd treat a hog bite with the first aid kit back at the cabin, how I'd get her back to the cabin, how I'd need to get her out of here and to a hospital before it got infected, how I brought her to help tag grouse and now she's facing down a fucking man-eating bone-crunching *feral hog*—

Andi says something I can't hear, her back still turned to me, and then there's a flash of snout above the boulder, just to one side of her foot, and then it's gone.

Fuck. Is it jumping? Is it goddamn *jumping*? Motherfucking hell goddamn son of a bitch—

"Andi!" I shout, already shifting my weight on the branch.

"I'M FINE!" she shouts back. "IT CAN'T REACH ME."

But then I see snout again, a quick glimpse above the boulder, and fuck *that*. I grab the branch sideways and half-slither, half-launch myself off it, scraping the shit out of my leg in the process and landing in the snow next to the knife. It's a folding pocketknife, the blade maybe three inches long, but I grab it anyway and run.

"*Whatthefuckareyoudoing?*" Andi yelps, high-pitched and all one word.

I don't answer her as I come up to the boulder, dart around the side, and brandish my knife.

"HEY!" I shout, and the hog looks over at me, its front feet up on the boulder. Even though it's big it's still a good two feet from Andi's shoes, and it's not getting any closer.

"Gideon?!"

"Shoo," I tell it, firmly as I can, sweating hard and shoulders heaving and panting for breath. "Go on. Get outta here."

It takes its hooves off the rock with a little bounce, settles them on the ground, and stares at me.

Shit.

The thing about being human is that most animals are scared of you, even the big ones. A black bear would far rather leave the area than get close to a human, and mountain lions are notoriously secretive. The worst I've ever really dealt with are deer who've gotten used to handouts, and even those are pretty skittish.

Then it trots for me, and I'm just about out of ideas, so I roar. It's somewhere between a scream and a shout and a bellow, and it works because the hog stops in its tracks and even backs up a little. Up on the boulder I can hear Andi say *holy fuck!*

When I stop, the forest is incredibly quiet, and I get the

distinct impression that every tree is staring at me, in addition to the hog and Andi. I think I could hear a single snowflake fall. The hog snorts, breath steaming in front of it, and inspiration strikes in the form of a fist-sized rock next to my right foot.

I get the hog right in the ribcage, and it squeals that horrible rusty-brakes squeal, backing off a little. The next one has it turned and trotting away, and I throw one more after it for good measure, thudding uselessly onto the ground in the half-melted snow.

Once it's gone there's a long, long silence. I'm still tense, still holding my stupid pocketknife, one more rock in my hand just in case. I'm panting and a little lightheaded with adrenaline and my heart's beating so fast and hard it feels syncopated, like it can't quite keep up with itself.

"Are you okay?" I finally ask Andi, once I'm pretty sure it's gone for good.

"I'm fine," she says. "What the fuck was *that*?"

"No idea," I say, carefully folding the knife. "I've never seen one act like that before, maybe it was—"

"No, what the fuck were *you* doing?" she asks, and her voice has a sharp edge to it, like broken glass. She's still standing on the boulder, four feet up in the air, her feet slightly apart and her back straight and behind her are the black fingers of dormant trees reaching for a steel-gray sky, and I don't have a good answer.

"I was doing exactly what you said, standing on this rock well out of hog-bite range, and I was perfectly *fine* and then you come running hell for leather and *point a pocketknife at it*," she goes on. Now her fists are balled at her sides and her voice sounds strange, all rough and strangled. I snap the pocketknife shut without looking.

"I thought you were in danger," I say, and I cross my arms

and puff my chest out a little because I *did*, she *was*, and now she's mad about it?

"I told you I wasn't."

"I know, but—"

"Do you think I can't tell when a glorified farm animal isn't gonna rock climb up to where I am?" she asks, and she's talking fast and high, panic and fury and something else threaded through her voice. "It didn't come within two feet of me! It was getting bored! It was about to leave until you ran over!"

"I wanted to help!"

"You did!" she says, and now she's shouting even louder and she waves her arms in the air, her voice breaking. "You helped by telling me what to do in the first place! Which I was doing! EFFECTIVELY! Which I told you!"

I clench my jaw and look away, my hands tightening into fists because how dare she, how *dare* she shout at me like this when I just risked life and limb to chase off an animal that could've easily killed her.

Could it have? A tiny, unwelcome voice in the back of my head asks. I ignore it.

"I was afraid you'd get hurt," I say through my teeth, not looking directly at Andi, all anger and righteousness, standing against the sky like some kind of Valkyrie. "So, I came over and dealt with the problem."

"By putting yourself in danger!" she says, and now her hands are over her face. If I didn't know better, I'd think she sounds shaky. "Gideon, that's not—that's so fucking stupid and reckless, oh my *God*. You can't do that."

I snort and roll my eyes, pissed-off and instinctual. "Of course, I can," I tell her.

When she doesn't shout again—when she doesn't say anything at all—I finally steel myself and look up at her. It's hard to see the expression on her face since she's backlit and I'm not used to this angle, but she's not happy.

After a long moment, she crouches, puts one hand on the boulder, and hops off.

"I need a minute," she says, and walks away between the trees.

I fight the urge to shout after her: that it's dangerous in there, that there's a hog, that she shouldn't get lost, that it'll be dark before too long, but I don't. Partly because she might strangle me herself if I do and partly because I know, deep down, that I don't need to. The hog's long gone, it's just a forest, and Andi's too smart and capable to get lost thirty feet away.

I pack our things instead of shouting. The hog rooted through it all, leaving some of it slick with pig snot and saliva, so I wipe that off as best as I can, put everything into our packs, and head down to the net.

I'm halfway done untying the destroyed net trap from the trees when Andi suddenly appears at the other end, on her toes, wordlessly untying the knot on the opposite side of the small clearing. When it's down we meet in the middle and she hands me a mass of tangled nylon, frayed and unraveling where the hog won its fight.

Andi's mouth is bright pink, her face flushed, her eyes red-rimmed. I don't question any of it, just swallow around the sudden tightness in my throat.

"Gideon," she says, voice low and controlled and tight. "You should take more care with yourself."

If you'd asked me to guess ten things she'd say, that wouldn't have been one. Instead of answering I crouch and shove the mess of ruined net into the backpack, because that's easier than looking at her right now.

"By which I mean don't do things that might result in you

losing a limb to an infected pig bite because you thought I wouldn't follow instructions," she goes on, still soft and a little shaky. I zip the backpack and stay down, staring at the muddy snow like it'll give me an answer.

It doesn't.

"That's not what I thought," I finally say and rise to my feet, slinging the pack over one shoulder. "I wanted you to be safe and you're my responsibility."

"I'm not."

"Andi—"

"I'm my own responsibility."

"I found you chained to a tree in a blizzard," I say, and it doesn't come out loud, but it comes out harsh, like rubbing alcohol on a skinned knee. Andi closes her eyes and her jaw flexes.

"I know," she says. "That was a dumb mistake and bad judgement."

"So maybe you can see why—"

"I don't want to see you get hurt!" she says, and now she's louder, that edge back in her voice. "I want you to be safe and whole and happy, okay, and I especially don't want you hurt because you think I'm fucking up." She swallows, hard, but her eyes don't leave mine. "I thought for a couple seconds back there that you were gonna get, I don't know, bitten or trampled and mangled and I just—I really don't want that, okay? I was terrified for you. That's all. Can we walk?"

I nod, silent, and Andi shakes her head and adjusts her pack on her back and crunches away, toward the cabin, through the half-melted half-refrozen snow, and I follow her.

She leads the whole way back to the cabin and doesn't falter or lose her way once.

TWENTY-SIX

ANDI

IT FEELS good to walk the mile back to the cabin. There's a small violence in hiking through the forest off-trail, and there's a small violence in making the only noise in silent surroundings, and there's a small, purifying violence in Gideon and I not saying a single word to each other until we reach the clearing with the cabin at the center.

The anger has bled out of me by the time we get there but the kernel of discord that preceded it is still there, pulsing and twisting. I want him whole and unhurt. I want him better than *fine*. I want him to tend to himself sometimes, but we're leaving tomorrow and I'm far from sure that I get to want any of those things.

I'm far from sure that whatever this is that we're doing, this spiderweb-delicate thing we've started, can withstand real-world conditions no matter how much I want it to. His whole family is fighting because his little sister has a boyfriend. What chance do *I* have?

"Do we have any leftovers?" is what I ask as I climb the porch steps, because anything else feels like too much.

"We should," he says. "And plenty of canned soup if we don't."

"We've got canned soup until the end of time," I say, hand on the doorknob before Gideon cuts me off.

"*Andi*," Gideon he says, all annoyed and rough. "Boots off outside."

I want to snap back at him, my temper flaring hot and expansive, but he's right so I grit my teeth and clench one fist and turn toward him without speaking. Gideon's kneeling behind me on the steps, furiously tugging his laces out of one hiking boot, gloves discarded next to him. Both his knees are soaked through with melted snow, his coat open, his hair curling at the ends with moisture.

"C'mon," he goes on, and looks up at me.

"Right," I finally say, and bend over to untie my own shoelaces. I'm still wearing gloves. It takes me longer than it should to realize I'm still wearing gloves and I have to take another deep breath at that because I'm thirty-two and this is no one's fault and I shouldn't scream *fuck gloves* into the silent forest like I want to.

Gideon sighs, runs a hand through his hair, and stands. He crosses the two steps across the porch, his own boots loose enough to step out of. He looks down at me for a moment, the space of two heartbeats, and I want to say something but I've got no idea what.

Silently, Gideon kneels.

"Oh," I say, when he grabs my shoelaces. They're double-knotted but he makes quick work of them, tugging them loose and pulling them around the eyelets, the quiet hiss of lace slipping through leather oddly loud in the snowy evening.

"No good tracking mud inside," he grumbles, and as he finishes with one shoe he runs his hand over it lightly. Wraps his fingers around my ankle, then my calf, his thumb moving gently over my shin.

Gideon looks up at me when I push my fingers into his hair. He lets his head go back as I run my fingers through it, my own gloves finally off. His eyelids go to half-mast but his eyes don't leave mine, even when I run a thumb over one cheekbone.

He's blushing, still kneeling, fingers still curled around my calf. Gideon swallows and I can hear the way his throat clicks, the way it makes his breath hitch a little. I want to tell him how beautiful he is right now, with his wide shoulders and thick thighs, all that power on his knees. I want to tell him he's worth caution. I want to tell him that I'm nervous about what's waiting for us at the bottom of the mountain, that I'm worried about how I'll slot into his life if that's even what he wants.

I want to tell him that he's so *pretty*, but I don't.

"Thank you," is all I manage to get out, and Gideon's eyes flutter shut as he leans in and plants a sweet, soft kiss on my thigh, then reaches for my other boot. I keep my hand in his hair, lean back against the door frame, and bite my lip against all the things I've got the urge to say to him.

This time when he finishes he kisses my thigh right above my knee, hand in his hair, and keeps moving up until he's at my hip, nudging my coat out of the way.

I unzip it. He pushes it open, strokes my other hip, and then he's sliding my shirt up past the high waistband of my leggings, lips on skin, beard spiky and ticklish. I make some kind of noise, a strangled gasp-moan-laugh, and Gideon smiles when he looks up at me.

Then we're kissing and I'm still backed against the door-frame. Gideon's got his hands tangled in my hair, the braid now a complete disaster, pressing our bodies together, his erection rubbing against my lower belly.

When I grab his hip and grind against him, he groans. I do it again, tug his head back with my other hand still in his hair, get my mouth on the long, exposed line of his throat. Gideon's not that much taller than me but he's wide and powerfully built and a minute ago he was on his knees, staring up at me through his eyelashes.

I bite into a tendon—gently—and he gasps.

"Fuck, Andi," he whispers, so I do it again and then lick the spot, our hips still grinding together. I'm seized with the sudden, wild desire to bite him harder, suck on his skin until I leave a mark so we've got proof of this later, but I don't. I behave, for once.

Gideon exhales and tips his head forward. His lips brush my ear and his hands drift down my sides, then up and under my shirt until he's gripping my ribs. I've spent a week watching him cage wild animals with gentle hands, soothing them while they fight, and I feel it now as he presses me into the door jamb. It's so much easier than *thinking*.

"Inside?" he rasps into my ear. I break into a whole-body shiver and he strokes the spot just below the band of my sports bra with his thumbs.

"Yeah," I whisper back, and with a kiss to the spot below my ear, he pulls back. We get our boots the rest of the way off and he opens the door, pushing me through with a hand on my back. Coats come off in the kitchen and Gideon wrestles the sweater over my head as he backs me into the living room, then gives me a deep kiss and goes to put more wood in the wood stove. I perch on the arm of the couch and *watch* until he closes the front of the stove and stands up, walks over, leans in.

I kiss him instead of an apology or an explanation, then pull back.

"Sit," I say, staring up into his face, my hand on his jaw.

"And if I don't?" he asks, all grit and growl.

"Please?" I ask, and give him my best wide-eyed ingenue look. Gideon snorts softly but sits on the couch, arms stretching over the back, knees wide. There's no light in here but the orange flickering from the wood stove and as I straddle him and settle my weight, he could be a painting.

"Thank you," I murmur, and lower my mouth to his. I kiss him hard, slow, and deep, my hands in his hair again. His mouth is lazy and focused, all at once; unhurried and thorough, like he's got the patience to last for hours. Gideon smooths his hands down my back, over my ass, down my thighs until his fingers catch behind my knees and he pulls wider, sending me off-balance and into him before he settles them on the backs of my thighs and gets me exactly where he wants me.

He's thick and hard, and I'm wearing leggings, and I swear I can feel every seam on his pants through them. I shift until I've got friction on my clit and then chase it, rolling my hips against him until he finally groans and presses his face into my neck.

"Still cold?" he asks, lips hot on my collarbone. Gideon's a furnace, casting off heat.

"No."

He makes a noise against my neck and pulls off the long-sleeved shirt I'm wearing, then hooks a finger under the lower band of my sports bra and pulls me in for a long kiss, my hands braced on his chest.

"Get this off," he tells me, giving it another little tug when we pull back.

I raise an eyebrow, and Gideon almost smiles.

"Please?" he asks, voice all honey and grit.

It goes better than the last time he watched me take a sports bra off and he pulls me back in as soon as I'm stripped, hands smoothing down my back, and sucks a nipple into his mouth. Gideon's good with his tongue, with his *teeth,* and soon I'm squirming on his lap, reaching behind myself to hold onto his thighs for balance, hips stuttering.

I open the button on his pants without thinking. His cock is even hotter than the rest of him, and when I stroke it, his head goes back and he bites his lip, eyes at half-mast, a cut-off groan dying in his throat. I put my other hand on his jaw and trace the lower line of his lip with one thumb.

"There's no one around to hear you," I tell him.

"Habit," he grinds out. He's already leaking precum and I slide my thumb across the head of his cock. Gideon shudders.

"Break it," I say, and he moans again, louder this time. I kiss him on the corner of his mouth. "Good."

"You make it easy."

I don't know what to say to that, so I kiss him again. I tighten my hand and there's an answering grip on my thighs, pulling me in.

God, I want to fuck him. I want to see his face when he slides in and feel the power in his body as I ride him or he fucks me into a mattress, either one, I'm not picky. But if there are condoms around, I haven't found them in my clandestine-but-thorough searching, and I'm pretty sure Gideon didn't bring any to what he thought was his solo getaway.

I twist my hand and thumb the head of his cock again and it wrings another moan out of Gideon, still fully dressed with his dick out, and it makes him look filthy. Maybe I don't get to fuck him yet, but I know what I want so I climb off the couch, get on my knees, and push his legs apart.

Gideon goes still and quiet, wide-eyed, almost deer-in-the headlights.

"Can I?" I ask, running the pad of my thumb along the underside of his shaft.

"Andi," he says, and he sounds rough. "You don't have to."

It's not the response I was expecting, and now I've gone still and quiet, except my hand is still around his dick.

"I know," I finally say. "I'm volunteering."

Great dirty talk, there.

Gideon leaks a little more, a bead of translucent white welling at the tip and sliding down the underside of his shaft. He swallows twice and glances from his leaking dick to my face and his expression is too complicated to read, but he finally nods.

"Yeah," he says, and clears his throat. "Yes. God, please."

I lean in and lick the droplet that slid down and then push my tongue into the slit. The noise that comes out of Gideon is *obscene*, a strangled gasp-growl that slides through me like lava. I push my lips over the head of cock, slowly, my hand still tight around the base. When I look up, he's staring down at me with a flush on his cheekbones and his pupils blown in the dark, breathing like he's just run a marathon, so I close my eyes, suck gently, and enjoy the way his gasp turns into a whimper by the end.

I pull off his dick with a wet *pop* that's loud on purpose in the small, quiet room and look up at Gideon again, my mouth half an inch away from his cock. He's beautiful like this and I can't help wanting to draw it out: the way he's half wide-eyed and ready to beg, half coiled, pulsing power, all pleading and demanding and ready to lose his mind.

Gideon doesn't say anything, but he reaches one hand down, cups my jaw, slides his thumb along my cheekbone in an echo of earlier, when he was the one on his knees. I tilt my head into his hand, eyes on his, and he swallows hard and moves his thumb until he's caressing my bottom lip. When I flick my tongue against it I swear his cock twitches in my hand, and then Gideon presses down softly, opening my mouth, his own breathing going ragged.

It doesn't take much for the head of his cock to touch my lips; the tiniest lift of his hips and he's there, leaking against my lip, and there are no words but this is Gideon asking me for what he wants, telling me, so I open my mouth and take him down as far as I can.

He throws his head back so hard on a moan that he hits it against the wall behind him, but he doesn't seem to notice so I keep going, sucking and licking and stroking with my fist around him. I can't swallow him but after a bit every time he hits the back of my mouth he swears, and God, it's good: Gideon louder and louder, losing control, letting himself get lost. He keeps one hand gentle on the side of my face, like he needs to feel me, the other clutching the back of the couch. His hips move in desperate little twitches and my own thighs are clamped together like it'll do anything about how turned on I am. For half a second I try touching my clit, but I'm nowhere near coordinated enough.

"Andi," he whispers, rough and choked-off, a little while later, and I push my mouth down onto his cock and look up. He's wide-eyed and open-mouthed and flushed. His cock twitches and Gideon makes a broken whimper, and I pull off just in time for him to come on my neck in a hot rush.

I stroke him through it and now he's fully gone, thrusting up into my hand with his head thrown back, moans echoing from the ceiling. Neither of us stops until he's going soft and suddenly flinches when I stroke him again, so I take my hand off and sit back on my heels, trying to be subtle about looking around for something to wipe myself off with. That wasn't exactly my plan, but I also didn't exactly *have* a plan, so this was as good as anything. At least my hair was pulled back.

"God," he finally says when he unclenches his fist from the couch and opens his eyes to look down at me. "Jesus."

Then his eyes fix somewhere around my collarbone and go a little wider.

"Oh," Gideon says, and his face does *something*, and he inhales sharply, and all that is very, very interesting. "Shit. I'm sorry. Um—"

I roll my eyes at the *sorry*, and he doesn't say anything, just smiles sheepishly before glancing around and then pulling off his shirt.

"Here," he says, and leans forward off the couch to wipe me off gently from my throat and down my chest, and the whole time he's got this *look* on his face. When he's done he kisses me gently, still sitting above me while he's on the couch and clothed and I'm kneeling on the floor and topless.

"Hold on," he says when he breaks the kiss, stands, and walks away. The floor's hard, so I flop onto the couch myself and when he gets back, he's got a washcloth in one hand and his dick is back inside his pants.

"Ooh, a gentleman," I say, half-teasing, and Gideon frowns a little and huffs out a breath as he sinks his knee between my legs and braces one arm next to my head.

"Well," he says, all frowny and pleased and embarrassed, and then he's over me and gently wiping the last sticky traces off of my skin, his clothed thigh brushing mine. "Sorry, it's cold."

"I don't mind," I tell him, tilting my head back and letting Gideon clean me off, thorough and gentle. The cloth is warm where he touches it but I shiver as soon as he lifts it away.

"Cold?" he murmurs.

"A little."

I slit my eyes open so I can see his face, focused and quiet in the dark, the way his eyes track along my body. Then he ducks his head and presses a white-hot kiss to the damp-cooled skin of my neck, and I shiver again. Gideon makes a little thinking noise somewhere in the back of his throat, *hmm*, then does it again: my collarbone, my throat, my chest. When he swipes the cool cloth over a nipple I gasp, then sigh when it's followed by his warm mouth.

I wonder, vaguely, how much he's done this before, a question I still haven't asked because I don't care beyond curiosity. There's something a little wide-eyed and wondering about him I find... appealing.

Then his lips are on the spot above my bellybutton, his beard prickling at my skin in a way that makes me feel it all over, and he's looking up at me with those pretty, wide eyes.

"Can I?" he asks, fingers hooked under the waistband of my leggings.

"Yes. Definitely," I say, and lift my hips so he can pull them off along with my panties in one very nearly smooth move. I'm still wearing socks, but my feet are cold so he's going to have to deal with that.

Once I'm naked except for socks, Gideon just—stops. He looks. He's on his knees on the couch, settled between my legs, still in pants and no shirt, and he *looks*. Even though he already came it's slow and heated, and he drags his fingertips up the inside of my left thigh, over my hip, up my torso until his hand is flat against my sternum, and he lets his gaze follow. It makes my breath catch and my breathing quicken and my pussy throb, because apart from my aborted attempt at masturbation while I was getting Gideon off, it's been very neglected so far.

I can't help but squirm while he looks, arching my back a little and shifting my hips. I draw my own fingertip along the top of my right thigh while I watch his face, just to see what he does.

"Jesus," he mutters, and chases my fingers with his own, all the way to my hip.

Then he slides his hand around the top of my thigh, squeezes, leans in, and kisses me before pushing my legs apart. I'm still on the couch so that means one goes over the back, my foot against the wall, the other on the floor. Gideon's got powerful, rough hands, his calloused fingers an odd counterpoint to the softness of his mouth and the soft scratch of his beard as he trails open-mouthed kisses up my thigh. I'm squirming under his hands, his mouth, aroused as hell and so fucking wet this couch is on its way to becoming a slip-n-slide.

Finally, *finally*, he strokes my entrance, dipping a fingertip inside, and I exhale on what might be a whimper.

"Fuck, Andi," he says, so low I can feel his voice more than I can actually hear it, and slides his slick fingers upward to circle… a random spot to the right of my clit.

"Left," I tell him, and it comes out a hoarse whisper. He moves his fingers and it's still not quite right, even as his mouth is on my inner thigh, doing something that almost hurts but feels incredible.

I clear my throat.

"Try, uh," I start, and he moves again, the thick pads of his fingers sliding over me.

"There?"

"Almost? Just sort of—" I say, then reach down and simply move his hand to where it needs to be. He moves his fingers and my whole-body jolts, pleasure fuzzing into my brain. "Yeah, there," I manage, and spread my legs a little wider.

It works for about twenty seconds, and then his hand drifts again, and before I can even say anything he huffs like he's annoyed.

"Hold on," he says, and *stands*, and what the hell, I'm trying to get off here. "I can't see anything, I'll be right back."

He disappears into the next room, leaving me naked and spread-eagled on the couch. I can hear him rummaging around, muttering to himself, as I wonder what he could possibly be looking for.

Maybe condoms? Maybe he brought just-in-case condoms, on the off-chance that he came upon a horny woman chained to a tree? Which, if he did, he should start playing the lottery. Also, I wasn't horny while I was chained to the tree. That came later.

The rummaging intensifies, and now I'm kind of cold, so I half-roll off the couch just enough to grab the sweater—his— that we pulled off earlier. It's sort of soft and sort of rough, and when I put it on with nothing underneath I can really feel it on every inch of my skin and especially my nipples, and— yeah. This was a good idea.

When Gideon comes back I'm lazily stroking my clit with one hand while I rub the sweater over a nipple with the other, and he immediately trips over something on the floor.

"You okay?" I ask, lifting my head a little.

"Fine," he says, and then under his breath, "Jesus *fucking* Christ."

With that, Gideon shines a fucking spotlight on me. I flinch and protest and throw an arm over my face, protectively covering my crotch with the other hand for some reason.

"Is that a flashlight?"

"No."

"Yes, it is," I say, even though I've got an arm over my face because that is *clearly a flashlight, Gideon*, and I'm not sure how I feel about it. Meanwhile his weight is back between my legs, rough fingers on the delicate skin of my inner thighs.

Then he leans in and bites my nipple through the sweater and it makes me gasp and swear and squirm.

"It's a headlamp. I couldn't see," he explains, and now he's pushing the sweater up my torso and that's his mouth on my nipple, hot and wet and teeth just this side of too much. "Keep going."

I swallow, and breathe, and I don't move my arm from over my eyes, but I start moving my fingers on my clit again in slow, slippery circles. He breathes in, ragged, and the sound makes me bite my lip and buck my hips.

"You look," he starts, hands stroking up my thighs, and I swear I can feel him watching me, like the light is heated. "Really good," he finally finishes.

Then he pushes my thighs a little wider again and I hear a tiny whimpering noise and Gideon's stroking my entrance, dipping a fingertip inside, and I don't have much leverage spread out like this but I try like hell to get *more* and Gideon rewards me by sliding his fingers knuckle-deep in one stroke.

"Good?" he asks, and when I nod and make some sort of confirming noise, he bends them just enough to send sparks up my spine.

"Nnnguh," I manage, and I'm still rubbing my clit, still trying to do it slowly but my fingertips keep brushing against his palm where he's got his hand inside me, his fingers moving —oh *fuck*—moving in time with mine.

Gideon leans in again, plants an open-mouthed kiss on my belly that makes me squirm. Another on my hip. Another on my inner thigh, and when he stops, I get brave and peek out from under my arm. I can't see very well because holy shit that thing is *bright*, but after a couple seconds I can make out Gideon's face, staring at our hands working together with a combination of wonder and concentration.

Then he leans in and I can't see what he's doing but a

second later his tongue, hot and wet and slippery, is at the juncture of the two fingers I'm using to stroke myself. He leaves it there for a moment before he slides it down the crease, the muscle working its way between my fingers until the tip is on my clit.

I cover my face with my arm again because I make a strangled, pleading noise as his mouth keeps going and I move my fingers apart, framing my clit for his tongue. Gideon takes the invitation and works it slowly at first, the tip of his tongue gentle and tentative, his fingers inside me stroking softly in time and it's good, it's *good*, and it's also not quite enough.

"You could go harder," I say in a voice that doesn't quite sound like mine. There's an answering rumble from somewhere between my legs and then everything is faster and harder and I choke on a moan, threading my fingers into his hair.

When I'm brave enough, I look down and I get treated to the sight of Gideon's face between my legs, the headlamp shining uselessly across my belly, the light already askew. He makes a noise when I pull it off his head and toss it somewhere else in the room, but he doesn't stop.

I watch him as long as I can, one hand still in his hair, but Gideon's tongue and fingers are relentless and God, he's following instructions and he's *focused*, sticking to the same rhythm and pressure and, holy shit, *suction* as I close my eyes and throw my head back and try not to crush his face against me as I slowly lose my mind.

I think I might kick him a little when I come, sparks exploding behind my eyes as a high, breathy moan escapes me. I definitely pull his hair and grind myself against his mouth, and Gideon takes it without batting an eye, licking me through it until it's suddenly too much and now I'm pulling his hair to get his head away and trying to scoot backward on the couch. I make another noise when he pulls his fingers out and then he's got his forehead against my belly, both of us breathing hard.

I flop my legs around his torso just because I can. After a moment he looks up at me, smug as anything, and I half want to roll my eyes and shove him off and half want to knock him to the floor so I can ride his face a couple more times.

"It's pretty hot when you wear my sweater," he says, lifting himself off me enough to lean against the back of the couch, my legs still awkwardly around him.

"You think so?" I tease, still breathing hard, because yes, I'd noticed he was into it.

"And it's *really* hot when you wear nothing but my sweater," he says, and tangles a couple fingers in the hem. I don't point out that I'm technically still wearing socks, but I do rearrange myself until I've got both thighs slung across his lap, and he settles his other hand there.

"Thanks," I say, because that's an appropriate response to a compliment. Gideon smirks, so I sit up on the couch and kiss him. He tastes like me.

TWENTY-SEVEN

GIDEON

IT'S BARELY dawn when we leave the cabin, packs heavy on our backs, breath fogging in the morning air, the curtains closed and the inside dark, everything folded up and packed away for whoever uses this place next. It feels like a different cabin, almost, like nothing could have ever happened here.

I lock the door, mostly because one should lock doors, and zip the key into my pocket. I remind myself that we've still got the day, ten long miles of being alone together on the trail, before the world breaks in and—well, before the world breaks in.

"You sure your ankle's okay?" Andi asks, breath steaming skyward, the floorboards of the front porch creaking under our feet.

I sigh and look down. I've got it wrapped, and I need to be careful, but it's no excuse.

"It's all right," I tell. "You're sure you're up for this? Ten miles, cross-country, and it's still pretty cold."

It's the closest I can bring myself to saying *we could stay here longer*. Life in the cabin isn't necessarily easier, but it's simple and I'm suited to it. Here, at least, I know what I'm doing nearly all the time.

"Yeah," she says, and gives me a jaunty little half-smile that's brighter than the sunrise. "C'mon. Don't you want to shower?"

"Good point," I say, and she's still smiling when she turns to go down the steps.

On impulse, I catch her wrist, and she stops. She's got on the same hat and coat and braid that she did when I first found her, and I almost tell her *never mind, it's nothing*.

"Wait," I say, instead, and my voice is slow and scratchy with the early hour and with a sudden desperation I can't explain. "Just—"

I kiss her there, on the cabin threshold, soft and chaste and lingering, and hope it says enough.

Then we follow the road out of the clearing where the cabin is, and at the last bend before it disappears, I look back. It's already so small, a deep brown dot on a white and gray landscape, closed up and cold, and I almost can't believe it felt like the whole world.

· · · · ★ ★ ★ · · · ·

THE PATH to the Hogswallow trailhead is easy, then hard, then easy, then not too bad. The first part is the road to the cabin, which is rutted and worn and badly in need of repair for a road, but wide and flat and pleasant for a trail. It's early and we don't talk much, or we talk about nothing, and I pretend that I don't want to turn back with every step.

About a mile and a half before the road comes to the spot where the avalanche closed it, we get to the tricky part: a long, fairly steep, off-trail hike to the trail itself. It's hard and made harder by everything we're carrying: Andi's got her frame pack on, and I've got a slightly smaller backpack that I insisted on filling with half her stuff. The footing is tricky for a lot of it, the forest filled with stumps and rocks under snow, not to mention plenty of impossible spots we can't get around easily. I have to check the GPS every few minutes to be sure we're still going the right way.

By the time we get to the trail it's midday, and we're both hungry and exhausted. Andi banged her knee pretty good on a rock when she fell, and I wrenched my bad ankle a little harder than I admit to her. I'm fine, especially because the hardest part is finished, but there's still six and a half miles to go and daylight is limited.

We argue about lunch—Andi wants to walk while we eat the sandwiches we packed, I want to sit for fifteen minutes because that'll do us more good in the long run. I win and we sit on a boulder next to a near-overflowing creek that makes me more nervous than I tell her, because what if there's a flood we can't cross? How do we get back? We're got her tent and sleeping bag, so I guess we share that, but it's not a good prospect and worry gnaws at me.

"You're quiet," Andi says after we've eaten and gotten back on the trail. It's wide and flat through here, next to the creek, though the water's closer than I'd like.

"Usually, I'm so talkative," I say, and she snorts.

"Point taken."

I take a deep breath, adjust the pack on my back, and discard the first three things that I'm actually thinking about: the creek, how late it is in the day, and what I'm going to do about Beth and Sadie's fight tomorrow, when I'll have to deal with it.

"I'm wondering whether Reid rendered the wild animals in my care unfit for release back into the wild," I say. It is, technically, a thought I've had.

"Vicky and Fluffy?" she asks. I only sigh in response, and Andi grins over at me. "You're releasing a three-legged fox into the wild?"

One of my boots sinks into mud further than I'd like, so I nudge Andi to step away from the creek.

"Probably not," I admit.

"Then why not let him name it?"

"It's a *wild animal*," I say, because that's the best and only explanation I've got, but it ought to be explanation enough.

"You don't want Vicky to get jealous. I understand."

I glance over at her, lips pursed like she's trying not to laugh, and it makes something small and secret behind my ribcage twist.

"Birds don't get jealous, Andi," I point out.

"One of my friends' moms growing up—in Jersey—had a very emotional parakeet," she says thoughtfully. I slide her a look, and whatever my face is doing, it makes her almost-laugh again. "Mostly it was angry," she admits. "Which I would probably also be if I had to live in a cage and poop on newspapers."

"Depends on the newspaper."

"You're not about to besmirch the Sentinel-Star, are you?"

"I would never."

"Because I'm reporting back to Lucia *tonight*."

"Is it her fault they keep running my father's letters to the editor?"

Andi makes a face and kicks a rock, which only makes it sink further into the squishy ground. "Yes and no?" she says. "It's her commitment to free speech and journalistic integrity, mostly, which means she thinks everyone should have a voice, and sometimes that voice—" she stops for a moment, like she's considering. "Isn't great."

"He asked her for an op-ed column once," I tell Andi,

something I've only just remembered. "Eight or nine years ago, maybe. She said no."

"Lucia's not really a fan of your dad," Andi admits.

"How much of an understatement is that?"

Andi doesn't answer right away, and when I glance over, she's scrunching her nose.

"Some?" she says, and it's obvious she doesn't want to answer truthfully, so I let it go and we walk in silence for a while and I try not to think about everything that's going to be waiting for me at the bottom of the mountain.

"Hey," Andi says, suddenly, as the trail swerves around a collection of boulders and away from the creek. "How long has Reid lived with you?"

There's a brief, complicated descent over some knotted tree roots, and I wait until it's done to answer her.

"Five years," I say, and then answer the next thing she's going to ask, too. "Since he was fifteen."

"Oh," she says, and takes a few more steps. "*Oh*."

I wait, the trail widening, and come up next to her.

"That's longer and younger than I thought," she says.

"It's been a while," I say, because when did it become five years since Reid moved in with me? From the way he leaves his shoes around it feels like he's still brand new.

There's another silence, and this one feels a little complicated. I can see her thinking from the corner of my eye, her back straightening while she does.

"Did they kick him out?" she finally asks.

"Not technically," I say, and she goes red in my peripheral vision, her jaw tight, and I think it's safe to assume that Andi doesn't like my parents, which is fair. It's their fault that her dad and Rick got outed twenty years ago, their fault that Andi's maternal grandmother went to family court and tried to have Andi taken away from her dad because of it, their fault that the Burnley County School Board fired him from his job teaching eighth grade science for "poor performance" after fourteen years of stellar reviews.

Of course, it's my fault that my parents knew at all.

"He had a rough time when he was younger," I say, my eyes on the trail ahead of me. "He started getting in a lot of trouble at school. Skipping, failing classes, acting out, mouthing off at home. I think they caught him drinking a couple times. Their solution was to be extra-strict."

I pull the GPS out and check it, because I need something to do with my hands and also a second to think about how to phrase all this.

"My parents kept ...punishing... him because he wouldn't act the way they wanted him to," I say. "He cut all his hair off, so they grounded him and made him go to church every day. They'd throw away all his pants and make him wear dresses, so he'd sneak out and walk to my house in jeans he stole from Jacob."

Andi frowns, still staring straight ahead. "How far is that?" she asks, sounding like she already knows the answer.

"Eight miles, give or take. I told him to call me and I'd come get him but most of the time he couldn't use a phone," I say. These are memories I hate to think of: coming home after work, or in the dark, to find my baby-faced little brother sitting on my porch, looking like shit. Knowing how many times I talked him into going back, only for the pattern to repeat.

"Did they ever come looking for him?" she asks, softly, and she doesn't need to say *I think your parents are monsters* for me to understand what she means.

"Once," I say, my voice surprisingly steady. "The first time. They called to ask if I'd seen him. I convinced him to go home." There's a heavy silence, nothing but the sound of foot-steps. "I convinced him a couple more times, after that. And then I stopped, and he stopped going back, and my parents stopped asking if he would. I don't think he's talked to them since then."

I don't tell Andi that I could have been a better brother to Reid back then. I let him live with me, got him to school, let him look how he wanted, but I also thought it was just a phase. I didn't even know he wanted to be called Reid—at home, at least—until Sadie told me. I made him too nervous. I still wish I could go back and be someone he could tell himself.

My parents ask me about him, sometimes, in their own way. My father will say *everything going all right at home?* and he'll mean *does Reid still live with you*. My mother will set her jaw and narrow her mouth and ask *How's everyone doing?* and pretend she means my friends or my animals, but she wants to know if Reid's changed his mind yet. I always answer the unasked questions aloud because I don't know what else to do.

"Has he been afraid of the cat the whole time?" she asks, and she's obviously changing the subject, and I'm grateful for it.

"Only since I got her."

"Wait, you got her *after* he moved in?"

"Two years ago, maybe?" I say. "Her mother was a stray who wandered into my friend Silas's cabin, took the place over, and had kittens. Silas still has the mom."

"So, you've made a habit of adopting strays," she says, and I sigh because no, I have not.

"One stray," I say, the trail in front of us narrowing. Andi goes in front so she can set the pace. "Reid is not a *stray*, and the other two are wild animals. Which I keep telling everyone."

"And Silas, and Javier, and Wyatt," she says, sliding a look back over her shoulder. "That's your freemason blood moon virgin sacrifice secret society, right?"

"It's none of those things," I say, even though my stomach gave a little lurch at *virgin*. I haven't been perfectly honest with Andi, and it's another thing we're hiking toward that I'll have to face at the bottom of the mountain. "And if anyone adopted strays, it was Silas."

That gets a laugh out of her, at last, crystal clear and bright. I want to take her hand, stop her, kiss her here while it's still just us. I want her to tell me that nothing I've just said matters.

I want to turn around and go back and keep the long tendrils of reality from wrapping themselves around us, but I know it's a futile thing to want. Instead, we keep hiking, and I watch the swish of her braid on her back, and I wish for things I probably won't get.

TWENTY-EIGHT

ANDI

WHEN WE FINALLY GET TO the Hogswallow trailhead parking, my feet hurt, my shoulders hurt, I have half a headache, my legs feel boneless, and the only car in the parking lot is a light blue Prius that doesn't look like it's a Forest Service vehicle.

I realize that I've got no clue who was supposed to come and pick us up. I figured Gideon would take care of it, and then didn't give it one more single thought, just... let him be the responsible one.

"Someone's coming, right?" I ask, going for *nonchalant* as Gideon swings the pack from his back and stretches his arms over his head.

"They said by five," Gideon says, unconcerned. "We've still got a few—oh, wait," he says as the driver's door to the Prius opens. A tall man in dark pants and a dark jacket gets out, and it'd be kind of ominous if he weren't grinning in the deep blue twilight.

"The hell?" Gideon asks, and the other man shrugs.

"Really, that's the greeting you give your rescuer?" he says. "You spend two long weeks battling the elements—"

263

"We were in a cabin."

"—fighting for your lives—"

"It had a refrigerator!"

"And when I brave the long, dark journey to come get you—"

"Jesus," Gideon mutters.

"That's my thanks?"

I'm trying to figure out if this is one of his brothers—maybe Zach or Jacob, one of the ones in the middle, though he doesn't look younger than Gideon—when Gideon sighs, thoroughly rolls his eyes, and then steps forward to give the other man an enormous bear hug.

"Thank you for rescuing us," he grumbles. "And for being such an asshole about it."

"Just glad you're back," the other man says. Gideon pulls away, glances over at me, and waves a polite hand in my direction.

"So, Andi, this is Silas," he says. "Silas, this is, uh, Andrea Sullivan."

"*Delighted* to make your acquaintance," Silas says as we shake hands, and from the look on his face, he really is.

"You text a lot," is the charming thing I manage to say after a full day of strenuous hiking.

"You chain yourself to trees," Silas says, that grin still on his face, and I snort because he has a point.

"Not that often," I tell him. "Only the once, actually. I probably won't again."

"Probably?" Silas asks. Gideon looks over at me with a thunderous frown.

"I like to keep my options open," I say, and Gideon frowns harder, and Silas looks from my face to his and looks like he's trying not to laugh, then jerks his head back at the Prius.

"C'mon," he says. "I borrowed Kat's car. Seemed like it would be more comfortable than my truck."

· · · · ★ ★ ★ ★ · · · ·

FORTY-FIVE MINUTES LATER, we turn into the driveway of Lucia's house. I spent the first five minutes of the drive making polite conversation with Silas, and then the next five minutes listening to the occasional murmur of their voices while watching the night slide past the car windows and trying not to think too hard about what was going to happen next, and then thirty-five minutes zoning out completely in a half-awake fog because holy shit, I'm tired.

"Thanks for the ride," I say, as Silas turns the car off, politeness on autopilot.

"Of course," he says as I unbuckle. "Happy to be of use."

"I'll walk you up," Gideon says, and Silas gives him some kind of look as he opens his car door.

Gideon's already gotten my pack from the back by the time I'm standing, and he's looking up at the sky—cloudy and starry in alternating patches—and then we stand in Lucia's driveway for a moment and look at each other. Suddenly, I've got no idea what to say because nothing that happened in that cabin seems *real*, right now, and I feel back to square one with this virtual stranger.

Then Gideon clears his throat and shifts the strap on his shoulder and looks at Lucia's front door, and there he is, again, and he's looking back at me and it's impossible to see in the dark, but I think he might be blushing.

"So," he starts. "I've never really done this before."

I glance over at Silas's car, then back at Gideon, unclear on what it is he's never done.

"Dropped someone off?"

He huffs a laugh and puts one hand to his face, and I think he's blushing harder. I want to frame him and hang him above my fireplace.

"I haven't dated very much," he says. "I've never actually had a girlfriend before."

I do not say the first thing I think, which is: *what?*

I do say, "Oh."

"And I know that most people figured all this out when they were teenagers and got over it then, but I just—I never was all that interested in it," he goes on, in an awkward way that feels oddly familiar, and—holy shit, am I getting dumped? I'm not upset, not quite yet, but it's close.

"So, you're not... interested?" I ask, mind suddenly swirling.

"No! Fuck, no," he says, wide-eyed, pushing a hand through his dark hair. "I'm saying I don't... know what to do. Because I've never really done this. I'm pretty sure that usually taking someone to dinner comes before, you know. Other things."

"Like eating me out while wearing a headlamp," I say, and now he's *definitely* blushing as hard as I've ever seen him blush.

"Right," he manages, bravely. "That sort of thing. We got it all out of order."

"And that's bad?" The evening after a ten-mile hike, it turns out, is not my best time to have this sort of talk.

"Ah, Jesus," he mutters, and rubs his face in his hands again. "It's not bad, I'm just—I wanted to warn you. About me. That I might do everything wrong."

He's not doing great so far, but I don't tell him that.

"I can't tell if you're trying to ask me out or trying to break things—"

"Ask you out," he blurts, wide-eyed. "No, not—God no. I like this."

Gideon clears his throat.

"Would you like to go to dinner sometime?" he asks, suddenly so formal I feel like I'm being asked to prom. "On a date," he clarifies unnecessarily.

I'm tired, exhausted, confused, and wrung out by the up-and-down of the last minute and a half, and I wonder for a moment whether I should be warning him about *me*, that if he's concerned about doing things in the wrong order then maybe I'm no good for him at all because I'm not sure I've ever done anything *right*, but this interaction has been complicated enough already.

"Yes," I say. "I'd like that."

He smiles. Gideon has a thousand micro-expressions, always hinting and gesturing at one emotion or another, but this is a *smile*, pure and pretty as sunlight on fresh snow.

"Good," he says, and the front door opens and a rectangle of light falls across us.

"Andrea!" Lucia shouts, both arms up in a victory pose as she stands in the doorway. "Frank! She's returned! In one piece!"

"How many pieces were we expecting?" Frank calls from somewhere inside the house.

Lucia comes out to where we're standing and takes my face in her hands. Gideon's off to the side, gone quiet again.

"If you ever pull something like that again I'll kill you," Lucia says, her earrings still wobbling. "I don't *care* that you're thirty-three—"

"Two."

"—I'll do it myself to save Rick and your father the heartache," she finishes, which doesn't make any sense, but it's not my place to argue. "God. I'm so glad you're okay."

"Me too," I say, hugging Lucia back and also acutely aware of Gideon, holding my huge frame pack, standing there blank-faced like he's at attention. "You know Gideon, right?" I ask when Lucia finally pulls back.

"I believe we've met," she says, her voice suddenly about ten degrees cooler. She holds out a hand. "Lucia Dawson. Thank you so much for keeping Andrea safe."

"Happy to help, ma'am," Gideon says in the same voice he uses to talk to Forest Service Dispatch.

"Can I invite you in? We're just about to have dinner and we'd be delighted if you would join us," Lucia goes on. She doesn't really mean for him to accept and everyone here knows it, but we've all been raised with the same intricacies of manners and politeness, so I let Southern Hospitality Theater play out.

"I'm afraid my ride is waiting on me and I've really got to get home as well," Gideon says. "Appreciate the offer, though."

"Maybe some other time."

"I look forward to it," Gideon says, then nods at me. "I'd best be going."

He hands over my pack, and he steadies me with a hand on my arm while I get the strap over one shoulder.

"Call me?" I ask, because I'm suddenly not sure what to say or what the rules are, here, on a front porch in what technically counts as polite society.

"Of course," Gideon says, and he sways a little on his feet and glances down at my mouth and there's a second where I think he's going to kiss me, in front of Silas and Lucia, but instead he smiles at me and nods at Lucia and then he's down the steps, striding back to his friend waiting in the car. I try not to be disappointed.

"Come on. I made pot roast with mashed potatoes and

there's ice cream for dessert," she says, and yeah, those are basically the magic words.

"You're amazing," I tell her as I let her herd me through the front door.

"I know," she says, and rests one hand lightly on my shoulder.

· · · · ★ ★ ★ ★ · · · ·

I'M MOISTURIZING the ever-living fuck out of my entire body after my shower when there's a knock on the bathroom door.

"I'm still naked!" I shout, because I like to give pertinent information first.

"Phone!" Lucia calls back. "Again!"

"How many times have they *called*?"

"What?"

I grab my robe, shrug it on, and open the door.

"For you," Lucia says unnecessarily, holding out the cordless phone.

"Civilization treating you well?" my dad asks after I take it. "Lucia's been having kittens all day."

Sure. *Lucia* has been having kittens.

"It's great. I love showers and running water," I tell him. "And I'm fine. Safe and sound, no worse for the wear, newly appreciative of electricity."

"It's great stuff," my dad agrees. We talk for a while, Rick getting on the other line eventually, and I end up telling him more than I mean to about the cabin: the water filters we used and the propane-powered fridge and the solar battery that was good enough to keep phones charged, because Dad and Rick love gadgets almost as much as they love discussing home repair.

"We ought to send a thank you note to Steve," Rick says, after a while, the slight twang that twenty years in New Jersey haven't erased crackling down the line.

It takes me a minute to figure out who Steve is. Shit.

"Not a bad idea," says my dad. "You wouldn't happen to have his address, would you?"

I should just tell them, and I know I should just tell them. I *know*. But I'm tired, and exhausted, and I don't feel like explaining the truth and then explaining why I didn't tell them the truth already and *then* explaining why the truth isn't a problem, really, Gideon's cool now and of course I'm certain of that after spending two whole entire weeks with him.

"I don't, sorry," is all I wind up saying.

"I'm sure we can find his work address, or at least close enough," Rick is saying. "I imagine we can just send a card to Steve Wheeler care of Cumberland National Forest and sooner or later it'll get to him."

"What are you talking about?" my dad asks. "You can't just address something to a forest and expect it to arrive at your intended recipient."

"I bet you could in this case," Rick says, and they're off again, casually bickering with each other the way they've been doing since I was six or so, familiar as the kitchen table.

TWENTY-NINE

GIDEON

"HEY," Silas says, when I get back into the car. "You good?"

"I'm fine," I tell him, which is true enough; I'm tired and a little rattled and the space behind my ribcage feels oddly wind-burned and raw, but all that is fine, honestly.

Silas keeps looking at me, like he's waiting for a real answer. I feel a little more wind-burned, so I focus on buckling up. There are a thousand things that he could say right now, probably: he could say *I'm here for you* or *you can tell me anything* or *something happened, didn't it*, but he's too smart and knows me too well for that.

Instead Silas says, "There's soup, those brussels sprouts you like, and brownies waiting back at your place," and he starts the car.

"Thank you," I say.

"Thank Wyatt, it was his idea," he says, and we drive through the dark for a while.

Silas and I met in a veterans' support group, and we both spent the first two months of it sitting quietly, talking when asked to, sharing all the expected trauma and horror. He was in for longer than I was, did more tours, saw more shit; Silas never quite shared anything too close to the bone but he was good at seeming like he did, good at welcoming the new people, good at making the circle of chairs in a church basement feel like a sacred ring of trust.

He's half a decade older than me. He might be wiser. He's sure friendlier, and it took me a couple months to understand that we'd become honest-to-God friends outside the support group. Before I knew it, we'd collected Javier and Wyatt, two other strays; when Silas floated the idea of building cabins on the site of an old campground still owned by the Forest Service, we all said yes and understood why.

Those three know almost everything about me.

They don't know the story with Andi. Half because it was water under the bridge, or at least I wanted it to be; half because I couldn't bring myself to do it. I didn't want to see the looks on their faces when I said *I drove my best friend away because her dad had a boyfriend* and most of all, I didn't want to admit how I'd felt about it back then. That I'd been so self-righteous and *proud* of myself.

But Andi's not angry anymore, and there's brownies and soup waiting at my house, and all that makes me brave enough to lean on someone.

"Andi and I were best friends growing up," I say suddenly, into the darkness of the country road, and Silas glances over at me.

"You were?" he says, and as he drives me home, I tell him everything.

· · · · · ★ ★ ★ ★ · · · ·

THERE ARE two extra cars in my driveway when I get home, and I'm greeted by Dolly, who sits a foot back from the inside welcome mat and blinks at me slowly.

"Thanks, I'm glad to be home," I tell her in a voice just above a whisper. I don't need to hear what Reid thinks about me having conversations with my cat.

"Mrrp," she says, so I come in, put my stuff down, get my shoes off, and scratch her under the chin. She accepts this as her due, tilting her head back and letting her eyes go closed. Voices drift in from the kitchen, and I ignore them for a moment.

"He treat you right?" I murmur, now down on one knee. "You can tell me if he didn't, I'll take care of it."

She just turns her head slightly and shoves a different part of herself against my hand, so I keep scratching her and glance around the entryway. The place started life as a farmhouse somewhere around a hundred and twenty years ago, and every successive owner has made sure to leave their touch in the form of questionable flooring choices, add-ons with puzzling geometry, one very ugly stained-glass window in the front room, and two gargoyles flanking the front steps. Of a farmhouse. In the country. They're awful and ugly, but I couldn't bear to get rid of them.

My entryway is shockingly free of Reid's shoes, or his hoodies, or his backpack, or any of the things he likes to leave around.

"Did you eat him?" I ask Dolly. "Come on, we talked about this."

She stands up and rubs her back against my hand, then walks away slowly until I'm scratching the spot above her tail.

"He *said* he was feeding you," I say, and she looks over her shoulder and trills at me just as Reid walks into the doorway.

"Don't listen to her, I fed that cat *so* much," he says, hands shoved into the pocket of the oversized hoodie he's got on. "And she still bit me like three times."

273

"Dolly," I admonish. She gives me a look that's the cat equivalent of a shrug.

"Anyway, welcome home," Reid says. "I'm glad you made it."

"Same," I say, and stand. Dolly vocalizes her irritation, and so does Reid when I hug him. But then he hugs me back even as he says *are you trying to squash me or something* into my shoulder.

"Uh, by the way," he says, pulling back and sort of gesturing with one elbow. "Sadie and Ariel are here. They can tell you why."

· · · ★ ★ ★ ★ ★ · · ·

MY SISTERS GIVE me a bigger and louder welcome than Reid, who was subdued even as a toddler. Sadie's obviously been crying but she still jumps up and hugs me, lets Ariel do the same, and then orders Reid to get me some spaghetti and meatballs. They go back and forth a couple of times before she rolls her eyes and says *please, Reid* and he rolls his eyes and says *fine, Sadie*, confirming my decision to have a vasectomy for at least the thousandth time.

"How is it?" asks Sadie, sitting across the table from me, practically a blur of nervous energy.

I poke the spaghetti a little more, then break a meatball in half and eat it before answering.

"It's good," I say. "You didn't use mom's recipe?"

Reid snorts and Sadie makes a face.

"I didn't," Ariel says, looking quietly pleased. "I didn't need to feed a zillion people, for starters. Also, her spaghetti is gross."

I don't point out that it's hard to make good spaghetti for fourteen people on a budget of approximately two dollars. I grew up making that recipe at least once a week. I think I know it by heart. I don't particularly like it either, but Ariel's spaghetti is actually good.

I take a sip of water, and then realize there's not only a water glass in front of me, but a whole place setting.

I sigh again, taking it all in. "What happened?"

The three of them look at each other. Sadie takes a deep breath, then lets it out.

"Beth's not talking to Sadie, and Matt's been hassling her boyfriend," Reid finally says. "And Ariel's panicking because she thinks Drew saw her kiss her boyfriend on New Year's and he's gonna tell everyone that they're *also* fucking."

"Reid!" says Ariel, blushing furiously.

"What? Are you not?"

"That's not the *point*—"

"It's definitely the point, are you kidding—"

"Stop!" I say around a mouthful of pasta. Miraculously, they do.

"Sorry," Ariel says, face still bright.

Sadie, Ariel, and Reid were all born in three and a half years—in that order—and they've been thick as thieves ever since they were all old enough to talk. Matt, the boyfriend hassler, is the second youngest, after me, Beth the snoop is the oldest girl, and Drew who saw them kissing is eighteen, the next youngest after Reid.

I still have to draw Andi that family tree.

"This is all still because Beth found ...things... in your bedroom?" I ask, twirling more spaghetti because it's very good and if my siblings are gonna feed me for once, I'm not gonna complain. "And now everyone's up in arms that you're having sex before marriage?"

"Yes," Sadie says, leaning her forehead in her hand, red as a stoplight. I'm pretty sure Ariel mutters *nosy bitch* and I

275

ignore it, mostly because I agree. "And now they all want me to either break up with him or bring him to church and pray for forgiveness and re-take my purity pledge in front of *everyone*. And he has to do it too."

"Maybe you shouldn't have worn your purity ring to church every Sunday until you were *twenty-five*," Reid says.

"Maybe you should shut up."

"I'm surprised it didn't sizzle off your finger."

Sadie flips him off.

"Guys," Ariel says, literally stuck in the middle.

"Thou shalt not lie," Reid says with mock sincerity.

"What was I *supposed* to do?" Sadie snaps. "Toss it in the gutter while they were watching?"

"Say you left it on the sink like a normal person," says Ariel, and Sadie sighs.

"I didn't, okay?" she says. "Also, they want us to get married, I forgot that part."

I sigh and scrub my hands over my face, which I still haven't washed today since I hiked over ten miles down a mountain before being accosted by my siblings. Who, in their defense, did make very good spaghetti.

And, truth be told, I get why Sadie kept lying like she did. I get why she wanted to be the golden good girl for my parents, going through the motions and saying all the right things. I stopped wearing my purity ring when I joined the army at eighteen, but for years, I did pretty much the same thing.

"Do *you* want to get married?" I ask Sadie.

"Not *now*," she says, sounding horrified. "I don't know, I mean, maybe later? We haven't talked about it? I mean, I really like James but it hasn't been very long and it doesn't seem like a good idea—"

"We know," Ariel says, putting a hand on Sadie's arm. "Shh."

"I'll ask Matt to stop hassling James," I say. "And I'll try to talk to Beth, but no promises there. And Ari, for fuck's sake, don't let Beth in your bedroom."

"God, no," Ariel says, and Sadie says, "Thanks," at the same time.

There's a long pause, and they all look at each other for a moment before Reid pipes up.

"I made cookies," he says.

THIRTY

GIDEON

I TAKE Andi to dinner that weekend, to La Taverna, a place with cloth napkins and pleasant lighting and a menu without decimal points. I'm strangely nervous about it, as if Andi will see me somewhere nice and realize that I'm barely fit for polite company, but three minutes into the meal she snort-laughs so loudly heads turn and at the end she sneaks leftover dinner rolls into her purse because *they're just going to throw them away, don't you have some poor rehab critter who'll eat them* and I tell her that refined carbs are generally not good for rehab critters and she says *fine, Reid then* and starts arguing with me about paying half the bill.

She comes back to my place and meets Reid in person, finally, and we all sit on the couch and watch a movie and after he gets tired of us and goes to bed, we make out until the movie ends. It would be the perfect time to tell her that I've had a vasectomy but I've never had sex, not technically, not *that* kind, and instead I pull her on top of me and let myself get lost in her warmth.

The next time we go to dinner, she excuses herself to the bathroom before the check comes, then returns looking like the cat who ate the canary and informs me it's been taken care of. I try to tell her that she shouldn't, that I like doing this and giving her things and feeling useful, but she puts her hand on my mouth and kisses my temple and says *let me take care of you for once*.

It's hard to argue with her then and impossible to argue with her later, in my bedroom, when she pulls her mouth off me just in time for me to come all over her chest, something else I probably shouldn't like but do. I must say that out loud because she rolls her eyes and says *just not the hair or face*, and I can't argue with the heavy peace that's settled in my bones or the taste of her still on my lips.

· · · · · ★ ★ ★ ★ · · · ·

"I CAN'T BELIEVE you made fun of Jesus," I say, and across the table Andi makes a face.

"I didn't *make fun of Jesus*. It was just a joke," she says.

"About Jesus."

"It was a *water into wine* joke! Come on, that's not even blasphemy. People must make that joke all the time at church stuff, right?"

I don't know anyone but Andi who could wind up at a women's bible study by accident when she thought she was joining a book club. Apparently when the flyer on the library bulletin board said the book club was *inspirational* and *uplifting*, Andi thought they meant *Tuesdays with Morrie* or *Man's Search for Meaning*.

"Wasn't my experience," I say, taking a sip of my coffee. "Tell me you didn't also make a 'spent forty days in the desert because men don't ask for directions' joke."

"Of course not. That's a terrible joke," Andi says,

perfectly straight-faced, and I can't help the grin that takes over my face.

Andi's got her chin in one hand, her other wrapped around some confection that technically contains coffee but cannot, in any meaningful way, be called *coffee*. We're sitting at a two-person table by the wall of The Mountain Grind, Sprucevale's premier and only coffee shop, the other patrons buzzing around us. It's late morning on a Sunday, so the church crowd is starting to filter in. Several of them are eyeing our table.

I lean back, take another sip of my own coffee, and remain comfortable.

"You going back next week?"

"I'm not sure I have anything useful to contribute."

"You could always try a regular book club."

Andi snorts and takes a sip of her confection. "I thought this *was* a regular book club," she points out. "I kept waiting for someone to talk about a different book. I stayed for the whole hour."

I start laughing, because I can't help myself.

"Shut *up*," she mutters, but she's grinning. "I felt guilty just leaving!"

"That's how they get you," I say.

"I didn't want to be an asshole at *bible study*," she goes on. "I didn't even have a bible, someone had to lend me their spare. Besides, they seemed really nice. Just confused about why I was there."

Sometimes it's easy to forget that Andi has been away long enough that she doesn't immediately realize *inspirational* is usually code for *Christian*. I'm not sure why anyone around here ever uses a code for that, but it happens sometimes. Maybe it's so unsuspecting women join their bible study groups.

"Also, I got the distinct feeling that they wanted to gossip but couldn't because I was there," she goes on. "So, really, I'm doing them a favor by not going back."

"I'm sure there's at least one secular book club in town," I say. "Lucia's not in one?"

"I don't think Lucia wants me tagging along to *everything* she does," Andi says. "I've gotta give her space to vent about me sometimes. Anyway, I signed up for a bike path cleanup project next month, so that should be fun."

I narrow my eyes at her and think for a moment, because I saw something about that project the other day, and—

"The one organized by Friends of the Chillacouth?" I ask.

Andi drinks her coffee and glances away.

"Chloe Barnes left you chained to a tree and had the *nerve* to ask for help again?" I ask, leaning forward, lowering my voice. I swallow down *and you said yes* because I don't police what Andi does, it's not my job, but—I want her to be okay and not *chained to a tree*.

"It's a group thing, it's right downtown," Andi says. "I promise to use the buddy system."

"When is it?"

"You hate these things, you don't have to go."

"I don't hate them," I grumble, and Andi reaches out to pat my arm. "These big group things are fine."

Andi, it turns out, has been enthusiastically throwing herself into new groups of people since she came back about six months ago. I never realized because I'm not in any of those groups of people; I have my friends and I have my family, but I can't say I go meet strangers for the sheer hell of it the way she does.

I should go with her more, though, if only to see the way it makes her light up. Andi's good at people in a way I'll never be, charming and engaging in a way I'll never be. I'm sure the bible study group she crashed would love to have her back.

"When you came with me last weekend it took you two whole days to get back to normal," she says, and she's leaning in, her eyes laughing, her hand still on my arm.

"You shouldn't encourage Chloe," I say instead of arguing that point. What I *really* want to say is *I want Chloe to never speak to you again after what she did*, but Andi will tell me I'm being unreasonable.

"She apologized," Andi shrugs. The apology wasn't nearly enough, but that's not my call to make. "And it's not like I'm not going anywhere alone with her ever again."

Chloe didn't see the way Andi was shaking in my truck that night, something I can't quite get out of my head when her name comes up.

"Promise?" I ask, as Andi drains the rest of her coffee confection.

"Of course," she says, and stands. "Be right back."

She tosses her cup on the way to the bathroom, and I set about finishing my own drink while definitely not plotting reasons why Chloe Barnes could, theoretically, be arrested for forest crimes.

I'm mid-plot when Mrs. Buckley seats herself in Andi's empty chair, puts her purse on the table, and smiles at me. It's a bad sign.

"Sure is a cold one out there today," she says by way of greeting. "Listen, sweetheart, I'm so glad I ran into you. How're you doing?"

I know an ambush when I see one, and only wish I knew what kind of ambush this was. Mr. and Mrs. Buckley are long-time friends of my parents'. I have no idea what their first names are. For all I know, it's Mr. and Mrs.

"Well, and yourself?" I ask.

"Thank you for asking," she says, and puts a hand on my arm. I liked it better when Andi did it. "I was just at the most wonderful worship service with your parents, and I have to tell you, they put in a prayer request for you."

"Ah," I say, because I have to say something. I wish this were news.

"Now, I *know*, but they really are concerned for your happiness," she continues. I don't like where this is going, but I'm powerless to stop her from saying everything she came here to say and we both know it. "If you don't mind me saying so, it's just no good for a man to be in his thirties and not married. You ought to have a family by now. Don't you want that? A wife, some sweet babies?"

"I've got quite a bit of family already," I point out, and Mrs. Buckley gives a little huff and arm-squeeze at my non-answer.

"You poor thing," she says. "Anyway, when I heard your parents' prayer request, I said, Lord, what can I do to help Gideon find himself someone who'll love him just as he is? Because here's a sweet young man who deserves exactly that."

Everything I'm thinking is far too impolite to say aloud.

"And then, do you know," Mrs. Buckley says. "The Lord laid it on my heart to invite you to dinner this Friday. Laura will be home from college for the weekend and I know she'd love to see you."

At the end of her sentence her eyes flick to something above my head, and before I can turn to look, Andi's hand is on my shoulder.

"Hi!" She says before I even open my mouth. Fuck, am I supposed to stand now?

"Hello," Mrs. Buckley says.

"Andi, this is—Mrs. Buckley," I manage, before this can

get any further without me. "Mrs. Buckley, this is Andi Sullivan."

"Deanna, please," she says, so I guess she does have a first name.

"*Lovely* to meet you."

"Thank you so much for the offer, but I'm actually busy Friday," I say, politely as I can manage.

"Oh?" Mrs. Buckley—Deanna feels too weird—says. "Saturday, then."

"I can't then, either," I say, apologetically as I can.

"Well, aren't you mister popular?" Mrs. Buckley says, smile wide and not particularly sincere.

"*Very* popular," Andi pipes up, giving Mrs. Buckley a smile so pure and angelic I expect a beam of light to fall directly on her. "He's practically got a waiting list."

"I see," says Mrs. Buckley.

"The prayer requests must be working," Andi goes on. There's practically a halo around her head now. "His parents will be *so* relieved."

It occurs to me, at last, that I failed to mention that Andi and I are dating. Christ, I'm bad at this.

"Hey, um, babe," I say, and look up at her. I've never called her babe before. She looks appropriately skeptical. "Do you still want to—do that thing? Before we head out?"

It would probably be easier to simply point at her and shout *girlfriend!*

"Oh, definitely, *babe*," she says. "That thing sounds great."

Across the table, Mrs. Buckley's face is pleasantly neutral, which could mean absolutely anything. I stand, my chair scraping back, grab my coffee cup, and drain it.

"Nice to see you," I tell her, because I have to say something.

"Absolutely lovely!" Andi gushes. Her smile's a little dangerous. "Tell Gideon's parents I say hi."

"Have a wonderful day," Mrs. Buckley says, and Andi and I leave the coffee shop.

"So," she says, when we're a ways down the block and there's no chance of being overheard. "Does this mean your parents know we're dating or don't know we're dating?"

"I honestly don't know," I say. "This isn't the first time they've put in that prayer request, though they backed off a little over the fall. They might have been putting one in for Sadie and remembered me at the last minute, or maybe someone told them."

It's not a secret that we're dating, obviously, but I haven't actually had a conversation with my parents about it. I don't think I want to hear anything they might say.

"You know, I almost admire the sheer..." Andi waves one hand through the air, like she's looking for a word. "Passive-aggressive audacity? Of it. Because that was honestly pretty effective and they didn't have to make any direct statements whatsoever."

This sort of shit is practically rote by now. Putting in a prayer that I'll get a date is essentially a request for the Mrs. Deanna Buckleys of the world to set me up with their daughters—who I doubt want to be set up with me, either—without admitting that anything in their family is imperfect.

They might also think there's a chance I can be seduced away from Andi, bless their hearts.

"How bad is this gonna be?" she asks, suddenly serious and quiet. "I know Sadie's miserable."

I shrug with a nonchalance I don't quite feel, because it's easy to know that I shouldn't mind my parents' disapproval about this and another thing entirely not to feel it like a lead weight in my gut.

"However they feel is their problem," I tell her, which isn't completely true, but I like the way it sounds. "Anyway, what are you doing Friday?"

That gets a lifted eyebrow and a smirk, just like I was hoping for.

"I thought you were busy."

"There's a roller derby match in Blythe," I say, and her eyebrows shoot up. "Want to go?"

THIRTY-ONE

ANDI

"OH," Gideon says when I walk into the foyer where he's waiting with my uncle Frank, making small talk. He clears his throat. "You look nice."

"Thanks," I say, and smooth my dress against one thigh and probably blush because I did, in fact, take an hour and a half to get ready for this roller derby group date. "So do you."

"Thank you," Gideon says, sort of stiff and formal, probably because he's standing there with my uncle and waiting for me and this all feels more than a little like we're sixteen and going to a school dance together. "Ready?"

"Ten p.m. and not a minute later," Frank tells Gideon, because he thinks he's a comedian. "And you, should I be letting you wear that out of the house?"

I roll my eyes at him, fondly, because I'm in my thirties and this isn't even the shortest dress I own, though it's close.

"Okay. Thank you," I tell him. "Don't wait up."

"Are they leaving?" Lucia calls, somewhere inside the house.

"Go," I whisper to Gideon, because any chance of making a quick escape is fading.

He clears his throat, looks slightly nervous, and nods at Frank like he's fighting the urge to call him *sir*.

"Bye," I whisper, and then Lucia comes through the door from the kitchen.

"Look at you two!" she says, all ebullience and reading glasses around a chain on her neck. Gideon's in jeans and a flannel shirt, his coat open, and I've got on a short-ish green dress, black tights, and flat knee-high boots. "Wait, wait. I need a picture."

"Someone's waiting for us in the car," I tell her, tugging at Gideon, who seems torn between duty and flight.

"It'll only take a minute," Lucia says, her phone already out. "Stand there and smile. Get *closer*, I thought this was a date."

I slide an arm around Gideon's waist and whisper *sorry* as Lucia snaps several photos, presumably for her scrapbook or something. I don't know.

"Was that so hard?" she says when she's done, and comes forward to give me a hug, then a kiss on each cheek. She repeats it with Gideon, who blushes furiously. "Have a good time and be *safe*," she says, in a way that makes it clear she doesn't mean we should drive under the speed limit. I wonder for a moment if she saw the condoms I put in my purse, then remind myself that it doesn't matter.

"Thanks," we both say, and manage to escape at last.

· · · ★ ★ ★ ★ ★ · · ·

"I THOUGHT I might need to send a search party," Reid says from the back seat a few minutes later.

"My aunt wanted pictures," I explain, buckling my seatbelt, and Gideon snorts.

"Ugh. Adorable," Reid mutters. "Now I feel even more like your chaperone. No funny business up there."

"*Reid*," Gideon says, but he's still blushing and he leaves it at that.

· · · ★ ★ **★** ★ ★ · · ·

I KNOW exactly the moment Gideon discovers the tights I'm wearing are actually the thigh-high kind with a built-in garter, because the car stops mid-parallel-park and he's staring at my lap in mild alarm. My skirt, which was on the short side to begin with, has ridden up during the hour-long car ride to Blythe, just enough that the top band is visible around my thigh.

He glances at Reid in the back seat, Gideon's hand still behind my headrest, then at me again, and finally clears his throat and continues backing into a parking spot. I pull my skirt down and try to make a demure face while Gideon blushes in the driver's seat and focuses on parking like no one has ever focused before.

It's adorable and sweet and makes me want to ride him like a pony all at once, because feelings can be multi-faceted.

"Izzy says they've got our names at the front," Reid says, disturbing the silence. "Are we done parking, or..."

The roller derby match is in an older building close to the edge of town, near the river, surrounded mostly by other old buildings. Warehouses or something, probably, the streets quiet and empty and dark even though it's only seven forty-five. Reid walks a good twenty feet in front of us, wearing a hoodie under a denim jacket and checking his phone every ten seconds or so, practically humming with nervous energy.

"Yeah, they should be here any—hey, guys, come get wrist-bands," he calls from the lit doorway when we walk up to the derby venue. "Here. Yeah. Gideon and Andrea? Thanks. Thank you."

Reid scowls at his lime-green *under 21* wristband for a second, but then we're inside and there's already a hubbub and Reid shoves his hands into his pockets and looks around in a way that reminds me, a little, of a meerkat. He pays no attention whatsoever to the crowd as we walk over to where Silas and Kat are standing, a little off to the side, and knocks into at least two people.

"*Reid*," Gideon says. "Fuck's sake, look where you're going."

"Sorry," Reid says, still not looking where he's going. "Izzy said she was—"

"Reid!" a woman exclaims, and a second later a short girl with blue pigtails elbows her way through the crowd and launches herself at him. "You came!"

They hug, and Reid is wearing the goofiest, dopiest grin I've ever seen in my life.

"Hey," he says, when the hug ends, and then shoves his hands deep into his pockets. "Yeah, of course. I like your—" he sort of nods at her entire being, which is wearing knee-high rainbow socks, ripped hot pink fishnets, short gold spandex shorts, a *Blue Ridge Bruisers* tank top, and an impressive amount of glitter. "Looks like a good turnout," Reid finishes, cheeks mottled pink.

"It usually is when we play Richmond," Izzy says, and then she's excitedly talking a mile a minute about roller derby stuff while Reid stays quiet and makes the biggest heart-eyes I've ever seen on a human. It's not what I expected from Gideon's sometimes-sweet, sometimes-surly little brother, but it does make sense.

"Is this why we're here?" I whisper to Gideon. "And are we chaperoning him? What are our responsibilities right now?"

"Don't let him get into any white vans that say *free candy* on the side, probably," Gideon says, his voice low and right in my ear. "But otherwise..." he shrugs.

· · * * ★ ★ ★ * * · ·

THE BUILDING where the derby is taking place is the old gym complex for the satellite campus of Virginia State University in town—the college built a newer one a few years ago, Gideon's friend Wyatt tells me—and it's got a charming, midcentury athletics feel to it. There are basketball hoops pulled up against the ceiling, padding at either end of the gym, and wooden bleachers that pull out from the walls. They're only halfway out right now, and between them the oval track is demarcated with thick black tape on the floor.

"I'd get a couple levels up in the stands at least," Wyatt is saying cheerfully, a beer in his hand, his orange hair flopping forward over his forehead. "Sometimes they lose control and go into the crowd, which is always kinda fun, but you probably don't want it to be you."

"How is that fun, exactly?" I ask as Gideon walks up silently and hands me a beer in a plastic cup.

"Oh, the crowd loves it," he says. "And everyone knows not to stand there unless they're willing to get knocked over, maybe, so it's win-win."

"What? No one is winning," Gideon says. "One person gets a penalty and the other gets plowed into."

"It's a win in the spirit of roller derby," Wyatt says confidently.

"Sure," Gideon says. He sounds utterly unconvinced. "You guys seen Reid?"

"I thought we weren't chaperoning."

"We're not."

I lift an eyebrow and try not to feel a little squishy inside at the way Gideon is looking out for his little brother while also acting annoyed about it.

"If it helps, I also haven't seen any *free candy* vans."

"There's a free candy van?" Wyatt asks, taking another sip of his beer.

"Yes. They lure children and kidnap them," Gideon explains, and Wyatt grimaces.

"Oh, that kind. Is that really a thing?"

"Probably."

"Anyway," I start. "I think Reid is—"

I am interrupted, again, by a hand mysteriously appearing from Gideon's other side and going for his beer.

"Hey. *No,*" Gideon says, glaring as the rest of Reid also appears. "You're underage."

"I'll be twenty-one in, like, five months," Reid says, tugging his sleeve over his lime green wristband. "C'mon."

"Then in five months you can have some of my beer."

"Really?"

"In five months, I'll buy you a beer," Wyatt offers. "We all know Gideon's not sharing."

"It's unhygienic," says the man who's recently discovered a fondness for ejaculating on my breasts.

"You spend way too much time in the woods for anyone to believe that," Wyatt says, cheerful as ever.

"I don't go there to share my drinks."

"You drink water with fish pee in it," I point out.

Gideon makes a pained face. "It's *filtered.*"

"I don't think you can filter out pee," Reid says.

"What do you know about filters?"

"I know that if I peed in one, when the pee came out the other side it would still be pee."

"Alchemy's fake, you know," adds in another voice, belonging to a man who's just inserted himself next to Wyatt. "Hi. If anyone says they can turn pee into gold, they're lying. Or very dehydrated."

Gideon closes his eyes briefly, as if maintaining his composure.

"Andi, this is Javier. Javier, my girlfriend Andi."

"Charmed," Javier says, grinning like it's true.

"Gideon doesn't want to share his beer," Wyatt says, as if that's an explanation.

"Does he need to?"

"*No,*" says Gideon. "He does not."

"The alcohol kills the germs," Reid says.

"Beer's not nearly that alcoholic," corrects Wyatt.

"Really?"

"Really."

Reid goes silent and looks very thoughtful.

"Anyway," Javier says. "Where are the best seats?"

· · · · ★ ★ ★ ★ · · · ·

"YOU KNOW HOW THIS WORKS?" Gideon asks me, so close his lips are practically against my ear. The derby players are lining up on the track, and the music is loud and the crowd is also loud and there's even a few spotlights swirling around.

"Sort of?" I say, because I went to the derby once in Brooklyn but it's been a couple of years.

Gideon leans in further and rests a palm on my thigh, right where my stockings end. I have no idea if it's an accident.

"So, it's divided into two-minute segments, which have a goofy name I don't remember right now," he says, his voice all rumbly and his hand warm. "See Lainey and the other woman with the star on her helmet?"

"I don't know who Lainey is," I remind him.

"Oh. Sorry," he says, pointing at the track. "She's the Black woman with the helmet star. I don't know the other one. Lainey is, um, friends with Wyatt."

I can't see her very well from here, but I'm pretty sure she's wearing rainbow fishnets and a lot of pink glitter, so she's probably cool.

"Sure," I say.

"They're the ones who score points," he says, "Which they do by skating through this pack of other women—" he points at a cluster further up the track, "—and then the goal is to lap the other team as many times as they can in two minutes by skating fast."

"That's it?"

He shrugs. "More or less."

Silas and his girlfriend Kat come sit in front of us right before kickoff, or skateoff, or whatever it's called. She's quiet but knows way more about derby than either Gideon or Silas, so I wind up sitting next to her on the bleachers, leaning back against Gideon's knees. He talks to Silas and keeps playing with my hair and then stopping, like he doesn't know he's doing it.

It's good, seeing Gideon like this: relaxed and happy in public. Ever since we've been back he's been stuck in the middle of all his siblings, trying to mediate The Sadie Situation. I'm not even sure any of them remember what sparked it, but I know that now they're arguing about whether Matt went to a wet t-shirt contest in college one time or if Jacob secretly dated someone before he met his wife, if Zach's wife is allowed to know the Secret Family Biscuit Recipe, or how Ariel might, sometimes, wear a two-piece swimsuit.

Watching over all this are William and Emma, Gideon's parents. They're either staying out of it (Gideon's words) or allowing their progeny to kill each other, *Lord of the Flies* style, until the final remaining child has proven his or her love for them by strict adherence to their impossible rules (my words, which I haven't actually said to Gideon). I've seen his dad twice and his mother once since I moved back to Sprucevale, both times in passing. We didn't speak. I'd be happy if we never spoke again, because as much as I can forgive Gideon for what happened back then, William and Emma can have my forgiveness when they ask for it on their knees and maybe not even then. So, yeah, I'm still mad.

My mom died when I was nearly three. Aneurysm. Her name was Gloria. I don't really remember her much, but I know all about her because my dad and Rick talk about her all the time, still. She grew up here and went to high school with Rick, then met my dad in college; after she died, her best friend and her widower spent a lot of time together and eventually started dating. I'm pretty sure that "started dating" is a polite euphemism for something else, but I'll never ask, and anyway, they're married now.

The other person who loved to talk about my mom was her mother, my Grandma Millie, whose house was full of doilies and throw pillows and ceramic figurines. She always had cookies in a jar, chocolate milk in the fridge, and let me watch as much TV as I wanted. Grandma Millie was *also* casually bigoted and racist in a way that I wouldn't realize until years later, when she found out from Gideon's parents that my dad and Rick were together and tried to have the state take custody of me away from them because of it.

Not the best time in my life. I had nightmares about being dragged away from my parents because my best friend had betrayed me. My dad lost his job teaching eighth grade science. We moved to New Jersey, where my dad's family is, the moment the court case with Grandma Millie was over, and I never saw her again. I didn't go to her funeral. I hope no one did.

I wouldn't be mad if I never saw Gideon's parents again, either, but for his sake I could probably force three or four minutes of politeness if I really had to. Maybe five if the situation *really* calls for it.

But right now, I'm leaning against him and he's half playing with my hair and talking to Silas about some movie I don't think I saw and Kat and I are trying to decide on our derby names, and this, I think, is what I want for him.

· · · · · ★ ★ ★ · · · · ·

"YOU LOOK GOOD LIKE THIS," I tell Gideon two hours later. I'm standing behind him on the bottom riser and I've got both my arms slung around his neck, pulling him back against me. It's dark in the gym, just the emergency lights on, the scent of beer and sweat and too many people slowly fading.

"Sweaty and a little tired?" he asks, voice buzzing through my palms where they're flat against his chest.

"You look happy," I tell him, the thing I've been thinking all night when I haven't been coming up with a derby name or lowkey ogling him because he's wearing a button-down plaid with the sleeves rolled up that is, frankly, very slutty.

Gideon reaches up and puts a hand around my forearm, then slides it down to my wrist, touching me like he's thinking. It's fascinating, the way I've learned his minutiae since we met again.

"I am," he says, and the words hang in the air.

We're still here because roller derby is a community activity as much as any church potluck, and if you know anyone on the team, you're getting roped into helping with cleanup. That means I got to peel tape off the floor while I watched Gideon and his friends stack chairs, carry them to a storage room, put away sound equipment, and generally lift heavy things in a way I found very pleasing.

"Where the hell did Silas and Wyatt go?" he huffs after another minute. "I'd like to get out of here."

"We could just leave," I point out, shifting a little closer. "Didn't Reid say he was getting another ride home?"

"Silas has a scratching post in his car for me," Gideon says, and I don't even ask why. Men.

I put my lips right next to his ear, because a scratching post? Is he serious?

"It's a long drive," I murmur, my mouth directly on the shell of his ear. "We should get started."

Gideon's whole body tenses, and he takes a careful breath.

"Especially if Reid won't be back until later," I go on.

"Why?" he rumbles, turning his head so our mouths nearly meet. "You got plans?"

Yes, I have plans. I'd like to get railed over the kitchen table while still wearing my garter tights, for example, but I physically can't make myself say that out loud, so instead I lick his ear and listen to the way he hisses.

"Andi," he says, and sounds a little pained.

"Mmm?"

Gideon doesn't answer, but he turns around, tilts his head up, and kisses me with a hand around the back of my neck. The angle is weird because I'm taller than him like this, sort of bent over, and I take my face in his hands and come down on his mouth with more force than usual.

He *groans*. It's quiet, but holy shit. I pull back and slide a thumb along his lower lip and he watches me, eyes mottled in the dark. I remember him on his knees, unlacing my boots, how he looked like this then, too.

"God, you're pretty," I whisper, and I don't really mean to, but Gideon swallows hard and pulls my mouth back to his. It's gentle for a second and a little feral after that, his teeth on my lip and my thumb gently tracing down the line of his throat. He presses himself against me then his hands are on my hips, my thighs, under my skirt. His hands are warm and calloused, and they scratch a little as he strokes the skin right above where my tights end, then finds both garters and snaps them.

It doesn't hurt. I can barely feel it, honestly, but I *know* it and then he snaps the ones on the backs of my thighs too and holy fuck, his house is *so far away.*

"You like the tights, then?" I murmur, my lips barely leaving his.

He frowns slightly. "Of course I like the tights," he says, very seriously. "I haven't thought about anything else since we got here."

"Nothing?" I tease, nipping at his lips again.

"You want an inventory of thoughts?" he says, and squeezes my upper thighs, skin on skin. "Fine. It was *tights, Reid trying to drink my beer, tights, roller derby, tights, tights, put away chairs.* Then *tights* again. Exactly like you wanted."

"I didn't mean—"

Gideon sighs, then wraps one arm around my upper thighs and lifts me off the bleacher. I squeak in surprise before he sets me down on the floor, at our usual heights, and then makes a whole show of pulling my skirt down.

He takes me gently by the chin and pulls my face up so we're looking at each other.

"Yes," he says. "You did."

"Then I'm glad it worked."

"You thought there was a chance it wouldn't?"

I take a tiny step closer in. He releases my chin, and my hands find their way under the bottom of his shirt, my fingertips on warm skin. Gideon makes a noise in the back of his throat.

I did think there was a chance it wouldn't work. For all his enthusiasm I swear sometimes I can see the tiniest flicker of hesitation on his face. I keep remembering him, in the dark, saying *sometimes this feels wrong, too*, and I know that for all his grumpy bluster and stone-faced exterior, Gideon's soft as a kitten on the inside and just as easily hurt. It's easy enough to feel one thing and think another, and some of my buried, latent fears are afraid he thinks I'm a harlot.

"There's always a chance," is what I say, and Gideon snorts, and then his mouth lands on mine again, more desperate than before.

The plan was, as far as there was a plan, to cheekily show him the garters on the drive back to his house, then launch myself at him once we were through the door. I didn't mean for him to grab my ass and haul me against him in an old high school gym, but plans change.

"Fuck," he mutters, and pulls away. He breathes like he's trying to catch his breath. "We should get going, it's a long drive."

"How well do you know Blythe?" I ask, and he frowns.

"Some," he says. "Why?"

I tuck my fingers below the waist of his jeans and slide one thumb along his erection before I realize I'm doing it, and he makes a noise in the back of his throat.

"Any good lovers' lanes?" I ask. "Your house is pretty far away."

"I think that's illegal," he says, voice hazy.

"Then we won't get caught."

Gideon's staring at me in the dark like he's trying to collect his thoughts and failing, pupils wide, lips parted. His hair's curling at the ends and he's not disheveled yet, all of him still in order, but everything about him is begging for it.

"How do you know?" he asks, sliding one hand up my body, along my jaw, one thumb featherlight against my lower lip, the way I did to him earlier.

"Be inconspicuous," I say, then lick his thumb. "And quiet." I close my lips around it, my tongue against the rough pad, and Gideon looks like he might pass out for a moment.

"You think—" he starts, and then we both freeze at the sound of a door shutting. It echoes across the empty gym, bouncing from the bleachers behind us, his thumb still between my teeth. There are footsteps. I bite down, gently.

"Fuck," he whispers, and I put a hand on his chest and push.

THIRTY-TWO

GIDEON

"YOU KNOW my car's the other way," I say, low enough that my voice won't carry.

"Oh, oops," she says, still pushing me backwards. There's a light in her eyes bordering on unholy, and she grins. "Let's take refuge in this dark hallway while I get my bearings."

"If you're confused, I could guide you."

"You know I'll never learn if I don't figure it out myself," she says, then grabs my wrist and tugs me along.

At the end of the bleachers there's a dark hallway that runs parallel to the back wall. It probably leads to locker rooms or ball storage or something, and it's lit by one emergency light all the way at the end. Andi pushes me against the wall in the darkest part, the painted-over cinderblocks cool against my back, her hand splayed over my chest. Another door opens, out in the gym, footsteps fading, and Andi stands up on her tiptoes and kisses me more carefully than I'm expecting.

Now it's slow and lazy, as if we've got all the time in the world. As if no one will come looking for us any minute now, as if we won't get locked into this building before long. I slide my fingers into her hair and tilt her head back as she presses against me, her warmth sinking through my clothes and lighting my skin on fire.

Andi licks into my mouth and settles a hand on my hip, fingertips sneaking under the waistband of my jeans, the backs of her knuckles against my skin. My breath stutters at it, my hand at her waist, thumb moving over the spot where the elastic of her tights digs into her. I can feel it through her dress, can feel the exact shape and dimensions of what she's got on underneath, and it makes me dizzy.

After a little while she pulls back, wide-eyed and red-lipped and breathless. The fabric of her dress is twisted between my fingers, I realize, and I'm tracing over the outline of a garter on her tights, and my skin feels electrified. I'm so hard it hurts. We shouldn't be here.

"Someone's gonna find us," I remind her.

Andi *shrugs*. "And?"

"And we'd get caught."

"We're two grownups kissing."

I run my thumb over her garter again, my brain sparking like a downed power line. "It's public lewdness," I say. "Or something." As if I've ever had to consider what sort of misdemeanor making out in public is before.

Andi gives a little grin and steps closer, between my legs, somehow, her body warm and solid against my very present erection. I don't groan, but I have to bite my lip.

"This isn't public *or* lewd," she points out. "Yet."

Yet? Fuck. I take her by the hips and run my thumbs down the front of her garters so I don't think about *yet* too hard.

"I like your tights."

"You said."

"I can't compliment you twice?"

Andi presses harder against me and mouths at the hinge of my jaw, heat and teeth and tongue.

"I like your shirt," she says, laughing.

"Thank you."

"I like your jeans, too," she says, and ghosts a palm over my dick, trapped behind the zipper. I grit my teeth so I don't demand more right now, because fuck, *fuck* we're still in this gym.

"I like your," I start, my hands now under her skirt. My fingers sink into the soft flesh at the tops of her thighs, the spot where the stocking cut into her a little, and I pull her into me. There's some gentle dry humping. I fail to think of a word that might finish my sentence, but I don't think it matters because her teeth are on my collarbone and it doesn't matter that she's being gentle and it doesn't matter how easily I could over-power her, I feel pinned against this wall.

When she pulls back a little I capture her mouth again and she's plastered against my front, her heat singing along my nerves. I had an objection but I can't think of it anymore, not when she's rubbing against me and pressing me into this wall and not when her fingers are tugging at the zipper of my jeans. I realize my hands are on her ass and her skirt's hiked up around her waist, the blue in her eyes nearly swallowed by black when she looks up at me.

"I think this is lewd now," she says, and gets her hand around my dick. I have to close my eyes and tilt my head against the wall and breathe, fucking *breathe*, Gideon, most people got their first handjob behind the bleachers before they were old enough to vote.

"We should go home," I say, and it's true but I don't mean it. Andi slides her thumb along the head of my dick, the fabric moving with it, and I break into a full-body shiver.

"Or," she says, and I slit my eyes open. She sounds rough

and velvety. "It's an hour back to your place, right? And we wouldn't get out of here right away, so more like an hour and a half. You've gotta get the cat scratcher or whatever. *But*," she glances over one shoulder, like she's casing the joint. "I bet I can find a room with a door that closes in under two minutes."

It shouldn't send a bolt of heat charging through my body, but it does. There's the usual low, constant drum beat of *this is wrong but my reasons are bad* but this wrong for real reasons, like *we could get caught* and *this might actually be illegal*. Even if it's not likely. Even if I doubt we'll get arrested. I should adjust myself and stop looking at Andi's devilish face and insist we make the long drive back to Sprucevale so we can do this in a bed, behind a locked door.

But Andi is adventure and excitement, heat and promise. It's always been like this with us, Andi pulling me along to places I wanted to go and didn't know to ask for. As kids we'd find a fence or a property line or a No Trespassing sign and she'd say, *do you wanna?* And I'd always say, *yes.*

So, I should say *that's a bad idea* but instead I say, "You think so?" and she laughs.

The third door she tries opens, we shove through it. The room smells like rubber and leather and old wood and it's dark as the grave, but I can still feel her smiling as her hands grab fistfuls of my shirt and pull me in. We bump together too hard in the dark.

"Ow," she says, and then laughs, softly. "Hold on, where's the—"

"Wait, don't," I say, voice low. "Too visible under the door."

I take my phone from my pocket and turn on the flashlight, blinking. We're in an equipment room, I think, shelves piled with basketballs and soccer balls and nets and those small orange cones, a metal crate of volleyballs and a stack of blue mats against the back wall.

I put my phone on a shelf, flashlight aimed at the ceiling, casting everything in strange, slanting shadows. Andi leans against the mats, half-sitting, legs wide enough to make her skirt ride up and show off the garters.

"I'm starting to think you have a flashlight fetish," she says, head tilted to one side.

"If anything, I have a *seeing what I'm doing* fetish."

"Weird," she teases, and I step between her legs and kiss her again. This time it's desperate and hot, her hand grabbing the front of my shirt, the other palming my cock through my jeans again. I get her under the thighs and hike her up onto the mats properly so she can wrap her legs around my hips.

"You look good like this," she says. "I wanted to tell you. This fucking shirt."

Her hand is on my dick again and I grind into it, swallowing a groan.

"My shirt?" I manage, and she laughs breathlessly.

"I don't know," she says, and her skirt's around her waist now, and she's wearing black lace underwear, too, and—God. Andi *planned* this. Hours ago. Getting ready in her bedroom at her aunt's house she thought about how she wanted tonight to go and she put on garter tights and black lace. No one has ever been luckier than me. "It just—shows off your arms and your shoulders look ridiculous and then you rolled up the sleeves and were just, like, standing around with *forearms*," she says.

I don't know what she's talking about, but I plant my thumb on black lace, right where I figure her clit is, and circle it. I must be right because she makes a noise and her head goes back, her throat working. When I kiss her again she groans softly, so I take a second and push my fingers under the lace, where she's hot and slick and pushes her hips into me.

"Fuck, Andi, you love this," I say, and even in the bad light I can see that she's flushed pink, her lips parted, her eyes glazed. I lean in even closer, push her thighs a little further apart with my other hand, and she arches her back, breathing hard. "You wanted it."

"Well," she manages. "Yeah."

I feel like there's something unspooling deep in my brain, some sort of instinctual logic. Some primal urge. I plant my hand by her waist and sink two fingers into her, crooking them harder than usual, the heel of my hand on her clit. Andi gasps and jolts and swears, but then she grabs my wrist and grinds herself against the palm of my hand and hisses, "Fuck, Gideon."

"You have to be quiet," I tell her. "No matter how good it feels. You think you can do that?"

"Maybe," she says. "Are you really gonna stop if I get too loud?"

Probably not.

"Don't," I say, and pop the button on my jeans. It's pure relief, and God, the look in Andi's eyes.

"But it feels so good," she says, and looks me straight in the eyes. My brain goes blank. "What if I can't help myself?"

I inhale, I think.

"If I'm saying your name and begging you to make me come, are you gonna stop?" she goes on, flushed and her eyes half-closed and teasing me like this. "I think you'd like that. *Fuck*," she adds as I grind into her clit a little harder, twist my fingers.

"Don't get us caught," I say, and palm my dick a little because God, it fucking *aches*. Sparks fly up my spine, and she's watching my hand as I close it loosely around myself and stroke. "God, Andi, you look—"

She's still got her hand around my wrist and one foot up on the mats, using the leverage to grind her clit against the heel of my hand. Her bottom lip is between her teeth and her eyes are going out of focus. I'm dizzyingly hard, leaking into the fabric of my boxers.

"There are condoms in my purse," she says, and I go still. She swallows. "If you want. I know we haven't, but..."

Andi makes the softest noise when I pull my fingers out of her, then points to the floor beside the mats. I grab her purse and hand it to her, because I know better than to rifle through purses.

In high school, I made a purity pledge, and I meant it. It's easy to mean things like that when you're fifteen and have no prospects, but standing here, at thirty-two, I take a second to let the last tatters of it float away. I feel a little bad about not keeping a promise, but I shouldn't have promised in the first place.

When she hands me the condom she's got this flushed little grin on her face, like we're getting away with something, like it's exhilarating. I put a hand on her jaw and kiss her, slow and hard enough that I can't help but groan into her mouth.

"This is a bad idea," I tell her. I'm already opening the condom.

"You can say no," she says. "I'd rather you say yes, but..."

I wrap a hand around my dick, boxers still on, and give myself a slow, hard pump. It makes my toes curl, makes my skin feel too small. Andi watches with bright-eyed lust, her thumbs hooked in the waist of her black panties.

"I'm saying yes," I tell her, my voice half-broken. "But I'm also saying this is a bad idea."

Andi gives me a smile and a shrug and then pulls her

panties off, somehow, and I blink like it was a fucking magic trick.

"Those just come off?" I say as she shoves them into her purse.

"If you put them on over the garters, sure." She reaches out and thumbs the head of my clothed dick, making me gasp.

"You should be quieter," she says as I push my pants and boxers down just enough that they're out of the way. Andi takes the condom from my hand and strokes my cock once, positions it on the head, then rolls it down. She strokes me again and I push her against the mats, kissing her.

"I *should* be driving us home," I remind her, and thrust against her again, heat twisting up my spine. God, we're not even fucking yet and I think I might be melting.

"Still time to change your mind," she teases me, then bites my lip. I have to swallow a groan and don't do a good job of it.

"No. Turn around," I tell her. After one last kiss, she does, bracing herself on the mats. There's a zipper down the back of her dress, and I pull it down to reveal a sliver of skin all the way down her spine, her skirt still around her hips, the fucking garters and the fucking tights bold against pale skin. Andi shivers. I have to catch my breath, and she looks over her shoulder at me, all flushed and teasing.

I put my hand on her hip and guide myself in, and Andi's warm and slippery and before I know it Andi makes a broken-off whimper and I'm open-mouthed against the back of her neck, my whole body hot and cold and shivery, her skin salty. I swallow and try to compose myself, sunk inside her, try to fight the sensation that I'm gladly drowning.

"Good?" I finally manage, and curve my hand over her hip, along her belly. Andi leans back and braces a hand against the wall, muscles pulsing around me.

"Good," she murmurs, and I start moving. I go slow so I

can watch, greedily, one hand locked around her thigh. It looks like a magic trick the way I disappear into her, the way it feels like falling, the way she sighs and catches her breath and swallows her noises. The way she rocks back against me and makes a louder noise, an *oh* that gets caught between her teeth, when I bottom out.

I stay like that for a moment, holding her hips back against me, and scrape my teeth along her neck.

"*Fuck*," she whispers, gasps, clenches around me, and from then on, I can't think. She's braced against the wall and the mats and I'm braced against her and I'm burning or drowning, it doesn't matter. She swears again and gets one knee up on the mats, so I find her clit, rub furious circles around it. Andi's making these small, soft, whimpering noises, and over the rush of blood in my ears I think I hear her say *fuck, yes, come on*. I think I say her name in response.

And maybe we haven't fucked before this, but I know how she sounds when she's getting close, know the specific way her body trembles. Her hand against the wall curls into a fist and I get a second of warning before she comes and I hold her tight and fuck her through it the way I know she likes. I ignore the white heat sinking down my spine until she's done, boneless and gasping, and then I finally let go.

Andi pushes back against me as I do, the muscles in her back knotting as I come so hard my brain turns to static and my ears ring. I probably say her name again, at least once, and when it's over I'm plastered against her back, both of us sweaty, half-collapsed on old wrestling mats. I have to remember to breathe once, twice, my face still against the back of her neck.

"I don't think we were quiet," she says, turning her head.

"Oops," I say, and she laughs silently. I feel it in my dick and shudder.

After a moment, I peel myself off her and deal with the condom. Andi pulls her skirt down and I zip up the back of her dress because I'm a gentleman, and then she scoots over and sits so I'm standing between her legs, leaning back against her, floating and lazy. People are waiting for us outside this room, probably wondering where we are. I'll care about it in a minute.

"That was a good time," Andi says, playing with my hair. "Thanks."

I lean back against her, eyes closed.

"You're welcome," I tell her, and then: "I've never done that before."

"Really? You've never had sex in the equipment room of an old college gymnasium?" she says, dryly, the tugs on my scalp curling down my spine.

"I've never had sex before," I say, and her hands go still. "That kind, at least."

There are a few seconds of stillness and silence, just long enough for me to open my eyes and wonder if I've breached protocol.

"You're saying I just deflowered you in a supply closet?" she asks, her hands still in my hair but unmoving.

"That's not the word I'd use."

"Sorry, an equipment room."

Another beat of silence passes, and then I start laughing. I feel melty and floaty and like all my problems are a million miles away, and Andi puts her forehead on my shoulder and starts laughing, too.

"You meant deflower?" she says.

"I did."

"If you'd told me I could've gotten you rose petals and candles."

"I didn't want rose petals and candles," I tell her. "I wanted you."

"Against old wrestling mats in a room lit by flashlight, apparently."

"Anywhere," I say. "Everywhere."

Her hands are moving through my hair again, my head against her chest. She's quiet like she's thinking.

"Were you waiting?" she finally asks. She doesn't add *for marriage*. She doesn't need to.

"Not on purpose," I say, and I sound lazy and slow, voice deep as the ocean. "And I'd done... other things. Before." Even though we just fucked halfway in public, I can feel my face heating at the admission. Jesus Christ. Maybe someday I'll get up the nerve to say *oral sex* out loud.

"Well, you were a pleasure to deflower."

"Andi."

"How's it feel to be flower-less?"

"You *can't* call it that."

"Call it what, deflowering?'

I sigh and try to make it sound as annoyed as I can when my brain is floating a foot above my skull.

"Cherry popping," she offers, and now she's definitely laughing. "Ooh. You swiped your v-card. Your virtue has been—"

I turn around and kiss her, both of us laughing, to shut her up.

THIRTY-THREE

ANDI

THE NEXT MORNING we sleep in and then I make extra-sure that Gideon has been properly deflowered when I get on top and ride him until he's incoherent, then slow down and get myself off before I finally let him finish. We're both loud and his bed frame isn't the quietest, but I'm drunk on the sight of Gideon beneath me, the way his arms flex as he grabs my thighs, the way he throws his head back into the pillow.

It makes me fiercely possessive. It makes me want to fuck him slowly while he's got that glazed-over look on his face and ask him who he belongs to. Whether anyone else has made him feel this good. I *know* virginity is a bullshit social construct—I *know*—but despite that there's a lazily pleased part of my lizard brain that his belongs to me now.

Which it doesn't, because it doesn't exist, and also, I'm not a feudal lord in Medieval Europe and that's not how any of this *works*, but I get to think dumb things during sex, okay?

"There's something else I should tell you," Gideon murmurs a little while later. Neither of us has moved, his face in his pillow, one hand splayed above my belly button, one leg twined around mine.

"You're secretly a porn star," I say, which is the first thing that comes to mind because, again, sex makes me dumb sometimes.

Gideon lifts his head just enough to frown at me.

"Did I somehow give you that impression?"

"No?" I say, and good thing I'm already flushed from exertion or I'd be blushing. If I ever meet God, I'm going to ask him why I've got no problem *performing* all manner of blush-worthy acts, but the second I try to talk about them I'm embarrassed to death. "I mean. It would be surprising. Given that until yesterday you hadn't..."

"If you use the phrase *v card* again—"

"Had intercourse," I finish, and stick my tongue out at him.

"There are plenty of kinds of porn," he points out, which, yes, true.

"Gideon," I say. "Either tell me you've been in pornography so I can go watch it or tell me whatever you were going to tell me."

He sighs hard, squirms a little.

"I had a vasectomy four years ago."

It's not *I'm a porn star*, but it's surprising enough that I have to think about it for a moment.

"They let you do that?" Is what I finally say. Gideon's expression doesn't change, sideways on the pillow. "Wait, is that why your ...semen... is sort of..." I make a hand gesture that I hope conveys *not quite the usual consistency.*

"Oh. Yeah," he says, blushing. "That happens."

I'd just thought maybe he was really well hydrated or something.

"It took some convincing," he goes on. "I had to find someone who was willing to perform one on a single guy in his twenties and sign a lot of forms."

313

"So, you *really* don't want kids," I say.

"I really don't," he says, and then takes a deep breath and finally closes his eyes, lashes dark against his cheeks. "So, if you really do, this probably won't work."

I've thought about having kids. Of course, I've thought about having kids; find me a woman in her thirties who isn't deeply aware of the possibility. At some point everything we're told flips from *you're too young, not yet* to *your eggs are going to dry up and then you'll be a tragedy*, and there's shockingly little space between the two things. One minute it's irresponsible and the next the clock is ticking, louder with every second that you don't have a man, a house, a dog and whatever else childrearing is supposed to require.

It's something I've never fully decided. I've never had the urge but I always figured that maybe I would, with the right person, the right circumstances.

Or maybe not. More than anything, this feels like relief.

"I never really did," I say. Gideon opens his eyes and narrows them at me, looking thoughtful and pensive, his thumb stroking over my belly. It kind of tickles.

"No?" he asks. "I know it's a lot to bring up this early, but I don't want to trick you, or trap you, or waste your time."

"You are *anything* but a waste of time."

"You know what I mean." I do, as if falling for someone and sharing kisses and lying tangled in sheets and all the moments in between is a waste if it's not leading to a goal. As if Gideon in all his delicate, brawny glory is nothing but a means to an end.

"I'm not as sure as you are," I admit, and he huffs a tiny laugh. "But you're, like, *very* sure."

"I know," he says, and rolls onto his back so he can look at the ceiling, muted sunlight pouring through a window. His bedroom's on the second floor of his house, and when it's late morning and beautiful like this, it feels like we're lying in the sky. "I've always known. I remember being six and thinking that I never wanted kids."

Six. I had no idea he was thinking about this when he was six. I was thinking about tutus and dinosaurs.

"You decided when you were that young?" I ask. I'm thinking, *when we still knew each other?*

"More or less," he says. "Back then it wasn't *I think I should get a vasectomy,* but I knew I didn't want what my parents had."

"You knew what you wanted even then?"

"Not all the way," he says, and turns his head toward me, and in the morning light his eyes are the color of a penny that's been left out in the rain for too long, shot through with darker spokes. "Not exactly. Not everything. But I knew this." He swallows. "I knew a couple things."

I try to imagine it: being sure about something for most of your life. Understanding the shape of it early and stepping into it, comfortable and secure, not guessing and second-guessing and winding up thirty-two and still uncertain. I *think* I want to stay in Sprucevale and I *think* I'd like to be with Gideon and I *think* I don't want kids, but certainty's always eluded me.

"Oh," I finally manage to say.

"Will you promise me something?" he says. I'm on my side, watching him, and he rolls onto his back again, staring up. "That if you change your mind, you'll tell me and not drag it out? Just—make it quick and clean, okay?"

"Of course," I say, softly, then reach an arm across his chest. "Hey."

Gideon turns his head. His body follows and then he's closed the distance between us and we're kissing and it's gentle but focused, single-minded, the way Gideon does sometimes. There's teeth but they don't hurt. Not yet. When he pulls back, his fingers are still tangled in my hair.

"I think about you all the time," he admits. "I wake up thinking about you, and I go to sleep thinking about you, and I think about you when I'm driving and cooking and tying my shoelaces and brushing my teeth and—"

Gideon takes a deep breath.

"And I think about us in five years, or ten, and I know that's a little crazy, but it feels really right, Andi, so if you're going to break my heart tell me. Just promise you'll *tell* me."

And that feels like relief, too, the future splitting open and letting the sunlight in.

"Gideon, I will tell you," I promise. "But I've spent way more time thinking about you than thinking about having kids."

He kisses me again and this time it's a little harder as he rolls me onto my back, one knee between my thighs. I'm breathless when we separate again and Gideon's on top of me, on his elbows, looking down.

"There's one thing," I tell him, and he goes perfectly still, like he's anticipating a blow. I bite my lip, trying not to laugh. "We should go get tested so we can bareback."

"Oh," Gideon says, and blushes again.

· · · ★ ★ ★ ★ ★ · · ·

"IS THERE a meaningful difference between clementine and mandarin oranges?" I ask, leaning on the buggy handlebar.

"Probably," Gideon says, flicking through the list on his phone.

"What is it?"

"They taste different?"

"Do they?"

Now he's looking thoughtfully at the display of clementines that's right next to the display of mandarin oranges, probably because I had a good point.

"I can't tell them apart," he admits. "I just buy whichever one is on sale. Same with apples."

"But apples taste completely different from each other," I say, and Gideon shrugs.

"They all taste like apples."

"You can't tell me you think Granny Smith and Red Delicious apples taste the same."

"Well, no," he says, and looks up, frowning. "But all the ones in the middle..."

"Also taste different."

"Which aisle is coconut extract in?" he asks, before I can bullshit any more about apples. We're at the grocery store on Sunday afternoon for no real reason beyond the fact that Gideon needs groceries and I don't want to go back to Lucia's yet. Weekends have been like this, lately, the two of us sticking together through the lazy hours until there's a reason to leave.

I worry, sometimes, that I'm underfoot, that I'm jamming myself into the cogs of the well-oiled machine of his life. Gideon knows what he's doing and knows what he wants and here I am, a river otter bringing a birthday cake to a beaver dam. He keeps inviting me, though, so I guess beavers like birthday cake even if it's not very waterproof.

Why am I thinking about cake? Right.

"Baking aisle, probably?" I hazard. "What do you need it for?"

"Reid put it on the list."

"Does Izzy like coconut cake?"

Gideon answers me with a calm, quelling look, as if to say *leave the children and their courtship rituals alone.*

317

We're passing the yogurt and I'm wondering if I should grab some of the Greek stuff Lucia likes when someone says Gideon's name. He freezes like a rabbit.

"What luck running into you here," says a middle-aged woman, coming up to us. Behind her is a young woman with her hair in a ponytail who is very, very studiously reading a shopping list.

"Hi, Mrs. Russell," Gideon says. He hasn't moved a muscle. "How are you?"

"You remember my daughter, Trish," she says, and looks over her shoulder at the girl who is now bright pink and staring at a grocery list like maybe she can fall into it, like the books in *Myst*. "*Trish*," the woman says, between her teeth.

This cannot be happening again. It's Sunday, so I guess Gideon's parents must have sounded the alarm on Gideon's alleged singleness again, but seriously? I step up beside Gideon, keep my mouth shut, and offer a polite smile.

"I believe we've met," Gideon says, all lovely, perfect manners. "This is my girlfriend, Andi, who I'm dating. Exclusively."

I almost start laughing with the sweet awkwardness of it.

"Hi," I offer, as Mrs. Russell's smile goes a bit brittle.

"Nice to meet you," she says. "That must be a recent development."

"Oh, not that recent," I say, five percent too cheerful.

"It's been a little while," Gideon says, taking my hand.

"I guess word hasn't gotten around yet, though," I add. He squeezes my fingers. "Which is weird, because normally news gets around *very* quickly."

Behind her, Trish hazards a faintly amused look in our direction.

"Well, Gideon, I just wanted to let you know that my home is open to you if you'd ever like to come for dinner," she says. "Trish here makes *wonderful* homemade sourdough. She captured the starter herself and everything."

Trish looks pained at this characterization of bread making.

"That's not quite how it works," she says, and her mom laughs a laugh that's not fully sincere.

"Oh, Patricia," she says. "Anyway, lovely to see you, Gideon, and nice to meet you—"

There's a blank space where my name is probably supposed to go, and she fills it with a smile before heading into the cereal aisle.

"I don't remember discussing exclusivity," I say, and get to watch Gideon's face go through several expressions before settling on *slightly frowny*. "My other boyfriends might be sad about it."

Gideon just huffs, tosses some cheese into the cart, and shoots me a frowny look.

"Come on, we still haven't found coconut extract," he grumbles. "Also, you're not funny."

I just grin and kiss him on the cheek.

THIRTY-FOUR

GIDEON

"THEY DON'T *KNOW,*" I'm telling Reid after dinner as he clears the table and I scrub a pot.

"No shit," he says.

"They don't know her," I go on, because I started telling him about this and now I can't stop. "They don't know anything about us. They don't know—"

I cut myself off, because I can't bring myself to say *that we're in love* or *how she makes everything brighter* or *sometimes it feels like I've been underwater for years and now I'm surfacing in the sunlight* in front of my little brother. Seems awkward.

"—fucking anything," is what I say out loud.

"Yeah," he says, and puts two glasses on the counter more aggressively than is really warranted. "No *shit.*"

"Try not to break things."

"Are they broken?"

"Not *yet,*" I snap, scrubbing harder. At this rate I might scrub directly through the stainless steel, which would fucking serve this pot right for getting cheese burnt onto it like this.

"Don't get pissed at me because our parents are assholes,"

he says, and there's more clinking near the table, and I grind my teeth together and rinse the stupid pot and put it into the dish drain.

Then I shut the water off and lean over the sink and force myself to take several deep breaths because, as always, I'm the adult here. Even when I don't really want to be. Even when I want to pick stupid fights and storm out of rooms and let someone else come after me to calm me down, that's not how it is.

"Sorry," I say, after a minute.

Reid walks over and—gently—puts two plates and silver-ware on the counter.

"It's okay," he says. "I know how bad they can be."

I turn and lean my back against the sink, fold my arms over my chest, glare at the opposite wall and feel guilty because of course Reid knows how awful they can be. He knows better than me. He probably knows better than anyone.

"I wish they weren't," I tell him. He snorts.

"Well," he says. "If wishes were fishes."

That one hangs in the air for a long moment.

"What?" I finally ask.

"It's a kids' book or something," Reid says, like I'm the weird one. "If wishes were fishes they'd swim away. Or whatever."

I give my brother a long, scrutinizing look, because I'm pretty sure he's just making up some bullshit.

"This is how they are," he finally says. "You know they're not gonna change."

"I know."

"Sorry you couldn't get them to."

"That's not what I'm trying to do," I say. "I'm not stupid."

Reid shifts on his feet, and now we're both leaning against

the counter and staring at the opposite wall, having this conversation without looking at each other.

"I mean," he says, and pauses. "Isn't it, though?"

There's another, longer silence, and I think about telling him he's wrong again but I don't bother. Dolly walks in, tail held high, and begins casually examining a spot on the floor.

"I just don't get it," I say. "I don't get how they can be like this and think this shit and it doesn't eat them alive." I'm gesturing vaguely in Reid's direction, and I mean how they're treating Andi, but I also mean Elliott, and I mean Reid, and I mean Sadie, and I mean every time they've forced their will on one of us with the weight of their disapproval.

"They're not you," he says, and thank you, Reid, for your brilliant insight. "You always wanted to be there for us more than you wanted to be right, and they'd rather be right."

I finally turn to look at him.

"You've thought about this," I say, a little surprised.

"*Yeah*," he says, all sarcasm and bluster. I tap into my reserve well of patience. "My parents basically kicked me out when I was fifteen and I moved in with my annoying brother, I've thought about it once or twice."

"Annoying? Seriously?"

"I've listened to your lecture about how to load the dishwasher *so many times*, dude," he says. "And then you adopted this giant murder cat—"

"Mrrp?" says Dolly, from where she's sitting on the floor. We both narrow our eyes at her.

"—you see?" Reid says, voice hushed, like it proved something. "Murder cat."

"You were telling me how annoying it was that I let you live with me."

Reid grins the same impish grin he's had since he was a toddler.

"Sorry," he says, not looking sorry in the least. "But, yeah. This is who they are. I was kinda hoping they'd never, like, point the beam directly at you but I guess they did. Or at Andi but that kinda seems like the same thing." He's looking away again, doing the thing where he acts like something doesn't hurt him but it does. I let him get away with it.

"I didn't think they would," I tell him, and push my fingers through my hair. I need a haircut. "That obvious, huh?"

"Andi?"

"Yeah."

I swear to god there is an *audible* eye roll.

"She's only over here basically every night and you're only texting her *all the time* and everything you say is 'Andi this' and 'Andi that'—"

"Okay, thank you."

"—and you get all *goopy* when she's around—"

I *glare* at that asshole.

"The other day you giggled."

"The hell I did."

Reid shrugs.

"Get as mad as you want, we both know the truth. She's cool, though. I like her."

That statement shouldn't make me nearly as happy as it does, so I try to hide it.

"She's good for you. I'm glad you've got her."

He's staring at the opposite wall again, braced against the counter, and in a sudden rush I realize that Reid is trying to take care of me. Sort of.

Reid's moving on, sooner or later. Probably sooner. He's been working and saving up and going to classes at the community college up in Blythe, and I know he's borderline desperate to get out of Sprucevale. I can't blame him.

But—he's been worried about leaving me alone when he

moves on, and that sudden realization feels a little like hairline cracks in my heart. It feels like I'm in a snow globe, flipped over and quickly righted, waiting for everything to settle.

"Yeah," I say, wondering what just happened. "Me too."

· · · ★ ★ ★ ★ ★ · · ·

"WHAT IF," Andi says, thoughtfully, waving a single french fry through the air, "you just told them about the vasectomy?"

I fight the urge to look around and see if anyone around us heard, but they're all either talking to each other or watching the basketball game on various screens around the bar.

"If I told who?" I ask, although my brain is helpfully supplying me with an endless stream of names about who she could possibly mean.

"The people who keep trying to give you six goats and a Chevy as their daughters' dowry."

"I'd never accept a Chevy as payment. At least not one being given away."

Andi grins, leaning her head on one hand, hair spilling over her knuckles and down her forearm. It's late, cold and raining outside, a Wednesday night, but I hadn't seen her in a few days and I wanted to. She'd agreed to cover a Chamber of Commerce meeting for the paper, so I offered to meet her at the only place still open at nine-thirty.

"Gideon," she says. "Don't tell me you're a Ford Motors loyalist or whatever. I'd have to rethink *everything*."

"I drive a Toyota," I tell her, the very picture of patience. "I don't *want* another car, and I especially don't want whatever rust heap one of my parents' friends would give away."

"That's actually a good point," she concedes.

"I also don't want their daughters."

"The goats, though," she says, and I can't help but smile

because she's not wrong. The goats are the only thing in that bargain I'd half-consider; the Chevy is an outright no and while I'm sure the daughters are lovely, nice young women, they don't interest me.

Also, no one has actually offered me a dowry. My parents and their church friends might have archaic attitudes about a lot of things, but I don't *think* they actually pay people in livestock to take their daughters off their hands.

"Goats can be useful," I admit. Then I remember what we're talking about. "Wait. Did I tell you about that?"

"Did someone literally offer you goats and a Chevy?" she asks, sitting up a little straighter.

"No," I tell her. "Would you stop—they're not *that* bad."

Andi raises one eyebrow and eats another french fry.

"Just more dinner offers," I mutter. "That sort of thing."

Since I last saw Andi, it's been two voicemails and one email. I responded promptly to the email but haven't tackled the voicemails yet because talking on the telephone can go fuck itself.

"Would they stop if they knew you weren't having kids? Could be an easy out," she says, and she's trying to sound casual but there's something about the way she's holding her shoulders, the set of her mouth, that makes me reach across the narrow table and tap the underside of her wrist with one fingertip.

"Hey," I say, and she looks at me, and I was about to say *there's no number of goats I'd rather have than you,* but the words shrivel up on my tongue. The look on her face is like ice over a river that might not hold; it seems sturdy but there's a lot swirling underneath.

"I'm not interested, so they'll get bored and move on to someone else soon, once I say *no* enough times," I tell her. My fingertip is sliding across her wrist, warm and soft. A tendon flexes, and I run my finger down it. "Though if I tell anyone about the vasectomy, they'd tell my parents instantly."

"They don't know?"

God, the thought of it. I snort.

"Fuck no. They'd be furious."

Andi's quiet, watching my finger on her wrist.

"Why?" she finally asks, and I can tell from her tone of voice that she thinks it's incredibly weird. I can't blame her. I'm not even sure I can explain myself.

"Because they think there's a right way to live and a wrong way," I say. "And the right way is exactly like them and the wrong way is everything else. They think I'm still trying for the right way and just... haven't made it yet."

"And if you told them, they'd know you were wrong," she says, and I sigh.

"Something like that," I admit. "And I'd rather—it's better for everyone if they don't know. They're happy, I'm happy, I can help when my brothers and sisters fuck up. Besides, they're a little nicer when they pity me for not being able to achieve the life they think I want."

I say that last part with a small, secret smile on my face. Andi doesn't share it, two fingertips now drawing circles on the inside of her wrist. I watch them for a moment, and when I look back at her, Andi's looking at me so intently I feel pinned to the booth behind me.

"What?"

She blinks and shakes her head.

"Nothing."

"Andi."

"Gideon."

I tap her wrist again. "Tell me."

She sighs, and makes a face, and scrunches her nose the

way she does when she doesn't want to say something but is going to anyway.

"I wish it weren't like that," she says. "I wish you could tell them about whatever life you want."

"It's this."

There's a beat of silence as Andi and I look at each other. I did mean to say it, but I didn't realize the weight it would have until it was out of my mouth already, hurtling across the table. I didn't realize that I'd feel like my heart went with it, out of my chest and into the air where anything at all can come along and damage it.

Andi watches me. She doesn't say anything. I don't, either, and finally she slides her hand into mine, raises them to her lips, and kisses my knuckles. I can't help but smile and blush and feel brand-new in this world, because there are *people* and we're in *public* but I don't stop her. I'd never stop her.

"Thank you," I say, and she shrugs, but strokes the knuckles she just kissed with the pad of one thumb.

· · · · · ★ ★ ★ ★ · · · ·

I THINK about it for days, and finally settle on: I can tell them something. It doesn't have to be everything. I can ask for mercy in some small way, and it will be granted, and everything can carry on almost as before, the delicate balance we've found not altered too greatly.

I've earned some kind of concession. This one small thing. Surely.

· · · · · ★ ★ ★ ★ · · · ·

"WE'LL PRAY ON IT," my father says. Standing in front of the stove, my mother doesn't say anything. I've still got my outdoor coat on, my hands in the pockets because they're clenched into fists. Elliott would hire security guards.

"That's not what I asked," I say, and the steadiness of my voice surprises me. It gets my father to look up from whatever he's reading on the table and give me a long, level look. "I asked you to stop. Not to pray about whether you should stop."

"And I said we'd pray on it," he repeats, and stands slowly, his hands still on the table in front of him. "I don't appreciate my own son thinking he can walk into my home and tell me what to do."

When I was four and he was three, I hit my brother Matt with a toy fire engine. He got a black eye and I got the first spanking I can remember when my father got home from work that afternoon.

I remember how much it hurt. I remember how hard I cried and how much I tried not to. I remember Matt watching from the floor in front of the chair where my father was sitting. I remember that Elliott, still a baby, started crying at the noise and my father was annoyed about that, too.

But the thing I'm thinking of, right now, is that when I thought it was over, I had to sit on his lap, give him a hug, and thank him. If it wasn't sincere enough, I'd get spanked a few more times, and over the years, I was plenty insincere.

I'm grown and he hasn't laid a hand on me in decades, but that queasy feeling is still there, the uncertainty over whether he'll hit me or not. The unsettling, unmooring knowledge that if he did, I'd stand here and take it. My mother, as always, is at the kitchen counter, her back to us.

"It's a waste of everyone's time and effort," I say, my voice still steady. "I'm already seeing Andi and I'm not interested in going on other dates."

"It's true, then," my father says. "I'd heard a rumor but I

thought, no, if Gideon were serious about someone, he'd tell us himself. Your sister at least had the respect to do that."

Something clatters on the counter, and we both look over, but there's no sign of it. Just my mother's back.

"It's serious," I tell him. "Now you know. Please stop trying to set me up on dates."

"You'll thank us," my mother says suddenly, and I turn. She's never hit me—not really, not more than a smack here and there—but she knew how to wield the power and terror of our father. It was up to her what he heard about and what he didn't, and up to her what counted as a grave misdeed and what counted as *boys being boys*. She chose which injuries and tears she'd soothe and which she wouldn't.

"Pardon?" I ask, when she doesn't go on.

"We're doing you a favor, sweetheart," she says, and turns, wiping her hands on a tea towel. She comes and puts a hand on my shoulder. "Girls like her don't know how to be with a good man," she says. The compliment, that I'm a good man, thrills me and I hate myself for it.

"But we're glad you're finally showing interest," my father goes on. "Listen, son, this thing won't last, but once it's over you'll be ready to find someone right for you and settle down."

"Girls like *what*," I say.

"You know," my mom sighs. "Here, sit down, I've got some—"

"No. I don't know."

"Gideon," my father says sharply. "Don't talk to your mother that way."

"You don't know her," I say, and I wish my voice weren't so tight. I wish I could control it better. "You don't know anything about her."

"Of course we do," my mother says, and she's got the gentlest face and the gentlest eyes, and even though I've got at least five inches on her my heart is pounding with a deep, instinctual fear. "She's been prancing around like a tart since she was in diapers. With those parents it's a miracle she's not selling her body on the streets by now, or worse."

It doesn't take much to make me speechless, and that over-does it by a mile. I stare at my mother, all soft smiles and a warm hand on my shoulder, and in silent desperation I look over at my father, who shrugs.

"We were so grateful when the Lord laid it on their heart to move away," he says, and I feel like my brain might implode.

"Don't," I say, the only word I can think of. I back away from my mother's grasp, and she frowns, and it's her frown but it's Reid's frown and Sadie's frown and I have to look away. "Don't you fucking dare say that about her."

My mother gasps and my father snarls, *"Gideon!* Apologize."

I inhale and automatically my mouth makes the shape of *sorry,* but it sticks in my throat. I swallow it, and there's no replacement.

I wish there was. I want to come up with something biting and clever to defend Andi. I want to laugh at their astonishing ignorance and I want them to understand how wrong they are, how perfectly fucking wrong, but I can't summon anything. I just stand there like I've been struck.

"Excuse me," I finally tell them, turn, and walk out of their house.

· · · · ★ ★ ★ · · · ·

I GO HOME and don't tell anyone what happened. Not Andi. Not Reid. I know, all at once, that it's not my fault and that there's no good reason to feel so ashamed about it, but at the same time, the guilt feels like a heavy coat on my shoulders, a scarf around my neck. At least it's still winter.

· · · · · ★ ★ ★ · · · · ·

THE NEXT NIGHT I'm elbow-deep in the dishwater when there's a knock on the door. I thought Andi couldn't come over —some volunteer thing at the library—but maybe it got canceled. Shit. Do I have to tell her? Will she know?

"I'll get it," Reid says, and heads off. The door opens and then slams shut half a second later, and I've just turned my head to see what's going on when Reid reappears, shoulders hunched and expression locked down. Every alarm bell in my head starts going off.

"Matt," he says, jerking his head toward the door and disappearing further into the house.

"The fuck does he want?" I mutter, but Reid doesn't answer.

Matt's still there, looking annoyed on the porch, holding a cardboard box. We haven't been on the best terms these last few years.

"Yes?" I ask, and have to bite back an automatic *would you like to come in*?

"Mom and Dad asked if I'd bring this over," he says, hefting the box a little. "Some things of yours from their house."

He's got on a polo shirt and khaki pants under an unzipped winter coat, a wedding ring, and a *you're getting in trouble* smirk on his face. I'm not jealous of him. I haven't been jealous of him in years, not since we were kids and I couldn't do anything right and he couldn't do anything wrong.

"Why?"

"They asked me to tell you not to contact them until you

apologize," he says, and the smirk deepens. "What did you *say?*"

They—what? Until I apologize? I nearly ask if it's a joke, but Matt has never been funny in his life.

"C'mon, it's heavy," he says. I take it without thinking.

"They don't want me to contact them? That's what they said?"

"Yes," Matt says, like he's annoyed. "Dad was pretty angry, so I'd wait a few days."

"I'm not apologizing."

For the first time, Matt looks uneasy. We watch each other in silence.

"You know they're not gonna come around," he says, voice lowered. "They haven't talked to—" he nods at my house, "—in three years."

It's the nod that snaps me out of it, the way he won't even say Reid's name.

"I know," I say, stepping back, and then: "Thank you," by accident.

Matt's frowning as I shove the front door shut, and then stand there. I stare down at the box without seeing it because —don't contact them? *Don't contact them?* Outside, footsteps fade, and I finally breathe again because of all people, I don't need Matt around for this. Fuck, I don't need anyone around for this, for—my *parents.* Jesus.

My fingertips are going cold where I'm clutching the bottom of the box, and I don't know what happened. I *know,* of course, I was there, but I don't understand. I was so sure I had more runway between *don't call my girlfriend a whore* and *we'll talk again when you apologize.* Or maybe I was further along on the runway than I thought, for the crimes of sheltering Reid and defending Sadie and still talking to Elliott. For not coming to Christmas. For not settling and not reproducing and never being sorry enough for any of it.

Seems like it should take more, though, for your own parents to stop talking to you, or maybe this is all much more and much worse than I thought because—how can you do something so wrong that *your own parents* won't pick up the phone?

They haven't spoken to Reid since they learned he'd come out and they haven't talked to Elliott for much longer than that, but that's because my parents are assholes. I thought I'd threaded that needle just enough to stay on everyone's good side, enough that I can be there for everyone who needs me, but—fuck. *Fuck*, now I can't even do that, I can't—

"He gone?" Reid asks, floating half into the doorway like a jeans-and-hoodie-wearing specter. He's got his hands shoved into the hoodie pocket and dark hair just long enough to get into his eyes, and he looks at the closed front door like there's a leopard behind it. Reid's short for a man, and he always will be, and right now his face is still more delicate and angular than mine, like it's always been. It took a year, but this summer he's finally got an appointment at the gender clinic in Richmond to start hormone therapy. I already took the day off work so I can drive him; Richmond is an all-day trip from Sprucevale. It's another thing I won't be able to tell my parents, because my parents won't talk to me.

"Matt, I mean," Reid clarifies, frowning, and I realize I haven't answered. I clear my throat.

"Yeah, coast is clear," I say, but he keeps frowning.

"What'd he want?"

"Nothing."

"You're holding a box."

He's right. I am. "Uh," I start. Fuck me, I can't even think. "Mom and Dad are cleaning out the attic, I guess."

Reid stands up a little straighter, eyes narrowing, but he's silent. I'm silent. The house is silent. Possibly, the world is silent.

"You okay?" he finally asks, at least a year later. "You look —" he pulls a hand out of his hoodie pocket and waves it in my direction.

Of all people, Reid would understand. Of all people, Reid would never blame me. He might even know the right thing to say.

"I'm good," I say, and head for the stairs, box still in my hands. "Just Matt."

"Ugh," he agrees, and disappears.

THIRTY-FIVE

ANDI

I HEAD up Gideon's driveway with my backpack over my shoulder, ninety-nine percent sure I'm welcome. Why wouldn't I be? He's my boyfriend. I'm his girlfriend, a fact that he's made hilariously clear to several hopeful matchmakers. We like seeing each other and he's been explicitly clear that my presence is always welcome—*just come over whenever, quit asking like you think it's an imposition*—so, what the hell, final one percent?

I knock on his door because he hates the doorbell and tell myself that just because he's been quieter via text and a bit monosyllabic doesn't mean I'm being too much and I need to back off or something. He's been working a lot. He said so.

It takes Gideon so long to answer the door that I almost knock again. The way the look on his face goes from thunderous to relieved when he sees me is... weird.

"Surprise!" I say, holding my arms out like a muppet, and finally, I get a smile. "School board postponed their meeting again."

"Hi," he says, and looks so quietly pleased that I forget what I was all in my head about. He lets me in and we kiss hello, chaste

335

and then a little deeper until I'm chasing his mouth when he pulls away. "Reid," he mutters, tilting his head toward the living room.

"Reid's seen it before," I point out. "Didn't he grow up with farm animals?"

"One, no," Gideon says, and then ghosts his hand to my face and gives me another sweet, thorough kiss. "And two, the only farm animals we ever had were chickens, and that's not a flattering comparison."

I laugh, lean in, kiss him. We're practically whispering. His beard is very soft and I like it.

"Is there a farm animal that *would* be a flattering comparison?" I ask, and something occurs to me. "Ooh, like stallions."

"They don't tend to be very generous lovers."

"Really? I thought that's exactly what they were known for."

Now he's blushing and glancing at the living room again, like Reid's never heard a sex joke in his life.

"It's one thing to be..." Gideon makes a gesture that probably means *hung like a horse*. "It's another to be good at it."

"So which animals *are* good in bed? I read somewhere that pig orgasms last half an hour."

"Not because pigs are good lovers," he says, his hand making its way down to my waist. "That's also more of an urban legend than anything. Sometimes, in the right conditions, some types of pigs will *mate* for that amount of time—"

"THAT'S ANDI, RIGHT?" an invisible Reid calls.

"Yeah!" I call back, then give Gideon one more quick kiss. "Tell me all the details about how pigs fuck later."

He closes his eyes, briefly, which is probably the correct reaction. I head toward the kitchen, where something smells good. From the next room, I can hear Reid saying, "*Quit* it, jeez," so I poke my head in.

"Don't *poke* me," he's saying as he looks up. He's cross-legged on the couch, in jeans and an oversized hoodie, and Dolly has one paw on his leg and one raised in the air, almost touching his chest. Reid's got one hand free and one holding a giant, floppy *Norton Anthology of American Literature* with a creased cover, frayed edges, and a bright yellow USED sticker on the spine. "Oh. Hey."

"Hi," I say. "Uh, you guys okay?"

In answer, Dolly maintains eye contact with me and pushes her paw into Reid's chest. He grumbles.

"Fine," he says, and then, "Just get in my lap or whatever, god, quit it with the weird mind games."

"Just pet her," I say.

Reid gives me a look as though I've suggested something unforgivable.

"That's just what she wants me to do," he mutters. "Then she'll think she can get *on* me, and do that weird purr-nuzzle where she kind of bites my hand, and when she gets really happy and starts kneading. Her claws are so fucking huge, you don't even know. Oh! Hey! GIDEON!"

Dolly's claws come out at the sudden volume increase, and Reid inhales sharply.

"Yeah?"

"We got mail. It's from Elliott. You should read it."

"Oh, is it his save the date?"

"Read it! *Ow*, you monster." Dolly chirps, and I leave her and Reid to their negotiations.

In the kitchen, Gideon's frowning at an off-white envelope addressed to Mr. Gideon Bell and Mr. Reid Bell, and even though I haven't seen Elliott in twenty years, I like him already.

When Gideon pulls the card out, a second piece of paper

flutters to the ground. For a long moment he looks at the card, then picks up the slip of paper and reads it.

"June twenty-first," he says, then glances up at me. Suddenly, I don't know where to put my hands. Gideon clears his throat. "You busy?"

"On June twenty-first?"

"This says I get a plus one," he says, and looks back at the card. "If you'd—um. Like to come. It's in Boston."

This is definitely quiet and subdued, even for Gideon, and it's making me wonder if something is wrong and if I'm the something, so I plaster on my smiliest smile and beam at him.

"Sure!" I enthuse. "Sounds great!"

"Did you see the note?" hollers Reid. Gideon rolls his eyes and glances at the other piece of paper again.

"What's he want?" Gideon hollers backs.

"You know you could go into the same room," I point out.

"Call him and find out," Reid says, ignoring my great suggestion. "Do it now!"

Gideon frowns at the paper, then frowns at me, then frowns in the general direction of Reid.

"Later," he tells me, shoving the note into his pocket, and then he smiles but it doesn't quite reach his eyes. "You hungry?"

· · · · ★ ★ ★ ★ ★ · · · ·

"HOW JEALOUS SHOULD I be of these prayer requests?" I ask Gideon a few days later, my head against his arm. I push one toe against the railing of his back porch, and the swing we're sitting in wobbles a little.

He grunts as an answer. He's been doing that a lot this week. I try not to get anxious about this one, but it feels like something is up and I hate it.

"And how come there's a huge hullabaloo over Sadie getting laid and nothing but passive-aggressive matchmaking attempts for you?" I go on.

"You know why," he says.

"They can't possibly think we're not fucking," I say, and Gideon turns the faintest pink. I can't help how much it delights me. "I mean, look at you."

That gets a huff and the world's tiniest smile, so I reach down and squeeze his right thigh. It's warm for late February, somewhere in the upper fifties, and Gideon insists he saw a golden eagle yesterday and wants me to see it, too.

"I don't know what they think," Gideon admits. "And I don't particularly care."

"Beyond people trying to set you up with their virginal daughters who bake cherry pies and know how to knit socks," I say, then swallow because shit, that came out differently than I meant it. Or, worse, maybe it didn't.

"Andi," Gideon says, and now he's frowning, and I feel like an asshole.

"Sorry."

There's a very long silence, and, fuck. I feel like I'm doing nothing but making waves in Gideon's life, and not the fun surfing kind, the violent kind with too much seaweed and flood the ground floor of vacation homes. I should keep my mouth shut about cherry pie.

"I talked to my parents about it," he finally says. Oh. There's another long pause. "I don't know if it'll help."

"You didn't have to," I blurt. "I mean, you're gonna have to do worse than that to make me jealous."

Gideon's frown just deepens. He was supposed to laugh. Shit.

"Well, they can't just do this," he finally mutters, and looks away, over the brown and gray of his winter back yard.

"I don't know how to bake a cherry pie," I say, because it's the only thing I can think of.

Gideon shrugs. "I do," he says. "It's not hard. You could learn, no problem."

We swing for a moment, watching the trees. We're supposed to be looking for eagles out here, all bundled up, swinging. Nothing moves.

"Or I could make all the cherry pies and you could mix all the cocktails and we could call it even," he says. "Which they'll never understand."

"That you can bake?"

"That I'm not missing some key ingredient of my life," he says. "They think I've been lonely this whole time and I'm with you because I finally got desperate and you were available, but I never was. I liked being alone until you showed up."

He swallows and looks over at me.

"And then I liked being with you," he says, and it sounds so simple when he does, like he'll never get tired of navigating the whirlpool-riddled channel between me, our shared past, and his family. Of *me*.

"I told my parents that we were dating and that you're not Steve Wheeler," I say, just to change the subject slightly.

"And?"

"And they took it pretty well. We talked about Captain America for a little while."

He lifts one eyebrow.

"They confused Steve Wheeler with Steve Rogers," I explain. "It was a whole thing, they're ridiculous."

"I always liked them," Gideon admits. He doesn't look at me. "I wasn't supposed to, but I did."

"They're not angry at you."

I think it's true. It feels true, even though I didn't ask them outright. When we talked they were clearly a little hesitant about Gideon, even though they're too supportive to say that to me. They'll come around. Gideon's looking out over his back yard again, green eyes darting from tree to tree, his hair a little too long and curling at the ends.

"I cleaned out a drawer in my dresser," he says, and glances over at me. "I was thinking that maybe, you spend a lot of time here, if you wanted, you could just keep some clothes here. It seems easier."

"A whole drawer?" I ask, and I can't help but smile.

"And some closet space," he grumbles.

Since being in the cabin with Gideon I've learned way more about bird mating behavior than I ever expected to. There are birds like peacocks, all bright plumage and displays of puffery. There are birds like grouse, who do calls and dances. And then there are bowerbirds, who spend days carefully crafting the perfect nest, hoping to bring their mate home.

"Can I have a hook on the key rack?" I ask, and he sighs dramatically.

"I guess," he says, so I lean over and kiss him on the cheek.

THIRTY-SIX

GIDEON

BEAST SEATS herself at my feet and looks up expectantly as I put a tortilla chip in my mouth. After a moment, her front feet wiggle impatiently and she blinks once.

"They're tortilla chips," I tell her. "You're a cat."

"Barry likes chips," Wyatt says. He's leaning on the kitchen island next to me, on the other side of Beast, also looking down. "And if I leave bread out she'll tear through a plastic bag to get to it? Especially pitas, for some reason. That can't be normal."

"I promise your cat isn't normal," I tell him, still watching Beast watch me. "She has a hidden nest of rubber bands."

"I should find her new one," Wyatt muses, taking a long drink of root beer. "I found a bunch a month or two ago and cleaned it out, so she's probably got another stash by now."

Dolly, alone among her family, is a completely normal cat. Beast, her mother, likes to lick the shower curtain while it's wet. Zorro, her brother, is obsessed with knocking things off the counter. Barry has a rubber band problem. All Dolly has ever done is enter into a long-standing psychological cold war with my little brother, which is perfectly acceptable cat behavior.

"You shouldn't feed her people food," I tell Silas, who's fussing over something at the counter in his kitchen.

"I don't *feed* her people food," he says over his shoulder. "Sometimes she *takes* people food. Also, Kat's still a little too nervous to admonish her properly, so she gets away with a lot."

"Tell Kat to take a firm disciplinary hand," I say, and Wyatt snickers. Silas turns and throws something at him—a mushroom stem, turns out—and Wyatt yelps when it hits him in the face.

"What if I were allergic?" he says. He bends down to pick it up, but has to wait until Beast is finished sniffing it.

"You're not."

"You don't know that."

"You ate mushroom pizza *last week*. Yes, I do."

"Adults can develop allergies," Wyatt says as Beast decides the mushroom isn't for her and goes back to watching me. "It happened to my sister. She's allergic to cantaloupe now."

There's the sound of Silas's front door shutting, and a few moments later, Javier brings the cold air into the kitchen with him.

"Cantaloupe? Bummer," he says, putting a box on the counter. "Though it turns out I'm allergic to pineapple? I just thought it made everyone's mouth itchy."

I give him a long, slightly disbelieving look as he shrugs off his coat and I dip another chip into the guacamole.

"You thought all people routinely ate a food that made them *itch*," I say, just to confirm. Javier shrugs and then grins at me, bright and easy, his dark hair down around his shoulders.

"People like spicy food and that makes you hurt," he points out. "Honestly, the itching seems less weird."

We all think about that for a moment, and Silas upends a cutting board into a pot on the stove, scraping it with a kitchen knife that's slightly too large for my personal comfort. Then he checks some things, wipes his hands on a towel, and comes over to the island with the rest of us.

"Okay, Javi's here, *finally*," he says, and Javier rolls his eyes, mouthing *five minutes*. It was fifteen, but Javier will be Javier. "Gideon, tell us this boat story you've been teasing."

· · · ★ ★ ★ ★ ★ · · ·

WHEN I FINISH, we're in Silas's living room. Wyatt and Javier are sharing the couch, Silas is in one armchair, and I'm in another, Beast sprawled on my lap. It'll give Dolly something to think about later.

"Your family's buckwild," Wyatt finally says. He has no fucking idea.

"James is still alive, right?" Silas asks. "Someone's checked in on him? Gotten visual confirmation?"

"He's fine," I say.

"I thought *my* family was a lot," Javier says.

"Different kinds of *a lot*," Wyatt says. "Though if I were banging your sister, I wouldn't get on a boat with your dad."

There's a beat of silence. I've only told them about Sadie's problems and the resulting talk I had to have with my idiot brother Zach. It's funny, sort of. From a certain angle. My brain keeps making the shape of *I made my parents stop speaking to me* but it never comes out of my mouth.

"Not that I'd bang your sister," Wyatt goes on. "I mean. Thalia's great, she's just not really my type?"

"Thanks," Javier says dryly. "Even if you were, I wouldn't

take you out onto a boat and make oblique threats about what might happen if you don't marry her."

The three of us look at each other, then all look over at Silas, who's frowning, one elbow propped on the arm of his chair.

"*What*," he says. "I didn't take him on a boat. That's fucked up. We hugged it out, like men."

"Not what I heard," I say. "I heard there was a black eye."

Silas sighs and rubs his face in his hands.

"Look, getting woken up at four-thirty in the morning by my best friend telling me he was banging my sister was not my finest moment," he admits, like we don't all know the story. "But that's way different from taking someone *out on a boat* to tell him that if he doesn't marry your sister her virtue is ruined, or whatever. I promise I don't give a shit about June's virtue."

"I assume Georgia's virtue is no longer with us," Wyatt says, looking both thoughtful and unhappy to be having this thought. "But I've never made it my business."

I scratch Beast between the ears and try very hard not to reflect on my own recent ruination. I might be blushing anyway.

"Did Zach say anything when you talked to him?" Javier asks, leaning back on the couch, hands laced atop his head. "I mean, I assume you had to talk to him."

"He promised not to do it again," I tell them. "But he also claimed it wasn't that big of a deal and James was being 'a total baby' about it, so we'll see."

I have no idea if my younger brother actually feels remorse about it or not, but he did get furious when I suggested that taking someone onto a boat and then issuing an ultimatum constituted a threat. Talking to Beth had approximately the same effect—that is, not much—and I've got a feeling that when she backs down, her twin will, too. But so far, I think Beth's too mad to back down.

"What about your parents?" Silas asks. My head snaps up and I stare at him, silent, Beast flopped over in my lap. He knows, God, somehow the rumor mill has already been at work and they all *know—*

"What about them?" I ask, forcing my mouth to start up again.

"They mad at Sadie?" he asks. "Or just *disappointed?*"

Right. Yeah. Of course. If these guys knew they wouldn't fuck around for an hour first, they'd have texted or called, they'd have come over. I know they would. I know it and I still can't say *actually, something else happened* because—well. Because.

"They're pissed," I say. Beast shoves her face into my knuckles. "And self-righteous about it. Especially since Sadie won't break up with James and re-take a purity pledge, or whatever the fuck it was they wanted her to do in the first place. And of course, Sadie and Ariel both think I can fix it, somehow."

There's silence in the room, the kind that whispers *we know all about your parents and we don't like them* because no one's going to say that out loud. I wish they would. I wish *I* would.

"At least when my dad kicked me out, my mom left him," Javier finally says, as if the events of that single sentence didn't earn him years of therapy.

"That would require my mother to ever disagree with my father. In public, at least," I say.

I've known for years that whatever my parents want in a son, I'm lacking it. I know that whatever they didn't see in me they saw in Matt, their next child, their perfect, shining example of how a son should be. I was never their favorite, never quite good enough, useful and dependable but never really *special*. I shouldn't be surprised at what's happened, not really.

Sadie was one of the golden children, and that's the real problem. When she fell out of their high esteem she fell fast and hard, and I know that must hurt.

"My offer to tell them to go fuck themselves still stands," Silas says. "You can consider it a perma-offer, even. Seems like you need it."

Despite myself, I smile.

"Thanks," I say. "I'll keep it in mind."

"Telling them off would be an honor," he says, and pushes himself out of his chair. "You guys want soup, or what?"

· · · · ★ ★ ★ ★ ★ · · · ·

A FEW HOURS LATER, after the potluck is finished and Javier, Wyatt and I are leaving Silas's house, Javier waves goodbye to Wyatt and turns to me on the street outside.

"Listen, Gideon," he says, and for someone who's usually got paint on his shirt and fidgets non-stop, he's got surprising gravity. "Parents can be really fucked up, and it's—it's fucked up how they treat you guys. But, you know, I get it. I still pick up the phone every time my dad calls, even when I swear I won't."

It's dark, past ten, the damp chill of a February night in the mountains. Clouds cover the stars and at the edges of Silas's street, bare tree branches poke against the sky like barely-visible fingers. Javier's taller than me, his hair gently lifted in a slight breeze, dark eyes and high cheekbones and a wide mouth that smiles a lot.

"Did he ever apologize?" I ask, because even though he's

talked about it plenty of times, I've never thought to ask that question.

Javier snorts and tries to smile, though it doesn't quite stick. "You think Admiral Raul Lopez apologizes?" he says, the cheer in his voice forced, too. "Nah. He'd have to think he had something to apologize *for.*"

"There it is," I say, and sigh. "Thanks. Get home safe, okay?"

Javier rolls his eyes, but now he's smiling for real as he walks toward his own car.

"You want me to text you when I get there?"

In lieu of an answer, I flip him off.

· · · · ★ ★ ★ ★ · · · ·

WHEN I EMPTY out my pockets before bed that night, Elliott's note is still in there. I still haven't called, even though Reid's hounding me, even though I know Elliott is depending on me to contact him.

It feels heavy, that note. It's been weighing on me, like I've forgotten to pull up an anchor before setting sail.

Elliott's going to ask me to tell our parents. He's going to ask me, in that careful, slightly hesitant way he has, to invite them if they seem receptive. To tell the rest of our siblings that he doesn't talk to any more. To see if some of them—any of them—might remember the brother who tucked them in at night and made perfect paper airplanes, and might want him to be their brother again.

And it'll be down to me to break the bad news to him: they don't. I tell them—told them, I guess, past tense—how he was doing, sometimes, but they never asked. I wanted them to, just once. Not that I could ask them now, either.

Fuck.

THIRTY-SEVEN

ANDI

AT THE ROUND table in the corner of Debbie's, the four of us are impressed into silence by the pies. Or maybe we're overwhelmed. It's a little hard to tell.

"Is this the amount of pie you were imagining?" Kat finally asks, breaking the silence.

"Of course," Silas says, and grins at her. "I know what eight slices of pie look like."

"You do now."

"I'm just having a moment of silence for my dream coming true at last," he says, and then kisses her on the cheek, his nose bumping her glasses. "Thanks for making it happen."

Kat manages to scrunch her face, push up her glasses, and look embarrassed and pleased, all at once. "Well, they were easy dreams," she says. "What's first?"

"I feel like we should have labeled them," Silas says.

"Too late. No one but God can help you now," I say, already sort of leaning over the table. "I think that one's key lime? And that one's chocolate for sure."

"Just pick a pie and eat it," Gideon says. "You'll get to them all eventually."

Silas leans in, tapping his fork against his lower lip, and examines each slice of pie one by one.

"Oh, for fuck's—"

"That one! Eat that one."

Silas listens to neither Gideon nor Kat, reaches all the way over the table, and selects a mystery pie. It's sort of pale and piled high with what's either meringue, whipped cream, or possibly cool whip, and it wobbles slightly as he brings it toward himself. I think Kat's trying not to laugh and Gideon's still pretending to be grumpy about how long this is taking, but it's Silas's birthday—well, his birthday week, which he's been using to his advantage—so we all tolerate him.

Silas slices a bite. He examines it. Finally, he eats it, chews thoughtfully, and doesn't seem to mind at all that three people are staring at him while he does it.

"Verdict?" Kat asks as he swallows.

"I think that was banana cream," he says. "What's our rating scale? Are we doing out of five or out of ten?"

"Five, it's easier," says Gideon, as I reach across the table and swipe a piece of what I'm pretty sure is lemon meringue.

"Three and a half stars, then."

"If you're going to give half stars, rate them out of ten," Kat says.

"Seven and a half stars," Silas says, scooping up another piece of pie and grinning at her.

Kat opens her mouth, closes it, sighs, and reaches across the table for the chocolate pie.

"You're impossible," she says.

"You like it," Silas says, looking pleased as anything with his mouth full of pie, and Kat laughs and rolls her eyes but doesn't disagree.

It's Friday night, and Debbie's Diner is pretty full, mostly with teenagers who probably have nowhere better to go in

Sprucevale. It's a little loud but in a bright, fun way that makes me think of house parties in the suburbs that I wasn't supposed to go to when I was that age and did. It's a far cry from the constant noise and light of Brooklyn, something I loved when I was younger.

I don't think I miss it, now. Sometimes I feel like I should, though.

Next to me, Gideon frowns, pointing his fork at a pie.

"That's not strawberry," he proclaims.

"What is it?"

"I don't know. An abomination," he says. "It's—grape, or something?"

Obviously, the rest of us all reach for it at once. It's sort of red-pink-purple and creamy, and I put it into my mouth while watching Gideon's face. He looks apprehensive.

It is not a good pie.

"I did warn you," he points out as I chew. I'm probably making a face.

"What *is* that?" Kat asks.

"It tastes *red*," I say, still wrinkling my nose and trying to figure out what that even means. "You know how sometimes candy or soda or whatever is strawberry or cherry or watermelon but sometimes it just tastes... red?"

"Like Gatorade," Silas says, and Kat looks profoundly unhappy.

"Right. This tastes like red pie."

Thoughtfully, Gideon pokes the remainder with his fork.

"Careful," Kat warns, and he snorts.

"Just curious," he says.

"That's pretty bad," Silas says, reaching for another bite. We all watch him put it in his mouth. "But a good kind of bad?"

"It's all yours," Gideon says, already moving on.

We eat the pies, and then we rank the pies. Silas places the red pie suspiciously high on his list, and I'm pretty sure he's doing it to get under Kat's skin, but he looks so happy when she tells him he has awful taste that I can't judge. I can't judge too hard, at least.

They're still debating pie rankings when I slide out of the booth to hit the bathroom before we leave. I'm at the sink, washing my hands and wondering whether that red pie dyed my tongue or if it's just my imagination when a woman appears behind me. She's staring hard enough in the mirror that I stop what I'm doing, the water running, for a moment.

It's been years and years since I last saw her, but way less than that since I heard her name. I think.

"Hi, Andi," she says. She's got this weirdly soft, quiet voice, but she steps a little closer to me than I'd prefer, eyes steely. I shut the water off and dry my hands. She smiles. On reflex, I smile back bigger. "We need to talk."

"Beth, right?"

"Yes. Gideon's sister. I'd like you to leave him alone," she says, all in one breath.

"Oh," I say, because that's a level of directness I wasn't expecting, and toss the paper towel into the trash. "Okay. No."

I cock my head and keep smiling my friendliest smile as Beth purses her lips slightly.

"He deserves better than someone who's just looking for a good time," she says, saying *good time* in the same tone of voice Gideon uses to say *cat vomit,* and it's a little disconcerting how much they sound and look alike.

"Hm," I say, and cross my arms over my chest. "Hard disagree."

"Then you don't know him."

I wish I knew she was wrong. I wish I were so confident it

352

didn't occur to me, even a little, that she might be right, but it does, and like hell am I telling her any of that.

"I know he deserves to have a good time," I say.

"He deserves a loving wife, and a comfortable home, and a family. Every moment you spend together deprives him of that for just a little longer."

"You don't think he's got plenty of family already?"

Now, Beth looks downright disdainful, so I push a little more.

"There's a whole lot of you," I say, all sunshine and rainbows because it's pissing her off.

"Is that why you're driving a wedge between us?" she asks, eyes narrowed. "You think he has *too much* family, so you'd like him cast out?"

Fucking hell, how does goddamn *Beth* know the shit I'm secretly worried about?

I don't crack and roll my eyes instead.

"I thought I was just a good time," I point out. "Which I think he's earned after all *your* bullshit."

"I'm trying to help my brother out of love," she says, which, debatable, in my opinion. "He's been blinded to the truth by—*lust*—" Beth blushes a very familiar blush, "and I consider it my duty to return him to the fold."

"Blinded?" I ask, delighted. "Aww, he likes me that much?"

"You're leading him astray."

"Very," I agree. I'm grinning like a madwoman, my heart thumping in my throat. Beth is bright red now, the only giveaway on her serene face.

"If you truly cared for him or his well-being, you'd let him go."

"Again, gonna disagree."

Beth grabs my forearm and holds on, her grip surprisingly

strong, and it shocks me out of my sunshine-and-rainbows facade. Shit, is she about to—am I gonna have to fight Gideon's sister in a diner bathroom? I don't *fight*, I'm not—

"I'm sure this is a fun game for a harlot like you, disappearing for years and then coming back for vengeance," she says. "I know how easily men are led down the wicked path by feminine wiles."

"Plenty aren't, actually," I say. It's basically a reflex.

Beth drops my arm with the smallest sneer.

"This is a favor to you," she goes on. Any veneer of politeness she had has melted away, and suddenly I can see the kid she used to be. The one who was always furious that her brothers got to wear pants and wander the woods, so she retaliated by enforcing the law wherever she could. "Soon he'll come to his senses and move on to someone who hasn't given herself away so freely. I know he thinks he wants you now, but he'll change his mind."

"Did you just call me a *floozy*?" is the thing I manage to ask. Beth stands up a little straighter.

"I know what kind of girl you are," she says. "And I know who—and *what*—raised you."

I've never had the visceral urge to slap someone before. I've never had to focus on holding myself back from physical violence, but I do now.

"So does he," Beth goes on, then takes a step forward. She's maybe an inch shorter than me, so she's staring right into my eyes, brown with tiny flecks of green. "And you may have successfully led him down the road to temptation, but he'll find his way back, and when he does, we'll be waiting to forgive him."

It's the last part that makes my vision white out with rage, my ears ring. Fucking *forgive him*, as if he's wronged them.

"Fuck you, Beth," I say, too furious to be eloquent, and leave the bathroom.

I don't go back to our table right away, because fucking Beth and her stupid fucking too-insightful bullshit has me way closer to rage-crying that I'd like to be, so I go through a side exit and stand on some cracked pavement, looking at the parking lot under blue-white fluorescent lights. It's cold, a little damp, a little windy, and there are still a few scraps of snow hanging around at the edges, all the trees naked, grasping branches.

It feels appropriate, somehow. I feel leafless and bare myself if I'm that easy to see through, if even fucking *Beth* can look at me and know what I worry about late at night in a complicated, tangled snarl. I worry that, somehow, Gideon will be compelled to pick between his family and me. That either I'll make him lose roots he's had his whole life, or I'll lose him. That there'll be a rift and I'll be the cause of it, and yes, his parents are bigoted assholes and I hate them, but they're still his parents.

And—if I lose, if he picks the hateful assholes over me, then maybe that's proof he never changed at all and the sweet, careful, loving Gideon who apologized to me that night in the woods never really existed.

God, *fuck* Beth.

When I slide back into the booth Silas is telling some story about trespassing, tree climbing, and falling into a creek. Gideon smiles at me and quietly puts a hand on my leg, and I try to listen.

"Did you at least get the hubcap back?" Gideon asks when Silas seems to be finished. Kat's half-smiling, looking fond and entertained but also somehow unimpressed all at once.

"Not that day," Silas admits. "We had to go back about a

week later and drag the creek for it, and of course by then it'd rained a whole bunch so it was quite an undertaking."

"Was it worth it?" Kat asks, and Silas grins.

"Only for the story," he says, and she rolls her eyes and he laughs and she mutters something about how ridiculous he is.

"Andi," Gideon says, voice low and close. I realize he's looking at me, a line between his eyebrows. "You okay?"

"I'm fine," I tell him.

He frowns harder. "Andi."

Shit. I don't want to make this his problem, but I also don't want to fight about whether I'm mad right now, so—"I ran into your sister in the bathroom and she was kind of a dick to me," I say.

Incredibly, he frowns *more*.

"Bethany?" he says, not waiting for confirmation. "What happened?"

I sigh and pinch the bridge of my nose. Across the table, Silas is quietly saying *Gideon's sister Beth kind of sucks* to Kat, which is honestly a good summary.

"She told me to dump you because I'm a harlot and a floozy and you can do better," I say. Across the table, Kat makes a *ha* noise and immediately covers her mouth. Gideon sucks in a breath and sits up straighter.

"Sorry," Kat says behind her hand, and I shake my head.

"Where is she?" Gideon says.

"Who cares," I say to him, and "No, you're right, it's funny," I say to Kat.

"I'm gonna go talk to her," says Gideon. "Excuse me."

"It's fine."

"The hell it is."

"Do you need backup?" Silas says, brushing his hands together.

"No, I need Andi to *move* so I can go *talk* to my *sister*,"

Gideon says, staring me down. There's silence for a moment. "Please."

"I don't need you to defend my honor," I mutter, but I slide out of the booth anyway.

"I'm not defending your honor, I'm telling her to stay the fuck out of things that don't involve her," he says, and gives me a surprisingly gentle forehead kiss, given how pissed off he is. "Be right back."

I slide back into the booth and look across the table at Silas and Kat. "Shit," I mutter. "Sorry about this, we were having such a lovely time with pie."

"You're not the one who sucks, she's the one who sucks," Silas points out, and Kat nods.

"Also, floozy?" she says and I snort. "Harlot?"

"One of Gideon's brothers called his other sister a Jezebel," I say, and that gets a laugh out of Kat.

"That's almost charming," she says. "Shitty, but I don't know if I could get mad about it."

"I could," Silas says. "I could get real mad."

"Arrrrgh," I say, shoving my hands into my eyes and remembering a little too late that I've got mascara on. "We were having such a nice time."

'That was fast," Silas says, and I look up. Gideon's back, standing by the table, and glowering.

"They left," he says. "Either that or they're hiding in the kitchen. You all ready?"

"Are we chasing them down?" Silas asks, and Gideon snorts.

"I wouldn't give Beth the satisfaction," he says, and we all slide out of the booth.

THIRTY-EIGHT

GIDEON

I WALK through the parking lot dreaming of arson and how I could get away with it. I don't want to murder my sister and her family—I doubt I'll ever be that angry—but God, I'd like to light something on fire and watch it burn. Beth's car, maybe. The shed behind her house. Her stupid garden that yields about three tomatoes per year but that she talks about like she's virtuously feeding the whole neighborhood. It wouldn't do a single goddamn thing to make her less of a self-righteous asshole, but I'd enjoy it.

"Sorry," I tell Andi as we get into the car. It's at least the third time I've said it. I might have said it more and already don't remember. "I'm sorry about them. She's—Beth's—"

"A raging bitch with a martyr complex?" Andi says, sharp-edged but bright as ever.

"That," I say.

"A fucking busybody who wants everyone to fall in line to validate her own life?" Andi goes on. "Pathologically inca-pable of imagining other modes of existence?"

I swallow hard and pull the car out, already driving a little too fast. On the road I take a glance over at Andi, and nearly crash.

She's... smiling. Smirking? That face she makes when she's up to something and about to start laughing.

"Yeah. Those," I say, swerving the car back onto the road. "Are you okay? She has no fucking *right*."

"Sure she does. This is America, we've got free speech and shit."

"Not what I meant."

"I know. Sorry," she says, and why is *she* apologizing, all she's done is light up my life for the past two months.

"Don't be."

"Gideon, it's fine," she says, for maybe the fifth time since the incident. "I can handle your sister saying something impolite to my face. She's disliked me since she was six and I made one of her knock-off Barbies drive around naked."

I want to say *that's not true* but I'm pretty sure it is.

"Maybe it's some kind of alpha female pissing contest since she's the oldest girl, I don't know," Andi goes on. "It doesn't matter."

"Yes, it does," I say, quietly, half to the headlight-bright road in front of me and half to Andi. Of course it *matters*.

"I don't really care that your family thinks I'm a harlot. Or a floozy."

"They can't just *say* it."

"Sure they can. By their standards they're probably right, too. Some woman comes along and seduces away their precious eldest son? In above-the-knee skirts with her bosoms threatening to spill out at the slightest turbulence?"

I glance over at her, and she's smiling but it's an edged, dangerous smile, like she's daring me to disagree with her.

"You do look good," I say.

"Thanks," she says brightly. "It's the third-sluttiest dress I currently own."

I look over again and the car swerves a little. Andi laughs, twisting around in her seat, her right elbow leaning on the windowsill.

"The sluttiest one is the one I wore to roller derby," she says, and I swear I can *hear* her grin at my blush. "The second sluttiest is a sundress I've got with a cutout in the back. I used to own a couple sluttier things but I hadn't worn them in while, so I gave them to my old roommate's little sister."

"Oh," I say, as my brain offers an image of Andi in very short cutoffs, a bikini top, and a cowboy hat. I don't know why the hat. I can examine that later.

"If this dress pissed her off, imagine what those outfits would've done," she goes on, that sharp note back in her voice. "Imagine if she'd seen us the other night in the movie theater."

I take a deep breath and clear my throat, glad it's physically impossible for me to blush any more. The movie we saw was terrible and the theater was practically deserted, but instead of leaving like the thirty-something adults we are, we stayed in our seats near the back and made out like teenagers. By the end of the movie Andi's bra was unhooked and I'd nearly come in my pants, which would have been embarrassing if it weren't so exhilarating.

"I'd rather not think about Beth seeing that, actually," I say, and I sound impressively steady.

"Why, she wouldn't approve?"

"That, and I wouldn't want my sister seeing us in—that state," I say, and Andi laughs.

"Good point," she says, and puts one foot on the dashboard, her knee almost knocking the window, her head back and her throat exposed and her dress puddling into her lap, hiking up higher on her left leg, too.

It's dark outside, and she's lit by dashboard lights and the backward-reflecting glow of the car's headlamps on the road in front of us. My mouth's gone dry and I can feel her watching me. I glance over every couple of seconds.

"You know what I think?" she says, and her hand's on her inner thigh, right where her skin is softest. Where I left a mouth-shaped purple bruise by accident a few days ago. It's half-faded now, and she circles her thumb around it.

"That we're seven minutes from my house?" I say, voice low. I accelerate a little.

"That if your family's going to treat me like a whore, I may as well act like one," she says.

Fucking absurd that my first instinct is to say *no, they don't*, thirty-two years of conditioning bubbling to the surface, the urge to defend them stamped into my hindbrain somehow. I tighten my grip on the steering wheel.

"Now?" is the only thing I can manage to say, and Andi laughs.

"I could wait until tomorrow," she says. "If that works better with your schedule."

There's a soft gasp at the end of that sentence, and in the corner of my vision, I can see the heel of her hand sliding over her underwear.

"Six minutes," I say. "Five, maybe."

"Okay," she says, voice neutral, and then lifts her hips off the seat and slides her panties off.

I swerve, ever so slightly, onto the shoulder, and we both jostle.

"Gideon," Andi says, and it's warm and teasing and still a little sharp, and she winds her underwear around the gear shift. "Please drive responsibly."

"How am I—" I start, then glance over at her, and she's got her seat back a little and her hand between her legs, moving beneath her skirt, her seatbelt still on. "You can't wait five minutes?"

"I bet I can get myself off first," she says. "I'll race you."

Jesus. Fuck. She's going to kill me. She's going to kill both of us, or at least embarrass us a whole lot when I have to call a tow truck because I ran off the road and into a tree. I don't want to find out what an airbag deploying can do to an erection.

"Andi," I say, and it comes out ragged.

"No speeding," she says, and I can see her move her hips again at the edge of my vision. "Eyes front. Hands at ten and two. *Oh.* Watch the road."

I shouldn't be driving with this little blood in my brain. My skin is hot and all of it feels too tight, like I might split it open at any moment. The heat's on in here and I have no idea how to turn it off. I'm lightheaded, my heart is beating out of rhythm, my knuckles are white on the wheel and then Andi groans softly.

"Fucking Christ," I say through my teeth. Andi laughs breathlessly, and I steal another glance.

"God*damn* it," I whisper when I do.

"Focus," she says, half-whispering. "On the road, not me. Pretend I'm not even—*mmm*—here."

She is torturing me and I am going to die. There are headlights in the distance, and I hold my breath until they pass us, Andi breathing faster, harder. The double yellow line sears itself into my retinas because I can't look away, not for anything. It's silent except for road noise and the tiny, slick sounds Andi's making as she rubs herself.

"Is it good?" I finally ask, my arms shaking from how hard I'm holding the steering wheel. Two more minutes, just a stop sign and a curve and a straightaway—

"Yes," she says, sounding a little bit strangled. "You're really hot like this, you know."

I have to remind myself to breathe.

"Like what?"

"Holding back," she says. "When you're all uptight and stern and using self-control."

"That's all the time."

"Not like this."

"You're not usually getting yourself off in my passenger seat where I can't even look at you," I say, executing a technically illegal rolling stop.

"Fuck, Gideon, it could be arranged," she says, and shudders out a breath. I feel like my hair's standing on end. "We could do this all the"—she gasps and makes a noise and oh *God*—"time."

"We're almost there," I tell—her? Myself? Who fucking knows. "Just down this hill and around that bend."

Andi turns her head toward me and I catch it in my periphery.

"Don't come yet," I tell her.

"We're racing," she says, all shaky. "I'm about to win."

"I forfeit."

There's a sharp, whimpering gasp from the passenger seat, and I swallow. I can feel sweat trickling down my neck.

"Please?" I ask, barely more than a rough whisper, and Andi exhales hard.

"Fine," she whispers, and in the corner of my vision, she pulls her hand away. "Because you asked nicely."

"You don't have to stop," I say. "You can go slow. You could make more noise, if you wanted."

"What if I make myself come by accident?" she asks, teasing and raspy. "I'm pretty close. Anything could happen."

"You won't."

"I could."

"I did say please, Andi," I tell her, and slow the car to turn into my driveway. There are oncoming headlights, and the wait for them to pass might be the longest five seconds of my entire life. "You like it when I say please."

"Such good manners," she murmurs as I turn into my driveway at last. I take it at a fairly reckless speed and she reaches her left hand out to stroke my beard. It smells like her musk, and I clench my jaw even harder. "So polite. *Fuck.*"

"Not yet."

"I'm *not.*"

"Almost there," I say, and reach up to catch her hand in mine, pressing a blind kiss to her wrist. "You're so patient. Thank you."

"Hurry *up,*" she whispers, and finally the gravel widens out into my small parking area, a clearing in front of my house. I slam on the brakes too hard and forget to put the car into gear before I turn it off, push it into park, shut it down. I'm shaking and frantic and feel staticky with arousal, like it's all-consuming.

It's cool outside as I come around the car, one hand on the too-hot hood. Reid's car isn't there and I say a quick prayer that he's not either, and then I'm yanking Andi's door open and her seatbelt's off and she tries to stand but I duck and push her back down. My mouth is hot and wild and desperate on hers and she goes back willingly, her hands in my hair. Something on the center console clicks or breaks when she puts her weight on it and I don't give a fuck.

My knees hit gravel and the buckle of the seatbelt smacks against the open door and Andi's legs are spread in front of me, the headlights so bright against the trees that it's nearly impossible to see anything else, but I know this by now. I drag my face up her thigh and feel her squirm, so I wrap my hands around both of them, my knees shifting against gravel, and it hurts but it's a good distraction from what my dick is trying to do.

I find Andi's clit in the dark, by feel, and she's already got one hand in my hair. It doesn't take long and it doesn't take much finesse before she's shaking and saying *Jesus fuck yes, fuck, Gideon* and I grab her thighs and hold her closer and stroke her through it gently as I can, even past the part where her thighs jolt and she lets me go. I taste her until she pushes me off and sits up, something else on the console clicking or snapping or breaking, and then she sits in the passenger seat, legs akimbo as I kneel in front of her.

She takes my face in her hands and kisses me.

THIRTY-NINE

ANDI

"STAND," Gideon says, and I do. My legs are a little unsteady but he pulls me to one side, props me against his car, leans in. The headlights go off. Something stops dinging. He shuts the passenger door and then he's kissing me again, slow and thorough, one hand on my thigh underneath my dress. I lean back a little and part my legs for him, and he takes the invitation, pulling back and gazing at me as he runs his fingers up the inside of my thigh, where it's still sticky.

"You can," I say, and I mean ten things at once: he could put his hand on me again, in me; his mouth. He could strip me naked. He could leave me clothed and fuck me against the back door of his Toyota, out here in the cooling night.

"That what you want?" he says, and he leans his forehead against mine. He's *teasing* me. "You're so impatient and greedy that you can't make it into the house?"

"No," I scoff, the rough pad of his thumb sliding over the thin skin of my hip. I breathe into the feeling. "I've never been impatient, even once."

I can feel him smiling as he kisses me again, bending me

slightly backward against the car windows. He's hard against my hip so I grab him and pull him against me until he groans.

"Come on," he finally says, and pulls back.

Inside he shuts the door, locks it, gets his shoes off, and slides a hand around the back of my neck to kiss me again, gentle and possessive all at once. I kiss him back and get my hands on him, grab his belt loops, haul him in. I bite his lower lip and push the heel of my hand against his dick, straining against the zipper on his pants, but he takes my wrist and pushes it away.

"No," he says, his mouth barely leaving mine.

"Because I forgot to say please?"

Gideon's breath catches.

"Can I please touch you?" I murmur, and he takes my hand and puts it on his back, pressing the length of our bodies together.

"Not yet," he says, kisses me, draws back. "Upstairs."

When we get to his bedroom I turn and sprawl on the bed, propping myself up on my elbows, skirt riding up and legs wide.

"Now?" I ask, as he closes the door.

"So *fucking* impatient," he mutters, but he crawls on top of me and puts his mouth to my neck. I tilt my head back, offering myself. "No, not yet. There's something I want to try first. Take your clothes off."

He gives my neck a final lick and sits back on his heels, his hair wild, the room lit by one bedside lamp. I push myself up on my elbows again, just to get an eyeful, and he skates a hand up my thigh.

"Please?" he says, before I can say anything. "I can make it worth your while. And I asked *so* nicely."

I lift my hips, tug my dress up, then sit and pull it all the way off. Gideon's watching me, on his knees, hands on his thighs, attentive and relaxed and a little predatory, all at once. His erection is straining against the zipper of his pants so hard it has to hurt—looks that way, at least, I've never had one and wouldn't know—but aside from a slight flex of his fingers, he ignores it. I toss the dress away, unhook my bra, get rid of that too until I'm propped up on my hands, watching him watch me.

"God, Andi," he says, all grumbly and whispery, one dark curl tumbling onto his forehead. "You look like—a painting. A sculpture."

"One of the *really* expensive sex dolls," I offer, for some reason, and I get a *look* in return.

"What is *wrong* with you," he mumbles, but then leans over and presses me into the bed with a kiss.

"Whatever it is, you like it," I say, anchoring my hands in his hair. It gets a smile, against my lips.

"Yeah. I do," he says. "Don't ever fix it. Please, don't ever fix it."

He pulls back enough to lean a hand on my sternum—not hard, just enough that there's solid pressure, the kind of command that's half polite request—and opens the sex drawer with his other hand. I wait while he rummages, my heartbeat ticking up, heat winding through my belly.

"Here," he finally says, and holds up the vibrator that lives here now. "Make yourself come."

It's blue, silicone, more or less phallic with a few extra bumps. Gideon's bright red—I probably am, too—in the low light but holds my eyes as he hands it over. He swallows hard, worries his lip and his eyes skip from the vibrator to my face and then down my body in his slow, feral way, like a predator getting ready to feast.

I turn it on low and draw it down his arm, where he's still

leaning on me. He pulls it back and goes back to kneeling between my legs, eyes on me.

"What are you gonna do?" I ask, because I want to hear him say it.

"Watch," Gideon says.

"That's it?"

"For now," he says, and takes a hand off his own thigh to put it on mine. So much for just watching. "I drove all that way and kept my eyes on the road. I want to see what I missed."

He swallows.

"Please."

I've done plenty, but I've never done this before; I've never been watched and scrutinized so hard it makes me feel like my skin is transparent. I've never *wanted* it, but I do now, heat pounding through my veins. Gideon wants a show and he's right about how greedy I am for him, how impatient. I wiggle my hips into a better position and brace my left hand against the headboard and slowly notch the vibrator between my legs.

The moment it brushes my clit I groan, because even though it's on the lowest setting I'm so turned on I think anything could set me off. Gideon makes a noise in the back of his throat, small and desperate, and I pull the vibrator back a little.

Someone's breathing hard and fast and ragged, and, oh, it's me. I gather my wits and rub the vibrator's tip in slow, slick circles around my clit and even that makes my toes curl a little.

"Does that feel good?" Gideon asks.

"Yeah," I manage, and bite my lip. I go a little slower because I can feel his gaze on me like electricity, sparks everywhere he looks.

"Does it feel as good as planting it on your clit and coming already?" he asks, more than a hint of growl there.

Just for that, I dip the vibrator lower, tease it just inside my entrance. It also feels fucking good but I'm not gonna come this way.

"You don't like this?" I say, and I'm trying to tease him but more than anything I just sound wrecked.

"I didn't say *that*," Gideon says, and he's got his knees spread wide with his shirt off and his pants on. I want him to touch me, but I don't want to ask. I want him to *want*. "I said I wanted to watch you come since I missed the show earlier."

I drag the vibrator up, a long oval around my clit. It brushes against it and I have to bite my lip.

"I came on your mouth earlier," I point out, my eyes closed. Gideon slides one hand around my knee and pulls my leg up, onto his thigh, then leaves his hand there. I roll my hips mindlessly.

"I know. The view was nothing like this," he says, and he sounds calm, but his breathing is ragged. "It's unfair that I have to choose."

"Such a struggle," I gasp out, because I'm trying to stay in control and go slow but also there's a vibrator near my clit and Gideon's eyes on me, and I'm losing it pretty fast. "You poor thing."

"Not at all," he says, running his hand up my thigh, and I can't help but arch my hips into his touch.

"Come on," I whisper, unsure what I'm asking for. "Are you really just gonna watch?"

Gideon's a mess, his hair tangled and wild, his lips parted, his face flushed all the way to his chest, one hand on my thigh and the other on his own, knuckles white.

"Yes," he says, and raises his eyes to mine. "I like it when you put on a show for me. I like being your only audience."

I slide the head of the vibrator right up against my clit, and I explode. It's eye-rolling and body-jolting and the whole time I swear I can feel Gideon's eyes on me like velvet, soft and warm and sumptuous.

"*Fuck,*" he says with feeling when it's over and I've moved the vibrator away from myself, because I need a break. When I look up, his pants are still on but he's palming himself, his hips rolling in a way I really appreciate. "God, that was good. Was that good?"

I snort, because I think I'm still trembling. "Yes," I confirm, boneless and lazy and yet, still interested in the way he's touching himself. Gideon doesn't answer me right away, just takes his hand off my thigh and plants it on the bed by my waist, leaning over me.

Then he dips his head and presses an open-mouthed kiss to my belly, right below my sternum.

"Do it again," he says, and when I don't answer, he raises his eyes to mine but leaves his mouth where it is, his beard somewhere between tickly and scratchy. "Please?"

I swallow and turn the vibrator up a notch. This time I come with my other hand in Gideon's hair, his teeth around one nipple so tight it almost hurts, a little, but it's a pain like a beam of light slicing through my body.

"Again. Please," he says, once I've stopped shaking, and follows the request with a lick. That time my whole body jolts when I get the vibrator back on my clit, but Gideon sits up to undo his pants, pull his cock out, and stroke himself slowly while he runs a hand up my inner thigh. When I come we both groan, and this time I don't even wait for him to ask, I just keep going.

I'm oversensitive, sweaty, my clit swollen. I turn the vibrator up one more notch—it's gotta be almost on high but I've lost track—and slide it over my lips, inside a little, just far enough I can feel it. Gideon puts his hand on my hip and brushes his thumb over my clit, and he's gentle but I jolt anyway, clenching around the vibrator.

"Too much?" he asks, husky and ragged, his cock still in his other fist. I can see him leaking onto the bedspread from here, enough that the whole shaft is slick.

"No," I say, and he does it again, and this time I don't jolt as much but I moan a little. "It's a lot. I like it."

"Show me," he says, as if I haven't been doing just that. "Please."

I pull the vibrator out of myself and press it against his thumb until it's right on my clit, the rough, warm pad buzzing. It's not enough to come for a fourth or fifth or whatever time, but it's good enough to make me feel floaty, like I could stay here forever.

I don't. Soon enough I come with the vibrator pressed right against my clit and Gideon's thick fingers buried inside me, stroking that spot I like. I'm borderline incoherent and he's swearing, his dick smearing pre-cum all over the inside of my thigh.

When it's over he stands and I take a break for a second, watching him as he finally pulls his pants and boxer-briefs off, his dick pointing skyward. He sees me looking and wraps a hand around it, stroking himself once. It makes all the muscles in his arms flex.

"I didn't say to stop," he teases.

"What if I break myself," I say from where I'm lying, legs spread wide, waiting for him to come back. "What if my clit never works again after this?"

"You can stop if you want," he says, and climbs back onto the bed, then over me, cock smearing pre-cum against my stomach. "But the human body is very resilient."

Gideon kisses me slowly, like we're not in a hurry, like he

hasn't been watching me fuck myself for ages, now. His tongue is still in my mouth when I start again, gasping with the pleasure/pain/pleasure of it.

When I'm close, shaking and making these desperate little whimpers that I don't like and can't stop, Gideon pulls back. He grabs the underside of one knee and pushes it a little wider, just to where I can feel the stretch, just to where I feel a little held and helpless.

"You're close again, aren't you?" he asks, his voice nearly a whisper, low and soothing. "Go ahead. Come again."

With that he fits the head of his cock to my entrance and I inhale hard, waiting, *anticipating*, but nothing else happens. When I open my eyes, he's looking down at himself—at us— raw lust and fascination on his face.

"Fuck, that's good," he says, so quiet and strained I can barely hear him. "God, Andi."

"You can feel it?"

"Yeah," he says, shaky. "I can—"

He breaks off when I pull the vibrator back, push myself up on one elbow, and look at it because there might be one more—yeah. I turn it up. Gideon's pupils are blown so wide I can barely see green as he watches me put it back on my clit.

"Fuck," I say when I do. I'm basically out of words. "Oh. *Fuck.*"

Gideon bites his lip and finally slides in, slowly, like he's testing himself. We ditched condoms after getting tested so he's bare, and I've never minded using them, but I also like the look on his face. As if he's seeing God or something.

He bottoms out and groans, his fingers sinking into my thigh hard enough to leave bruises. I wrap the other one around his hips as he presses himself into me, and—

"Ow," I say, the vibrator squashed against some weird spot.

"Sorry," Gideon gasps, then moves, groans and thrusts again and that doesn't work *either*, goddamn it.

"Here," I say. "Try—"

He wraps both arms around me and rolls us over. I yelp, unsexily, and my foot gets tangled in the bedspread and the vibrator jumps out of my hand and I have to lunge after it, but then I'm suddenly on top, kneeling over Gideon. I'm breathing hard, shaking, my clit is throbbing from the over-stimulation, but I still sink onto him in one greedy stroke.

"Please," is all he says, hoarse and wrecked.

It's easy, from this angle. All I have to do is stay upright and let Gideon grab my thighs and push my knees a little wider. I gasp and clench when I touch the vibrator to my clit again, gently at first. Gideon's breath stutters.

"I'm not sure it's gonna work again," I say. I've got my full weight on him, grinding down, pressing my clit against the vibrator. It's the kind of *good* that I can feel in my bones but I don't know if it's the kind of good that'll let me come again.

"I think you can," he says, his hands on my hips as he angles himself, pulls me down, and I make a gasping whimper noise I'm not proud of. "Doesn't that feel good?"

I sigh and shudder in response.

"That's it," he murmurs, pulling me down again, gentle but firm as anything. "Just the way you like it. Lean back."

I just do what he says, because he's right that I like this and I'm aching and buzzing and the vibrator pressing against my clit *hurts*, almost, like I'm gently poking a bruise but it's also fucking wonderful, and his cock is wonderful, and yeah. I can come again.

Just as gently, he takes the vibrator out of my hand without ever moving it from the right spot, and I let him go to put both hands on his thighs behind me, and fuck. *Fuck.*

"There you go," Gideon says. "I love it when you use me."

I try to disagree, say I'm not *using him*, but he bucks up a little and pushes the vibrator a little harder against me so instead I make a choked-off sobbing sound. God, I'm close, I'm so fucking *close*—

"Shhh," Gideon is saying, like he's soothing me. "It's okay if you don't. It's okay if it just feels good."

"It's good," I hear myself say. "Gideon, it's so good."

"That's it," he says, and he sounds like he's cracking apart under the strain. "You're perfect. I—*fuck*, Andi, I can't--"

I stop moving. Gideon makes a noise like he's dying but I settle myself and grind down, feel him fill me and stretch me and press the vibrator so hard against my clit I think it might pop and then, in a burst, I fucking *come*.

I see stars. I see galaxies and black holes and the end of time itself, and when I open my eyes again Gideon is pulling me in, up, grabbing my hips, fucking me hard and fast with my face against his shoulder before he shouts and goes still, throbbing inside me.

I feel flattened and sun-warmed. I feel like I could melt into the cracks, live a simple and thought-free existence. Soon, my breathing evens out and Gideon's fingers start at the knob of my neck and trace, gently, all the way down my spine.

"You okay?" he rumbles. He sounds like I feel.

I heave myself to the side and roll off him, both knees cracking. The vibrator is still going, somewhere across the bed, and it'll just have to run out of battery because I'm not getting up to turn it off.

"I'm good," I say, and we're on our sides, our legs still tangled. I push a sweaty curl off his forehead. "Are you okay?"

Gideon scoffs and smiles, secret and shy. "I'm fi—"

"Don't you *dare*," I tell him, shoving a couple fingers against his lips. His smile widens behind them, even as he rolls his eyes.

"I can say whatever I want," he says, and kisses each of my fingertips in turn, matter-of-fact and delicate, but also says, "I'm great."

"Agreed," I say, and after all that, he still blushes.

· · · · ★ ★ ★ ★ · · · ·

"YOU KNOW," I say later, after I've brushed my teeth and done my skincare routine, though I haven't put on clothes. "There are vibrating cock rings."

Gideon's already in bed, on what's become *his side*, reading a paperback that's seen better days.

"Really," he says, his attention snapping to me.

"Really," I confirm. "You know. If you were interested."

"Might be worth checking into," he says, and he's making a serious face but he's got that note in his voice, that crinkle around his eyes and it almost hurts, what a gift he is. When he's like this, quietly happy in a way that feels like walking on sun-warmed stone.

"Might be," I agree, and steal his robe from the hook on the back of his door, just in case Reid got home while we were busy. "I'm gonna go grab some water."

When I come back five minutes later, he's swapped the book for his phone, and I crawl under the covers and get nosy.

"Shit, that was fast," I say as he scrolls through vibrating cock ring after vibrating cock ring. He taps on one and—yep, he's reading the reviews.

"Never leave for tomorrow what can be done today," he says.

I blink at the phone for a second.

"Did you just quote Thomas Jefferson at me? About sex toys?" I ask, and he turns his head. Our faces are two inches apart.

"Fuck no," he says. "I quoted Benjamin Franklin at you."

"Is that better?"

"Of course it's better," he grumbles, then gets his arm around me with only a little shoving. "Here. This one's well-rated and waterproof, tell me what you think."

FORTY

GIDEON

THE CAGES OUTSIDE ARE EMPTY. I can barely see them in the dark, faintly moonlit, clouds wandering over the night sky. It's good when they're empty, because it means that there's no hurt wildlife out there with no place to go. Critters only wind up here when the real wildlife rehab centers are too full, or too understaffed, or too underfunded. Too still and too quiet, but good.

It's been a couple weeks since the two of them went back, the eagle to the wild and the fox to be an Educational Ambassador at a wildlife refuge, but I haven't quite gotten used to it yet.

I never meant to start taking in critters, but a few years back—after Reid but before Dolly—I got a call about a Great Horned Owl who'd nearly died from ingesting rat poison and needed a safe place to recover, so I built an enclosure big enough for an owl. Then another, and another, and then a few years had gone by and I was a sometimes-waystation for wildlife who needed it.

It's good, I remind myself, that they're empty right now, even if it looks and feels a little wrong. Even if the empty cages are a little like a gentle itch somewhere in the back of my brain that I can't scratch. It's nice to have fewer responsibilities and creatures who depend on me. It's relaxing when the cages are empty.

"Hey," says Andi's quiet voice behind me. I turn and watch her vague shape pad across the kitchen, wearing pajama pants and the same sweater she kept borrowing at the cabin. It still looks good on her. "You okay?"

"Fine. Just woke up and couldn't get back to sleep," I say. "You can go back to bed if you'd like."

Andi makes a sleepy, noncommittal noise, and walks over to me. Next thing I know she's got one arm slung over my shoulder, her chin on the other, her arm wrapped around my waist. She sways against me like she's on tiptoe, and I plant my feet a little more securely.

"Anything out there?" she asks, her voice all dreamy and rough from sleep.

"The usual," I say, covering her hands with mine, sliding my fingers between hers. It feels good, letting her drape herself over me like this.

"Hm."

"Was I an asshole for not giving them heating pads?" I ask. The question takes me by surprise almost as much as it does her.

"Fluffy and Vicky?"

They didn't have names, but, "Yeah."

"No. They were wild animals, that's what they do."

"But this isn't the wild," I point out.

"But that's what they were going back to," she says, and she sounds like she's frowning.

"Maybe I should have been a soft place to land," I say. "Tough love is kind of bullshit."

"Tough love is *definitely* bullshit. For people."

"But not animals?"

Andi slides away from me, her hand drifting over the back of my neck and down my arm until she takes my hand and faces me, leaning against the sliding glass door, her face in front of the darkness. She looks at me for so long I start to feel transparent, and it makes panic fizz somewhere behind my sternum for the first time since—

Fuck. Since the cabin.

"Different beings need different kinds of care," she finally says. "Eagles need to be treated like eagles. Foxes need to be treated like foxes. People like people. You'd have given a person a heating pad."

"I wouldn't have kept a person in a cage," I point out, and she grins.

"True. Reid's even got his own bathroom," she says, and I snort.

Then I lean forward and press my forehead to the cold glass over her shoulder, my mouth going close to her neck, to the knit of my sweater. I keep thinking about how I'd apologize to my parents. How I would start. Where they would both be: in the living room, my father in his armchair, my mother on the couch while I stood? In the kitchen, newspaper and sink, dish gloves on? On the front porch, in the foyer, outside in the driveway?

I've thought of a hundred starting lines, easily, and they all feel like sand on my tongue. The whole thing feels like tissue paper in my mind; I could tape it once, twice, a million times, but it would just tear around the tape. I can't fix the fact that I'm the child they chose to cut off.

I think, for a moment, of telling Andi but the words stick in the back of my mouth. *My parents stopped speaking to me and I don't think I'll ask them to start again*, but Andi would never understand. If Andi murdered someone, her dads would come hug her in prison.

"I wish Bethany hadn't said those things to you," I say. "I'm sorry."

Andi swallows, her other hand drifting to the base of my skull, where she twists my hair in her fingers.

"It's fi—"

"Don't," I cut her off. Her chest heaves once with a laugh or a snort or something.

"I also wish she hadn't, then," she says. "But she did, and it's not really our problem."

"I wish she wasn't like this," I say. My eyes are closed but I know my breath is fogging the glass, blocking the view of the backyard. "But she always has been. I remember her being three years old and lecturing us that we weren't putting together the Tinkertoys the way it said to in the instruction manual."

"Those were suggestions."

"Tell Beth that," I say. "I remember once me, Matt, Elliott, and Zach all went fishing, and Mom made her stay home because they were making strawberry jam. She was so pissed that she reported back to Dad every single time one of us took the Lord's name in vain for the next month."

She and Zach are twins. I wonder if she would have been less angry if they weren't.

"I'd have resented you, too," Andi says. "You know it's not your fault, right?"

She knows, I think for a moment, and the panic fizzes and my heart kicks. *She knows and she's about to be too gentle and incorrect with me*—breathe.

"I know," I say, and my voice doesn't shake.

"I don't envy her," Andi goes on, quiet and low, her fingers tugging gently at my hair.

"She lashes out," I say, which is probably obvious. "She's got no right to, but she does."

Andi doesn't answer.

"I'm not excusing her."

"I know."

"I'm just..." I don't know. I feel like this is a knot made of smaller knots, the ends looping back into themselves. It feels infinite.

"You're being her big brother," Andi says after a while. "You still love her, even if she's an asshole."

"Yeah," I say. "It sucks."

Andi laughs, and it's loud and warm in the dark kitchen. My eyes are still closed but the sound feels bright behind my eyelids, like the rosy glow of dawn. She always feels like that.

"I love you," I say, and I didn't quite mean to but it's true. I say it too fast, too urgently, but I need to say it before she finds out what kind of person I really am, someone not even my parents can love. Before I tell her. Which I will, soon, just not tonight.

"I know," she says, and places a gentle kiss to my neck, right below my beard, the part of me closest to her mouth. The tiniest shiver slides down my spine. "I love you too."

"Thank you," I say, and shove *would you if* and *maybe you shouldn't* away, wrap an arm around her waist, pull myself closer. The glass door behind her radiates cold and she radiates warmth, her face buried in my neck, the dark settling like a blanket around us. It's so quiet. It's so still.

Here, in the dead of night, it's so simple.

· · · ★ ★ ★ ★ ★ · · ·

THE NEXT DAY I go over to Beth's house to tell her, in no uncertain terms, that if she's ever rude to Andi again we'll no longer be on speaking terms. It feels easier than I thought it would when I tell her that, and maybe that's the trick: family is like a rope, and once you cut a little the whole thing frays.

She looks tired and harried while she stands in the front door and listens to me. I can't stop thinking about the little girl who had to stay behind and make jam, her perfectly righteous fury. I wonder if I could have talked my parents into letting her join us, but it's decades too late for that.

But she doesn't back down. She calls Andi a harlot again, to my face, and I've never itched so badly to hit a woman. I don't let her finish talking, I just turn and walk away. It's the first time I've ever done that to a sibling.

It feels much better than I wish it did.

· · · ★ ★ ★ ★ ★ · · ·

I'M at work a few days later, on a conference call about isopods, when Elliott texts.

Elliott: Hey, did you get my note?
Elliott: I specifically told Reid to make sure you saw it, don't tell me he forgot

"Shit," I mutter out loud, alone in the office I share with the outreach coordinator, then immediately check that I'm still on mute.

I am. I've been on mute for fifty-three minutes. We're not even talking about isopods in my district, but the higher-ups in my department wanted to make sure we had "a seat at the table," so here I am, not quite paying attention.

I stare at my phone. I think about the note he left, the way he addressed the card *Mr. Gideon Bell and Mr. Reid Bell*, and I hate how much of a relief that was even though Elliott has always been one of the good ones. I think: if anyone understands why I can't talk to our parents, it'll be him. Even if Reid still doesn't know.

I decide it's a great time for a bathroom break.

"Hey," Elliott answers the phone, half a minute later. "Finally."

"Sorry," I say, shoving my other hand into my pocket. I stepped outside for the phone call, into the grassy little picnic area the Forest Service offices have out back. It's cool but not too cool, the sunlight weakening with the afternoon. "Thanks for the invitation."

There's a noise that might be static or might be Elliott in Boston, snorting.

"Yeah, sure, you're welcome," he says, blustery and almost sarcastic. I miss him. "I basically had to invite you two, right?"

"I didn't say I was coming," I tell him. "Maybe I'm busy that weekend."

"Too busy to be a groomsman?"

"Oh," I say, because that somehow hadn't occurred to me. I didn't think he'd want me to be, not after I abandoned him for years. "No. I mean, yes? Fuck."

That gets a real, honest-to-God laugh, the same one he's always had.

"Perfect," he says, and I sigh. "Reid didn't tell you?"

"Tell me what?"

"That I was asking you two to be groomsmen."

"He didn't."

"I guess the kid can keep a secret," Elliott says. "Remember when he cut his own hair and somehow kept anyone from noticing for two full days?"

"He'd been wearing the hat anyway, so it wasn't that weird," I say, and Elliott laughs. "Who got in trouble for that one? It wasn't me."

384

"I think it was Beth," Elliott says. There's a short, cool silence as I stare into the woods and feel warm inside. "I'll let you go, I know you hate the phone."

"That was it?" I ask before I can tell myself not to.

"What, you want to be the ring bearer instead?"

"I'd be great at that," I mutter.

Another pause.

"You okay?"

"Yeah, of course. I'm fine."

Elliott waits, and I don't know what's happened to me lately that I can't bear things any more, but I crack.

"I thought you wanted me to call because you were going to ask me to talk to our parents and maybe invite them," I say.

"Oh," he says, voice crackling a little as it comes down the line. "Oh. Fuck no."

He says it so definitively. With such *certainty*. Like this is a matter that's been decided years ago, like he barely thinks about it any more. It makes my voice stick in my throat. I stare at the trees. Somewhere inside me, a knot comes undone.

"Right," I say.

"If there's some sort of chance they might come, you have to tell me so I can hire bouncers, or security, or something," Elliott says. "I will *not* have them ruining my big day."

"*Big day*, Jesus Christ," I mutter, and Elliott laughs.

"Someone asked me what color napkins we wanted," he says. "I don't fucking know, napkin-colored? Wedding planning is a nightmare and I'm in hell."

"I can't wait," I tell him, and it's true.

FORTY-ONE

ANDI

I REALLY HOPE the Sprucevale Sentinel-Star hires someone soon, because Lucia keeps asking me if I'll cover school board meetings, and I keep saying yes, and it sucks. I get paid, yeah, but school board meetings are the worst.

Case in point: tonight's. It started at 8pm on a Wednesday, which is fine, but they always start late and go late. They take place in the cafeteria of Sprucevale High School, which has bad acoustics, so it takes extra concentration to hear everyone. The chairs are uncomfortable. The lights make everyone look like zombies and the one in the corner by the front office keeps flickering, which is driving me mad.

Oh, and William and Matthew Bell are here, and I hate them. I haven't covered a school board meeting since I started dating Gideon, but tonight, while the school board spends forty-five minutes discussing what brand of plastic chair they're going to purchase for the middle school's band room, I take a handful of notes and glare at the sides of their faces.

Last time I was here, they were trying to get sex ed out of the curriculum altogether. Never mind that the one week per year that kids learn *anything* on the topic is already absti-

386

nence-based, he thinks it should be gone. He's also pushed for a stricter student dress code, a stricter *teacher* dress code, student-led prayers before football games, and the disbanding of the high school's Gay-Straight Alliance, which has seven whole members. I hope they're burning him in effigy.

Tonight, it's books. He would like to ban a lot of them, and surprise surprise, they're mostly queer kids' books. Or, at least, he starts off there and then manages to get the entire school board into a flurry by bringing up *Lolita*. How, he demands to know, is a hypothetical parent supposed to explain the very problematic content of this book to a hypothetical first-grader who's brought it home from Sprucevale Elementary?

It works. Everyone wastes twenty minutes arguing about a book that Sprucevale Elementary obviously doesn't have in its library, and by the time we're back on track everyone is thinking about creepy Humbert Humbert, and I'm furious. I'd be shocked if William Bell has even read *Lolita*, and I'm also trying to secretly text Gideon because he's picking me up after this so we can go grab late-night snacks since I haven't seen him in four days, but the meeting has gone thirty minutes over already.

At least the motion to ban the books doesn't pass, though I'm sure we'll all have to hear it again, and again, and he'll eventually succeed at some part of his plan.

After the meeting I have to stick around a few extra minutes to clarify some stuff about the proposed school bus situation for next year, and *then* I get turned around finding a bathroom, so by the time I'm finally heading to the parking lot to wait for my boyfriend, the high school has mostly emptied out.

Which is probably why it sounds so loud when someone says, "Ah. Andi," in the hallway as I'm walking toward the school's front lobby.

"Hello," I say as Matt Bell, Gideon's younger brother, walks up to me. He's clean-shaven and has brown eyes, but other than that, it's a little unnerving how much he looks like Gideon.

"I never did say welcome back," he tells me. Out of polite habit, I wait for him to catch up to me. "Must be a big change from... Washington?"

"New York."

"Ah, yes. Well. You'll find we prefer things at a somewhat slower pace, here."

I grab the strap of my messenger bag and give him my brightest, fuck-off-est smile.

"I remember," I tell him.

"More old-fashioned," he goes on, like I'm not talking. I've never liked him. "A very family-oriented place, Sprucevale. Tradition is important to us."

To my credit, I don't ask him if being a dickhead is traditional.

"Hmm," I say, mostly to fill the gap.

"Just something to keep in mind," he says, and thank God we're almost to the lobby. "Have you talked to Gideon lately?"

I finally glance over at Matt, eyes narrowing. He's got his hands in his pockets and his shoulders thrown back, and he looks like Gideon but there's none of the easy assurance in his stance, none of Gideon's bone-deep gravity.

"Is that a trick question?" I finally ask, exasperated with this man. "Yes. I texted him ten minutes ago. He's picking me up."

"How's he doing?"

"He's great."

Matt has the nerve to look surprised, dark eyebrows going up. "Really? With everything that's happened?"

"Yes, really." A sideways, skeptical look, and the fuse of

my patience is burning low, so I put on my most chipper smile. "He's spectacular. Incredible. Thriving. Wonderful. Do you need more adjectives, or...?"

"We worry about him," Matt says, and I can hear the royalness in the *we*. Ugh. "He was always easily so swayed. Particularly by you."

We're almost to the lobby, white walls with green-and-white tiles on the floor, an uncomfortable bench, two ficus trees that may or may not be fake. I roll my eyes because if I don't, I might start considering violence.

"If you're also going to call me a harlot, do it now," I say. "We're nearly to the exit. Or, fuck, what was the other one? Was it *strumpet*? *Tart*?"

I *know* I shouldn't keep going, that being an asshole to Gideon's brother won't help shit, but it's been a long school board meeting and a long month since we left the cabin and a long twenty years before that. Matt's glaring at me, his face going red.

"Floozy!" I proclaim, snapping my fingers and grinning at him. "That's it. I like that one, because it makes me sound like a fun slut, not one of those boring, dour sluts—"

Dour sluts is barely out of my mouth when I turn the corner to find William Bell, Gideon's father, standing in the lobby. He's got his hands in his pockets and disapproval on his face. I slam to a stop and can feel my face go beet red. I feel like I'm nine years old and just got caught swearing, and I hate it.

"Andrea," he says, and *smiles*, and if I were a cat my fur would be standing on end. I gather my nerve and stare at him and if it takes me a minute to answer him, so what?

"William," I say, voice steady. I've never called him by his first name before.

There's a moment where I'm certain he's going to correct

me—that he, an adult, is going to tell me, another adult, to call him *Mister*. When we were children, Gideon was afraid of him; afraid of what he'd do if Gideon displeased him and afraid to flinch at the thought. That meant I was afraid, too, but not like Gideon had to be. If William Bell told me I ought to call him *Mister*, I'd still do it and be furious the whole time.

"It's been such a blessing to see you at these meetings."

"Likewise," I echo, my mouth on autopilot, the sense memory of *in trouble* ringing through me.

"Ever since I saw you at the last one, I've been praying for you," he goes on, smiling and friendly and folksy. "That the Lord would see fit to change your heart—"

"Don't," I say, and we're both surprised.

"Sorry?"

Breathe in, breathe out. Be civil to him, for Gideon's sake. "Don't pray for me. Please."

"We all need someone to pray for us," he says, but the smile is fading, the accent hardening. William Bell never had much of a mask.

"All the same, I'd prefer you not do it for me," I say, perfectly polite. My hand is sweating where I'm gripping the strap of my messenger bag.

"Still the same stubborn, wicked girl," William says, shaking his head. Something inside me flashes white-hot. "Still a lost lamb, turned away from the Lord—"

"Whatever you're asking for, I don't want it," I snap, and my heart is hammering, my palms sweaty. "Whoever listens to your—" *Bullshit.* "—prayers, I don't want anything to do with them."

"Forgive her, Lord," he murmurs to—himself? "She doesn't mean it."

"Yes, she does," I say, and walk for the doors, calling back over my shoulder. "Good to see you!"

"I know what you're doing."

"Leaving the building after a school board meeting?"

"You're only with Gideon to exact revenge on our family," he says, and I swear everything in the cosmos goes still for one single, silent moment. I turn, slowly.

"That's all you think of him?" I say, my voice rising. "That I don't—that he's not—"

"Dad," Matt says. He is ignored.

"You think the only reason I'd date Gideon is to get to you," I go on, and I think I'm shouting now. "You think I'd do that? *To Gideon*? You think Gideon wouldn't know? You don't think he could do a million times better?"

"I know you came back to tear our family apart," William sneers, and it's the ugliest thing I've ever seen. "You, Andrea, are a test of our faith, but Gideon will see you for what you are and return to us."

That one drips down my spine like tar, finding that secret place where my fears live. My hands are in fists.

"I'm with Gideon because I want to be with Gideon," I say, and I'm quiet now but my voice is shaking. "That's it. That's all. I don't give a fuck whether your family gets torn apart or not."

It's not true, but the lie feels great.

"See?" Matt says softly, and something registers in my brain.

"What do you mean *return to us*?" I ask.

"I mean that once he is rid of your influence, we will be waiting with open arms—"

"Say it normal!" I shout. Matt clears his throat.

"Gideon is cut off until he apologizes to our parents," Matt says, and he looks—smug? Pleased, in a way that can't be Christlike. Like he's won something at last. I feel like my heart might punch its way out of my chest.

"What," I say, and swallow, trying to sound normal. "Did Gideon do that you think he needs to apologize for?"

I'm afraid I know the answer, and it feels like the bottom dropping out, like tiny barbs in my heart. *Cut off.* Oh fuck. Oh, god.

"For you, mostly," Matt says, just as William says, "He was disrespectful."

"Good," I say, and feel like someone else is talking. "You don't deserve his respect."

William gives Matt a significant look. "Told you," he says, softly.

"You're going to die alone," I tell William, because I can say whatever I want now. "You're going to drive away anyone who's still got the ability to love you, and when the shriveled husk of your heart finally stops beating, you will be alone in this world. And I hope I can feel it when it happens."

There's a blanket of silence in this over-bright high school lobby. It settles and stretches, my brain echoing, and I try to convince my feet to move out the door but William is staring at me, ugly with anger, and Matt is staring over my shoulder and looking slightly alarmed and—

I can sense what's happened a moment before I actually turn to see it.

It's Gideon. He's standing in the doorway, the door slightly propped behind him. I didn't hear it open, and I have no idea how long he's been there, and I've been shouting at his family and doesn't that prove what they've been saying about me?

"Hi," I manage, my chest clenching so hard I can barely breathe.

"Hi," he says, wide-eyed and stock still.

I stare, desperately trying to think of something to say that isn't just *fuck fuck fuck fuck*. His eyes flick over my shoulder and then back to me and he's—wary and uncertain and maybe hurt and a whole lot of ways I didn't want to make him feel.

"Listen," I say, and jerk a thumb over my shoulder, toward the school. "I'll just call Lucia—"

"Andi—"

"—it's fine, don't worry about it, I'll. You know. A ride." I'm babbling and walking backwards, and then I point haphazardly toward a hallway and power walk toward it before I can think or speak or do anything else.

"Andi!" he calls, but I don't slow down because all I want is to be *away*, to hide in a hole and not come out maybe ever because I did this. He's not on speaking terms with his parents and it's my fault. If only I had been better, somehow. A little less me and a little more of a sweet, smiling girl who bakes pies and keeps a household running smoothly.

Behind me, William or maybe Matt says something I can't quite hear, but I do hear Gideon snap *I thought we weren't talking* and it doesn't make me feel better. I don't hear whatever else he says because I'm off, turning corners and pacing through hallways, closed door after closed door in the high school I never attended.

I think, wildly, that I could really run. I could escape upstairs or out a door. I could walk into the woods that surround the school on three sides and Gideon wouldn't be able to find me, probably. I could move back to New York and go on with my life and never have to look into his pretty eyes again. I could live my life and never face up to the fact that I'm exactly who his family thinks I am, and he's the worse for it.

But then I turn another corner and it's a dead end, tile and cinderblocks and closed doors and forest-green lockers. Fluorescent lights and drop-tile ceiling. I wish I'd never seen William Bell again, and I slump against the lockers.

They're cool behind my shoulder blades. Breathe in, then out. I just need a few minutes, that's all. I'll collect myself and go back and apologize and it will be fine, perfectly fine, like it was before. In, out. Except: how long has Gideon not been on speaking terms with them? How could I not *know*, not tell? This happened because of me and he never said anything?

Why the hell didn't he say anything?

I'll fix it. I just—need a minute so I can calm down and fit the lies to my mouth so they don't sound quite so outrageous. It's not lying, not *lying* lying, if it's for a good reason right? Not *lying* if no one can prove it. I know how it is, with family, how you dislike them and also need them and how complicated and totally fucked it can be.

"Andi," says Gideon's voice from the end of the short hallway.

I drag a breath into my lungs. "Hi," I say.

"I don't think we're supposed to be here," he says, because of course that's the first thing he says. I roll my eyes without really meaning to.

"You're welcome to leave."

"I'm not letting you get locked in a high school overnight."

"That's not what would happen," I say. "It's got the doors that push out or whatever. I'd escape just fine."

He sighs and pushes his hands a little deeper in his pockets and looks around like he thinks a SWAT team is going to descend at any moment.

"There aren't even metal detectors in this high school," I point out. I sound a lot sharper than I mean to. "No one is going to come arrest you for standing in a hallway a little while after the school closes, so just chill the fuck out."

"*I* need to chill out?" he asks, low and gruff. "Andi, what is —fuck, did I do something?"

"You didn't tell me your parents *disowned you*!" I say,

waving an arm in his direction. "You didn't say anything! And you let me just carry on, bitching about your sisters and every-thing, and--fuck, Gideon, what the hell?"

"I don't have to tell you anything," he says.

"You should have told me this!"

"Why? Does it matter?"

I don't have an answer for that, so I stare at him. Gideon glowers back, and somewhere in the back of my mind, the part of me that's been paying attention in therapy for twenty years is saying *this is a very stupid argument that you're only having because you're in emotional distress.*

"I don't know!" I shout anyway, and push myself to my feet. "If my parents had stopped talking to me when I told them we were dating, I'd have told you about it!"

"That's different."

"How?!" I shout and Gideon glares harder, his jaw flexing under his beard. Now we're three feet away from each other, both standing. Despite myself, I think of all the ways that my parents and his are, in fact, completely different. I take a deep breath.

"Seriously?" he asks, and I scrub my hands over my face.

"I can't do this," I say, and everything goes dead silent.

FORTY-TWO

GIDEON

THESE BIG MUNICIPAL buildings sound strange when there's nothing to hear. Clicks and groans and sounds echoing from God knows where; sighs and the sound of vents shifting, the ghosts of sneakers scuffing on linoleum.

"What does that mean?" I ask her, twenty seconds later, in the cacophony of silence.

"This," she waves an arm around as if that explains fucking *anything*. "I can't—look, I'm fucking it up, this is going so bad. I'm sorry. I just—sorry."

It feels like there's a bird trapped in my throat, all panicked fluttering, and I can't get words out around it.

"Okay," I say, even though it's not. I can't feel my finger-tips. "Are you—?"

The bird panics harder, claws at my throat and I can't bring myself to say *breaking up with me.* Is this how it happens, then? You think something is good and then your family fucks it up and you get dumped in a high school?

"I'll be fine," she says, and my heart gives an ugly twist. "I just need some time."

She's bright red, her blue eyes pink around the rims, like

she's been trying not to cry and failing. Andi's clenching her teeth and not quite looking at me, holding her shoulders back like she's bracing herself.

"How much?" I ask. I'm still as a statue and I feel like one.

She blows out a breath and rubs her eyes, then grabs her hair with one hand. "Can you give me, like, ten minutes? I think if I just calm down a little—"

My brain feels like a car ignition that won't turn over.

"Ten minutes?" I ask, just making sure I got it right.

"Yes," she says, her voice still tight, and she snaps her eyes up to mine. "If we keep going like this I'm just going to shout at you more, and that's obviously not helping shit."

I stare at her for slightly too long again.

"Is that not cool, or did you really want to—"

"You're not breaking up with me?"

Now Andi stares. We're all staring. It's a hell of a night.

"No?" she says, then frowns. "Are you... breaking up with me?"

"*No*," I say, and it's probably a little to forceful, because she goes a little more pink. "But you said—you couldn't do this, and it was going bad, and I thought..."

Andi's face is in her hands and she makes a noise that kind of reminds me of the mating call of certain members of the cervidae family.

"I meant this conversation," she says, muffled. "Not *us*."

"Oh," I manage, and that syllable doesn't go very far toward expressing the dizzying relief I feel, but it'll have to do. "Good."

"I'm gonna take a walk around the school," she says, her face out of her hands. "I just need a minute. I'll be back, okay?"

"Of course," I say, because if there's anything I've understood in my life, it's needing a minute alone. "I'll be... here?"

Andi doesn't answer, just gives me a peck on the cheek and disappears around a corner.

· · · · ★ ★ ★ ★ · · · ·

THREE MINUTES IN, my heartbeat's finally returned to normal. I'd feel like an idiot, but I'm too relieved, all of this still a little alien to me. I can't shake the feeling that most people got this out of the way as teenagers and would understand what they're doing by now, not almost fucking it up in a high school hallway.

At seven minutes, it occurs to me that we could have also done this in my car, which is parked outside. I'm slumped against the lockers in the spot she abandoned, and it's kind of uncomfortable.

At nine or so, I'm drawing up a mental list of places we could move together that aren't Sprucevale. Where Beth will never corner her in a restroom and Matt will never swing by my house and I'll never get accosted in a grocery store for being offensively single.

At twelve, I start to worry that she *did* get arrested for trespassing or something and maybe I should go try to explain the situation, or at least also get arrested in solidarity. Or something.

At about twelve and a half—but who's counting—she comes around the corner, shoes squeaking a little on the linoleum, and stops.

"Hey," she says.

"Hey," I say, looking up. Her eyes are still a little red-rimmed and puffy, and the lighting in here isn't doing anyone any favors, but my mouth still goes dry and my heart feels like it trips over something. "Feel better?"

"Kinda," she says, comes over, and slides down the lockers

next to me. "Sorry for getting into an argument with your dad and telling him he was going to die alone. And for getting mad that you didn't tell me you weren't talking any more. And for being the reason you're not talking, and for being a being a mess and crashing into your life like that cartoon of the Kool-Aid Man—"

"I like Kool-Aid," I interrupt, and what I mean is *most of that's not true and I don't mind the rest* and what I mean is *everything is brighter when you're here* but it's not what comes out of my mouth.

Andi, for her part, blinks at me for several seconds.

"No, you don't," she finally says, and I put a hand on her thigh.

"No," I admit. "But I like you."

Andi slides her hand under mine and tangles our fingers together.

"I like you too," she says. "And I'm sorry I made you think I was breaking up with you. I really didn't mean to."

"Yeah. I think that one's on me," I say, and look down at our joined hands, at the way the pads of my fingers fit between her knuckles, the bones right below the surface. It's incredible, how delicate humans are, how easy they are to break. I slide my thumb over her skin and it feels like a small miracle, Andi here with me, putting her complicated, break-able hand in mine like it belongs there. "And you're probably right that he's going to die alone."

"Doesn't mean I should have said it."

"Well."

"He's still your dad," she says, tapping her index finger against my knuckle.

"He's my father."

Andi raises an eyebrow at me, but leaves that thread of conversation alone.

"When did they..." she gestures with her other hand. "Cut you off?"

I snort because *cut me off* sounds like I'm a rich kid whose parents stopped making the payments on his yacht.

"About two weeks ago," I say. Her hand tightens, but she watches me like she's waiting. "Not long after the match-making proposals started rolling in. I asked them to stop trying to set me up with someone else and they... declined."

"I told you I don't care," she says, and there's a note of panic in her voice, her fingers squeezing mine. "I'm not worried, it's not like I think it's going to work—"

"I care."

"Oh."

I settle my head against the lockers and they make a soft *clang* of metal on metal and I try to find some words for why I hated it so much.

"They act like you don't matter to me. Like you're incon-sequential and unimportant and—like I might not want you just because they toss some other girl in front of me. But I don't want *someone*. I've never wanted *someone*. I want *you*."

Andi thunks her forehead against my shoulder, so I kiss the top of her head.

"I'm sorry," she says.

"I don't accept your apology."

She thunks her forehead against my shoulder again, a little harder, and I wonder if she's been spending too much time with Dolly.

"I didn't want to be the reason your parents stopped talking to you," she says, her voice a little muffled. "It's not like we were ever going to get along, but I didn't... want to be the one who did that to you."

"Well, it was them," I say, then think about it for a moment. "Actually, it's me, because I'm welcome back if I apologize. One quick and easy *I'm sorry* and we're back to how we were."

She pulls back to look at me, and there's a raw, anxious, hopeful look in her eyes.

"Not a fucking chance," I say, and kiss her forehead.

"Why didn't you tell me?" she asks, softly, then closes her eyes. "Not that you have to. It's your choice and everything. I just—I want to be someone you can tell things to and I wish I had been."

"My own parents stopped talking to me because of something I did," I say. "You're not supposed to be able to do something that terrible. If you murdered someone, your dad and Rick would visit you in federal prison every weekend."

Andi rearranges herself, lowers one knee to the floor, shifts her back against the lockers.

"Yeah, probably," she finally admits.

"I hate that I couldn't be good enough for them," I say, and close my eyes. Some things are easier in the dark. "And I know who they are, and I know how they've treated Elliott and Reid, so I hate that I wanted to be. And—I was afraid it would make you realize everything wrong with me, and you'd change your mind."

The silence stretches on so long that I finally open my eyes and look over at Andi, who's staring at me. Sometimes her eyes are so blue I feel like I'm falling into the sky.

"Gideon, I already know what's wrong with you," she says, and her other hand slides around the back of mine so she's sandwiching me. "You like animals better than people. You show affection by grumbling. You've got an inflated sense of your own self-importance when it comes to your siblings. Even though you don't like most people, you want their approval so much you're willing to lie to get it, even when it's to your own detriment."

"Okay," I say, frowning at her.

"And I still love you and I'm not changing my mind," she says. "And I'm sorry—"

"Andi—"

"—*that it happened*, and I'm sorry that it had to be about me, and that I brought all this... mess into your life."

"You didn't."

"I kind of did, though."

We look at each other. She's wearing her *trying to be brave* face.

"I missed you so much, for so long," I tell her, my voice suddenly rough. "There was an Andi-shaped hole in my life for twenty years, and I didn't even know that's what it was until you showed up again. There are a lot of people I'd cut out of my life if it meant keeping you."

"Please don't," she says, and I shrug.

"That's really up to them," I say. "If anyone else makes me choose, I'll pick you. Not even a question. They can fucking try me."

Andi presses a kiss to my shoulder, then leans her temple into it so I kiss her hair.

"I love you for all the good reasons," I murmur, her hand tensing in mine. "I love you because my life's better with you in it, not because I'm supposed to. Remember that."

Andi clears her throat, softly.

"And I love you for who you've become, not despite it," she says, raises our joined hands to her mouth, and kisses my knuckles. "Remember that."

We sit there for a few minutes, backs against the lockers. If I listen hard enough, I can hear the buzz of the overhead lights. I wonder if there are security cameras in here. There used to be mirrors in the stairwells so teachers could see students trying to make out in private.

"My butt's a little numb," Andi finally admits. "Sorry to ruin the romance."

"Want to go home and see if my brother loaded the dishwasher wrong?" I ask, and she snorts.

"It's like you're composing a love sonnet."

"I could."

"You don't have to."

We both heave ourselves off the floor. Several joints pop.

"There's a rhyme scheme, right?" I say. "What rhymes with *please ride my cock?*"

Andi makes an explosive squeaking noise and turns to me, eyebrows all the way up, already blushing. I'm also blushing, mostly because I said *cock*.

"You went straight to that from loading the dishwasher?"

"You still haven't given me a rhyme," I point out.

"I'm trying not to encourage you," she says, and we head to the parking lot.

· · · · · ★ ★ ★ · · · · ·

IN THE BOX Matt brought over, there's a picture. An old one, a little faded, worn and wrinkled in a few spots like it's been touched a lot, looked at, treasured and loved in a hands-on way.

In it: two toddlers, sharing a bathtub, both covered head-to-toe in mud. One light-haired and one dark; grinning and frowning.

It's been a long time since I was sure what I believe in, but I know I don't believe in fate. I don't believe that my life had a set path for me to follow or that what's happened was always meant to happen. Certainty is for the faithful.

But when you lose your faith, you find possibility. Sometimes it's terrifying, a gaping maw of *everything* that feels like it could swallow you. Sometimes it's wonderful, a map of all the places you could go. Awful and freeing. Falling and flying.

The photograph is older than my memory, and there she is. It's strange to think that I've known Andi longer than I've known myself, but it makes sense that she's there, intrinsically woven through my life; it makes sense that after she pulled at her thread, the rest started to unravel.

It isn't fate. There's nothing inevitable about us: we could be anywhere, with anyone, but we're here, together. A thousand choices, and I chose this one; a hundred ways to be happy, and I wanted her.

· · · ★ ★ ★ ★ ★ · · ·

REID DID, in fact, load the dishwasher wrong.

FORTY-THREE

GIDEON

ANDI AND REID may be the two least sneaky people on the face of the earth, and they're both currently in my kitchen, trying to casually convince me to come to whatever it is they've been "secretly" planning for the last week and a half.

"It'll be fun!" Andi is saying. "Dwayne Wayne's Honky-tonk Orchestra is playing tonight, and you can just throw your peanut shells on the floor—"

"Neither of those things appeals to me in the least," I point out, just to be difficult. I'm going to say yes sooner rather than later, and we both know it.

"There's allegedly line dancing after eleven," she says, waggling her eyebrows.

"You know how you like line dancing," Reid deadpans. "And peanut shells."

I'm not exactly sure what, but they're Up To Something.

"I haven't electric slid in years," I say. "And I'm sure my boot scoot is rusty."

"No time like the present to practice," Andi says, grinning, and tilts her head a little to one side. "C'mon. It'll be fun."

"You've heard of fun," adds Reid.

No one is dressed for line dancing. Andi's got on a long-sleeve shirt with one of those wide necks that keeps falling open over her shoulder, and Reid's wearing a short-sleeved button down with multicolored triangles over it and jeans. It's the first time in a while I've seen him out of oversized hoodies, and I'm still trying to figure out how to tell him he looks nice.

"Neither of you is dressed for the honkytonk orchestra *or* line dancing," I point out. "Though you do look nice."

"Yeah, is that a new shirt?" Andi chimes in, and Reid shoves his hands in his pockets.

"Um. Yeah."

"It looks good on you."

"Thanks."

"Okay, great!" Andi says, as if something's been decided. "Let's go!"

"To the country western bar with the honkytonk band," I say, knowing full well that something else is going on here.

"Yeehaw," Reid says, and Andi grabs my wrist. I let her pull me along. It's what I do.

· · · · ★ ★ ★ ★ · · · ·

SHOCKINGLY, we don't go to what I'm sure is a standout performance by Dwayne Wayne's Honkytonk Orchestra. Instead Andi drives us out of town while singing along to Taylor Swift, and once we're past Sprucevale limits, it takes me about five seconds to figure out where we're going.

"I don't think there's *any* honkytonk here," I complain as she parks in the lot for Loveless Brewing.

"It could probably be arranged," she says, and she's smiling so wide and bright that I can't imagine someone not giving her what she wanted. "C'mon."

I admit, my mind goes right to worst-case scenarios. Andi's

cooked up some harebrained scheme to reconnect me with my parents, with Matt, or Beth, or my other siblings who took their side. She's arranged an intervention. I'm going to get inside and discover this is all an elaborate ruse to get me to buy a timeshare in the Catskills.

Or, the worst because it's the most likely: it's a surprise party with all the trappings. It's not even my birthday.

"It's not my birthday," I point out when we reach the doors, and Andi gives me a confused frown.

"I know?" she says, and then pulls me in.

It looks like every other Saturday night at Loveless Brewing, and I let out a secret sigh of relief at the lack of confetti and balloons and people shouting my name. Andi pulls me to one side of the big, high-ceilinged room, looking pleased with herself, and after a moment I see why: sitting there is Silas and Kat and Javier and Wyatt and Lainey and Sadie and James and Ariel and her boyfriend and my sister Hannah.

"Surprise," Silas says, then stands and comes over to give me a hug. "What are you drinking?"

· · * * ★ ★ ★ * * · ·

"YOU'VE GOT MOTHMAN AND BIGFOOT," Sadie is saying thoughtfully, her chin resting on one hand. She's halfway through her second beer and taking this very, very seriously. "You know about Deepwood Dave?"

"Of course," Javier says.

"I can't believe they named a monster *Dave*," I tell them.

"I like it. Approachable," says Sadie.

I sigh deeply. "Monsters shouldn't be approachable," I remind her. "They're monsters. Please don't approach them, for the love of God. Don't approach any wild animals."

Sadie narrows her eyes and takes another sip.

407

"Not that they're real," I say, belatedly, but the two of them already look far too amused. "I'm just saying, if you see something monstrous, don't approach it."

"Maybe you should look into the vaults at Forest Service HQ," Sadie tells Javier. "Sounds like they're hiding some cool shit."

"We don't have vaults," I say, which may or may not be true.

"That's what I'd say if I had vaults," Javier says.

"Hmm," Sadie intones seriously. Then she snaps her fingers and sits up straight. "Hodags! Do you know about those?"

"Hodags?"

"They live in caves and have bright red eyes," Sadie tells him. "And eat people or something. That part was actually never clear."

Javier has his phone out and is writing down *Hodags caves red eyes*.

"What else?" he asks.

· · · · ★ ★ ★ ★ · · · ·

ANDI'S AUNT Lucia and her uncle Frank show up a bit later, and there's hugging and cheek-pinching and not once do they mention my parents. Lucia calls me *sweetheart* and Frank calls me *champ*, and I'm pretty sure he's not even kidding.

No one has ever called me *champ* before. I'm not quite sure how I feel about it, though I don't think I feel too bad. It's been a week and a half since Andi and I sat on the floor in the high school, and I've slowly been telling people the truth: I'm estranged from my parents.

The response has been considerably more positive than I

was expecting, which comes with its own set of Goddamn Complicated Feelings that I'm currently trying to wash away with beer.

Complicated Feelings like: I should have known, shouldn't I? I should have stood up to them for Reid. For Elliott. I should have done this years ago instead of telling myself that I was helping, somehow. I should have been a better big brother.

I drink some more beer.

"They're real assholes, aren't they?" I ask the people currently standing near me.

Wyatt frowns and looks over his shoulder, like he's trying to figure out who I mean.

"My parents," I say, and Wyatt and Lainey exchange a *look*.

"I don't really know your parents," Lainey says, polite as anything.

"Well," says Wyatt.

I sigh.

"Kinda," he admits, then shoves a hand through his shock of orange hair. "I mean. They did kick your brother out."

"And whatever's going on with your sister," Lainey adds, as diplomatically as she can.

"Does everyone know they're assholes?"

"Define everyone," Lainey says, and Wyatt snorts. She elbows him.

"*Ow,*" he mutters. "Those are pointy."

She grins and holds one up, waving it at him in half a chicken dance, while Wyatt makes a face and tries to duck away, even though he's nearly a foot taller than she is. They're both laughing, until he finally grabs the offending elbow and whirls her into some sort of elbow-lock that also involves an embrace.

I sip my beer politely and glance away, because this is Not My Business. Twenty feet away, Andi gives me a pointed look and raises one eyebrow. I shake my head. She raises the other one.

"Don't spill my beer," Lainey is saying, still laughing. Wyatt's barely holding onto her, but she doesn't move away.

"Don't elbow me," Wyatt answers.

"Sometimes you need to be elbowed."

"I didn't even *say* anything."

"You were thinking about it."

"I'm allowed to think," he says and she finally pulls away, tucking a stray loc into place and a hand into the pocket of her jeans.

"Sorry," she says to me, and I shake my head and sort of shrug all at once, because I'm sort of drunk and sort of floaty in the best way, and also if I say something it might be about her and Wyatt and whatever's going on there, which is none of my business.

While I'm doing all that, someone slings an arm around my neck.

"Yes," Javier says, casually leaning against me. "Your parents are assholes, which I would know because I'm an expert. What other questions you got?"

· · · · ★ ★ ★ ★ ★ · · · ·

ANOTHER WHILE LATER, I'm sitting on a bench, facing away from one of the long tables and leaning against it, while Andi's draped over my lap, one arm around my shoulders. She's half-playing with my hair, and I'm sitting as motionless as I can, because we're really not a *sit on laps in public couple* and if I move, she might realize what she's doing and stop.

"So you're Sprucevale's Queen Victoria," she's saying to Silas, who's sprawled in a chair opposite.

"Yes. Tons in common, me and her," he says, waving his beer in a *sure, what the hell* kind of gesture.

"At some point she was related to, like, two-thirds of the reigning monarchs in Europe," his sister says from where she's leaning against another table.

"I'm only related to you," Silas says.

"You're related to the brewery by marriage," June explains very patiently, and then gestures at her very prominent belly. "And also via this guy, like, any day now."

"Should you even be here?" Silas asks, eyeing her. "Are you *sure* you don't want a chair?"

"Yes, and where else would I be? I either sit around and wait at home or do it here, and here is way more interesting," she says, and Silas sighs. June's due date was a couple days ago, which I know because Silas has been kind of a basket case about it.

"I bet if you had the baby in the brewery he'd get free beer for life," I say, and June looks thoughtful. Silas looks horrified.

"So your unborn child has an ownership stake in the brewery? Or did I miss something," Andi says, getting us back on track. "Is there a line of succession?"

"I'm married to that guy," June says, pointing across the room, "and his brothers own it."

"One of whom is engaged to Wyatt's cousin," I say.

"Javi's sister is also married to one of them," June says. "Though not one of the brewery owners, a different one."

"I'm pretty sure they're just living in sin," says Silas.

"How many of them *are* there?" Andi says. "This feels like one of those brain teasers, like, if *John has a black dog and Tammy's cat is not orange then what color is Reginald's car?*"

I pat her thigh a little above the knee. "I'll make you a chart."

"You know," she says, turning to me, her fingers still twisting in my hair. "We're probably, like, fifth cousins."

"I really hope not."

"Fifth cousins isn't a big deal," June says. "Just means you had a common ancestor in the early 1800s or so."

"Still cousins," Silas says, and June shrugs.

"Genetically speaking, it's fine," she says. "Actually, even first cousins isn't a big deal so long as they don't reproduce repeatedly over generations. That's the mistake Queen Victoria made."

"So don't fuck your cousin," I tell Silas, who sighs and rubs his face.

"Thanks," he says. "Thank you for that great suggestion."

· · · ⋆ ⋆ ★ **★** ★ ⋆ ⋆ · · ·

I'M STANDING at the edge of the room, leaning against a wall and feeling a little hazy, when someone wraps themselves around me from behind.

"I hope that's you," I say.

"Or what?"

"Or my girlfriend's gonna be *so* mad," I tell Andi, and she laughs.

"I wouldn't be *mad*," she says, resting her chin on my shoulder and nuzzling her face into my neck a little. Shivers work their way down my spine. "I'd just feel bad for whatever poor, misguided person thought they could steal your affections away."

I turn and kiss whatever part of her face my lips reach. Her temple, I think, and she hums into my neck.

"You wouldn't be even a little jealous?" I tease, keeping my voice low. "Not the tiniest bit?"

I can feel her smile against my skin, her arm around my waist going a little tighter. I'm exactly drunk enough to want her to slide it under my shirt even though we're in public.

"Should I be?" she asks, and then licks the spot below my ear. *Licks* it. "I could try, but I can't see you straying."

"Me either," I say, and swallow hard against the twist of heat that slides up my spine at Andi's casual possessiveness. She strokes her thumb across my belly, over the fabric of my shirt, and it fizzes through me like champagne.

"We should probably head out soon," she says. "Let them clean up and go home."

"Yeah," I agree, and slide my fingers over hers, look around the room at all the people who are still here: siblings and friends and relatives-by-marriage and coworkers, and for once, I stand there and let myself feel warm and fuzzy without questioning it.

"Thanks," I tell her. "Love you."

"Love you too," Andi says, and kisses my neck.

FORTY-FOUR

ANDI

"OKAY. SOME GROUND RULES," I say in my bossiest voice, adjusting the rear view mirror until I can look Rick in the eyes.

"I know how to act," my dad protests from the passenger seat.

"She thinks we're gonna misbehave," Rick tells him.

"Or embarrass her."

"No, I *know* you're going to embarrass me," I say, because it's an important distinction. Rick sighs. "I'm just trying to make this go as smoothly as possible."

It's mid-April, and my parents are visiting for a week, which seemed like a good idea when they suggested it. I'm starting to doubt my judgement on that point.

"You don't trust us?" my dad asks.

"Remember when you met my roommate and told her she looked like Andy Warhol, and then tried to pass it off as a compliment?" I ask.

"Andy Warhol was a visionary," my dad says.

"Was he, though?"

"Not the question at hand!" I say, before they can get into

it. "The *point* is that telling a twenty-five-year-old woman that she *looks* like Andy Warhol is not very complimentary and she didn't appreciate it, so please give some thought to any comparisons you might make today."

"Of course, pompom," my dad says. I don't quite trust it, but it'll have to do.

"Thank you," I say. "Also, please don't question the structural integrity of the floors or ceilings, and don't ask questions about the plumbing."

"What are we supposed to talk about, then?" Rick asks dryly.

"Some suggestions," I say, and hold up my right hand, thumb out. "The owl currently rehabbing in his back yard."

"What kind of owl?" my dad asks.

"That's a great starter question to ask Gideon," I say. "What a way to spark conversation."

I glance over at my dad. He looks unimpressed.

"Two: the bat box he recently put up," I say. "Three: the hand-carved mantle over his fireplace."

"Did he carve it?"

"What's a bat box?

"Again, these questions are a great way to enter into conversation," I say, and I know I'm being kind of bossy and a bit much right now, but I'm nervous as all hell. Gideon and my parents have talked some via FaceTime—including at least one long conversation while I wasn't present—but this will be the first time they've actually been in the same room in twenty years, so forgive me if I'm nervous. I want this to go well.

I slow the car to turn into Gideon's long, wooded driveway, car tires crunching on gravel.

"Pompom," my dad says, turning to me. "It'll be fine. We all love you."

I blow out a deep breath and can feel myself turn slightly pink. "Thanks," I say, and pull up next to Reid's car.

Then I kill the engine, and before they can get out, hold up a hand.

"Wait," I say.

"What more could there *possibly* be?" Rick grumbles, half-kidding.

"There's a cat," I tell them. "Her name is Dolly, she's the size of a Great Dane, and you *have* to be nice to her."

My dad closes his eyes and exhales through his nose, because he's slightly allergic to cats and also thinks they're haughty, stuck-up sociopaths. He is not wrong.

"I brought allergy meds for you," I tell him, and it gets a half-smile.

"Thanks," he says.

"Seriously. Be nice to the cat. If you follow one rule today, it *has* to be this one."

"We'll be nice to the cat," Rick promises.

· · · · ★ ★ ★ ★ ★ · · · ·

HOURS LATER, once my parents have been wined and dined and packed off to Lucia's house again, I flop bonelessly onto Gideon's couch. Dolly, who's curled up on the opposite end, raises her head exactly enough to glare at me, then settle back into her own fluff.

"Sorry, your majesty," I say. She doesn't respond. "They treat you right?"

Her ears twitch, but Dolly doesn't open her eyes. Naturally, the moment we walked through the door, she chose my dad to be her favorite for the night and spent most of the time no more than three feet away from him while he handled the situation with the aloof politeness of the allergic. Rick tried valiantly to tempt her away and give my dad a break, but it didn't work. Cats.

"Stop doing dishes and come relax," I call.

"I'm just—"

"Stooooooop!"

Dad and Rick, because they're polite guests, also brought over a couple bottles of wine. Those bottles are now gone.

"So *bossy*," Gideon's muttering, but he's also shutting off the water and his footsteps are moving through the kitchen, so that's fine.

"You like it," I say as he walks into the living room and flops next to me on the couch, grunting in answer. Dolly lifts her head again, but this time she yawns, stretches, and stands.

"That went well, right?" Gideon asks softly as Dolly pushes her face against his hand. I squirm into his side.

"It did. You did great," I tell him, because sometimes Gideon needs reassurance. "Dinner was amazing, and you actually knew which walls were load-bearing when they asked."

Gideon gives me an *of course I know which walls are load-bearing, who wouldn't know that* look I choose to ignore.

"It was so strange to see them again," Gideon says. Dolly's now purring like a thunderstorm in the distance. "They're *exactly* the same, just with a few more gray hairs."

"I *know*."

"Like. Exactly the same."

"Trust me, I'm aware."

Gideon's quiet for a moment, fingers buried in Dolly's fluff.

"How are they doing, being back here? With you staying?"

I blow out a breath and pull my feet onto the couch, because even though I've been to hundreds of hours of family therapy with my parents, their feelings still tend to be a grand mystery.

"Okay, I think," I say. "A lot's changed in twenty years. Not enough—like, I don't think they'd hold hands in the Kroger—but it's getting better. And it's not like I'm gonna get run out of town for being cis and straight, so, there's that."

Gideon sighs his *I worry about Reid sometimes* sigh, so I wriggle until I can get an arm over his shoulder and play with his hair.

"They were so... nice," he says, after a long pause, like this is the thing he can't get over. Like despite everything, he wasn't expecting it.

"You *are* dating their favorite daughter."

"I'm dating their only daughter."

"A completely irrelevant detail."

"Also, isn't the opposite supposed to be true?" he asks. Dolly's now flopped over his lap, which puts her half in mine. I got the tail half, which is very twitchy, but if I touch it she'll get mad.

"Would you rather they bring a shotgun along?"

Gideon snorts. "I'm not complaining," he says.

"Most people prefer to have good relationships with their in-laws," I tease him, fingers still drifting through his hair. Something occurs to me. "Wait, did your parents do that?"

"I wouldn't know, I left home before Beth was old enough to date," he says. "Besides, I think she only ever dated David."

"Really?"

"They got married when she was nineteen."

I make a noise somewhere between a snort and a questioning grunt, because *nineteen*. When I was nineteen I was reduced to tears multiple times trying to decide on a major in college and briefly dated a man who always played the bongos after we had sex. Even at three in the morning. We didn't date long.

Still, those are the choices I was making.

"They always did like you," I tell Gideon, changing the subject back. "I think they're glad you turned out well. They probably think it was their influence, actually, but that's just how they are."

Dolly stretches, and she's now longer than both our laps. I swear this cat is six feet tall.

"They're not *wrong*," Gideon says, slowly. "You remember the time you stepped on glass in the creek and had to go to the emergency room?"

I twist until I can show him the long scar that's still on the bottom of my foot. Dolly *mrrps* and gives me an irritated look.

"Of course. You got me back home."

"I was terrified," Gideon admits.

I must have known that, deep down—we were kids, there was lots of blood—but it's not what I remember at all. "You didn't seem like it," I say.

"I thought your dad and Rick would be *furious*," he says, drifting his fingers through Dolly's long belly fur, something no one else is allowed to do. "If you'd been one of my siblings and I'd brought you home like that, I'd have—"

He stops for a moment.

"Been punished," he finishes. "And, I mean, Rick wasn't *happy* when we showed up, but he gave me a hug before you left for the hospital. Then a couple days later they gave me a really nice pocketknife as thanks for getting you home safe."

I choose not to examine whether a pocketknife is a good gift for an ten-year-old.

"You were so good that day," I say, running a hand along Dolly's back to see if I'm allowed. I think I am. "I was being a dumbass, walking around barefoot, and you still took care of me and got me home safe, and the whole time you were so... sweet, and calm. I'd have been so much more scared if you hadn't been there, taking care of me."

Gideon's silent for a long time, running fingers through Dolly's fur. Both of us remembering different sides of a sun-soaked summer afternoon.

"It never felt like that, with you," he finally says, voice soft as anything.

"Like what?"

"Like I was taking care of you," he says. "It still doesn't."

"Even when I do something dumb like chain myself to a tree in a blizzard and you're very definitely taking care of me?"

Gideon shrugs, glances over at me with this sweet, shy smile on his face.

"It was always different," he says. "You would take us places and I'd get us home safe. None of it ever felt like a burden. It just felt like... us."

"I used to want to rescue you," I say, suddenly, a feeling I've never quite put into words before. I must pet Dolly too hard, because she lifts her head, glares, and then decides she's done with laps for now. "Sometimes you'd come over out of the blue, and you'd look so tired and kind of lost, so I'd microwave popcorn and we'd watch one of those bootleg Disney movies we had, and half the time you'd fall asleep in the middle."

"I thought *Aladdin* always had commercials in Spanish until I was about thirteen," Gideon says.

"Or sometimes," I say, and swallow, because this is a little hard. "My dad or Rick would gesture somehow and you'd flinch away, or if we got in trouble with them you would just... shut down, like you powered off or something."

Gideon's staring down at his hands, like I've done it to him just now. Shit. After a moment, I turn, drape myself into the corner of the couch, and pull him on top of me.

"Mmph," he says, mostly into my boobs.

"So I used to concoct these daydreams where you had to come live with us instead of with your own family," I admit, something I haven't thought about in years. "I'd get a brother, you'd get a way cooler sister, and you wouldn't have to live with your parents or your siblings any more."

There's another long silence.

"I think you did," he finally says, both of us sprawled across the couch, his weight warm and heavy on me as I trace fingertips along a shoulder blade. "Rescue me, I mean."

I process that for a second.

"Shit," I say. "That's not—"

"It worked," he says, and I can tell he's laughing. "I don't have to deal with my parents or half my siblings any more, and you basically live in my house. Though the way I think of you sure isn't sisterly."

"Well, that's good," I say. "And you did bring me home safe."

Gideon moves up the couch a little until his face is in my neck, his beard tickling my collarbones. He gives one a slow, warm kiss and I wrap my arms around him a little tighter.

"It's good to be us, again," he says.

"It's better than good," I murmur. His lips press against my throat.

"The best," he says, and nuzzles against me, and I hold him a little tighter.

We're home, safe and warm, in the house he shares with his brother and his cat, but I've never been here before. I've never wanted so badly to wrap someone in my heart and I've never felt this urge to push onward, to be brave, to drop my defenses and just *be*.

EPILOGUE

GIDEON

Summer

I stare at myself in the full-length, gilded mirror and try not to think too many thoughts. The midday sun streams through the windows and the breeze lifts gauzy white curtains. It smells like recently-cut grass, lemonade, and toast.

In the room behind me, there's a yelp and then a squeal, but I don't turn around. If I turn around now I'll *never* be done with this and I would really, really like to be done.

"Just try to act natural," the photographer suggests, as if that's possible. I don't know how I usually act, I just do it and hope no one notices.

"Okay," I say, and... try a slight smile. She makes a noise that isn't exactly positive.

Behind me is a crash, then lots of swearing, followed by my sister Ariel hissing, "I told you not to stand on that!"

"It looked sturdy!" Sadie hisses back.

"Are you drunk *already*?" Reid asks, and I shoot the photographer a pained look. She sighs.

"They're all right, don't worry," she says of the slapstick

422

comedy act apparently going on behind me. "I just need a few more getting ready shots. Did you have a young lady...?"

"Andi?" I call, and turn around.

I almost regret it.

Elliott's wedding is taking place at some sort of large, old inn in the country about an hour outside Boston, and the traveling circus of his wedding party has taken over some sort of large room with lots of mirrors and a chandelier. He's standing off in a corner with his best man, Adam, and the other photographer, looking slightly nervous but mostly calm and... happy, actually, which is good.

Meanwhile, the rest of the room is strewn with tables and chairs, most of which either have drinks on them or clothing draped over them, an impressive state of chaos given that we've barely been here for forty-five minutes.

Sadie, Ariel, and Reid are standing next to a chair that looks far more decorative than sturdy, whisper-shouting at each other. There's a balloon in the corner of the ceiling above them, about twenty feet up. I ask no questions.

They're being glowered at by my sister Hannah, off to the other side, who's standing very still while Andi does something to the back of her dress.

"One second, sorry," Andi calls back. "This button got loose but I think I can..."

Hannah just gives me a thumbs up as Andi trails off.

"Totally under control!" she calls, and while I'm not sure I'd call it that, the chaos is oddly comforting and familiar, at least.

"Usually there's a few toddlers running around, spilling apple juice on someone," the photographer says, shrugging. "This is a walk in the park."

A minute later, Andi comes over and gets directed to

stand in front of me and, quote, "do something to my suit." She opts for poking at my tie and messing with my corsage, and since I don't know what to do with my hands, I settle them on her waist as the photographer snaps away.

"Your hair smells good," I say, because I'm running out of compliments to give her today. I've already told her, in both polite and impolite terms, that the one-shouldered pale turquoise dress she's wearing looks very nice on her, as well as her earrings, necklace, and hairstyle.

"Thanks. I washed it," she says, still poking at the flowers pinned to my chest as she looks up at me through her lashes.

That look should probably be illegal.

"Perfect. You're doing great," the photographer says. "Just a few more, act natural."

"She keeps saying that," Andi whispers, ducking a little closer.

"I know."

"Do you know what it means?"

"Not a clue."

She plucks at something on my shoulder.

"How did you get cat fur on a tuxedo you rented in Boston?" she murmurs.

"She has to track her loyal subjects somehow," I say, and Andi snorts.

"Okay! Great, thank you," the photographer says. "You're free to go until after the ceremony."

I give Andi a quick kiss on the forehead before we separate. For lipstick reasons, we're not allowed to kiss on the lips until all the family pictures are finished, and I'm pleased enough that Elliott and Connor wanted her in the family pictures that I don't mind.

"I'm gonna go keep Sadie's poor boyfriend company

before he disintegrates," she says. "See you later. You look good."

She squeezes my hand, and gives me a smile, and it's such a beautiful day.

$$\cdots \ast \ast \ast \bigstar \ast \ast \ast \cdots$$

"I DON'T KNOW!" Ariel says, turning in a complete circle like that'll help. "He was right there!"

"How did you *lose Reid*?" Hannah asks.

"I didn't *lose Reid*, Reid... lost himself," Sadie says, scowling.

"Connor's mom might actually kill us," Ariel says, already texting. "I wouldn't put bloodshed past her."

"Where did you last see him?" I ask. The ceremony is supposed to start in about seven minutes, and Ariel's right about Elliott's mother-in-law-to-be.

"He was right there!" Sadie says, pointing, as if Reid is a purse she'd put down. "He seemed kind of nervous, and then he was gone, I don't know."

"Stay here," I tell the two of them, not that they were offering to go search.

It doesn't take long to find him, in the dressing room we all left about ten minutes ago, still in an impressive state of chaos. The balloon is still on the ceiling and it smells a little like someone spilled champagne, but it's a lovely, warm kind of chaos.

Reid's in front of the mirror, scowling at his tie.

"You need help?" I ask, even though I know the answer.

"Yeah," he says, letting the sides go and shaking out his hands. "It was probably fine, but I thought it looked kind of lopsided so I went to go fix it and then I just made it *more* lopsided and—" he finishes by gesturing at himself.

"Here," I say, and he turns to me.

"Thanks."

"Don't thank me yet," I say, and set about tying. Reid closes his eyes and forces his hands to his sides while I work.

It doesn't take long. I'm probably better at tying other peoples' ties than my own, after years of helping all my younger brothers and then years of helping their kids, too.

It occurs to me, as I finish Reid's, that I've never helped him with a tie before. I don't mention that thought to him since he already seems plenty anxious.

"There," I say, and turn him to the mirror. "That better?"

Reid doesn't say anything. He blinks at himself, and stares, swallows twice. The breeze blows through the curtains and he stands up a little straighter, then smooths the tie and his lapels and swallows again.

It strikes me, suddenly, how glad I am that he's here. He told me, in the car on the way to Richmond a few weeks ago, that he came closer to not being here than I ever realized.

There's a lot about Reid I'd never realized, but I'm trying to learn. Our roles are oddly reversed these days; after all, he got through this when he was fifteen. It's his turn to guide me.

"You look good," I tell him, and his eyes flick to me.

"Thanks."

For a moment, I almost put my arm around his shoulders so I can kiss his head, but I stop myself and settle for squeezing his shoulder instead.

"Don't be long," I say, because he seems like he might need a minute. "Connor's mom might kill someone."

Finally, that gets a half smile.

"Sure," he says. "I'll be right there."

* * * * * ★ ★ ★ * * * * *

THE CEREMONY IS PERFECT. For all that both Elliott and Connor have huge wedding parties, the ceremony itself is borderline casual, performed by a woman with short gray hair and a full-sleeve tattoo. Ariel and Sadie are excellent flower girls, none of the groomsmen trip over anything, and both grooms are so busy grinning at each other that they keep missing their cues.

Everyone cries. In the audience, I can see Andi handing James a tissue while Hannah sniffles behind me.

Afterward we get plied with champagne while we take even more pictures, but it's stopped being awkward. Andi and James are in some of them, Elliott and Connor are over the moon, and Connor's huge Irish-Catholic family's chaos makes our chaos look positively calm by comparison. Elliott even insists on a "just brothers" picture of him, me, and Reid, and I might cry again.

· · · · ★ ★ ★ ★ · · · ·

LATER, after dinner, I'm drinking a beer and watching people dance when Elliott comes over and throws an arm around me.

"Hey," he says, listing into me a little. "Thanks for coming. Like, seriously. I'm really glad you were here. I know you hate —" he gestures around, as if indicating *people*.

I throw an arm around him in the hopes it'll keep him upright.

"I'm glad you invited me," I say.

"Of *course*," he says. "I wasn't gonna get married without you."

"Good," I say. "I'd hate to miss this."

We both go quiet for a moment, but we don't have to say anything to know what we're both thinking.

"And Reid," he says. "I'm glad he made it."

"Being asked to be a groomsman made his month, by the way," I tell Elliott. "Not that he'd ever admit it, but."

"Good," Elliott says, watching Reid across the huge room, talking to someone with lavender hair. "How many drinks has he had?"

"I'm not his chaperone."

Elliott takes a long sip of his own drink.

"Mhm," he says.

"Two, I think. We had a discussion earlier about pacing."

"Probably a good idea."

"I thought so."

"Oh. Incoming," Elliott says, moments before Andi's on my other side, hooking her arm through mine.

"Come dance," she says, flushed and grinning.

"I'm talking to the groom," I protest. It's pretty half-hearted.

"Don't decline on my account," Elliott says.

"Gideon," Andi says, my hand firmly in both of hers. "We both know I'm going to win, so could you please finish your drink and we can skip to the part where you give in and come dance with me instead of pretending you're not going to?"

On my other side, Elliott starts laughing. I sigh.

"She has *always* had your number," he says.

"I know," I say, and let Andi guide me to the dance floor.

· · · ★ ★ ★ ★ ★ · · ·

"WHY ARE WE HERE?" I ask, again.

"Because Connor's cousin said there were fancy roses, and I want to see fancy roses," Andi says. "Don't you want to see fancy roses?"

"I don't think we're gonna see much of anything," I say,

but I'm going along with her, obviously. Of course. Always. It's something like midnight and I've spent the day drinking and basking in reflected joy, and right now, like this, it's easy to feel like I was made to go along with her.

If I was made for anything at all, it was this.

"Maybe they're night-blooming roses," Andi says. "Those exist, right?"

"What gives you the idea I know anything about roses?"

"You know about some plants!" Andi says, and she's already laughing. "You know what trees are."

"Yes. I know what trees are," I deadpan.

"Don't sass me while I'm taking you to see fancy roses."

"You're not gonna have any idea which roses are fancy and which aren't," I say, because it's dark, the moon is just a sliver, the lights back at the inn not reaching this far. The sort of darkness that makes you feel nearly invisible, like you're made of moonlight and gossamer.

"We just established that you also don't know the fancy roses, so I can tell you whatever I want and you'll have to believe me," she says, and it's nothing like the moonlight.

"I don't *have* to believe you."

"Well, you should," she says. "And—"

Andi pitches sideways and stumbles into me out of nowhere.

"Fuck. Ow," she says, leaning into me and looking at the bottom of one foot.

"Didn't you have shoes?" I ask. She did, I'm sure of it; they're probably with my tie and jacket, wherever they are.

"Somewhere."

"You came outside with no shoes?"

"It's a civilized outside," she says, brushing off the sole of her foot. "It's all nice and stuff."

"Then what did you just step on?"

"A rock or something, I think."

I heave my biggest, most dramatic sigh.

"If I step on glass, I've got exactly the right person to take care of me," she says, and she's grinning about it for some reason.

"Please don't step on glass."

"It's fine. I'll just swoon into your arms," she says, like this is a desired outcome or something.

"Since when do you swoon?"

"I could swoon at literally any moment."

"Not really a swooner."

"Ready?" she asks, and I frown at her. "I'm gonna—"

Andi practically flings herself to one side, arms over her head, and I barely catch her, and then I nearly drop her because we're both a little sweaty.

"You *have* to warn me," I tell her. Neither of us makes any move to let her up, though I shift until my hold is a little more comfortable.

"I literally just asked if you were ready."

"*Better* warning," I say.

"That's the thing about swooning," Andi says, serious in her tipsiness, winding an arm around my neck. "Could happen any time."

"Still, seems like it could be avoided by wearing mmmmmph."

Andi levers herself up and presses her mouth to mine, which doesn't count as winning the argument but does make me stop talking. She's warm and pliable and tastes a little like champagne and wedding cake, her skin damp with the humid night and sweat from the dance floor. I work my fingers into her hair at the nape of her neck, slightly wet and sticky with whatever was in it.

I like her like this: flushed and overheated, gloriously alive. I like the tang of salt on her skin and the way it sounds when she's panting for breath in my ear, the way droplets of sweat look when they slide down her neck. I want her when she's picture-perfect, like earlier, and I want her when she's devilish and disheveled, like now.

We kiss until I hear voices getting closer, so I pull her upright and she gives me a satisfied look while she wipes the corner of her mouth, as if she has any lipstick left to mess up.

"So. Fancy roses," I say, and she points in a random direction.

We wander. We never do see the other people we heard, and instead of fancy roses we find a wall with a gate in it, a grassy yard outside. I lean against it, and somewhere in the back of my mind I know the brick might stain the back of my shirt, but I can't bring myself to care.

"I've been lied to about fancy roses, I guess," Andi says, stepping between my feet.

"Can't trust anyone," I agree, and she leans into me, elbows on my shoulders.

"You look good like this."

"Sweating through a shirt?"

"Happy," she says, and—she's right. I am. "Also, the whole *rakishly disheveled groomsman* thing is really working for you."

"It's been a good day," I tell her, my hands on her waist again, the spot where it feels like they belong. "A good—what is it, six months?"

"Has it really been six months?" she says, and is quiet for a minute. "It has! Huh. Think we can do it again?"

"Have six more good months?"

"Mhm."

I want to say I think we can have six good years. Sixty. As many as I've got left, but that's a thing to say sober, not drunk in a garden with no fancy roses.

"I like the odds," I tell her instead. Andi wriggles, her elbows still propped on my shoulders.

"What's that saying about the odds?" she asks.

"I cannot even pretend to *begin* to have any idea—"

"The odds are good but the goods are odd!" she yelps, and then starts laughing.

"How much champagne did you *have*?" I ask, but I'm smiling so hard it hurts.

"I have no idea," she says, gazing up at me, her blue eyes a little dreamy. "People kept coming around with it on a tray, and it would obviously be rude to refuse."

"I'm gonna have to pour you into bed."

"Oh, *please* do," she says, and now she's grinning, leaning in. "I brought the dick vibrator," she says. "And the regular vibrator. And the one with the straps so you can have your hands—"

Suddenly there are voices again and Andi's not talking quietly, so I press my mouth to hers. She makes a noise but slides her tongue into my mouth, and then her body's pressed even harder against mine and everything is her.

She feels like going somewhere I've never been and realizing that it's home. Andi's been part of me for longer than I can remember, a sliver of sunshine and quicksilver lodged so close to my heart I wouldn't survive pulling it out. She's made me brave, always; she showed me the path that led me back to her.

I'd choose it, again and again. Whatever it took, I'd always come home to her.

The voices fade, and after a bit we pull away.

"We should probably head back," she says, voice low and secret, just for me.

I kiss her on the forehead because I can.

"I know the way," I tell her, and we walk off, hand in hand.

THE END

ACKNOWLEDGMENTS

This book, like all my books, would probably not exist without the gentle-yet-firm guiding hand of Becca Hensley Mysoor, aka the Fairy Plotmother. Thank you for being my book-writing North Star, and also for the time you shut me in a dark room with snacks and said I couldn't come out until I'd finished the chapter I was stuck on.

An enormous thank you also to Julia Jarrett and Theresa Leigh, who have been tireless cheerleaders, irreplaceable brainstorming partners, and who sometimes make me laugh so hard I think I might asphyxiate. Sorry for all the times I laid on the floor and word-vomited into a voice memo, but also, thank you for listening to all those and responding so reasonably.

Thanks to Alec J. Marsh for the incredibly helpful sensitivity read, and especially for doing it at the eleventh hour.

None of this would be happening at all without my husband, the talented and lovely Mr. Noir, who knows exactly which TikToks will make me laugh and who reminds me about things like "time" and "lunch."

And finally, thanks to everyone who's read and enjoyed my books in the past, especially the other Wildwood Society books and the Loveless Brothers series. When I decided to write some romcoms set in my home state I didn't quite realize the scale of what I was getting myself into, but I'm so glad I did it.

ABOUT ROXIE

Roxie is a romance author by day, and also a romance author by night. She lives in Los Angeles with one husband, two cats, far too many books, and a truly alarming pile of used notebooks that she refuses to throw away.

Want to be the first to hear about new releases and giveaways? Sign up for her newsletter and join her reader group!

www.roxienoir.com
roxie@roxienoir.com

Made in the USA
Las Vegas, NV
19 December 2024

14969820R00256